The Phoenix Inheritance

By

Derek Rossitter

Visit us online at www.authorsonline.co.uk

An Authors OnLine Book

ISBN 0 7552 0286 4
ISBN 978-0-755202-86-7

Authors OnLine Ltd
19 The Cinques
Gamlingay, Sandy
Bedfordshire SG19 3NU
England

This book is also available in e-book format, details of which are available at www.authorsonline.co.uk

For my late and much loved
Wife and our children

ABOUT THE AUTHOR

Derek Rossitter was born in 1923. After war service in the British Army throughout most of World War Two he entered industry as a trainee works manager. Some years later he was called to the Bar of England and Wales. Thereafter he served for many years on the legal staff of a large international industrial organisation. After retirement from this position he became President of a company specialising in intellectual property research. He is now fully retired but remains Honorary President of a worldwide society specialising in the legal aspects of branding. In addition to *THE PHOENIX INHERITANCE* he has had published another novel entitled *SPLENDOUR POSTPONED* as well as an illustrated book of children's verse entitled *THE GREEDY PIGEON AND THE HUNGRY PORCUPINE AND FRIENDS*. He is now a widower, having lost his much loved wife in 2005. He has three daughters and eight grandchildren.

BY THE SAME AUTHOR

The Greedy Pigeon and The Hungry Porcupine and Friends

ISBN 0-7552-0142-6

Splendour Postponed

ISBN 0-7552-0141-8

These books are available from Authors OnLine

www.authorsline.co.uk

Come, let's away to prison
We two alone will sing like birds i' the cage
When thou dost ask me blessing, I'll kneel down
And ask of thee forgiveness

King Lear

Will you walk into my parlour? said a spider to a fly
'Tis the prettiest little parlour that ever you did spy

Mary Hewitt   The Spider and the Fly

When people wish to attach, they should always be
ignorant. To come with a well informed mind, is to
come with an inability of administering to the vanity
of others, which a sensible person would always wish
to avoid. A woman especially, if she has the misfortune
of knowing anything, should conceal it as well as she can.

Jane Austen   Northanger Abbey

"...let us pay the penalty not to our bitterest enemies, the
Romans, but to God - by our own hands. It will be
easier to bear. Let our wives die unabused, our children
without knowledge of slavery: after that let us do each
other an ungrudging kindness, preserving our freedom as
a glorious winding sheet."

Josephus (tr. G.A.Willliamson)   The Jewish War

PART ONE - DAWNING

CHAPTER ONE

BERLIN

The letter was datelined Bayswater, London, January the tenth, 1871. Josef Aronberg was holding it in his hand with dismay written on his face. His normally severe expression began to assume such grimness that his wife, Ruth, usually respectfully silent whilst he read his breakfast mail, exclaimed, "Whatever is the matter, Josef? Has something terrible happened to Reuben?"

"Indeed, something has happened to Reuben," growled her husband, handing the letter to his son, Isaac, to pass down the table to his mother.

"Why, it's from Julius Roth," said Ruth, looking first at the signature, "surely he wouldn't send you bad news?"

"Read it, Ruth, read it!" said her husband irritably.

She read it carefully. Then she put it down and said, "It must be a false report he's been given! This is malicious talk! I don't believe it! It's impossible!"

"You know perfectly well that Julius wouldn't send me a false report. You know he'd check and recheck on such a thing. I'd already heard rumours. I tried to ignore them. I didn't want to distress you. That's why I asked Julius to investigate for me. This is certainly true."

The Aronberg international textile import and export business had both its headquarters and main residence of the family in a large mansion in the Charlottenburg district of Berlin. Josef had established the firm there in 1838 and had since seen it grow to its present importance. He, together with his family, had renounced Judaism some years ago and been baptised into the Lutheran church. This prudent act had effectively removed certain problems, which had been preventing business expansion. He had, however, insisted on retaining both the family name and continuing the practice of using Biblical first names for the children. "Never, never, are you to abandon my name of Aronberg!" he enjoined his son. "If any member of the family ever renounces my name they, too, must be renounced. Make me that promise!"

1

"I make that promise, Father, and shall see it is observed by my own children and by theirs."

The Charlottenburg offices Josef managed himself. Although, in 1871, still only fifty-four years old he already had the appearance of a greybearded patriarch. He was a tall, dignified man, always dressed in suits of fine dark cloth, wing collar and carefully tied cravat, gold pince-nez dangling at his waist from a silken cord. There were two other main offices. One in Munich, managed by his younger brother, Moses, and the other, more recently established in 1850, in London. This latter was, at the insistence of his wife, whose family had put a great deal of money into the business when they had married, managed by her younger brother, Reuben. In 1850 Reuben had been twenty-five and had shown much more enthusiasm for a literary career than a commercial one.

"All the more reason," Ruth had said to her reluctant husband, "to give him a proper job. Give him enough responsibility and he'll prove himself a capable business man!" Unfortunately she had been wrong but nothing would make her admit to it. Reuben ran the London office with such little enthusiasm that Josef despaired. Reuben's aspirations were always elsewhere.

Breakfast was an important meal in the Charlottenburg household. It was mandatory that everybody be seated in his or her appointed place by seven o'clock. At the head of the massive oak table was Josef. At the opposite end, behind the great silver coffeepot, sat Ruth Stein, two years younger than her husband. She had been a noted beauty in her youth and this was still apparent. She invariably dressed in black. Her only concession to personal adornment was her wedding ring and a large cameo brooch at her neck. Her fine black hair, just showing traces of white, was firmly encased in a black lace cap. On Josef's right sat their only son, Isaac, then thirty-two. Ruth had intended he would be the first of many children but his birth had been attended by such grave complications that he had no siblings. He had grown to adulthood aware that he would one day succeed his father and was passionately devoted to the firm. He was a tall, dark, sallow man, heavily bearded, soberly dressed and generally considered handsome. At twenty-four he had married Miriam, three years his junior. She was seated next to her husband, to the left of her mother-in-law. By some quirk of ancestry she had a much lighter complexion than her husband's family and grey-green eyes. She, too, dressed only in subdued colours and, apart from her wedding ring, never wore any jewellery other than the pearl necklace given to her by Isaac as a betrothal token. She, also, had

2

brought into the business a very considerable dowry. Opposite their parents were seated the two children, Samuel, then aged six, and Eli, a year younger.

Isaac and Miriam had been listening to the exchange between Josef and Ruth with bewilderment. "Father," said Isaac, at last, "what is it that is so distressing you both? Can we be told?"

"Isaac," responded his father, gravely, "I have just received news which is going to change the lives of you and your family. Reuben has involved the business in very considerable financial loss and problems through his incompetence. I can no longer tolerate his remaining in charge of the London office. You must go to London and take over from him as soon as possible."

"But Josef," exclaimed Ruth, "at one stroke you condemn my brother unheard and exile my children! You should make further enquiry before acting so precipitately!"

"Indeed, my dear," responded Josef, " in this matter you must, I fear, defer to my business judgement notwithstanding your natural affection. This must be so!"

Isaac and Miriam sat silent, stunned by the suddenness with which all this had descended upon them. Neither had any desire to quit Berlin and live in a foreign country.

Ruth, for her part, suddenly rose from her chair and swept out of the room, her eyes brimming with tears.

"I think you and the children should go to her, Miriam," said Josef. "I must speak alone with Isaac."

Left on their own Isaac took up the letter and read it. Then he looked at his father questioningly.

"The business relies on mutual and absolute family trust, Isaac," said his father, "we can no longer put any reliance in Reuben's judgement. I shall give him a generous inducement to go that I know for certain he will not resist. Please remain on friendly terms with him when you go to London. That is the least I can do to compensate your mother. He must, however, be kept completely out of the business. I am afraid you must go, Isaac!"

"What will Reuben find to do, Father?"

"He always had a consuming desire to own and run a bookshop. Indeed I truly believe he'd rather read than marry! I suppose that must be why he never has married! I shall, therefore, provide him with ample means to acquire such a shop whilst making it quite clear to him that he must never again interfere with the running of the London office. You will have no trouble with him. You will find you are dealing with a much happier man!"

"That's more than I can say for myself! It is going to be very difficult. How am I, who has always regarded himself as a loyal Prussian subject, going to adjust to being a British subject?"

"There are many types of loyalty! It is, I know, often hard to reconcile them all. Isn't it only realistic to recognise that blind obedience to any particular principle or person may, according to circumstance, be actually harmful? In the present case I could have placed consideration for my wife and her manifest natural affection for her brother before my loyalty to the business. In the end that, surely, would have led to the decay of the London office and, quite possibly, the downfall of the entire business. In such circumstances should not prudence overrule emotion? I am well aware of your commendable patriotism. No doubt, one day, when I am gone, you will return here, to Berlin, to take charge. In the meantime find comfort from the knowledge that you are still only thirty-four. It must be to the Queen of England you must give your allegiance whilst you live there. As for your other loyalties, to your family, and the business, these are and always shall be beyond question."

"Father, I shall always remember what you have said! I cannot, however, pretend that my devotion to both the city of Berlin and Germany will not always remain. These feelings both Miriam and I shall certainly pass on to our children. I leave with the certain knowledge that, one day, we shall return to live where we truly belong."

CHAPTER TWO

LONDON

Julius had known Reuben since childhood. He had been seeing him regularly ever since he had been in London where he had been asked to go by Josef to investigate at first hand just what Reuben was doing. He had always been aware that Reuben was a square peg in a round hole, frustrated by his London commercial responsibilities and nursing a consuming desire to devote himself to books. The day Josef's letter arrived he had already arranged to accompany his friend to the literary club, where he spent all his free time, and dine with him afterwards.

They met, as arranged, at Reuben's bachelor rooms, which were in a large house in Gardens Square in the Bayswater district, and walked together up Queensway to Kensington Gardens. They began to make their way along the Broad Walk, for Reuben's club lay on the other side of the park in Knightsbridge.

"I have had a letter from Josef, Reuben"

"Oh, what does he have to say? He never writes to me about anything else than the wretched business! I sometimes wonder whether he ever thinks about anything else than his textiles. "

"He has asked me to tell you, Reuben, that he has decided to provide you with the necessary funds to buy the bookshop he and Ruth know you have always really wished to possess!"

They were at that moment just approaching the Round Pond. Reuben stopped dead in his tracks and gazed without speaking at a small boy who was carefully launching his toy boat. His friend watched him anxiously.

"You know, Julius," he said after a long pause, "I think I feel like that young man! I have, it seems, been released from the nursery and given the chance to engage, at last, in something I have always yearned to do as my own master. But, alas, look here comes the nursemaid to supervise him! Will I still be supervised do you think? What shackles must I wear? Tell me, Julius, what has brought about this remarkable volte-face in Berlin?"

Julius had given the mission that he had been told to carry out a great deal of consideration. On the one hand he had no desire to cause Reuben unnecessary distress by baldly telling him that Josef no longer considered him competent to run the business. Conversely he could not see how he could avoid making it quite plain that, in return for the gift of the bookshop, he was expected to have no more to do with the running of the London office. He had banked on Reuben's pleasure at the news outweighing all other considerations. He had just decided that the only way to handle the matter was to tell the plain truth when Reuben pre-empted him.

"It is of course obvious, isn't it? I have always been a hopeless misfit. I was only given the position because of Ruth's insistence. I never wanted it but what alternative did I have? I had no other way of making a living. I can only conclude that Josef has at last realised that I am losing the business money, although why this was not evident to him ages ago I really cannot understand!"

"There is a difference, Reuben, between not making as much money as one should and actually losing it. It seems that Josef was prepared to tolerate the one but not the other."

"So that's it, is it? Well, it certainly suits me, but what is to happen? Is the office to be closed?"

"No. He has asked me to work alongside you for the moment so that, as soon as you are able to put your shop on a working basis, I shall have sufficient knowledge of the business to hand it over to Isaac."

"From that I can only infer that Isaac, Miriam and their children will be moving to London. That really surprises me. I should never have believed Isaac, that patriotic Prussian, would ever agree to come and live with his family in England."

"I do not think Josef gave him any option, Reuben!"

"Where are they going to live?"

"That, Reuben is left to us. We have been given the job of finding, buying and even adequately furnishing a house here ready for them to occupy when they arrive, which, I calculate, will be about this July!"

"So we have two tasks ahead of us. We must find a shop for me at a price which is agreeable to Josef, and then a house for Isaac and his family. Has he given you any idea how much he is prepared to pay?"

"Yes, he has. He has given me upper limits. I have already made tentative enquiries through some agencies and I predict we are not going to be worried on that score. I do not know where he obtained his information but it does seem to have been reliable. He has probably been scrutinising advertisements in The Times!"

"As a matter of fact, Julius, I think I know of both an ideally situated house and, you will not be surprised to hear, suitable premises for myself. Shall we arrange to see at least one of them tomorrow?"

Julius smiled. "Nobody could accuse you of not co-operating!"

The house that Reuben had noticed had recently been placed on the market by the executors of the former occupant. It was situated in Gardens Square, close to his own rooms, in excellent decorative condition, and exceedingly spacious.

"It seems ideal to me," said Julius, after they had been given a very thorough tour by the house agent. "It is, perhaps, a little large but then it is always possible, I suppose, that they may have more children. In any event it would be very convenient if the London office work could be carried out by Isaac from his own home. The price is right and the situation ideal. I shall certainly recommend Josef to conclude the purchase. The sooner the better. Then we can instruct Maples to furnish sufficiently for their arrival. I suppose Miriam will wish to complete furnishing herself."

"I hope you are equally impressed by the premises I have my own eyes on, Julius. Would you be willing to come along with me and see them tomorrow? I have already spoken to the agent and made an appointment in anticipation."

"Reuben!" laughed his friend, "You are like an excited schoolboy!"

"I have already admitted to that, haven't I. Remember, I have waited over twenty years for this to happen, and never seriously thought it would. I think I am entitled to a little show of impatience!"

"And so you are. Certainly I shall come with you to see your heart's desire tomorrow."

They took the omnibus from Bayswater, along Oxford Street and almost as far as Tottenham Court Road. Here, trembling with excitement, Reuben said, "We alight here, Julius, it is just over there. Look, there's the agent waiting for us."

The shop had been empty for some time and was in need of a coat of paint but, as soon as he saw it, Julius knew why Reuben had his heart set on it. It was absolutely ideal. A great glass window opened on to the street, thronged with passers by. On the ground floor was an enormous room from which led off a smaller rear room, itself leading to a small delivery yard. From the main room a staircase led to the upper floors, for the entire building was available.

"Can you visualise it, Julius? Shelves and shelves of books, with people browsing, as they say. Here at the back a little sanctum. Upstairs first store rooms and then, at the top my own residential rooms. Why, I may even marry and have a family, who knows? I'm still young enough at 46 am I not? What a place to rear a family!"

"Reuben it would take a much harder hearted man than I not to support you. I shall certainly recommend Josef to buy this for you, and wish you many, many happy years here, old friend!"

"God bless you, Julius!" and they shook hands on the thought.

"The business will prosper, Julius. I was made for books not textiles. When it does I shall pay Josef, or Isaac if he has succeeded by then, back every penny. I want this to be my own in every way."

"Are you going to give the shop a name?"

"Yes. Since my surname is Stein, a stone, I shall call it Bibliopola Petrae."

In July 1871 Isaac and his family finally arrived in Bayswater and took up residence in the now partly furnished house. They found integration into their new community even more difficult than they had anticipated. Their new neighbours were not at all to their liking initially, for not only were the Aronbergs extremely austere in their lifestyle but they still obstinately persisted in speaking German whenever possible. This latter practice, in particular, created a substantial barrier to social intercourse from the very outset. Even the usual means of contact arising from children seeing each other at school was lacking for they had engaged a private German speaking tutor for the two boys. The local community saw them but seldom.

Had it not been for Reuben and Julius they would have made virtually no social contacts outside the business. Reuben, they discovered, was completely happy. His shop had quickly become well known in scholastic circles and the business was prospering accordingly. Proudly he showed them over the shop but they showed little interest in it and never visited it again. Nevertheless he was always made welcome at the Bayswater house and he and Julius dined there at least twice a week.

In 1874 Miriam conceived again. It had, by this time, already become increasingly difficult for them to maintain their self-imposed isolation. Reuben and Julius both had from time to time brought friends to the Bayswater house, thus enlarging their circle, whilst other acquaintanceships had proved unavoidable. The daily intercourse of everyday life had compelled resort to an ever-increasing use of the English language. Samuel and Eli, now respectively nine and eight, began to demand the company of boys of their own age. The two children now ventured where their parents had hitherto been reluctant to tread.

As the months of Miriam's pregnancy went by more and more people came to the once so rarely visited house. The two boys had by now persuaded their parents to allow them to attend a select private school in the neighbourhood. Here they soon struck up further friendships. Mothers brought their children to the house to play and then stayed to chat to Miriam. The boys were invited back. Miriam then called to collect the boys and in that process met still more mothers. As her time approached friends, thus acquired, came round ever more frequently. By the time Sarah, as the new baby was named, arrived on October 15th, 1874, the bastions of self-exclusion had begun to crumble. Julius, however, was recalled home.

With Julius gone some of their old ways began to reassert themselves. Their adaptation to London life had always been half-hearted and they had never felt able to accept complete integration. Likewise the two boys, having been so subjected during their most formative years to their parents' prejudices, inevitably acquired some of these themselves. Both grew up feeling in some not very clearly defined way that they were really German and not English. This was much reinforced by their annual and extensive visits to see their grandparents in Berlin.

In Sarah's case, however, matters were turning out otherwise. She grew up regarding herself as English. The German speaking tutor had departed and she was allowed to have an English nurse, and then governess. When she grew older she attended a local private school where she mixed with other girls from the locality. Whilst, inevitably, she had acquired fluency in German it was as a second language. She hated visiting her German grandparents in what she regarded as the great gloomy Aronberg Berlin mansion. By the time she was ten Josef seemed to her a terrifying old man, best avoided. Her grandmother, with her severe face and black rustling silken dresses, frightened her. She began to make every effort to find excuses in order to avoid the dreaded Berlin visits. She persuaded sympathetic schoolfriends to have their parents issue invitations to coincide with the intended dates. For their part, the grandparents took not the least interest in her, they were completely bound up in the boys.

The gulf widened between Sarah and her brothers and her parents as each year passed. She feared but felt no love for her remote, heavily bearded father in his dark suits. He rarely smiled and such pleasantries as he might utter were always directed to the boys. For her mother she had some natural affection but she rarely felt any reciprocal warmth. The boys were already nine and eight when she was born and had lived, at that time, the greater parts of their lives in Berlin. In that austere household the lively little girl found no companionship. She was, she felt, alone in the midst of an otherwise closely-knit family.

By the time she was ten Eli had been sent back to Germany. On his eighteenth birthday he departed to live with Moses in Munich to learn the business there. Moses, a life-long bachelor, died four years later and Eli remained to run the Munich office. Sarah never saw him again. Moses, however, left each of his brother's grandchildren substantial legacies. Sarah's was of sufficient size to yield her quite a worthwhile income that she was free to use as she wished once she achieved the age of twenty-one.

Samuel, now working in Isaac's office in London, she saw scarcely at all. Her mother had become closely involved in charity work and Sarah was left very much to her own devices.

The gloom and restrictiveness of the house became increasingly irksome to her. Families with whom she stayed during school holidays were so much more liberal in their outlooks. Nevertheless whilst they were invariably polite and friendly to her she could not fail to be aware of the barriers and problems caused by the foreign origins of her family as revealed by her name. These she furiously resented. She regarded herself as being just as English as her friends. Her name, as she saw it, distinguished her as foreign, and this she resented.

When he reached seventy, in 1887, Josef, deciding it was time to reduce his workload, summoned Samuel back to Berlin. Here Samuel, now twenty-two, married a childhood friend, Naomi. Shortly thereafter these two had a son, Aaron, born in 1888.

Sarah, now thirteen, was thus alone with her parents. Puberty had arrived early and with its onset there welled up within her ever more strongly her spirit of discontent. The oppressiveness of the house and all its customs weighed ever more and more strongly upon her. She did, however, have one great solace in Uncle Reuben. In him, she had early discovered, she had found a kindred spirit. She adored and admired him in equal measure.

He was so utterly different from her father. He was a cheerful, totally anglicised man, still young at seventy, whereas her father seemed to her to be infinitely old, though not yet fifty. She loved his pleasantly clean-shaved face. She had grown to detest beards and sidelocks. Her young spirits lifted at the sight of his bohemian style dress, his not over well pressed trousers, his baggy jacket, his carelessly tied cravat. She loved the smell of his cigars. She had never been permitted to visit his shop but in her imagination she saw all his clients in similar mould. It was only to him she felt able to confide her innermost thoughts. He never criticised her, never attempted to impose a view. He listened, considered, and then commented. In this way he had early learned of her worries about her name and its real or fancied revelation of her German-Jewish origins. He was the only person in the world she had ever told. Their discussions were cathartic experiences for her. Reuben was her window on an as yet unexperienced world.

On her twelfth birthday he had given her a copy of Sir Thomas Malory's "Morte D'Arthur". This had become her most treasured possession. She had him write an inscription on the title page. Below this she kept a note of her favourite passage in the book. She would, she determined, never be voluntarily parted from it.

CHAPTER THREE

DECISION

Always their discussions reverted to her foreign background and name and the problems she believed to stem from them. In truth the subjects obsessed her. She had begun to convince herself she had been born with them as a ball and chain.

"My surname was not of my choosing," she said one day to Reuben when they were sitting together in the old schoolroom, somewhere they were sure never to be disturbed. It was then October, 1893, and she was newly nineteen. "Yet it seems to dominate my life. Wherever I go, it goes with me. Why should I be so enslaved? We were reading Rousseau the other day. You remember, "Man is born free: everywhere he is in chains." Was I born free? When they hear my name I am convinced people immediately begin to regard me differently. I don't feel different and I am not different. Furthermore I am determined not to be different. I want to be free to choose for myself, Reuben. In particular I want to marry whom I choose. I want to be able to act according to my own choice and conscience."

"Sarah, you cannot so easily renounce your background. You must learn to live with it. People must love you and respect you for what you are, not what you pretend to be."

"We could have changed our name when we came to England. Why did we have to keep a German name and behave as though we were German when we live in England? "When in Rome do as the Romans do". Lot of people alter their names in such circumstances."

"That your grandfather has specifically forbidden. You know how proud he is of the Aronberg name."

"You give in too easily, Reuben," she flashed. "I'm going to do what I feel is right for me. You wait and see."

He smiled. "I prefer to say I'm a pragmatist."

He sat back and studied his niece carefully. "You always were a pretty girl, Sarah. My goodness, though, you are now the kind of maiden who must have inspired the Song of Songs."

"Thank you, sir. That is the best compliment ever paid to me in this house. A most agreeable experience."

She settled back into her chair and gave her mind to his earlier remark about pragmatism. He continued his study of her.

She had inherited her mother's grey green eyes. These sparkled deliciously below her dark eyelashes. Her complexion, though perhaps a shade darker than that of some of her friends, was wonderfully attractive. Her young figure had formed into what, he thought, was surely an artist's ideal. Yes, he pondered, it was surely one of your ancestors who so inspired Solomon.

She, meanwhile, had come to a conclusion. "We are two of a kind aren't we?"

"Don't be over-concerned on that score. You have a determination to pursue your own path that, I fear, was sadly lacking in me when I was your age and faced with the same kind of problems."

She looked at him questioningly. A thought had occurred to her. "How did it come about, Reuben, that my father took charge of the London office? How was it that you came to acquire your bookshop? Has it something to do with what you said about your being a pragmatist?"

"Yes, Sarah, it has. Before you were born I, too, wanted to follow my own course. Josef, Miriam and the family soon put a stop to that. But, eventually, I made such a hopeless mess of things that Josef, mercifully, removed me from the firm. Strange, isn't it, that what was, perhaps, intended to signal my disgrace was the best thing that ever happened to me? The arrangement Josef made was highly satisfactory. Without his assistance I could never have secured the shop. It has been so successful that I have been able to repay every penny he loaned me. When I did that I really did feel I had lost a ball and chain. That is except in one respect, which you may be surprised to hear. I, too always wanted to change my name from Stein to Peters - not only to match the name I chose for my shop but for the same reasons as motivate you. However I felt to do so would be a betrayal of my sister, who was, I have always believed, instrumental in persuading Josef to make the offer."

"I never knew that. Well now I know why you say you are so 'pragmatic'. I'd still like you to answer my question, though. How can I divest myself of my ball and chain? Is there no way?"

"In a few years time, Sarah, the twentieth century will dawn. You will be entering a new era. Look to the future, not the past. Be, as you say you will, mistress of your own future. You won't have any second chance. Above all don't be deceived by spurious notions of loyalty. I'm afraid that if you follow such advice you may end up hurting people, perhaps even me, certainly your parents. That is often the price of self-fulfilment."

This conversation made a great impression on her. She turned over its import in her mind for many weeks. Then she made a decision. As soon as she was of age she would at the very least anglicise her name, whatever her parents might think and do.

One year later, Josef and Ruth followed each other to the grave in rapid succession. Isaac and Miriam at once returned to Berlin to attend the funerals. Sarah, however, to her great relief, was left behind. Isaac forecast a protracted absence. "Somebody," he said, "must remain in charge of the house. That responsibility devolves on you, Sarah."

When they arrived in Berlin, however, both Isaac and Miriam were overcome by a desire to remain there permanently. Since Samuel would not agree to return to London, and Julius was no longer available it was finally decided to put the London office under the temporary supervision of a trustworthy clerk. Isaac took up residence, as head of the firm, in the Berlin mansion. Samuel was put in charge of the Berlin office and Eli in charge of the one in Munich. In consequence the Bayswater house was now considered to have become redundant and could be sold. Nobody even thought of asking Sarah what she felt about these decisions. It was taken for granted she would join her parents in Berlin.

" It is high time Sarah was married," said Miriam. "I'm already looking out for a suitable match. Her husband can then take over at the London office. It should be in the charge of a family member. Then Sarah can move back to London with him."

A month later Isaac and Miriam returned to London and, over dinner that first night, with only Reuben also present, informed Sarah of the decisions which had been taken in Berlin. Sarah, now being of age, was in possession of her legacy. This knowledge, together with her natural resolve to remain in England, considerably fortified her.

"Under no circumstances will I agree to go and live in Berlin," she said heatedly, flushing with anger. "You may all consider yourselves German. I know I am English. I shall remain here in England."

Her mother put down her knife and fork and looked at her in amazement, whilst her father began to show signs of being on the verge of explosion. Reuben held his tongue.

"But Sarah, the house is to be sold. There is already a prospective purchaser waiting. As soon as you are married your husband will come back to London and take charge here. In the meanwhile you must come back with us."

Isaac, a man always, at the best of times, hovering on the brink of irascibility, was having immense problems retaining his self-control. Miriam sat back, puffing slightly, obviously feeling her argument was unassailable. She waited, in vain, for Sarah's expected capitulation.

Reuben who had long foreseen such a development, and had devised a plan accordingly, now decided it was time to intervene before matters escalated into a major catastrophe.

"Would it be an acceptable solution if Sarah were to come and live in the vacant apartments I have available over Bibliopola Petrae now I have resumed living in my former bachelor quarters in Gardens Square? She would be such a help to me there. You can trust me to care for her as though she were my own daughter until such time as she marries."

"There is nothing in the world I should like so much, Reuben." cried Sarah

Isaac, who was in fact greatly relieved to be so unexpectedly offered such a convenient escape route from what had been threatening to turn into a major problem, looked at Miriam. "Your Mother must make the decision," he said, "and by that you must abide."

Miriam had already eagerly embraced the proposal. "Very well." she said, as though making a concession, "until you are married."

Sarah was content to keep her own counsel on that score. She had what she wanted. Isaac and Miriam, their business in London completed, returned to Berlin in January 1896.

As soon as they were gone Sarah joyfully moved out of the Bayswater house and into her new accommodation over Bibliopola Petrae.

CHAPTER FOUR

REUBEN

It was Wednesday, fifteenth January, 1896, that Sarah first saw Bibliopola Petrae.

"I have never before been in such a wonderful place!" she exclaimed as she excitedly paced up and down the corridors of books. Every now and then she would pause and reach down some volume that chanced to catch her attention, savouring it like some exotic fruit. Reuben watched her with delight.

That first evening they dined at a little nearby restaurant, the haunt of people much like Reuben. He was obviously highly popular. Sarah at once felt herself amongst friends. "Let us come here together every evening, after the shop closes," he said, "it will be a pleasant end of the day for each of us. Furthermore it will considerably assist your catering problems!"

The meal over he escorted her back to her rooms over the shop, a task he performed faithfully every evening from then on. Then he made his way back to Gardens Square, seated on the top of the omnibus, which went along the Bayswater Road.

Bibliopola Petrae opened promptly each morning at nine. Sarah now took her place beside Reuben behind his desk. In a matter of weeks she felt totally at ease with all the customers. She had soon acquired almost as comprehensive knowledge of the contents of the shop as had Reuben himself.

The window display was arranged so that passers-by had a clear view of the interior of Bibliopola Petrae It consisted of a display of rare and beautiful books, opened at pages carefully selected to excite interest and thus entice prospective customers to make further enquiries within. Beyond the table stretched the book-laden shelves. At the far end was Reuben's desk. This was a large mahogany affair, leather topped with ball and claw feet. It was always piled high with books and pamphlets, awaiting despatch, or for reading, or for classification, or for repair, or for putting back on the shelves. Behind it sat Reuben, a veritable fountain of information. He seemed to know the location and provenance of every book in the place. A feeling of quiet, scholastic dignity pervaded Bibliopola Petrae. In the winter it was lit by gaslight. This, together with the distinctive, rather musty, smell of the volumes, gave the premises that special atmosphere so beloved of bibliophiles.

Beyond the desk lay the sanctum. Here the more precious books were kept. Here took place all special negotiations. The sanctum was furnished with a desk at which to work and two old but very comfortable leather armchairs. Its window looked out on to the delivery yard at the back. It was regarded as a high honour by the regular clientele to be invited into the sanctum.

Upstairs were the storage rooms and, of course, Sarah's new home.

It was over dinner one evening early in March 1896, at the little restaurant where they now regularly dined after they had closed the shop, that she finally plucked up the courage to tell Reuben that she had just changed her name by deed poll to Avondale.

"Reuben, I have something important to tell you!" She saw a flicker of concern and correctly guessed the interpretation he had put upon her remark. "No, I have not made an unfortunate liaison!"

The relief on his face was almost comic.

"It concerns that conversation you and I had just after my nineteenth birthday, do you remember what we discussed?"

He did. "Are you still worrying away about your name, Sarah?"

"Reuben, I've been in touch with a lawyer and obtained and acted upon his advice. I've changed my name, by deed poll, to Avondale. I feel that I've escaped from my cage!"

He carefully poured out a glass of wine and held it up to the light as though examining it. Then he said,"" I don't suppose they know about this action of yours in Berlin yet?" Not that there was the least chance they did, as he well knew, but it made an opening gambit.

"No, they don't, I simply didn't know how to set about telling them. As you know old Josef had made them all swear they would never do such a thing!"

"Well, Sarah, what's done is done! You've crossed your Rubicon. I cannot say I can foresee any possibility of forgiveness or understanding in Berlin but, if you don't feel able to face it, then I suppose I must do so. I did say I would be responsible for you."

"Dear Reuben!" she said, and her obvious relief was sufficient reward for him.

"Well," he said with a wry smile, "we're both about to enter the fiery furnace!"

That evening he sat on the omnibus, as it bumped its way along the Bayswater Road, and composed in his head letter after letter. He finally resolved upon what he felt were the right words and sent the result off to Berlin by the first available mail. When his letter arrived in Berlin it was as though the household there had been visited by the plague. It lay, as had Julius Roth's, on the breakfast table. Isaac was sitting in the same chair, in the same place, in the same room, at the same table, and at the same time as had his father. His reaction when he opened and read the contents was much more extreme than had even been his father's. He read it silently but, as he did so, his features became contorted with a mixture of rage and anguish. Miriam, Naomi and Samuel watched in astonishment. Unlike his father Isaac now turned to his son not his wife. He felt he could not rely upon Miriam's judgement where her daughter was concerned. He passed the letter, with a shaking hand, to Samuel. "Read this!" he commanded.

Samuel digested the contents, then looked at his father, who simply said, "Let us go into the study and discuss what we are to do!"

Only then did he address his wife. "Miriam, a matter of great concern is in this letter. I must first discuss it with Samuel. Would you, Naomi and Aaron please all go and wait in your sitting room? I cannot bring myself to tell you more until I have had a further discussion with Samuel. I shall send somebody to tell you when we have resolved what we feel should be done." So saying, and without giving the astonished Miriam any further chance to say anything, the two men adjourned to Josef's old study. There they remained in consultation for a full hour. Finally a maid was sent to request the presence of the ladies and Aaron in the very rarely used morning room. This was a gloomy room, even by the sombre standards of the Berlin mansion. It was furnished with dark, velvet hangings, lined with dark oaken panelling and equipped with heavy mahogany and leather furniture. It was used only for the most formal of occasions. The last such gathering had been to hear the reading of Josef's will.

Miriam seated herself on one of the uncomfortable high-backed chairs. Naomi sat down on the equally uncomfortable sofa with Aaron by her side. To Naomi's surprise Samuel came over and sat down next to her, holding her hand and putting his arm protectively round Aaron.

Isaac took up a position before the unlit fire, the letter in his hand. The room was deathly cold. "I received this letter this morning, from Reuben," he announced in sepulchral tones. "I shall now read it to you." This he did, in the process reducing Miriam and Naomi to tears. Then he folded it, returned it to its envelope, and locked it away in a small drawer of the desk. He resumed, "She is no longer our daughter or a sister to you Samuel. She has renounced us and we renounce her. She has betrayed the trust my father placed in my hands. From now she is non-existent! No member of this family shall ever see or speak to or of her again!" He turned and left the room.

He re-entered the study and, seating himself at Josef's old desk, he took up his pen and wrote to Reuben. He directed him to remove Sarah from her apartments and to comply with his edict. For the moment he sought to attach no blame for what had happened to Reuben. He could not bring himself to believe that his mother's brother could lend himself to such a proceeding willingly.

But Reuben, when he received the letter, curtly refused to comply. He would, he wrote, under no circumstances reject Sarah. In fact he had meanwhile taken the necessary steps to change his own name to Peters. He, himself, was thereupon included in the ban. From that day on neither Sarah nor Reuben ever again had any communication of any kind with the rest of the family.

"Well, at least they won't try to marry me off now!" said Sarah.

"I suppose that's as good an epitaph on this part of your life as could be spoken!" said Reuben.

It was April, 1896.

CHAPTER FIVE

THRELFALL

The Threlfalls were one of those ancient English families who had lived quietly and unostentatiously on their estates for generation upon generation. They were solid county folk, with considerable wealth. They were greatly respected but seldom ventured into the worlds of politics or fashion. On rare occasions a younger son had been known to represent the constituency in Parliament. In such a manner the family had survived since before even the Norman conquest. Civil wars, religious schisms, the industrial and agricultural revolutions had all made but little impact. Their interest and fortune lay in their land.

The family seat and only principal residence was at Loughbourne Manor. Originally little more then a fortified farmhouse it had, over the centuries, changed continuously. By 1880 the original structure had vanished, submerged in a welter of architectural styles, late Tudor, Anne, Regency and some quite pleasant early Victorian additions. The result was surprisingly attractive. The house was approached by a mile long, gravelled drive, bordered by great chestnut trees, which gave way beyond to open fields. At the end of the drive stood the Lodge, a Regency flight of fancy more pleasant to look at than to live in. Here lived the coachman, Wilfred Mitchell, with his family. The manor house itself was for the main part built in a warm red brick and on three principal floors. It contained numerous bedrooms, a fine drawing room, a formal but pleasant dining room, a breakfast and morning room, a billiard room, the squire's study, the chatelaine's private room, a conservatory and a large, relatively well stocked but rather dark library. Behind the manor house and across the stable yard were the outbuildings, stables, estate office, coach-house. For the most part the servants' quarters were in a separate building, some small distance from the main house.

Formal and carefully tended gardens surrounded the house but the family were more interested in agriculture than horticulture and the gardens soon gave way to fields on which grazed sheep and cattle. Some small distance away from the main dwelling lay the Dower House. This had had as its original purpose the housing of surviving widows, for the Threlfall males tended to predecease their wives with alarming regularity. However, in 1880 the Dower House, not being required for any surviving widow, had been let on a long lease, to the estate's land agent, Frank Morton. There he lived with his wife, Beatrice, and their infant son, Alan, born that year.

Loughbourne village was owned in its entirety by the family and consisted of some forty houses, an ancient and extremely large church, St. Ethelred the Martyr, and the vicarage. The church had originally served the entire surrounding district including what had originally been the hamlet of Crufton. However when the railway came the line went through Crufton completely bypassing Loughbourne. In consequence Crufton had grown rapidly, soon dwarfing its neighbour and acquiring its own complement of churches. London was sixty-five miles distant and, for most of the local inhabitants, little more than a place of legend. Nobody ever ventured further than Crufton.

Here, in 1845, Robert Threlfall had been born. He was educated, as had been his father, grandfather and great grandfather, at Bushfield Abbey School. In 1869 he had inherited the estate and title, a baronetcy, on the death of his father and immediately immersed himself in its management, with the able assistance of Frank Morton. The following year he had married Mary, the daughter of a neighbouring squire. By her a son, Frederick, was born in 1871. Lady Mary never again produced a child that lived for more than a few weeks. By the time she was thirty, in 1878, the estate management was being left almost entirely in the hands of Frank Morton whilst they devoted themselves to foreign travel. Frederick, by that time eight, was a boarder at Bushcome School, the preparatory school that served Bushfield Abbey. If his parents were, as was almost invariably the case, away on their travels when he came home for the holidays he either invited school friends for company or went to stay with them at their homes. He saw very little of his parents and they took minimal interest in him. Both Sir Robert and Lady Mary had been only children. He had, in consequence, no aunts, uncles or first cousins. Sir Robert's mother had died when Frederick was six. His maternal grandparents had died when he was still a baby.

When he was twelve Frederick entered Bushfield Abbey, which was exclusively for boarders. He was a bright, diligent boy and showed considerable promise in classics, history and English literature. By the time he was seventeen the then headmaster recommended to Sir Robert that his son be encouraged to enter Cambridge. Here he did much better than might have been expected considering the small amount of work he appeared to do. He left university with a lifelong love of literature and an ambition to improve the quality of the Loughbourne Manor library. As soon as he had graduated he expressed a desire to his father to be allowed to enter the army or, failing that, to stand for Parliament.

"Nonsense," said his father when he broached these ideas. "You've already wasted quite enough time at Cambridge! I really cannot understand why I ever agreed to your going there! You must remain here with Morton and learn how to run the estate. It will all be yours, you know, one of these days!"

"But, Father, you're only forty-six. I most sincerely hope I shall not be inheriting for a long time yet! Surely there's plenty of time for me to do something else before I settle down here?"

"Well, there's something in that, I admit. For the moment, however, your mother and I intend to continue to extend our travels. When we finally decide to settle down again here I'll see if I can't have you fixed up with a seat in Parliament. I'll speak to Sir Gilbert Winslow about it. He's the local party chairman. In the meantime you are to stay here. Get to know the ropes, the tenants and so on. Morton's a first class chap, learn all you can from him!"

"I'll still be able to spend a couple of days a week in Town? I'd like to continue to keep in touch with a few friends from university?"

"Don't get the idea I want to imprison you! Of course you need some time off the leash! That reminds me, it's high time I increased your allowance."

There was no question of his changing his father's mind. He gave up the attempt. In due course he fell in love with the family estate, as had all his ancestors, but he dearly valued his weekly London visits. His passion, when in London, was to hunt out interesting bookshops, where he looked for additions to the manor library. It was thus that he discovered Reuben. He first entered Reuben's shop on Wednesday, May 12th, 1896. The first person he saw as he opened the door was Sarah.

Every Wednesday from then on he caught the early train from Crufton. He checked in at his club and then went directly to Reuben's shop where, under the guise of book hunting, he observed Sarah, although he never actually spoke to her.

It was soon quite evident to Reuben that it was Sarah who was the focus of attention of his new, obviously aristocratic, client's attention. Sarah, however, seemed to be oblivious to Frederick's interest in her. In the meantime an increasingly satisfactory number of quite valuable books exchanged hands. Reuben reasoned that this was good for business and that no harm was likely to result. As far as he could see there was no conceivable future in the affair. Sarah, he was certain, would not be entrapped into anything foolish. The young man would eventually grow tired of such a one sided courtship and transfer his affections elsewhere. He still, however, had no idea as to his identity. He always paid in cash and took his purchases away with him. He obviously had an educated taste and such conversations as Reuben had with him were interesting. The two even became quite friendly. Sarah, however, never appeared to take the least interest, and the admirer never attempted to speak to her, even, in fact, apparently deliberately avoiding any possibility of addressing her directly.

The truth was that Sarah had realised what was happening from the very outset. She had at once felt a reciprocal attraction but, like her uncle, had written the position off as hopeless. "Sooner or later he'll come to his senses!" she said to herself.

But he didn't.

Threlfalls had not retained their lands and position through a thousand years of turbulent history from lack of resolution or enterprise. For the moment Frederick recognised his goal was apparently unattainable but he was quite certain he would eventually overcome the problems. He was in no hurry. He enjoyed Bibliopola Petrae. He liked talking to Reuben. He had no reason to go elsewhere. He kept coming.

At that time he was haunted by the prospect of the future which seemed to be his inevitable lot. He was only just twenty-five. Even allowing for the notorious propensity of Threlfall men to die before their wives it was unlikely, barring accidents, that he would inherit under twenty years. Inevitably it would become increasingly difficult for him to resist agreeing to marry some suitable county girl his mother would find for him. In fact he was quite sure this would be Eleanor Winslow. She was a handsome girl, well fitted for the role of chatelaine of Loughbourne and he was a good friend of her brother Humphrey one year older than himself and also still unmarried. She would, however, be most unlikely to approve, let alone share, his literary enthusiasms. He felt utterly trapped. He wanted to be free to marry whom he chose.

This frustration had been deepening for some time. His discovery of Sarah greatly increased his despondency.

In June that year a letter from an Italian friend his parents had met on a previous trip to Italy arrived at Loughbourne. Sir Robert opened the letter at breakfast and read it with obvious pleasure before passing it across to his wife. "There, that's a pleasant surprise, Mary, eh?"

"Why, it is from the Marinis inviting us to join them at that beautiful villa of theirs on the shores of Lake Como in July. I suppose it will be very hot, but perhaps those trips he promises on his yacht will keep us all cool."

"They know how to deal with hot weather, Mary! There will certainly be many lake expeditions. They will be most enjoyable. Luigi and Maria Augusta are so pleasant. I shall accept at once."

He turned to Frederick. ""Your mother and I met these people whilst you were still at Bushfield. They have always hoped that we might be able to go over and spend some time with them, but until now Luigi has been too occupied with his business affairs. Their villa is absolutely superb, we have been there once before and enjoyed the lake with them, for he is a keen yachtsman. He has, he says, now retired and is longing to see us again."

"How long shall you be away, do you think?"

"We are asked for two months. After that your mother and I may well extend the trip to take in ancient Pompeii, Naples and Assisi. We should be home again by late October."

"You could well employ your time whilst we're away finding yourself a wife! I'm sure they'd make you more than welcome at Hardstone Place. That would really be an excellent match!"

"Indeed," said his father, approvingly, "no need to ask my consent in that quarter! That would very much please us both!" Hardstone Place was the family seat of the Winslows.

Sir Robert and Lady Mary departed for Italy late in June 1896. Frederick waved good bye to them as they boarded the boat train, and then wandered off to his club. There was nobody there of the least interest. He ate a solitary lunch and then made his way to the by now familiar surroundings of Bibliopola Petrae.

Although he had been presented with no gateway to everlasting freedom the prospect of such a lengthy parental absence had somewhat lightened his spirits. He entered Bibliopola Petrae with a firm resolve to speak, at last, to Sarah. There could, he told himself, be no possible harm in striking up the same kind of relationship with her as he had already achieved with Reuben.

CHAPTER SIX

MEETING

He had no idea what he was going to do as he entered the door. He saw Reuben and Sarah standing, as usual, behind the desk at the far end of the shop. It was still early afternoon and there were, in consequence, very few people around, just a few customers scattered among the shelves browsing. The Monday departure of his parents had changed his normal routine. His arrival was, therefore, unexpected. "Something's happened," said Reuben to himself. Out of the corner of his eye he could see that Sarah was also observing the young man's entry with interest.

Quite unexpectedly she suddenly said, "I think that customer who has just entered looks as though he needs some assistance!" Before Reuben could utter a word she had walked straight up to Frederick who, in the meanwhile, had begun wandering rather vaguely round the shelves picking up books in a desultory way and then putting them back again. At the moment she approached him he chanced to be holding in his hand, why he knew not, a copy of Malory's "Morte D'Arthur".

"Excuse me, sir, can I be of any help to you?"

It was scarcely poetry but, for Frederick, these mundane words could well have issued from the Poet Laureate. His heart missed a beat. She was actually speaking to him! His response, however, was equally banal.

"How kind of you! Yes, I was thinking of buying this book. It looks most interesting."

She knew perfectly well that it was in herself, not the book, he was interested, but she simply gave him a charming smile and said, "I'll have to ask the price from the owner, my uncle. But what is the name of the book, please?"

He gave her the book with a slightly shaking hand. "How fascinating! This is my own very favourite book! My uncle gave me a copy when I was twelve. I read a little every night. I adore it. I have favourite passages I read again and again! Do you know, you are the very first customer, since I began working here, who has ever asked for a copy?"

He grasped this opportunity for a conversation as a drowning sailor might grasp at a proffered rope. "Do show me one of your favourite passages. I should be most interested!"

She turned over the pages. "Ah, yes, here's one. The light here is so poor though. This old fashioned print is so hard to read. Come along into the sanctum. There's much better light in there and we won't disturb other customers with our conversation." Without waiting for his reply she proceeded to lead the way to the back of the shop, carrying the book. She smiled sweetly at Reuben, who was looking astounded, and beckoned Frederick to follow her in to the room. She put the book down on the desk and proceeded to read, "Chapter twenty five of book eighteen, "How true love is likened to summer"."

He leaned over to look. As he did so their heads touched very lightly. He straightened up quickly as though he had been stung. She gave no sign of having even noticed. She continued to read from the passage in her soft, educated voice, "For then all herbs and trees renew a man and a woman and in likewise lovers call again to their mind old gentleness and old service and many kind deeds that were forgotten by negligence." She paused and looked at him.

"There, isn't that beautiful?"

Under his breath, or such was his sincere intention, he said, "But not as beautiful as you." Her sharp ears picked up the words but she gave no sign she had heard them.

He flicked nervously through the pages. His eye chanced on a half line. This he read out, "...said Sir Palamides, for love is free for all men."He smiled at her and said, "Well spoken, Sir Palamides, I agree with you!"

There was a discreet cough behind them. A rather apprehensive Reuben had decided he really had to intervene. Frederick realised he would have to take some immediate and determined action if he were to have any hope of seeing Sarah again. "Your niece is so interesting, sir. She has been explaining this book to me. I am so interested in the Arthurian legend. I wonder whether, as the shop does not appear to be too busy this afternoon, I might have your permission to discuss the book further with her over a cup of tea at the little place opposite? I should see we were not more than an hour. I have to catch a train back to the country this evening."

It was not a very convincing tale. Sarah gazed demurely at Reuben. Reuben, very puzzled by her behaviour, very reluctantly gave his consent.

Frederick promptly paid for the book. Sarah collected her coat and hat and the two left the shop. In the little cafe they selected a table and, as soon as they were seated, he proceeded to pour out his heart to her. He had never had such a sympathetic listener. Each had been instinctively attracted by the other. Both greatly wished to develop this sudden relationship into something special whilst only too well aware of the obstacles which would confront them. Both were very determined people.

Throughout July from then on they met each Wednesday and had tea together. By the end of the fourth meeting each knew every last detail about the other. Sarah, however, considered herself much more practical than Frederick.

"Frederick, surely you are aware there is absolutely no chance whatsoever of your family ever accepting me socially. You are an aristocrat and I, whatever I may call myself, would be a shop assistant with a German Jewish background to them. I may have changed my name, but the facts would be certain to come out. It has been wonderful meeting you and talking to you but I am sure that if we continue to see each other than on a simply casual and friendly basis, like this, for occasional chats, we shall both be badly hurt!"

He sat fidgeting with his teacup, saying nothing.

She continued, "If you were to cease seeing me you will soon forget all about me. After all you've only known me four weeks, in fact really only four days!"

"It could just as well have been four centuries. I'm jolly well not going to stop seeing you when and where we choose. Threlfalls don't give up. Just you wait and see, something will turn up. It always does!"

"I'm afraid this Threlfall has tackled something even he can't handle," said Sarah, gently.

"And what might that be?"

"The power of prejudice!" she responded, with a touch of bitterness.

CHAPTER SEVEN

INHERITANCE

That evening he returned to Loughbourne. Since they had been away he had had only two communications from his parents, both postcards. Letter writing had never been their strong suit even when he had been at boarding school. It was, therefore, with some surprise he found a letter with an Italian stamp on it awaiting him. It was addressed in an unfamiliar and foreign hand. He turned it over and saw that it was from a Domenico Marini. He felt sure that he recollected his father's telling him that they were going to stay with a Luigi Marini. Perhaps he was being asked to join the party? With considerable puzzlement he opened the letter.

It was datelined Como, Italy, July twenty-third, 1896. It was from Luigi's brother, Domenico. By it he was informed that Luigi and his wife, together with their houseguests, his parents, and their crewman had all perished by drowning. A violent and most unusual and totally unexpected wind had capsized the yacht in the deepest and most dangerous stretch of the lake. Domenico had witnessed the tragedy from the lakeside through his telescope. All efforts to recover the bodies or the yacht had so far been unsuccessful. It was, indeed, feared that both the wreck and the bodies might be irretrievably trapped at the bottom of the lake. In consequence, Domenico wrote, there seemed little practical purpose in Frederick's at once making the arduous journey to Como. He was arranging for the erection of a memorial on the promontory, part of the Marini's property, which overlooked the lake at the point where the accident had occurred. This would be complete and ready for dedication by November. He suggested that Frederick should instead come across to attend the dedication ceremony. The villa, at which Domenico was currently living, whilst seeing to his late brother's affairs, was, of course, at all times at Frederick's disposal.

Frederick had never felt any genuine emotional attachment to either of his parents. Indeed sometimes he felt he had scarcely ever known them. He knew he should mourn them, more particularly because of the dreadful circumstances in which they had met their deaths. Try as he might, however, he found he immediately related the news to his desire for Sarah. He was tired and not thinking as straightforwardly as he might have done. It was almost as though he been told of the death of two strangers. He said nothing to anybody that evening. He simply took himself off to bed and, surprisingly, slept soundly.

The following morning he wrote to the family solicitors and asked them to send a partner down to the manor house as soon as possible to see him and discuss all the implications. Then he replied to Domenico. He composed an obituary notice and posted it off to the Times and the local press. Then he went round to see the Mortons, the vicar and the doctor. He wrote letters to all he felt should be informed. He had the butler assemble the staff and broke the news. Both the manor house and the entire village went into mourning. The vicar arranged a memorial service.

Over the next days local gentry and tenantry called. The solicitor arrived and went over the legal position with Morton and himself. In no possible way was he able to leave Loughbourne and go to London. By the time he finally managed to extricate himself it was already mid-September.

By this time Sarah had told Reuben everything that had occurred.

"You handled the matter well, Sarah!"

"Too well, perhaps! He has taken flight!" She busied herself with some trifling task but Reuben could see she was weeping.

"It will pass for her," he thought. "Love is as blind as justice; and certainly as foolish."

It was, therefore, with great astonishment that Reuben beheld Frederick re-enter the shop one Wednesday in mid-September. It was apparent from his demeanour that something had happened of great significance.

The fact of the matter was that, in such brief intervals as had been available for him to put his mind to the matter since the news of his parents' death had broken, Frederick had come to a firm decision. He was going to marry Sarah and nothing was going to stop him.

He had caught the first train from Crufton that morning and proceeded from the station directly to the shop. It was only ten o'clock when he arrived and there were no other customers present. As he entered the premises, Sarah simultaneously appeared coming down the stairs from her own apartments. For a moment both of them stood stock-still looking at each other. Then Frederick said to Reuben, who, as usual, was seated behind the desk, "I should be much obliged, sir, if you would permit me to speak privately to your niece, in the sanctum. I have something of great importance to say to her."

Reuben looked at him in bewilderment but silently gestured for them to enter. The door closed behind them.

CHAPTER EIGHT

PROMISE

"This is most unexpected! I had not thought we should be seeing each other again. Your absence over the last weeks made me quite sure of that. Why have you decided to return?"

"Sarah," he burst out, without further preliminaries, his growing excitement mastering his other feelings, "I have extraordinary news! Whilst it is sad it carries gladness for us! Sarah! Both my parents are dead! They were drowned at the end of July whilst on holiday in Italy. I am afraid that, in consequence, I have been absolutely unable to escape from Loughbourne ever since. There has been so much for me to do!"

She gave a little cry. "Oh, poor Frederick! I had been thinking such unkind things! Oh, I am so sorry!" She had been standing looking at him with concern. Then, recollecting his words, she said, "But what possible gladness can there be in such terrible news?"

"Sarah! I have spent hour upon hour with the lawyers. The position is absolutely certain and clear. I am the sole inheritor of both the estate and the title. I am absolutely my own master!"

"Indeed, Sir Frederick!" she replied, very deliberately emphasising the title, "I see you may well have some gladness from that, but what about your poor parents?"

"Look, Sarah, I have no grandparents, no uncles, no aunts and no cousins. For any other relations I may have I don't care tuppence. It may sound unfilial but I have no intention of allowing whatever might have been my parents' views on your and my relationship to interfere with us from beyond their graves. Surely you, of all people, will understand that? You didn't allow your parents to deflect you from your chosen course, did you?"

Fully appreciating his viewpoint she replied, as calmly as she might, for she knew perfectly well what he was going to say, "What is it that you have determined upon then?"

"That you shall be my wife!"

"Indeed!" she said, speaking very slowly in an effort to keep control of her voice, "but you have yet to ask me if I am willing!"

He was in no mood for these conventionalities. "Well, you will be, won't you?"

"We have already had this discussion. Apart from your altered circumstances has anything, as between us, really changed? If anything, as I see it, things are now even more difficult. You have become a baronet. I am still the same shop assistant with just the same background. Do you honestly believe such a marriage is either sensible or practicable?"

"I have been considering that aspect of things. In fact I have given it all a great deal of thought. Threlfalls have always been realists. That has been the secret of the family's survival over the centuries. I can see no point in taking a high moral line over all this. As for your working here in your uncle's bookshop, that does not concern me at all. I do admit that the Jewish part of your ancestry, were it known, could cause problems. It most certainly does not worry me, but it is true that there are many people who are absurdly prejudiced by such trivia. We had some boys of Jewish origin at Bushfield. They had to put up with a good deal of unpleasantness from some elements there. One of them, an exceptionally good athlete and scholar, went up to Cambridge with me. Even at Cambridge he encountered problems. ."

"Well, there you are! Why should you and I escape?"

"Why should we reveal anything to anybody? We can side-step them by being married in Marylebone Registry Office. I have no wish whatsoever for a church wedding. Lots of my friends have been married like that recently, to all sorts of supposedly unsuitable people. Not one of them has experienced any consequent difficulties. I can tell you that once you are Lady Threlfall of Loughbourne it will be a bold and very foolish person who would question your position in my county! You are self-evidently a well-bred gentlewoman whom, I know, the servants will respect. In these matters, you know, it is the servants who count! If they respect and like you then so will everybody in the county and the village. Leave me to deal with the vicar! He'll be very upset by the registry office marriage, but I have already thought about how I am going to handle that problem with him."

Sarah carefully considered this argument. She could see all the flaws and was completely unconvinced. Nevertheless she had fallen deeply in love with him. Her heart overruled her head. She raised one final objection. "What about our children? We couldn't keep such information from our children!"

"Why not?"

"Because it would be wrong!"

"Fiddlesticks! It is no business of anybody's except ours. It is of no more importance than if you were French. Such information is only important to silly people with silly prejudices! It must remain private to us. Why bother our children with such irrelevant information? It simply confers a spurious importance on the matter which it does not merit!"

She was sure he was completely wrong in his reasoning but she accepted the position and agreed. Her desire to marry him was too strong.

He opened the sanctum door and said to Reuben, "We should be greatly obliged, sir, if you would be good enough to join us. We have something very important to tell you."

There was nobody in the shop. Reuben went to the shop door and hung up the "Closed" sign. Then he joined them.

Sarah was still seated in the chair. Frederick was standing by the window, with one hand in his jacket pocket. Frederick removed his hand from his jacket pocket In it he now held a small leather case. This he now proceeded to open with great deliberation to display a magnificent diamond ring. He knelt down and placed this on Sarah's finger. Sarah, meanwhile, seemed to have gone into a trance. Frederick stood up and kissed her lightly on the cheek.

"Sir, may I introduce you to the future Lady Threlfall!".

Frederick had already wired Morton to tell him he was spending that evening at the club and would not return to Loughbourne until later the following day.

To Reuben and Sarah he said, as he took his leave from them that evening, "I must return to Loughbourne. I must be there tomorrow. I shall return to you within a week. Look after her for me, sir!"

CHAPTER NINE

INTERLUDE

On his return Domenico's reply was waiting for him. No trace of the bodies or the yacht had yet been found. The monument had been commissioned. The dedication, as had previously been suggested, would definitely take place toward the middle of November. If Frederick could manage to be present then the villa would be at his disposal until the first of December. Domenico and his own family would also be there but would then have to close it and return to Rome for the winter.

Frederick at once replied telling Domenico that he was just about to be married and that he and his wife would certainly attend the dedication. He would confirm the exact travel plans as soon as possible.

He then paid a visit to the Mortons in the Dower House. "I am going back to London tomorrow, Frank. I have some people to see there. Then, at the end of October, the Marini family have asked me to go over to Como to attend the dedication of a memorial to my parents and the others drowned in the yacht disaster. I plan to remain with them until the end of November and to be back here, at Loughbourne, by the latter part of December. You will be able to contact me through my club.

When I get back I think that should mark the end of the mourning period and I should like the coming Christmas to be a merry one for everybody. I shall probably bring a couple of friends back with me. By the way I should like you to arrange to revive the servants' Christmas Ball in the Old Barn. Could you see to that? I know I can leave everything safely in your hands!"

Then he returned to London.

"You know I have a feeling that he may have found himself a wife!" said Frank to his family."Well, we shall all find out soon enough, Frank!" said Beatrice, his wife. "Goodness knows the place could do with a mistress! If he marries anywhere other than at the church here in Loughbourne, though, the Reverend Tapping is going to be upset!"

"True enough! But he's been making remarkably regular visits to London. He's up to something, I'm sure. Anyway I must go and tell

Mrs.Faming and Goodenough that the servants' ball is to be revived! That will please them, they always resented its abolition by Lady Mary after that little spot of bother some years ago!"

Their maid had overheard this exchange. It was only a matter of hours before a rumour had swept the manor house, and then the village, that the squire was courting and was expected to bring back his bride in time for Christmas.

CHAPTER TEN

MARRIAGE

He checked in at his club and told the secretary he would be staying there for at least four weeks. From the club he made his way to the Marylebone Registry Office where he found out the formalities required for marriage by licence. He satisfied himself that there would be no problems and then proceeded to make a booking to be married there on Tuesday, October the twenty-seventh. It could have been earlier but he wished to avoid any appearance of undue haste. It was already late in September. Then he went to Bibliopola Petrae..

He was full of plans. "I've fixed the wedding date!" he said.

"But we've only been engaged a week!" she laughed.

"Waste of a perfectly good week! Marriage or nothing!"

"When, may I ask, is it to be?""

"Tuesday, October twenty-seventh, at 10 o'clock in the morning at Marylebone. I would have made it even sooner but I felt I had to show some constraint! Anyway there is so much to do between now and then!"

"One month! Just one month!"

The following morning he cabled Domenico to inform him that he and his wife planned to arrive in Como on November the fourth and stay until the villa was closed. This done he said to Sarah, "Now, we are going to set out and buy you the best trousseau in London!"

The next four weeks passed rapidly. Most of the time was spent shopping but they also contrived to visit an amazing number of concerts, art galleries and theatres. Each evening they dined quietly and unostentatiously at some delightful but unfashionable restaurant where Frederick was unlikely to encounter anybody he knew. Reuben was leaving them on their own. He had very happily reverted to his pre-Sarah days. He had for a long time belonged to a literary club and this he now again frequented virtually every evening. Whilst he missed his meals with Sarah he was now of an age when he enjoyed the company of men of his own age and inclinations. He knew all would be well with Sarah and at seventy-one he felt at peace with himself and the world.

The civil ceremony at Marylebone was attended by just the three of them, the Registrar supplying them with a second witness. The simple formalities were certainly in complete contrast with the elaborate service and ensuing reception which Frederick's parents would have arranged had they had their way. As they unobtrusively left the building, Sarah happily on Frederick's arm, Reuben said, very quietly, "Good fortune, Sarah!" Then he kissed her lightly on the cheek, shook Frederick warmly by the hand, and abruptly vanished into the crowd. A fine learned looking man, dressed in rather old-fashioned formal clothes, for he had put on his best, rarely worn, suit for the occasion, he strode briskly back to his shop. He would be seeing them again when he saw them off on the boat train, on November the second. The trip to Como would also be their honeymoon.Until then and against their return they had booked in at a small hotel backing on to Green Park. When they returned they would be staying there for a few days, to see him and give him all their news, before they made their journey down to Loughbourne. In spite of repeated invitations he had resolutely refused to join them there for Christmas or subsequently. He knew the real testing time for Sarah would come when she finally took up residence as mistress of the manor house. "No, Loughbourne Manor would not agree with me nor I with it. That is for you. That is your life." Nothing they could say would change his mind.

The following morning a telegram from Frederick to Morton was delivered at the Dower House. The excited boy who brought it up from the village post office on his bicycle already knew the contents. The postmistress had been unable to contain herself. For this lapse of duty she was severely reprimanded by Morton. "In future keep these matters to yourself if you wish to retain your position! The entire village and all my own staff at the manor house knew of Sir Frederick's marriage before I did myself!"

The telegram stated that Lady Sarah and he would be home in time for Christmas and would attend the servants' ball. The exact date of their return would be communicated a little later. He would explain matters to the Reverend Tapping on his return, but Lady Sarah and he would be attending divine service on Christmas Day at Loughbourne church.

CHAPTER ELEVEN

ARRIVAL

A postcard with a picture of Como on it arrived at Bibliopola Petrae. It announced their safe arrival but nothing more. It was not until November the twenty-fourth that a letter from Sarah arrived. She sounded ecstatic. "Domenico met us at Milan station," she wrote, "with a most magnificent equipage! From there we drove through the most enchanting countryside. The first sight of the lake and the mountains beyond was thrilling beyond my belief! The Marini family have received us with the greatest kindness. They have given us a room with absolutely breathtaking views across the lake. The monument to those who perished in the disaster has been completed and is in the best of taste, carrying inscriptions recording the event in both Italian and English. The day after we arrived there was a service of dedication. This was, naturally, conducted by a Roman Catholic priest but both Frederick and I found the service most moving and appropriate."

In a post script to Sarah's letter Frederick wrote that they would be stopping off in Paris on their way home, where they would spend one further week. They would be back in London on December the ninth.

In due course they returned and a telegram was then sent to Morton. This time the postmistress carefully kept the contents to herself. In it they announced their intention of arriving back at Crufton on the afternoon train on Tuesday, December the twenty third. Frederick, anxious to ensure that Sarah's arrival at Loughbourne was attended by the maximum ceremony, instructed that Mitchell was to meet the train with the family coach.

The intervening two weeks they passed in London, taking the opportunity to dine with Reuben each evening. Then, at last, came the time for them to make the journey to Loughbourne. As the train wound its way deeper and deeper into the Norsex countryside the consciousness of the great responsibilities which were now hers began to weigh ever more heavily upon Sarah's spirits. However, by some mysterious means, this near panic evaporated as the train finally pulled into Crufton. When she alighted, to be greeted by a deferential stationmaster, she felt able to cope with anything.

Outside Mitchell was waiting with the coach. This had been used but rarely of recent times and Mitchell had taken the opportunity to make it look quite wonderful. Her eyes immediately fell on the Threlfall coat of arms emblazoned on the door, her first real experience of her new social status. The attendant footman opened the coach door, put the steps in position and said, "Welcome, my lady!" the first time she had been so addressed by a family retainer. Frederick quickly stepped up to assist her mount and before she knew what had happened she and her husband were seated side by side jolting along the country roads.

It was not really a very comfortable ride. The roads were not very good and the coach springs had difficulty dealing with some of the ruts. Furthermore it was late and since it was pitch black outside it was not possible to while away the journey by looking at the unfamiliar countryside. Loughbourne village was silent as they drove through. The cautious Morton, realising that were the villagers to discover that the squire and his lady were returning that evening they would insist on greeting them in some way, had sworn Mitchell to secrecy. He correctly guessed Sarah would be tired and that Frederick would not wish her to be seen like that for the first time by the villagers. He had, however, alerted both Mrs. Faming and Goodenough to the imminent arrival and the manor house staff were in a state of readiness. For this purpose a boy had been stationed at a vantage point from which he could see the coach approaching whilst it was still some distance away. Being given, by this means, adequate warning the staff were marshalled, in proper order, outside the main entrance of the house by the time the coach arrived. Fortunately, although a chilly evening, it was neither snowing nor raining.

At last the great wrought iron gates came into view, standing wide open to welcome them. Mitchell swung the horses through them and they began to approach the house up the winding, gravelled drive. Behind the great chestnut trees the dark fields beyond could be dimly discerned in the faint moonlight which was by now illuminating the scene. Quite suddenly the coach rounded a small bend in the drive and the house sprang melodramatically into view, its windows all alight in greeting. Frederick had often attempted to describe it to her and she had formed quite an accurate picture of what to expect. The reality, however, transcended anything she had imagined. Involuntarily she gave a little gasp. As she did so Frederick whispered to her, "Welcome to Loughbourne!" and squeezed her hand.

Mitchell expertly brought the coach to a halt in front of the assembled staff, and the footman jumped down and opened the door, placing the steps in position. Then Frederick eased his great frame out of the coach and stood by the steps ready to help her alight. The manor house staff waited breathlessly for their first sight of her.

She was wearing the fur coat and matching hat and gloves they had bought in London for the Como trip. On her feet were a pair of shoes they had discovered in the Rue de Rivoli in Paris. Her only visible jewellery were two pearl earrings which matched the necklace Frederick had given her as a wedding present. The bumpy journey, combined with the present excitement, had given an extraordinary radiance to her face. A low murmur of approval arose. Then a little girl came forward, curtsied, and shyly presented a bouquet of flowers her father, the head gardener, had that morning selected from the hot house.

Sarah at once bent down and kissed the child to the great approval of the watchers.

Frederick said to Morton, standing there with Beatrice and his young son, Alan. "Thanks Frank! A pleasant thought! Well done, Victoria!" The child blushed crimson, gave another curtsey and tried to hide behind Beatrice. She was gazing at Sarah with unashamed adoration. This, she was thinking, is one of those ladies from the storybooks!

"Sarah, may I present Mr. Frank Morton, our land agent, and his wife and son, Mrs. Beatrice Morton and Mr. Alan Morton to you?"

These preliminary courtesies over it was the turn of Mrs. Faming and Goodenough to present the manor house staff, and then that of the head gardener to present the outside staff. Nobody seemed to notice the cold. It was the most exciting event that had happened for a very long time. For everybody, from the most senior footman to the gardener's boy, Sarah found a suitable word. No mistress could have more speedily found her way into the hearts of the staff, yet she had not yet even crossed the threshold of the house.

This was soon remedied. Frederick suddenly and to the great delight of everybody lifted Sarah up bodily in his arms and carried her into the house. Then in full view he kissed her.

Such was the manner in which Sarah took up residence at Loughbourne Manor the week before Christmas, 1896. In due course there would have to be a visit to the Winslows quite apart from those to the neighbouring gentry and tenant farmers. These, Frederick had decided, would have to wait until after Christmas. In the meantime there were the twin and urgent matters of her introduction to the village and the Reverend Edward Tapping. He was well aware that the manner of his marrying would have upset the vicar. That fence would have quickly to be mended.

He had given much thought to the matter. It was an essential element of his strategy that Sarah should be well received in the county and the village from the outset. Fortunately the imminence of Christmas afforded an ideal opportunity for a formal appearance at morning service at St. Ethelred's. That morning, he knew, the church would be filled to overflowing, notwithstanding its size.

He sent for Morton. "Frank, to celebrate her first Christmas here Lady Sarah has requested that every village household and individual member of the manor staff should receive two guineas, every child in the village of twelve and under a shilling. Could you see this is arranged by tomorrow morning? Please make it quite clear that these gifts are made by her."

"That is a great deal of money, Sir Frederick! Fortunately it so happens I have just about enough in the safe! It is a most extraordinarily generous gesture!"

Sarah's stock rose ever higher.

On Christmas Day the family coach drew up outside the packed church. The vicar, the Reverend Edward Tapping, then forty-six, was waiting outside to greet them, looking rather apprehensive. The news that they were already married had fallen on the vicarage like a thunderbolt. All Threlfalls had, from time immemorial, been married at St. Ethelred's. He had heard some excellent reports on the village grapevine but he was instinctively disinclined to trust this source of information. It was, therefore, with enormous relief that he felt all these anxieties evaporating as he saw her descending from the coach and come towards him with a charming smile and outstretched hand. Frederick, watching, at once knew she had made a complete conquest.

There was no time for more than the most cursory of introductions. The congregation was waiting. Certain prearranged signals having been given they entered, preceded by the vicar. A deacon hurried forward to conduct them to the family pew. The congregation stood and the organ thundered out "Hail to the Lord's anointed". As they made their way up the aisle a subdued murmur of approval was distinctly audible. The gifts had already been distributed in the village, but these alone would have been regarded as bribes. It was Sarah's personality that mattered. Her appearance and bearing confirmed all previous good reports.

The vicar pronounced his blessing on their union and had chosen his text from Corinthians in order to be able to preach on the twin themes of charity and love. As they left the church the two of them walked down the aisle bowing and smiling to everybody as though they had just been married there. Then they waited outside with the vicar. As people emerged they were greeted individually. For everybody Sarah found some pleasantry. Not one person's hand, in all that congregation, remained unshaken by her.

From that day on she was as one of their own.

CHAPTER TWELVE

HAPPINESS

For the next five years the only cloud in the otherwise blue skies of their married happiness was Sarah's failure to conceive. Frederick's concerns about the Winslows ' reactions proved to be unfounded for Eleanor had been being courted by a peer and meanwhile accepted him. Sarah was given a fine welcome at Hardstone Hall and the rest of the county took her to its heart. She was adored in the village. She was always a welcome visitor in the homes of the tenant farmers. She proved to be a pillar of the church. The servants vied with each other to please her. Wilfred Mitchell's wife, Violet, became her personal maid, and she took a great interest in the welfare of her daughter, Lily, who had been born in 1901. Beatrice Morton, although fourteen years older than her, became her closest friend and confidante.

In 1901 she finally conceived. It was a very difficult birth but the baby, George, was fine and healthy. Sarah, however, was warned by the doctor that it would be exceedingly dangerous to have another. Sadly she and Frederick agreed that George would, therefore, be their only child.

It was in 1902 that Frederick decided to commission an artist to paint Sarah's portrait. This he took six months to complete. It showed an exceedingly beautiful woman, seated in the manor rose garden, with just a hint of tragedy showing through an otherwise happy scene. In her hand she had an open book. If one looked very carefully the title of this could be made out. It was the "Morte D'Arthur", the very copy that had brought her and Frederick together in Reuben's bookshop. This book, together with her childhood copy, given her when she was twelve by Reuben, stood near her portrait, where it hung in the library. The portrait seemed to illuminate the otherwise rather dark room.

In 1905, by which time Sarah was thirty-one, there was a terrible fire at Bibliopola Petrae. Nobody ever discovered exactly what had been the cause but it did appear as though he might have fallen and broken a gas mantle. He was by that time eighty. He had always been in the habit of climbing up the library steps he kept in the shop to replace and examine books. As he grew older he was repeatedly cautioned about this practice but he was a creature of routine. The large amount of very dry paper combined with the age of the building to ensure the fire spread rapidly and very fiercely. It proved impossible to bring it under control. Bibliopola Petrae and Reuben with it were reduced to ashes and his body was never recovered. In his memory they created a rockery garden at Loughbourne. This they called Peter's Garden for it would always remind them of the rock on which they had built both their marriage and their happiness.

In 1908 Violet had another baby, a boy, Donald. "I would like him to grow up to be a skilled motor mechanic, Sir Frederick," said the proud Wilfred. "I am sad to have to admit that the days of horses are going. You mark my words it will be them motor cars everywhere soon. You should have one, Sir Frederick!"

"Do you know, Sarah, Wilfred's right! It is high time we caught up with the times! I'll buy one and you, Wilfred, can learn to drive it! I'll have the Daimler Company send somebody to teach you, then you can teach me!"

She did not pay much attention to his words. She had by this time seen many motor cars but had never felt any great desire to possess one. It was, therefore, a considerable surprise to her when he announced, one day, that they were to go to London to see one. He was in a state of great excitement.

They arrived at the motor car show rooms. "Look! There it is!"

She had not known quite what it was she had expected to see. By this time there were plenty of cars around in the London streets but she had never paid much attention to them. She had never, consciously, seen anything as glorious as the object at which he was now pointing an excited finger.

It was magnificent and black, with beautiful red leather upholstery. She gazed at it in awe. "You are thinking of buying that?"

"Only the best is good enough for Threlfalls whether it be their wives, children or motor cars! Come on let's have a closer look!" The salesman had been expecting them and had come forward bowing respectfully.

"Would my lady like to sit in it?"

He handed Sarah in.

"What do you think of it, Sarah? Would you like us to have it?"

"It's wonderful!"

"It's ours! I've already bought it!" Frederick was laughing like a schoolboy.

"But neither you nor Wilfred can drive!"

"No, as I told you before, we are both going to learn! The Daimler

43

Works will deliver it to us and the man who brings it will stay on with Wilfred and teach him everything. Then Wilfred will teach me!"

It was in this manner that Wilfred, the coachman, became Wilfred, the chauffeur. The coach, however, remained, side by side with the new car. Both were equally lovingly tended by Wilfred, who always sat Donald in the front seat of the car when he was working on it.

"He'll be a great driver when he grows up!" he prophesied.

That year George went off to Bushcome, the Bushfield Abbey preparatory school, as a boarder. Here he acquired two great friends, also destined for Bushfield. These were Francis Preston, son of a Yorkshire textile magnate, Sir William Preston, and William Hyslow, son of a Church of England clergyman. In 1913 all three friends finally entered Bushfield Abbey School.

In 1914 war was declared on Germany. Sir Frederick, by now forty-three, had always been a keen Territorial, holding a Territorial commission with the Prince's Own Carbines. Very soon, thereafter, he left for active service in France.

"It won't last five minutes!" he assured a tearful Sarah, as she waved him goodbye.

In 1916 Major Sir Frederick Threlfall was killed at the front fighting with the Prince's Own Carbines, his Territorial Regiment. He was just forty-five and George was sixteen.

Sarah, absolutely devastated with grief, had to cope on her own. Frank Morton, now himself sixty, proved a tower of strength and between them they kept things going until George, now nineteen, most unexpectedly announced he wished to marry Humphrey Winslow's daughter, Ann, forego university, and settle down to managing things himself.

The very strong attachment which had always existed between George and Sarah had been greatly enhanced by her widowhood. However, as a result of his father's death, George had acquired an unreasoning dislike of all things German. From then on he obstinately maintained that all Germans were responsible for his father's death. Nothing would change that conviction. He had completely overlooked the fact that his fiancée's mother was herself German.

Aware of this prejudice of her son's and only too conscious of Frederick's injunction not to reveal her family origins Sarah said nothing. She was, as she always had been, unhappy with her secret but, for the moment, it did seem to her to be the better course to follow. She consoled herself with the thought that she had so promised Frederick. She reflected to herself that it was indeed ironic that George had decided to marry a Winslow, whereas Frederick had been so concerned at such a prospect.

PART TWO - DARKENING

CHAPTER THIRTEEN

SEARCH

Although the Winslows had initially been disappointed by Frederick's choice of Sarah rather than Eleanor this had not disrupted their relationship for long, since it transpired she had been being courted by a member of the peerage whom she soon afterwards married Thereafter Eleanor and Sarah became as great friends as were Humphrey and Frederick. In 1900 Humphrey married Louisa, the younger daughter of Count Heinrich Von Runing, a member of one of the minor German princely houses. She so thoroughly assimilated into Norsex county life that it never occurred to George, as he grew up, to think of her other than as thoroughly English as he considered himself. In 1902 Louisa had a daughter, Ann. Two years later when Sir Gilbert died Humphrey inherited.

George and Ann, being both almost of the same age and such close neighbours, saw a great deal of each other as small children. This friendship continued into adolescence, George frequently spending much of his school holidays in her company. This friendship began to ripen into love and, by the time he was nineteen, in 1920, completely overlooking, indeed oblivious of, her German connections, George proposed to her and was eagerly accepted. Her parents were delighted with the match. Sarah, who strongly disapproved of George's prejudice, reasoned that, although he did not know it, he was in a similar position himself. If the marriage eventually changed his views once he realised the truth of the situation then it was all for the best. Happily abandoning any thought of university George prepared to settle down to devote himself to his wife, anticipated fatherhood, the running of Loughbourne and to the Territorial Army, for he had secured a commission in his father's old regiment, The Prince's Own Carbines, as soon as he had left school.

The Winslows were immensely proud of their direct descent from a Norman ancestor. To this was now added the quasi-royal Von Runing dimension. The union between their family and the ancient Threlfalls was, therefore, particularly welcome to them. Sarah, well aware of the consternation which would have resulted had she revealed her own secret, kept silent.

The new Lady Ann was just eighteen. She was eager to exploit her new rank and spread her social wings. George, however, was equally determined to devote himself virtually exclusively to the management of Loughbourne and the Prince's Own Carbines. He had no time at all for social affairs and resolutely refused to attend anything whatsoever outside the county, let alone going up to London or any of the fashionable watering places abroad. In consequence Ann began to visit her aristocratic German cousins by herself more and more frequently. By 1933 these cousins had all declared unconditional support for Adolf Hitler and his now dominant Nazi Party. These views Ann, without any understanding of them, began vociferously to support, even going so far as to apply for membership of Sir Oswald Moseley's British Union of Fascists, in 1936.

In 1921 John was born. From the day he arrived she resolutely refused to take any interest in him. Sarah took over and Ann happily acquiesced in the situation. George, for whom family was all-important, protested vociferously but to no avail. The German connection was now thrust at him with all its implications. He had given no thought at all to her cousins whom he had never met nor desired to meet. Quarrel succeeded quarrel. By 1936 the marriage was virtually non-functional. They put up a show of unity for the outside world but, within Loughbourne, they lived separate lives.

John, in consequence, grew up loving Sarah as though she were his real mother. His own mother he scarcely knew existed. So far as he was concerned she was simply a remote and rarely glimpsed figure in gorgeous gowns, much better avoided. It was Sarah who read him his bedtime story at night. It was to Sarah he ran for comfort. When he went to boarding school it was Sarah who wrote him letters. It was Sarah who visited him and welcomed him home for the holidays.

Late in 1937 Sarah, now sixty-five, began to read very disturbing reports in The Times of events affecting the Jewish community in Germany since the rise of Hitler to power. Although it was now forty years since she had had any contact with her family she had never been able to put them entirely out of her thoughts. Both Samuel and Eli still made appearances in her dreams. She assumed her parents were dead but had never, of course, had any confirmation of this. Her brothers would by now be in the seventies and, since the family were noted for longevity, most likely still alive.

She began to worry about them. She was feeling isolated. No longer did she have either Frederick or Reuben in whom to confide.

She longed to discuss her worries with George but felt inhibited by her promise to Frederick.

By July 1938 the rumours of impending war with Germany coupled with renewed reports of Jewish persecution by the Nazi regime brought her suppressed anxieties to fever pitch. Ann, as usual, was away in Germany. Sarah made a sudden decision. She would go up to London, on the pretext of a shopping expedition, and seek out Reuben's old lawyer and ask his advice.

"I'd like Donald to drive me into Crufton, George. I've decided to give myself a day in London looking at the shops there!"

"Goodness, Mother, you haven't done that for ages. I'm so pleased! It will be good for you to have such a change of scenery. I'll have Donald meet the evening train."Donald had succeeded his father as chauffeur in 1926, now driving a Rolls Royce, although the old Daimler still remained, standing by the coach. Neither Sarah nor Wilfred would agree to parting with it.

As soon as she arrived in London she sought out Reuben's old solicitors. The senior partner, whom she had known well, had long since died, but her crested card worked wonders. She was seen at once."Please understand that this is all in complete confidence. That is why I have come to you and am not using the Threlfall family solicitors. Any correspondence is to be directed to my bank in Crufton for my personal and private attention, and marked to be collected by me there and not forwarded to the manor house. Under no circumstances am I to be contacted by telephone. I shall be in constant contact on a daily basis with my bank manager.

"Your instructions are noted, Lady Threlfall."

"I wish you to make enquiries, on my behalf, about the welfare and present circumstances of a German Jewish family called Aronberg. This family, when I was last aware of them, was resident in Berlin, with a branch in Munich. They had a considerable business in the textile trade."

"You will appreciate, Lady Threlfall, that the existence of the present regime in Germany may make this a very delicate mission. Would you agree to our entrusting the matter to a very reliable private enquiry agent? The gentleman in question, a reserve army officer, is very familiar with Germany and, if anybody can act satisfactorily in such a matter, it is he. It may, however, be rather an expensive undertaking."

"Within reason money is no consideration."

She returned to Loughbourne suitably laden with shopping.

For some weeks she heard nothing. Then the bank manager told her he had a letter waiting for her.

"We have information for you. It is of such a nature that we feel you should hear it at first hand from Major Tomkins. Could you telephone and make an appointment as soon as possible?"

She was in the solicitor's office the following afternoon.

The solicitor had with him a well built, florid faced, man of about forty. He was soberly dressed in a dark pin stripe suit, and wearing a regimental tie. His face was strong and soldierly. Sarah took an instant liking to him. She knew instinctively he was honest and compassionate, the kind of man of whom Frederick would have approved.

"Before Major Tomkins makes his report, Lady Threlfall, I feel I should, in all fairness, ask you whether you are in any way emotionally involved in the subject matter of this enquiry?" remarked the solicitor.

"Very much so," she replied, beginning to feel real alarm.

"Then I must tell you that the news is bad."

"Oh, dear!" She suddenly felt as though she were about to faint but she quickly regained control and said, "Please proceed with your report, major."

"Isaac and Miriam, the two older persons concerning whom you asked me to make enquiries, both passed away in 1925. I understand their passing was peaceful. They were buried in Berlin. However it would seem that in April, this year, three adult male members of the family, all normally resident in Berlin, and all well known and respected members of the commercial community there, put their names to a protest, lodged with the civic authorities, concerning serious damage being done by hooligan elements to Jewish owned property. The Aronbergs, themselves, were members of the Lutheran church, but they were of Jewish descent. The three persons concerned were Samuel, aged about seventy, who had succeeded his father as head of the family business, his son Aaron, aged about fifty, and his son-in law, Benjamin, aged about twenty-six. In addition it seems that Benjamin had been involved in a complaint concerning alleged victimisation of his six-year-old daughter, on the grounds of her racial origins, by her schoolteacher. This teacher was married to a senior Nazi official. These circumstances had serious repercussions."

"What happened?" She felt faint again.

"The following month, May, all three men were suddenly arrested and have since disappeared. The Aronberg mansion, in Charlottenburg, has been sequestrated and the business has been closed."

48

"But, surely, there must have been wives and children of these people? What has happened to them? And where are the men themselves? With what offences have they been charged?"

"As for the offences, the answer is I do not know. I have been unable to find out. This kind of action against Jewish origin people is quite common. My guess is that they are at present in a new kind of prison or concentration camp, called Dachau, just outside Munich. This is a very secret place. It is almost impossible to discover anything about it or what happens there. It has a very terrible reputation though. As for the wives, there were, as you have suggested, three of them. I have, so far, been unable to trace them with any certainty but, so far as I can ascertain, they were not arrested. My guess is that they have probably gone to Munich, to join Samuel's brother, Eli, who managed the Munich end of the firm and had a large house there. I have not, so far, extended my enquiries to Munich. I wished to report to you first. I am somewhat concerned that if I begin enquiries in Munich I may stir up a hornets' nest. It might be more advisable to leave things alone for the moment. This latest meeting between Hitler and our own Prime Minister might herald a change in German domestic policies."

"You have not mentioned any children. Were there any children involved?"

"The six year old I mentioned, the child of Benjamin and Rachel, Aaron's daughter, who was allegedly being bullied at her school, seems to have vanished. I could find out nothing about her."

"What do you suggest we should do, now?"

"As I have said, it might be wiser to do nothing more for the moment. It would certainly be advisable to act with extreme caution. There are certain channels open by which people in such a predicament can, sometimes, be extricated from Germany. I shall look into this aspect for you if you so wish. It would in all probability involve very considerable expense."

"I must return home and discuss all this with my son."

By the time she returned home she was experiencing her chest pains. She was on the verge of collapse. She had already decided that she had no alternative but to confide everything in George. Frederick could never have foreseen such developments.

She found him working, as usual, in the estate office.

"Hullo, Mother! Had a good shopping trip?" He looked up cheerfully and saw her.

He jumped up in concern. She was white-faced and shaking. "My God, Mother, what is the matter?"

"George, my darling, I have something I must tell you!"

The whole story poured out.

He sat back and digested all she had told him.

"So, you are of pure Jewish descent! That means my beloved, fascist, wife has a half Jewish husband and a quarter Jewish son! Dear me! She isn't going to like being given that information!"

"George, why do you have to tell her? Things may so work out that you never do have to tell her. Frederick may still be proved right. However, I should like you to tell John, that's different. In fact if he could possibly be excused school for a day or so I should very much like him to come home and see me here."

And so Sir George sat down and wrote John the most difficult letter he had ever written in his life. It was posted on Wednesday, October the fifth, 1938 and was received at Bushfield by John the following Friday.

By the same mail he wrote to the headmaster of Bushfield Abbey, Dr. Wisley, an old friend and a fellow officer in the Territorials, to tell him that Sarah had been taken ill. He asked him to give permission for John to come home and see her and suggested he could come up by car to collect his son on Monday, the tenth, and return him to Bushfield the following day. He and Ann had already been invited by the Wisleys to stay at their house at the school in order to be able to attend some very special football match which had been arranged for the following Thursday. The proposal, therefore, would only involve one extra night for them at Bushfield.

Ann was due back from Germany that Sunday. He did not look forward to her return with any pleasure.

CHAPTER FOURTEEN

ANN

Late that Sunday Ann returned from Germany. She came into the house closely followed by her personal maid, Janet. Janet was a village girl, eighteen years old, who had been highly recommended by Violet. George greeted his wife, thinking to himself what a pity it was that their early love seemed to have faded so completely. She was still only thirty-six and had retained all her early beauty. Desperately he clung to the hope that, by some miracle, he would never have to reveal his mother's story to her.

In many ways Ann was now even more attractive than she had been at eighteen when he married her. Her hair was still golden and her complexion clear. Her eyes were the deepest blue. Her height enabled her to wear clothes to the best possible effect. Her tastes in clothes and jewellery could not be faulted by him.

He followed her up the stairs and into her private rooms. This was so unusual that she said, "What ever is it that you want, George? You know I have to have a bath and then change for dinner! You can tell me anything important over the meal. Oh, do be careful, Janet! You really are too careless! I simply cannot imagine what it was that made Violet recommend you to me!" She looked round and saw her husband still standing in the room. "Really, George, what is it? Surely it can wait?"

"Mother has been taken rather ill, Ann! She is confined to her bed."

"Oh, dear, what a bore! I do hope it is not infectious! Do I really have to go and see her now? Surely it could wait until after dinner? I am so hungry and tired!"

"It may be quite serious, Ann," said George, controlling his rising irritation with some difficulty.

"Oh, well, I expect it will all turn out to be a storm in a tea cup! You always exaggerate these matters. I'll go in and speak to her as soon as I have had my bath and dressed as you seem so insistent. Tell them to wait dinner for half an hour, Janet. Oh, how glum making! What a welcome after I had had such a jolly time!"

With that he had to content himself.

51

A little later a bathed and dressed Ann knocked on Sarah's door and entered. Sarah was sitting propped up in bed looking pale and drawn.

"Oh, my dear, you do look poorly! What have you been doing?"

"I rather think I may have over-exerted myself. But never mind about me. How did you enjoy your visit?"

"It was wonderful! Germany is so well run since Hitler took over! A model country! Everybody was so delighted about this Munich agreement! They were all dreading having a war with us instead of those awful Russians. They said the crisis had been caused by the Jews. But they know how to deal with those wretched people!"

"I really do not like you to talk like that, Ann! You must learn not to condemn people in such a biased manner! I was always of the belief one should think the best of everybody until one knew for sure they deserved opprobrium!"

"Oh, really, Sarah, you are quite impossible!" said Ann, and abruptly left the room without a further word.

By the time she entered the dining room she had regained her composure. She immediately launched into an euphoric description of her German visit for George's benefit.

"It was terribly exciting!" she chattered. "All my cousins are now really high up in the Party. In fact one of them has just been given a senior appointment at the German Embassy in London. I must go up there some time and look him up. They all look so smart and dashing in their polished jackboots and uniforms! Hitler's policies have absolutely transformed the country. He is everybody's hero! I do wish I could meet him. There is just a chance that I may be able to do so next time I go across. I was introduced to a general who said he might be able to secure me an invitation. That would be really thrilling...."

George had been growing increasingly restive during this monologue. He suddenly interrupted the flow. "Do you really approve of all these appalling people, or are you just fantasising?" he growled.

She stopped in mid-sentence and stared at him in unfeigned astonishment. Then she put down the silver fruit knife with which she had been beginning to pare a peach and said, " Do I approve?" in icy tones.

"Yes, that is what I asked you? I have been hearing the most unpleasant reports about your fine friends and their abominable activities. I hope you aren't mixed up in them!"

"I presume that you may possibly be referring to their efforts to rid Germany of parasitic elements such as Jews, gypsies and morons?"

"I had not heard about the morons and gypsies. I am certainly sorry to hear that gypsies are being persecuted. I have always rather liked

52

them. They have always been welcome here. Furthermore, I had no idea morons were being targeted. They do not seem to me to be very well equipped to protect themselves. Sounds like vicious bullying to me! I have, however, heard some very nasty tales about what is happening to their Jewish citizens. I do not like that kind of thing. Not the Threlfall tradition at all to mistreat people in that manner! I have been told that they have been excellent citizens for nearly a thousand years, as long as we have been here! Anyway what reason have you to voice such dislike? What experience do you have of them?"

"Excellent citizens, indeed! This general described them to me as "lice on the body of Germany". Since you ask me, George, my answer is "Yes, I do approve. In fact I earnestly hope the same policies will soon be adopted here. The sooner the better. Nobody of Jewish origin will ever be welcome in this house so long as I am here"

"I would recommend you to consider your choice of words more carefully! You never know to whom you may be speaking! Furthermore, in the minds of many ordinary English people these days Nazis are synonymous with Germans. However much you may imagine your fine German cousins and their friends are to be admired please remember that it is only twenty years since we used to say "The only good German is a dead German". There are still plenty of people around who still believe that. If war does come again, and I think it will, notwithstanding all this hullabaloo about Chamberlain and Munich, which I think is all nonsense, there will be people we know saying just the same thing again. Don't forget my father died fighting them. If war comes where will your loyalties be? Just remember that when you married me you became a Threlfall. Anyway you were born a Winslow not a Von Runing." This was an unusually long speech for George, a normally reticent man.

"This is quite preposterous! First of all Sarah presumes to lecture me. Then you bully me like this!" She rose from the table and swept from the room in tears.

Grimly George realised he was going to be faced with an even more difficult position than he had already anticipated if Sarah's story had, eventually, to be revealed.

CHAPTER FIFTEEN

ARBITANT

"I am delighted to notice that there seem to be very few Jews here these days! I really never did understand why the school admitted them! My golf club doesn't!" said Harold Arbitant.

The Reverend Alistair Strong, school chaplain at Bushfield Abbey, to whom this remark was addressed, gave up all pretext of reading The Times, behind which he had vainly been trying to hide. Wearily lowering this protective shield he remarked, "Really, Harold, has it never occurred to you that Our Lord was the child of a Jewish family?"

"He was among them but not of them," replied Harold, who had been carefully checking that very point in certain literature he had just been sent.

"H'rrmph!" said Strong, rapidly re-raising his newspaper.

"Their betrayal of Him proves that they knew He was not one of their own," said Harold, undeterred.

The newspaper remained resolutely in position. He waited for it to move but there was no sign of any further response. He glanced around the staff common room, where this conversation was taking place, and became acutely conscious of the amused looks being exchanged by other members of the staff, also taking their coffee there during mid-morning break. Angrily he left the room and returned to his classroom.The carefully constructed veneer of self-confidence, in which he habitually sought to encase himself, as in a suit of armour, had been cracked. He had, as he was well aware, lost control of the situation. All the inhibitions he was continually trying to suppress, in his struggle to find acceptance within the closed society of Bushfield Abbey, welled up with renewed force. Such a decadent society needs reshaping, he thought to himself. What better model than the new Germany? Now, there was a society in which he would find and be accorded his proper place.

He was twenty-eight. He had joined Bushfield directly from university, in 1932, six years previously. His appointments, at that time, had been as assistant languages master, specialising in German, and under-housemaster in Chaplain's House, with Strong as his housemaster. Chaplain's House was one of the eight houses into which the pupils were divided at this famous and exclusive school. By 1938 he had progressed to the position of senior languages master, but he still remained as Strong's assistant. He had, however, become the Commanding Officer of the school's Officer Training Corps, which was affiliated to the Territorial Battalion of the Prince's Own Carbines in which he held a commission.

Strong and Harold had little love for each other. Initially the fault had seemed to lie mainly with Strong. Strong was a traditionalist. For him the only universities worthy of the name, at least in England, were Oxford and Cambridge. These two universities had always been the sole source for recruitment of academic staff for Bushfield. Harold was a product of one of the University of London colleges. Of this Strong greatly disapproved.

He had hotly disputed the appointment with the then headmaster, Dr. Archibald Williams. Williams, however, having made a promise to an old friend, who had happened to be Harold's tutor, to find his protege, a place at the school, was inflexible.

"He has secured a first class degree, Alistair. You should start to move with the times! London is producing excellent graduates! You are far too set in your ways! He will breathe fresh air into Bushfield! I rely on you to mould him for us!"

Strong, therefore, had to make the best of it. He was a most sincere Christian with two principal loves in his life. These were his religion and Bushfield Abbey, where he himself had been educated. He always wore long out of fashion clerical dress. However, behind the outwardly forbidding appearance that this gave him, there was known to exist a kindly presence. He was very popular with the boys and most of the staff, notwithstanding an alarming propensity to express himself in no uncertain terms if he was provoked, as was often the case.

From the beginning the partnership had been uneasy. Strong had never again raised the matter of Harold's Alma Mater, in any context. Nevertheless when they found themselves in disagreement, and this was frequent, the fact the man was not from Oxbridge obtruded itself into his reasoning. In all other respects he was a fair minded and tolerant man, almost obsessively so. He was frequently reproving himself for his bias. After all, he instructed himself, the man would presumably still have possessed the same objectionable characteristics even if he had been to Oxbridge. Obstinately he remained unconvinced by his own reasoning. He felt ashamed of himself for such moral weakness. He would lie awake meditating on the nature of prejudice.

55

Perhaps this was not a case of mere prejudice, he wondered. Perhaps there was some evidence to support his feelings that, for the moment, he could not put his finger upon? Was there such a concept as inherent evidence?

The personal insecurity of Harold served to exacerbate the position. He had been over anxious to set his mark on Bushfield, but Bushfield was an alien world to the Wimbledon shopkeeper's son. His upbringing had not equipped him to deal with the aristocratic tolerance of certain aspects of life, which he regarded as in need of correction if not eradication.

He lacked upper class attitudes to the sexual mores prevalent at that date in British boarding schools for boys. In consequence he was continuously, with the best of intentions but invariably disastrously, rushing in where most of his colleagues, who had grown up with such things from childhood, would have hesitated long and carefully before venturing to tread. He was, in truth, sincerely shocked at Strong's casual treatment at some of his more startling revelations. He mistook Strong's experience for hypocrisy.

Moreover Strong, having had first hand front line experience of war, as a chaplain, was a self-proclaimed pacifist. Arbitant regarded such views as anathema.

More recently the deterioration in their relationship had received a new impetus. Arbitant had, by chance, re-encountered an old university friend, almost the only friend he had made there. This was a man called Gregory Schumacher, of Anglo-German parentage. On leaving university Schumacher had found employment within the London German embassy. Here he had rapidly embraced Nazi ideas. Eventually, relying on his deceased father's original nationality, he had asked for and been granted full German citizenship. He was now an aide to a very senior official on the Ambassador's personal staff. He encouraged Harold to be far more open in his support for both Hitler and Moseley than had been the case hitherto. When this became widely known at Bushfield there was a good deal of disapproval, particularly on the part of Strong.

Harold was a man of medium build, somewhat short of six foot in height. He had a shock of reddish hair, which he endeavoured to keep in check by the liberal application of a proprietary hair dressing, and a small well-clipped military style moustache. His face was of ruddy complexion with two bright blue eyes. When on duty, or for other formal occasions, he always wore one of his only two suits, white shirts with detachable collars and either a university or regimental tie. The two suits he alternated daily, pressing the unworn pair of trousers nightly under his mattress to ensure razor sharp creases. At weekends, or when he felt sufficiently off duty to relax his dress code, he wore a tweed suit, a Fairisle pullover, and occasionally carried a walking stick of curious design.

Ostensibly he had all the attributes of an excellent schoolmaster. He was well versed in his specialist subject and had been very competently educated. He normally maintained good discipline. His personal appearance, apart possibly from the Fairisle pullover and the walking stick, gave little scope for ridicule. He was reasonably proficient at all games. His position as O.C. of the O.T.C. entitled him to respect. Yet, he contrived to be unpopular with almost everybody. He had the most remarkable ability to upset people. In childhood he had suffered greatly under his martinet of a father. His mother had been utterly submissive to her husband. Gradually he had grown himself a kind of protective shell. This had taken the form of holding and expressing dogmatic and usually highly controversial views, which seemed to be invulnerable to reasoned discussion. His recently adopted Nazi-Fascist views were a typical example. People, initially interested and inclined to be friendly, soon became impatient and repelled.

Tom Riding, the school janitor, was waiting outside the classroom door with a note for him from the headmaster, Dr. Wisley. This requested him to present himself at the Headmaster's private residence, always known as The Lodgings, as soon as might be convenient after classes. These written summonses were Dr. Wisley's usual methods of communication with his staff. They did not necessarily presage trouble, but they more than often did.

Dr. Wisley was a relatively young headmaster, just thirty-eight. He had been brought in to replace Dr. Williams, who had recently retired. Previously he had been a housemaster at Franklin's Court, a progressive school, catering for wealthy intellectuals' children. He was a tall, genial, rather military minded man, inclined to the expression of deep emotion on occasion. He was a Territorial Army officer, in fact second in command to Sir George in the same battalion as that in which both Harold held a commission and to which the Bushfield O.T.C. was affiliated. By the time Wisley was appointed headmaster, however, Harold was already in command of the Bushfield contingent and this remained the position.

Classes having ended Harold made his way over to The Lodgings. The headmaster's residence lay between the Great Tower, which dominated both the school and the surrounding countryside, and the chapel. On arrival the maid showed him into the study where Wisley

57

was waiting for him with some impatience. Wisley was dressed in his invariable garb of black coat, striped trousers, winged collar, white spotted black tie and gold rimmed spectacles. He was standing with his back to a blazing coal fire.

"Afternoon, Arbitant! Good of you to come across so promptly. Much appreciated. Take a chair."

Slightly taken aback by such a warm reception Harold sat as bidden.

"Have something I want you to do, Arbitant. Think you will like it. Tell me first, though. What is your opinion about this Munich Agreement Chamberlain's just concluded with Hitler? Do you approve? Do you think it gives us peace with honour, peace in our time? Eh?"

Harold was taken by surprise. He had certainly not expected such a question or discussion. His professed political convictions had to dictate his response. "Shouldn't every right thinking person be pleased? So far as I have heard its only critics have been Jews and communists!"

Wisley carefully considered this reply, taking off his glasses and polishing them. Harold uneasily wondered whether he had been lured into some kind of trap. Cautiously he adjusted the knot of his tie. Wisley replaced his glasses and looked at him through them. "Don't know about that, Arbitant! I am quite aware of your strong political views and I know others agree with you. However, I would advise you to be more guarded in your expression of them! There are many people who either disagree with you strongly or whom you might unwittingly offend, you know! Anyway, yes, I agree this Munich affair does seem to have had a good press. Personally I was a little unhappy to see our Prime Minister hastening over to Munich like that!"

"But surely the end well justified the means, sir! Something like "Paris is well worth a Mass!" in a modern context?"

"An unfortunate comparison, Arbitant! I had always thought that to be one of the more discreditable actions in the history of France!"

An uncomfortable pause followed. Then Wisley resumed. "I do sometimes wonder what members of the crowd I remember rejoicing outside the Palace on Armistice night would have thought if they had been able to know this was going to happen twenty years on!"

"But we are no longer dealing with the Kaiser, sir!"

"Now, what is that saying? The more things change, the more they remain the same. I have been hearing nasty stories about this Nazi regime."

"Really, sir, I am quite sure such reports are without any real foundation. My friend at the German embassy tells me they are the product of those very sources you have just warned me against criticising too publicly!"

The man's words do seem to reflect public opinion, thought Wisley. He had just been reading a report in The Times that the crowds, watching the Chamberlains driving to the Palace to report to the King on the outcome of the recent negotiations in Munich, had observed a rainbow forming in the sky over the Palace and hailed it as a good omen.

In the staff common room this Munich Agreement had, in general, been well received. The younger members were relieved by the promise of peace. The older members, veterans of the Great War for the most part, had no wish to see a repeat of those dreadful years.

At the foot of the Great Tower, which was almost the only remaining part of the original Abbey building, facing across the gravelled space, now called Heroes' Yard, was the school war memorial. The long roll of names of dead boys and staff inscribed on the brass plaque affixed to its base was enough to dampen down the militant ardour of most people.

For a second or so Wisley remained silent, lost in such thoughts. Then, pulling himself out of his brown study, he said, "Right, Arbitant! Enough of all this! I want to tell you that last Friday I was invited as a guest to a meeting of the London Teachers Association. This was addressed by Anthony Eden. During his speech he said something that greatly impressed me. He said to us that there has never been a time in our long history when the responsibilities and opportunities of teachers is so great as today. He asked us what kind of England it is that we teachers are guiding our younger generation towards. What kind of England are we trying to create?"

"Fine words, sir. I certainly intend to play my part in the creation of a better England!"

"Yes, indeed! Now it so happens that, just before Chamberlain's historic trip to Munich, the Governors of this school received a letter from the London German embassy inviting us to meet a German boys' soccer team here at Bushfield. Their idea was that this would provide a bridge for understanding between the young of our two nations on the sports field."

"What a splendid idea!"

"In view of the serious international situation then existing the Governors very reluctantly declined. It was felt that, if war did eventually break out, the fact that we had so recently entertained such a team here, however good our motives, might be misconstrued to the detriment of the school. We did not decline absolutely, we just suggested the decision might be deferred for further consideration."

"And now we have the Munich Accord and all should be well, sir?"

"Just so. The Governors have now agreed that the invitation can be issued. This is where I should like to have your assistance. I rang the German Embassy and I have been informed that the matter will be under the supervision of this friend of yours there, a Herr Schumacher, I understand."

"Yes, sir. He was a great friend of mine at university. We renewed our acquaintance a little while ago."

"What I should like you to do is to act as our liaison officer and get things moving. I'd like you to go up to London, as soon as you can, and see him. Within reason use your discretion, but keep me informed."

"I'd be very pleased and honoured to be given such a task, sir! I shall telephone Gregory as soon as I can." He began to make preparations to leave, assuming the interview was now over.

"Just a moment, I have something else I should like to tell you about."

He sat down again, wondering what else was about to be revealed.

"I have been thinking about the immense impact this conclusion of the agreement at Munich could have on the lives of the boys and staff. After discussing the matter with the Governors and, in particular, the Bishop and Mr. Strong, I have now decided that next Sunday's chapel service will be designated as one for special thanksgiving. I shall be delivering the sermon and, provided, of course, that you have been able to confirm the arrangements by that time, I shall use that opportunity to announce the German fixture and the motives underlying it. It seems the correct context for such an announcement."

"So my mission is to be kept confidential until then, sir?"

"Yes. I do not wish the news to be made public until this is done by myself next Sunday. All the Governors have agreed to attend the service and the Bishop himself will read the first lesson. It so happens that it is young Threlfall's turn to read the second lesson. I feel this is very appropriate as he is really our best player. Now I must tell you that I have not yet felt it opportune to tell Mr. Strong about the German match. I am deferring telling him until you can reassure me there are not going to be any unexpected hitches. I intend to tell him that I have requested you to go up to London on a special job for me. I feel quite confident your friend will be able to see you on Wednesday. The embassy were very enthusiastic about the idea. I'll organise matters so that your classes are covered. I must say, Arbitant, it really is most opportune that you have this friend in the embassy!"

Harold left The Lodgings in high spirits, his depression quite gone. He felt he had recovered the dignity he had lost in his earlier encounter with Strong in the common room.

He immediately put through a telephone call to Gregory, who proved still to be working at his desk at the embassy. "I rather thought it would be you who contacted me about this business, Harry! Can you come up here on Wednesday? We can have lunch together and work out the fine details. I'll be able to introduce you to my chief. He is sure to join us for lunch."

CHAPTER SIXTEEN

EMBASSY

This was the first time that Harold had ever visited his friend at the embassy. He was very much aware that Gregory held an important appointment there and was anxious to make a good impression. He took particular pains to appear as well dressed as possible. He took out the better of his two suits and closely inspected it for signs of stains and wear. He put on a clean shirt and collar and carefully knotted his regimental tie. Then he wheeled out his bicycle and set off for Bushfield station where he caught the ten o'clock train to London, Waterloo.

Here he decided it would be a good idea to be seen to arrive by taxi. This made rapid progress through the London streets, finally turning into Carlton Terrace. There was a slight breeze and this caught at the red and black swastika emblazoned flags draping the building, sending them billowing out, almost creating the impression the place was on fire. There could be no doubt as to the identity of the embassy housed within. He stood for a moment gazing at the scene. He began to feel a kind of vicarious pride. He was, he thought, in the very presence of the New Order. With a little trepidation, for he had never before entered such a place, he went within and approached the smartly dressed receptionist.

"You are expected, sir," she said, consulting a list, "I shall at once tell Herr Schumacher you have arrived. Whilst you are waiting perhaps you would care to take a seat over there?" She indicated some chairs by a window.

He began to walk across the room in the direction of the indicated chairs when he was brought to a halt by the sight of the enormous portrait of Adolf Hitler which completely dominated the entrance hall. He stopped and looked at it in awe. He simply could not tear his eyes away from it. He was still so engaged when he felt a light tap on his shoulder, He turned round and found himself face to face with Gregory. Next to his friend was standing another man of about forty. This man was exceedingly handsome, with well brushed, slightly waved hair and steely blue eyes, into one of which was firmly clamped a monocle.

Both men were wearing beautifully tailored suits with swastika emblems in their lapels

"I see you are admiring the portrait of the Fuhrer, Harold!" said his friend, approvingly.

"Yes, I was absolutely overcome by it! It is magnificent! What a leader to have!

I just wish we had somebody like that here! The country could do with it, I can tell you!"

"Allow me to introduce you to my chief," said his friend, smiling broadly. "This is Herr Rudolf Von Rohrbach, a special aide to His Excellency the Ambassador."

Von Rohrbach clicked his heels, bowed slightly, and shook hands. He then proceeded to give Harold an almost frightening look of appraisal, finally saying, "Welcome Mr. Arbitant. The Ambassador has asked me to convey his personal pleasure to you at the prospect of our German boys being given the opportunity to play your famous school at football." His English was faultless.

"It is an honour for us, Herr Von Rohrbach!"

"May I suggest we proceed directly into luncheon, Schumacher. That is if Mr. Arbitant is agreeable."

He proceeded to lead the way to a door that opened off the main hall. He politely stood aside so that Harold could enter first. Within was a table on which had been set out luncheon for three. A waiter hastened forward and pulled out a chair for Harold and the other two seated themselves on either side of him.

The waiter now produced a bottle of wine for Von Rohrbach's approval. He took it in his hand and looked at it. "Do you enjoy white wine, Mr. Arbitant?"

"Most especially German white wines, sir! In fact, sir, I find I have a liking for everything German! Above all perhaps for your Fuhrer!"

"Your friend has excellent tastes, Schumacher!"

"He was always a fine fellow, sir! We are fortunate to be dealing with him. I am afraid not all his compatriots are so well disposed towards us!"

"Do you speak German, Mr. Arbitant?"

"It was my subject at university. I am at present the senior languages master at Bushfield and my special subject is German. If you would agree it would give me the greatest pleasure to continue our conversation in German."

"You are a most excellent young man! I congratulate you on your friend, Schumacher!"

63

When the meat course arrived another bottle of wine was produced.

"This is a red wine, Mr. Arbitant. We do have excellent German red wines, you know, although many ignorant people do not know this, believing we produce only white. However, on this occasion I have selected a French wine. In a way, I suggest, we might regard this as symbolic! As you know we have had our disagreements with France in the past, just as we have with you. However, since the Munich Accord, all three of our countries are in friendship. Thus Schumacher and I can drink the health of our English friend in both the white wine of Germany and the red wine of France! We have, as it were, here at this table our own mini-Munich!"

"Indeed, sir," said Harold quite carried away by the occasion, and with a little too much of the wines inside him, "perhaps under the Fuhrer's guidance the white wines of Germany can mingle with the red wines of France to establish an Europe working in harmony with Britain and to the detriment of international communism!"

"A most interesting analogy, Mr. Arbitant! The red and white wines can thus complement each other! Excellently put is it not, Schumacher?"

"Certainly, well said Harry!"

Luncheon ended. Von Rohrbach pushed back his chair and extended his hand again to Harold. "It has been a pleasure to meet you, Mr. Arbitant. I am sure we shall soon meet again. I suggest you both now adjourn to Schumacher's office and complete your arrangements. Let me know everything you decide, Schumacher! I bid you good day, Mr. Arbitant!"

Schumacher's office was by no means one of the grander ones in the embassy but it did possess a view across the Mall and a fine oak desk. It was certainly a great deal better than that to which Harold was entitled at Bushfield and he was greatly impressed with it. He nodded towards the picture of Hitler."I see you have your own copy."

"Yes, we all have one. We are all under his eye. It keeps us alert!"

He opened a silver cigarette box and offered it to Harold, then took one himself. He proceeded to light the cigarettes with a swastika engraved lighter. They puffed away silently for a moment or two. Then Schumacher said, "Our team is still in Germany. We can easily have them over here to meet your boys by Wednesday, October 12th. However I can't see how I can get them to Bushfield until the afternoon. Do you have any suggestions?"

"We could accommodate them at the school over the Wednesday night, without any problem. They could be entertained by the Bushfield team that evening. Then they could play the game on Thursday. How would that suit you?"

"It would have to be on the Thursday morning. They would have to return to London immediately after lunch as they would be due to meet the Ambassador here that evening. We have taken rooms for them at a Bayswater hotel. Yes, this all fits in well. Shall we agree to proceed on those lines, then?"

"I suppose you will accompany them?"

"Yes, I shall come down in an embassy car. Probably Von Rohrbach will come with me. The team will come down in their own coach. I suppose you can arrange for Von Rohrbach and myself to be given suitable overnight accommodation?"

"I am quite sure the headmaster will put you both up at his private house. Now, I have another idea. Do you think it would be a good idea if we agree to fly our respective national flags at either end of the pitch during the game? To emphasise its underlying purpose."

"That is a really excellent proposal! But do you have a suitable German flag at Bushfield? I could arrange for you to be loaned one by the embassy, but you would have to look after it! They are very particular about flags here!"

"Yes, I was going to ask you if you could lend us one. You know you have my assurances about its safekeeping. I know how much importance is attached to such matters in Germany, Gregory!"

The necessary instructions were issued. In a few minutes a messenger entered the room with a neat parcel containing the flag. With this precious package safely secured they shook hands and parted.

Harold made his way back to Waterloo. His head was already spinning with elaborate and largely impractical plans for the German team's reception at Bushfield.

Schumacher went up to Von Rohrbach's very much grander office.

"Well?"

"I hope you agree with me, sir, he would be excellent material for our purposes!"

"It certainly seems that way!"

"I think you had better have him thoroughly checked out by the section and then double checked by Munich. You can never tell just from appearances!"

"Right, I shall see to that at once."

Von Rohrbach was the most senior representative of the Gestapo at the embassy. Schumacher reported directly to him. One of the most important tasks upon which they were engaged in London was that of cultivating contacts within Britain, through an organisation called the Aryan Friendship Society, which could be useful in the event of war. Schools such as Bushfield, to which so many important people had been themselves, and to which they sent their sons, were of special interest to them. In addition the section was meticulously working through records at the Births, Marriages and Deaths Registries to establish racial origins of all people whose names came up in the course of these investigations.

Harold boarded his train. He sat wrapped in dreams. He was imagining a Britain governed as he supposed was Germany. He saw himself achieving a position of great authority. He felt sure the Munich Accord would inevitably result in a combined crusade by the Axis powers, together with Britain and France, against communism and, since the two were inextricably, if inexplicably, bound together in his philosophy, international Jewry.

He began to plan an elaborate welcome at Bushfield for the German team. He would, he thought, involve the O.T.C.. the school band, the flags, the Governors. He nodded off.

Arriving at Bushfield station he once again sought out his bicycle, carefully strapped the precious parcel to his carrier, and pedalled happily back to the school.

CHAPTER SEVENTEEN

WISLEY

Dr. Wisley was a curious combination of liberal middle class thinking and early twentieth century social attitudes. He had been born in 1900, just as the Boer War was ending. His family had been deeply imbued with ideas of Empire and patriotism. His mother had been an early champion of women's rights and closely involved with the suffrage movement, then in its infancy.

As a boy he had lived through the Great War, seeing the wounded return and sorrowing with friends who had lost fathers and brothers. At the end of the war he had seen his father return home gravely disabled by poison gas.

In 1922, as he was taking up his first teaching post, Mussolini's Fascisti were making their march on Rome. In 1926, notwithstanding his utter detestation of militarism, he decided to join the Territorial Army. The ferocity of the passions revealed to be underlying an apparently tranquil society by the General Strike had greatly alarmed him. He became convinced that a fresh world crisis was rapidly gathering and that such action on his part was a patriotic duty. He proved to be an excellent part-time soldier and earned rapid promotion. By 1932 he was second in command of his T.A. battalion of the Prince's Own Carbines, serving under Sir George Threlfall.

The 1931 economic crisis had been followed by the emergence of Sir Oswald Moseley's British Union of Fascists the following year. For this and all its alleged principles he rapidly formed a special dislike.

In 1935 Harold Arbitant, then twenty-five, had joined Wisley's battalion, holding a reserve commission. Harold had always elected to hold extreme right wing views but, at that time, he had not contemplated actually seeking membership of the B.U.F. A rather uneasy kind of relationship developed between the two men, based mainly on their mutual scholastic and army interests, but this was marred by the facts that they disagreed about almost everything and Harold's impenetrability to reasoned argument.

Late in 1937 Harold received a letter from the only person with whom he had ever formed any really close relationship since childhood.

This was Gregory Schumacher. Gregory wrote to inform him that he had now become a German citizen and had been given a permanent appointment working in the German embassy in London. He suggested that at some date they might have lunch together, perhaps during the school holidays. Harold replied enthusiastically. It was during this lunchtime reunion that Gregory had raised the question of Harold's political views.

"I, personally, have never had any doubts whatsoever, Harry! I am now a full member of the Nazi Party. From what I remember about you at university that would have been the natural course for you to take had it been open to you. To my way of thinking you do not fit at all comfortably into current weak- kneed British Conservative philosophy."

"That's all very well, Gregory. You are fortunate enough to have been granted full German citizenship. I live here. I can't join your Nazi party, can I?"

"No, Harry, but you could give your full support to Moseley and his British Union. This wretched Public Order Act that your Parliament saw fit to enact last December has been a real thorn in his side. He needs more support from the British intelligentsia. Why don't you go along to one of his meetings? See if you could meet and speak to some of his better educated supporters."

Harold was doubtful. "I'm nobody of any importance. I don't see why they should much benefit from my active membership. However, I don't mind going along to a meeting and listening to what they have to say. Would you come along with me?"

"Yes, I should be pleased to do so, and to give you some introductions."

Early in 1938 Harold joined the B.U.F. For the time being he kept the news of this decision to himself. He was by no means sure that Wisley, of whose quite contrary views he was well aware, would look favourably on the matter. For not only was he his T.A. superior but, by a curious twist of fate, he had also just been appointed headmaster of Bushfield Abbey.

In 1936 Dr. Williams celebrated his forthcoming seventieth birthday by announcing to the Governors his intention to retire in September 1937. For this reason a special Governors' meeting had been convened, meeting early in 1937, to discuss the appointment of a suitable successor. At that date the Governors were Sir Hubert Polesden, the chairman, a retired general, whose own son was currently Head of School; Sir Graham Harrap, the local Member of Parliament; the Right

Reverend Joseph Baldock, the diocesan Bishop; and a distinguished Old Bushfielder, Sir David Parker, K.C.

Each of these people, with the sole exception of the chairman, had come to the meeting armed with their own pet proposal. The chairman, however, had a shrewd notion that Dr. Williams had already formed his own firm ideas. He had no inkling what it might be but, whatever it was, he was resolved to support it against all comers. Sir Hubert had entered Bushfield in 1885 at the age of twelve. That was the year that Archibald Williams was just ending his final and triumphant year as Head of School. To the young Polesden he had seemed godlike. The awe in which he held him had never subsequently worn away. The idea of arguing with him about his choice of successor was unthinkable. The other three members of the board were all between six and eight years younger than Sir Hubert. In consequence they were themselves completely dominated by him for just the same reason. They were all Old Bushfielders. Such was the effect and result of the hierarchical system in which they had been educated. The loyalties formed at school were to all intents and purposes ineradicable. The general, notwithstanding all his subsequent distinction, had never been able to bring himself to refer to Dr. Williams by his Christian name, either directly or when discussing him with other people. He was always "Dr. Williams".

"We should be most obliged to you, Dr.Williams," he said, opening the meeting, "if you would first of all give us your own recommendations, if you have any, as to whom you feel might make a worthy successor for you

"Gentlemen, I do have one proposal. Before I tell you who this is I should like, if I may, to explain why I have made such a selection. We are living in difficult times. There is even the possibility, notwithstanding all efforts to the contrary, that we may once again find ourselves at war. It is for this reason that I am most strongly of the view that we should recruit somebody well fitted to face up to such a task. Academic distinction, whilst essential, is not of itself sufficient. You must direct your minds towards finding some person possessed of pronounced qualities of leadership and, preferably, younger than is often the case when making such a choice. I believe I know of such a person. Nevertheless before I announce his name I consider it only courteous that the other members of the Board should be heard first."

The other three Governors were silently reviewing their own proteges in the light of Dr. Williams's criteria. Each regretfully had come to the conclusion that they failed to meet them. They remained silent as the general looked enquiringly round the table.

"Well, Dr. Williams", he said, after a second or two had passed with no proposals forthcoming, "it seems we all wish to receive your own advice, first!"

"I have in mind Dr. Richard Wisley. He is currently a senior housemaster at Franklin's Court. I believe he would exactly fit the bill!"

The Bishop, who privately was more than a little put out at the way the proceedings seemed to him to be being manipulated, seized on an objection. "Isn't that an, ahem, somewhat liberal establishment? Should we not be seeking somebody from a more, shall we say, orthodox background?" He looked around at his colleagues, confident that they would support him.

However, before Sir Graham, who certainly was of the same mind as the Bishop, could utter a word he was pre-empted by an interjection from Sir David.

"I know Dr. Wisley very well! He is my sister's boys' housemaster at this moment. A most excellently run school, with first class results, most impressive! Everybody speaks most highly of him. I agree he fills the bill exactly. He would be much better than the man I had in mind to suggest myself!"

"That's spiked the enemy's guns", thought the general to himself. His admiration for Dr. Williams as a strategist had never stood higher. "I'll wager he knew Parker's nephews were at Franklin's Court, in Wisley's house! Clever move, pretending to defer, whilst setting up those criteria!"

However, as chairman, he felt he couldn't let Dr. Williams have a completely uncontested victory. He had a duty to preserve the Board's dignity and at least go down with colours still flying. "I am sure, Dr. Williams, your choice is based on the soundest principles and Sir David's endorsement is most persuasive. Nevertheless we should seek some special relationship with Bushfield, if possible. Does Dr. Wisley have any kind of special connection with us?"

"He is currently the second in command of the Territorial Army Reserve battalion of the Prince's Own Carbines, commanded by Sir George Threlfall, and to which our own O.T.C., under Mr. Arbitant's command, is affiliated. "

"Most persuasive!" said the Bishop, relieved to be thrown this face-saver, "He has my approval."

The other two nodded their agreement.

"He'd kept that trump card up his sleeve," thought the general admiringly, as he recorded the decision.

CHAPTER EIGHTEEN

REPORT

It was seven in the evening by the time Harold arrived back at Bushfield Abbey. Notwithstanding the excellent lunch he had received at the embassy he was by now famished. Although he knew perfectly well that the headmaster would be expecting him to present his report immediately he felt he could not do so until he had eaten. He was just in time for staff dinner and he accordingly made his way directly to the staff dining room. His arrival back had, however, been noted by the ever observant Tom Riding, who had duly reported it to Dr. Wisley.

Over the meal one or two people, consumed with curiosity as to the reason for his absence, tried to quiz him. He gave nothing away, maintaining a mysterious air of importance. "I can report only to Dr. Wisley!" was all he would say. Then, his supper finished, he made off to the Lodgings, leaving behind a number of highly irritated colleagues and, for him, a satisfactory degree of speculation.

"Evening Arbitant! I had heard you had returned. Hope you enjoyed your supper!" He glanced at the clock but the gesture seemed to be lost on Harold. He was far too pleased with himself to apologise for keeping Dr. Wisley waiting for over an hour since his return.

"I had a most satisfactory visit, sir. I was introduced to and given lunch by a senior aide to the ambassador, a Herr Von Rohrbach, a most charming gentleman. He has delegated full responsibility in the matter to my friend."

"Excellent! Now let me have the details!"

"The proposal, sir, is that their team, which is at present still in Germany, should arrive here, at Bushfield, by private coach, on the Wednesday afternoon. That would be October 12th. They would have had lunch. I said that I was confident we should be able to entertain them for the afternoon and evening and then put them up at the school for the night. The match, however, would have to be played the following morning. This is because they are due to be addressed by the ambassador at the embassy that evening, the only time he is available. This would mean they would have to leave immediately after lunch. Of course, this is all subject to your agreement, sir."

"You seem to have done well. This is all excellent. I shall tell Mrs. Jason to find them accommodation in the spare wing of the sanatorium, mercifully it has no occupants at the moment! They can also have their meals there, with our own team. I wonder whether they speak enough English to mix in with our fellows? Perhaps you had better look out a few of your star German speakers and have them join the group? Have them shown round the school on Wednesday afternoon and we'll see what we can arrange for the evening to keep them amused. Anything else?"

"Gregory will definitely come down with them. He will be travelling in one of the embassy cars, probably accompanied by his chief. He will let me know whether or not his chief can come when I telephone him to confirm your agreement. That means that we shall have to find both him and, probably, Herr Von Rohrbach, accommodation here for the Wednesday night. There will also be the chauffeur and the coach driver to consider".

"None of that presents a problem. The two German officials can stay with me. I shall have two spare rooms as none of the Governors will be staying here. The Bishop and Sir David have appointments elsewhere on the Thursday and General Polesden, if he comes, lives locally."

"I had wondered, sir, whether it might not be a good idea to invite Sir George and Lady Threlfall to attend the match? Lady Threlfall has, I believe, very close ties with Germany and I am sure Sir George would like to watch his son playing? What do you think, sir?"

"Good thinking! As it happens Lady Threlfall is away in Germany right now. I know that because I invited them both to attend the thanksgiving service next Sunday, to hear John read the lesson. Sir George declined for that reason. However I am sure they would be pleased to come along and see the match. I have another guestroom here they can have. Any other ideas?"

"They have loaned me a German flag, sir. They suggested we should fly this at one end of the pitch during the game and our own flag at the other to emphasise the purpose of the match, Anglo-German friendship on the sports field. If you agree, sir, I shall arrange for the erection of flag posts."

"Well, I cannot really say I am very enthusiastic about flying a German flag here, but if they specially asked for it to be done I suppose it would be churlish not to comply! Frankly I have a hunch some of the senior staff and even some of the parents, if they find out, will not be very pleased! I take it that it will be one of those swastika flags and not the imperial eagle?"

Harold had anticipated a certain amount of opposition to the idea of flying the flag. There was, as he well knew, considerable anti-German sentiment in the staff common room. Too many of the senior staff still had bitter memories of the Great War. Also, notwithstanding his earlier remarks to Strong, there were, in fact, quite a number of boys in the school of Jewish origin, although not religion, with highly influential parents. For this reason he had taken care to attribute the flag flying proposal to the embassy and not himself, although it had been entirely his own idea.

"The flag I have been loaned, sir, is the official Nazi Party flag, identical with the ones flown at the embassy."

"Very well! Arrange for the flag posts. However, please do not hoist the flags until just before the match starts. I have just remembered that there is a great deal of anti-German sentiment in Bushfield village. They lost almost all their adult male population in the course of the Great War. To make matters worse a Zeppelin dropped a bomb on the village, certainly in error, but nevertheless it did a great deal of damage to both life and property. I wouldn't put it beyond some village hotheads to try and rip it down and damage it if they saw a chance!"

"I am so glad you warned me about that, sir! I have been most particularly warned to look after it and return it in good condition as soon as possible. I think, on reflection, they should be lowered as soon as the match is over. That would mean that we should have them under constant surveillance."

"Do that!"

"I have another suggestion, sir. Would you agree to my organising a guard of honour from the O.T.C. to greet them on arrival?"

Rather to his surprise Wisley liked the idea. "I think that's a good proposal. That sort of thing should appeal to them. Also it will show them that we, too, are training our young people to defend our country. A guard of honour, mind you! Not a full parade! You can support them with the school band but make sure they only play British marches, we don't want any attempts at the German national anthem! Right, I think that wraps things up for the moment. I can go ahead with my plans for the service on Sunday and also tell Mr. Strong about this match. Perhaps you would be good enough to ask him to come over and see me? If you see Tom on the way back would you ask him to find Mrs. Jason and ask her to come and see me this evening? I know it is getting late but I must get things moving!"

Mrs. Jason was duly summoned. Then he went over to tell the Reverend Strong of Wisley's request.

Alicia Jason was the widow of Henry Jason, who had formerly been the school's senior classics master. Henry had been invalided out of the army in 1917 as the result of gas poisoning on the western front. In hospital he had been tenderly nursed by Alicia and had made a partial recovery. He thereupon had resumed his teaching career and immediately married her. In 1920 she had born a son, Brian. Shortly thereafter, however, he had succumbed to the after effects of the gas and died. Dr. Williams, then the headmaster, had promptly appointed her as school matron. When Brian had reached the age of twelve the Governors had granted him a special bursarship to enable him to enter the school to complete his education there.

By the time Harold knocked on Strong's door, through which could be clearly heard the classical music of which he was so fond, it was nine o'clock. Strong made no attempt to conceal his irritation at being summoned at this late hour . He was a tall, gaunt man of about fifty. His hair whilst entirely grey was still plentiful. He was immensely learned and of intense religious sincerity. He had gone directly from Bushfield Abbey, where he had been educated, to Cambridge and from there into theological college and thus into the church. In 1918 he had been old enough to enlist as a chaplain with the Prince's Own Carbines and served with them in the mud and desolation of Flanders. He absolutely detested having his established routine disturbed, especially through the agency of Harold. Very reluctantly he took the needle off the record he had been playing and stopped the gramophone.

"Anyway where have you been all day? Other people have had to carry your workload you know?"

"I'm sorry, sir, I went up to London on a special mission for Dr. Wisley."

"Well, yes, he did tell me he'd asked you. What is it now? I hope it is really important."

"I've just made a report to him concerning the London mission I have been engaged upon on his behalf. He wishes to discuss some aspects with you, if that is convenient."

"Convenient, indeed!" He reached for his clerical black hat, jammed it on his head, and departed, muttering crossly to himself.

Alicia Jason was already there when he arrived. He approved of Alicia and her presence somewhat appeased him. Together they both listened in silence as Wisley explained to them about the forthcoming match.

"Well, Headmaster, so far as I am concerned everything will be done as you require. I shall make quite sure the catering and accommodation is all in order. I am pleased to do anything that may help to avoid another war, however small the contribution. I have been thinking how dreadful it would be if Brian were to be caught up in one as was his father.

I must say, however, I don't particularly relish the idea of having all these Germans staying here!"

"Yes, I am afraid a lot of people may feel like that. The object of the exercise is to try and demonstrate that the present situation is quite different from that which obtained twenty years ago. We cannot undo what has already been done but we can show the way to a co-operative and hopefully war free future by meeting each other and laying the ghosts of the past."

She took her departure.

"And so what is your view about all this, Alistair?"

"In one way it makes some sense to me and in another it seems to be nonsensical!" said Strong with characteristic directness. " I am completely unconvinced by all the optimistic twaddle being spoken and written concerning the importance of the Munich meeting and its outcome. Naturally I am pleased that it has given us a respite from a war for which we were quite obviously completely unprepared. But I must say that I do feel this conclusion to which you appear to have come that it is going to usher in a period of peace has very precarious foundations. I fear you are in danger of making a mountain out of a molehill. But, no matter, the Bishop has already told me the thanksgiving service has his total backing, so I am, as usual, in a minority of one!"

"Am I to take it from that that you do not feel that this match can possibly make any significant contribution to healing the rift that has persisted between us and Germany since the Great War? " Wisley asked the question almost wistfully. He had been hoping for a rather more enthusiastic reception for his ideas. The "molehill" jibe had been particularly apt and had struck home with him. He was uneasily wondering whether his judgement really was as sound as he had, until this moment, firmly believed. Strong often had this disturbing effect on people.

"Well, Headmaster, I really cannot, in all honesty, say that I am rejoiced by the news that Bushfield Abbey is set to welcome a team of German boys all of whom, I am reasonably sure, will have been selected because they are members of that undoubtedly pagan organisation, the HitlerYouth. The ostensible purpose behind this reconciliatory game may well be praiseworthy but my suspicions as to the motivation of the German sponsors are by no means allayed by your own obvious sincerity. I fear they have, more probably, been sent to "spy out the land". If you are expecting our own boys to be facing a team which intends to play by our British standards of fair play then I believe you are likely to be disappointed! I suppose there may be an outside chance one or two of them may benefit from their brief exposure to our ways, although I think even this is unlikely. At least I feel confident they won't contaminate our British lads."

"Well, Alistair, you have certainly made your views crystal clear to me! You may be surprised to hear me say that not only do I respect them but, to some degree, I share some of them. However, I feel I have a duty to do all I can to promote such international accord by whatever means I have available to me. The alternative, of war, is too awful to contemplate. I am going to call a staff meeting tomorrow to explain matters and we shall see then what reactions there are. Whatever one may think about the terms and methods of securing this Munich Agreement it has, or so it would seem, prevented, for the time being, perhaps for ever, the imminent outbreak of a terrible war. If a war did occur many of our colleagues and pupils would be affected. Surely this is reason enough to make even such a puny effort as this?"

"Headmaster, please be assured I have no qualms as to your personal sincerity, as I have already said. I only pray, however, that your faith in both the outcome and efficacy of this Munich agreement and the susceptibility of our young visitors to British ideas of decency and toleration are not disappointed!"

With these words he took his departure.

Wisley, left on his own, sat for some time reflecting. He was feeling unsettled and despondent. He was, for the first time, beginning to wonder whether he had overreacted to the news of Munich. The ideas of the service and the match had both seemed so good. Surely, he reflected, it was only right that he should make some such positive attempts? Anything was better than war. Then he began to wonder whether even that was still true.

CHAPTER NINETEEN

MEETING

The promised staff meeting took place in the masters' dining room after classes on Friday. In addition to the teaching staff all school prefects and Alicia Jordan had been told to attend. Such a comprehensively attended meeting was unprecedented. A buzz of speculation filled the room. The majority opinion was that it must have something to do with the current world political crisis.

The noise subsided as Wisley entered. Then, to general astonishment, he was immediately followed in by Harold, who proceeded to take a seat on the prepared dais, immediately behind him. Harold was trying hard to appear nonchalant but his unease was quite visible.

"Thank you all for coming. I have some matters of importance to explain to you. First of all let me make two things clear. The Governors have already approved and, for the moment, you are specifically requested by me not to reveal, what I am now going to tell you, until after morning service, next Sunday, which I shall expect everybody to attend. Mr. Arbitant has been carrying out an important mission for me. He has performed this duty excellently and I take this opportunity of thanking him in public for his efforts. After I have made my preliminary remarks he will be available for further comment and questioning."

Harold was generally unpopular. Uneasy glances were being exchanged. Perceiving this Wisley decided to proceed with the business in hand as rapidly as he might.

"You are all well aware that the threat of war is once again hanging over all of us. The smouldering embers of enmity between ourselves and Germany once again look as though they may spring back into life! I know only too well the feelings and bitter memories so many of you hold arising from those terrible years when we were last at war. I know, too, that many of you, although too young to have suffered personally, hold strong views concerning recent similar events in Spain and Abyssinia. As you all know, from the radio and the press, last Thursday, September 29th, our own Prime Minister, together with M. Daladier, acting on behalf of France, concluded an agreement with the

German Chancellor and the Italian Duce, Herr Hitler and Signor Mussolini. In the subsequent words of our own Mr. Chamberlain this agreement gives "peace in our time, peace with honour". Now, we in Britain are a free people, free to hold whatever political views we consider appropriate. There are those amongst us who, for whatever reason, believe in the ideologies which have currently found favour in Germany and Italy. There are others who hold them in abhorrence. In this country of ours each man must decide such things for himself. That is how we order things here. Such decisions must, of course, always be subordinated to our overall loyalty to our country. We here, at Bushfield Abbey, like all teachers everywhere, have, however, another loyalty of a different kind. This is to the pupils who have been entrusted to our care by their parents. This loyalty must always be uppermost in our considerations. We may or may not approve of all the things which were agreed at Munich. We may, privately, perhaps regard ever closer ties with a country with which we were, in recent times, at daggers drawn in the most literal sense, with the greatest suspicion.. Nevertheless, so long as we are presented with the possibility of honourably, and I stress honourably, avoiding a war which, as we must all know, would inevitably result in terrible destruction we must remind ourselves that the victims of such a conflict will include not only our own colleagues but, inevitably, our pupils. For that reason alone, and there are many others of course, we must do all we can to preserve peace and create the right conditions in which peace can flourish. We only have to stand for a moment in front of our Bushfield Abbey war memorial and read the names on it to realise how important this is."

There was absolute silence in the room. He paused, for a moment, and looked around. He could see that many of the senior staff were mentally reliving the horrors of the trenches. He observed some cynicism on the faces of some of the younger staff, motivated by youthful conviction. Then he looked at the young prefects, seated together at the back of the room. Lambs for the slaughter, he thought. He knew how eagerly their fathers had enlisted and how few had returned. Was all that sacrifice to have been in vain?

He continued. "I have to tell you that, shortly before the Prime Minister made his trip to Munich, this school received an invitation, via the German Embassy in London, to meet a team of German schoolboys, here at Bushfield, and play them at soccer. The purpose behind the proposal, so it was stated, was to further the cause of national accord by providing the opportunity for young people of our two nations to get to know each other on the field of sport. However, at that time, the political situation at that time was so uncertain that it was felt better not to accept.

However, after the Munich agreement was signed the invitation was reissued and, this time, the Governors decided the time was opportune and accepted. It was urged that if governments can come to agreements then so can schools. I, therefore, delegated Mr. Arbitant, as senior German language master here, to make contact with the German Embassy in London. His negotiations with them have been outstandingly successful. He will now tell you what has been agreed. Before he does so, however, I have one further matter about which I wish to tell you.

As I hope you all know, next Sunday's morning service will take the form of one of special thanksgiving for the respite of peace we are now enjoying. I shall be preaching the sermon and it is in the course of this that I intend to announce the forthcoming match and the purpose underlying it. This seems to me to be the correct context in which to make such an announcement. That is why I do not wish you to talk about this until then. All the school governors will attend the service, to underline the importance attached to what I have said. The diocesan bishop will read the first lesson."

He sat down and Harold rose. It was as well that Harold was enjoying Wisley's support. The audience at once became decidedly restive. Wisley had been listened to with quiet respect but, privately, there were many present who felt far too much importance was being attached to the German visit.

When he began to explain about the flying of the two flags there was an expostulation from a senior housemaster. "Do you mean we are expected to fly that dreadful red flag with the crooked cross on it, here, at Bushfield?"

"We have been loaned the swastika flag, by the embassy, sir."

"I object, most emphatically!"

"Hear! Hear" exclamations were to be heard from various quarters of the room.

"That is the flag they have provided."

"Why fly anything. We have never done such a thing before?"

"This is a quasi-diplomatic event. We must comply. To refuse to fly it would amount to a diplomatic rebuff to the embassy."

Heads were shaking in disbelief all round the room but Wisley's presence stifled further discussion on the point. Wisley sat there, rather glumly, wondering whether Strong was right.

The road to hell, he was thinking, was truly paved with good intentions. Had he taken such a road?

CHAPTER TWENTY

JOHN

In 1933, at the age of twelve, John Threlfall, together with William Hyslow and Gordon Preston, had entered Bushfield Abbey School, as boarders in Chaplain's House.

He was a tall, brown haired boy, green eyed and generally reckoned to be outstandingly good looking. He had what seemed to be a permanently sunburned complexion. . He excelled at all sport and, by 1938, was generally reckoned to be the school's best soccer player.

That year all three were in their first year in the Lower Sixth. John was specialising in classics and literature, at which he was showing great promise. The others had opted for science .All three had just been appointed school sub-prefects. Their form master was Harold Arbitant, an appointment he held by virtue of his status as senior languages master. Thus he was in nominal charge of their studies, although in practice he met with them only once a week, when the entire class had a session with him. All three were considered to be of university calibre and had their hopes set on Cambridge.

John was a sensitive, liberally minded boy, much given to emotional outbursts. He held very strong views on a number of diverse subjects. More often than not these seemed to be diametrically the opposite of those expressed, equally forcibly, by Harold Arbitant. Neither would ever yield to the other. Considerable antipathy existed between the two. Clashes, when the class held their weekly joint session with him, were commonplace. Such disagreements usually arose from causes that seemed ridiculous to everybody else, but were none the less almost savage in their intensity.

Harold never felt completely at ease with John. He came from that sector of society to which Harold had always wanted to belong, but from which he felt utterly excluded. The Threlfalls were Bushfielders through and through. There had, in fact, been a Threlfall at the school ever since its foundation, an event that had taken place shortly after the restoration of the monarchy, some three hundred years earlier.

After the suppression of the monasteries Bushfield Abbey had passed into the possession of the then newly created Earl of Bushfield, a creature of Thomas Cromwell's. This parvenu magnate had at once proceeded to demolish the larger part of the original abbey, sparing only the Great Tower and the chapel. With the stone so secured he had built himself a magnificent house. This itself was later demolished, but from what had remained of it The Lodgings had been carved out in the seventeenth century to provide suitable housing for the headmaster of the new school. The Earl had adopted as his arms and motto the device of a phoenix arising from the flames, subscribed with the English words, "I was, I am, I shall be". This device still appeared on the stone shield carved on the side of the Great Tower, immediately below the clock. A later Earl had made the mistake of backing the King against Oliver Cromwell. He had had to flee into exile, where he had died, leaving no heir.

.When Charles II returned the now ownerless estate reverted to the Crown. Charles granted it to a charitable trust which proceeded to establish a school, ostensibly for impoverished sons of gentlefolk, but which quickly became popular with the aristocracy. From the very outset the Threlfall family had been involved with the establishment of the school. The first chairman of the Governors was a Threlfall and Threlfall males were always thereafter educated there. The school then adopted the phoenix and the motto as their own crest.

The Great Tower, with its steeply sloping conical roof, surmounted by a flagpole, dominated the surrounding countryside. It stood, in all its grandeur, at the end of a long gravelled drive leading up from imposing wrought iron gates. Here it looked across a wide-open space that extended between its base and the facing school war memorial. This space had, in 1919, at a dedication ceremony, been named Heroes' Yard and this was the name by which it was always called. On the plaque attached to its base were inscribed the names of all staff, pupils and staff connected with the School who had died as a direct result of the Great War. It was a lengthy listing and among the names was that of Major Sir Frederick Threlfall, John's grandfather. The majority of the fallen had served with the Prince's Own Carbines.

The Threlfalls were very considerable landowners. Their lineage was ancient, preceding even the Norman conquest. The incumbent of what was then the estate had been prudent enough to foresee the possibility of William's victory and had hedged his bets accordingly. In consequence when Harold was defeated and many neighbouring thegns dispossessed he had been left alone. The family had prospered quietly ever since. The family seat, and only residence, was Loughbourne Manor, in the county of Norsex. This was neither too far from nor too close to Bushfield, a most convenient arrangement.

John's grandfather, Sir Frederick, had been killed in the Great War in 1916, whereupon the title and estates had been inherited by his son, George, John's father, then still a schoolboy. Frederick's widow, Lady Sarah, had managed the estates thereafter until George, then still only nineteen, had married and taken this upon himself, foregoing a place at Cambridge. Lady Sarah, who had never fully recovered from her grief over her husband's early death, was, in 1938, sixty-six and, so far as anybody was aware, in excellent health. She was John's idol. He absolutely adored her. For his own mother, Lady Ann, he had virtually no affection and received none in return. She was frequently away from Loughbourne, visiting her aristocratic German cousins. These had all been early and fervent Nazi Party members and had prospered accordingly. All were now in high positions.. Ann had eagerly embraced their opinions and had made no secret of the matter, much to her husband's displeasure.

John's father was a genial man, greatly loved and respected by his son, but totally immersed in the running of his estates. He left Loughbourne as little as he could contrive, his only other real interest being his command of his Territorial battalion of the Prince's Own Carbines. Although he had had a particular hatred for Germany ever since his father's death, he had married Ann, who had a German mother, without giving that aspect of her parentage any thought. He had fallen so madly in love with her when she was eighteen that nothing else seemed to matter at the time. Ultimately, however, this fixation of his, coupled with both his wife's far too frequent absences in the hated country and her professed political views (which he abominated) had led to a serious breach between them. The more Ann preached her creed the more George grew to dislike it and her relations.

So far as John was concerned his mother scarcely existed. He regarded Sarah as his mother. She was the member of the family with whom he corresponded whilst away at school. Apart from instinctively siding with his father he took no notice of his mother's opinions. He had absolutely no idea what it was that was happening in Germany or any interest in politics.

His immediate ambition was to go to Cambridge and read English literature, a subject that fascinated him. He rarely set eyes on his mother, even when at home during the school holidays. When he did see her he did his best to avoid her. He spent his time either with his father or his grandmother or with friends.

Gordon Preston came from the younger branch of an extremely wealthy Yorkshire family, of Viking descent. Their fortune came from

82

textile manufacture. His father, Horace, was, in 1938, fifty-five and chairman of the board of Prestons' Textiles, the family owned business. This appointment was, however, for the main part, ceremonial. He took no active part in the management of the business. He had been badly gassed in the Great War and had never recovered his health since. In 1919 he had married Jessica Thomas, the nurse, who had cared for him during his convalescence. Gordon, born in 1921, was their only son. The business was effectively under the control of Gordon's cousin, Sir Francis, twenty one years older than himself. Gordon had a burning ambition to succeed Francis as either managing director or chairman of the family concern, since Francis now seemed unlikely to produce a male heir and, in any event, as William's grandson, Gordon considered this was his rightful entitlement.

The Viking origins of the Prestons were clearly evident from their appearance. The marauding ancestor had landed in Whitby and then decided to settle, marrying into and integrating with the local population. They were all very tall, fair-haired, blue eyed and immensely intelligent.

William Hyslow was a slightly built and introspective boy. He had light brown, slightly wavy hair, a freckled face, and hazel eyes behind steel frame spectacles, for he was slightly short sighted. The family was socially well connected but his father was a younger son with only a very small private income. This was supplemented by the inadequate stipend he received as a vicar. The Reverend Hyslow had good hopes of eventual substantial preferment but, for the moment, things were financially difficult. The family had just been able to manage to pay for him at Bushcome Preparatory School, but were at their wits' ends as to what to do about meeting the much higher Bushfield Abbey fees. Old Bushfielders' sons with a Church of England connection were eligible to apply for a Clergy Scholarship but the amount on offer was still too little to make much difference. At the critical moment William's godparents, appreciating the problem, stepped in with a proposal. Provided, they diplomatically suggested, carefully sugaring the pill, William secured a Clergy Scholarship, and provided they were given an undertaking that he would follow his father into the Established Church as an ordained minister, they would guarantee all his fees, right through to ordination. This offer William's parents joyfully accepted on his behalf, without, however, thinking it necessary to consult him. All efforts were then concentrated on securing the scholarship. This was no problem for William. He was then able to accompany his two friends to Bushfield Abbey. It was not until some five years later that the exacting nature of the undertaking which had so freely been given by his parents on his behalf dawned on him.

"Oh, well, I suppose my birthright was sold for a mess of pottage!" he half joked to his friends as they discussed their future plans.

"I expect you will become a Bishop!" said Gordon, comfortingly.

"That's more likely to be my father! I'm more likely to end up as the housemaster of Chaplain's House, here!"

"Many a true word spoken in jest!" said John

"H'm!" said Hyslow, "but I am jolly well going to go to Cambridge and take a degree in science before I am ordained!"

As school sub-prefects they had been at the staff meeting. In view of Dr. Wisley's injunction against public discussion of what had been said they walked back to their house almost in silence. It was agreed that they would meet again for a private discussion in John's room the following evening.

"We are allowed to talk about it in private, surely. After all the three of us already know about it. It is only in front of other people we are not allowed to mention it, "said John.

The following morning, Friday, October the seventh, John received a letter from his father. Since George never wrote to anybody, even his son, if he could help it John looked at the envelope, written in his father's characteristic hand, with considerable surprise. Then he opened it and began to read. As he did so he felt his world changing about him.

It was a lengthy letter and it had cost his father much effort to write it. John studied it very carefully, then he sat down and thought about its content for a long time, especially in the light of Dr. Wisley's recent remarks, which now assumed a significance for him they had not previously possessed. Then, very carefully, as though it were something very precious and delicate, he reinserted it into its envelope and put it into his inside pocket. There it lay, by his heart, for the rest of the day. He felt as though he were carrying an unexploded bomb around with him.

It so happened that that morning the Lower Sixth were due to have one of their weekly combined sessions with Harold. This always took the form of what was called free discussion, the subject being chosen by the combined class. On this occasion they had elected to spend the time talking about two Shakespeare plays they were all studying, Hamlet and The Merchant of Venice. Almost at once trouble arose between John and Harold. This was not unexpected, it usually happened, but, this time, it was much worse than usual and found its genesis in most unexpected fashion.

It began gently enough. Harold made a joke about Polonius.

"Why should we believe he is a dotard, deserving his fate? I think he was a good old man. It seems obvious that both Ophelia and Laertes really loved him. I think the advice he gave Laertes when he was going off to university was jolly good. Just because he is old doesn't mean he was stupid. If we live we'll all be old one day and probably much wiser not sillier!"

"Well, he does agree with Hamlet when he's asked whether a cloud in the sky looks like a whale " said Harold, slightly taken aback by the vigour of John's attack.

"I would have done so, too, if I'd been in his position! It wouldn't have been very wise to argue the point with an obviously mad sixteenth century prince, heir to the throne!"

The fickle class tittered. Harold felt he was losing control. "Oh, well, I suppose we must always make allowance for age," he said, rather weakly.

Then John suddenly said, "He reminds me of my grandmother!" He stared at Harold and round at the class so fiercely as he made the remark that nobody sniggered and Harold decided not to utter the sarcastic, "Well well, fancy that!" which had formed in his mind.

From then on matters deteriorated rapidly. The discussion had moved on to The Merchant. This was a play Harold especially enjoyed discussing. It gave considerable scope for the expression of his well-known anti-semitic views under the guise of literary criticism.

"So," said John, his tone more aggressive than ever," we are asked to accept that Shylock, like Polonius, deserved the abominable treatment to which he was subjected. I suppose that was simply because he happened to be a Jew?"

"Well, partially," responded Harold, " but he also happened to be a cunning, bloodthirsty rogue. But since you point it out, yes, he was a Jew. That doesn't really help his image much, does it?"

There were some sycophantic sniggers. John glared round the room and they stopped abruptly.

"Well, I have come to a different conclusion," he said.

"And what might that be, Mr. Threlfall? What is this amazing contribution to the study of Shakespeare you are about to make known to us?"

"When Shakespeare wrote the play he did so on two levels. The first, most obvious and, frankly, vulgar level played on the known prejudices of the ignorant mob. But Shakespeare himself really knew better than that. That is why he makes Shylock say that speech in the first scene of

Act three. The one that begins "Hath not a Jew eyes.." Those, I am sure, are the true feelings of such a learned man. He knows perfectly well that Shylock has been compelled to take the action he did because of the ridiculous prejudice he has encountered. The play is an illustration of the iniquity of acting upon prejudice and not reasoned judgement. Wouldn't you agree, sir, that such prejudice is the antithesis of decent behaviour?"

Harold had listened in startled silence. He could feel his control of the class slipping even further away from him. He resorted to more sarcasm. He should have known better. "Dear me, I don't think our clever friend here would find much support for that interpretation of the play, except of course, from Shylock's own kin, who would, doubtless, be only too happy to agree."

"Probably not," snapped back John, "but that is because prejudiced people are so blinded by their own opinions they don't take the trouble to think things through. Pearls before swine!"

"That's enough of that," said Harold hastily. "Class dismissed!"

"Anyway," said John, as he collected his books together, "Shylock reminds me of my grandmother!"

Harold practically fled from the room. Either the boy was mocking him or he had gone mad. Either way he simply had no idea how to handle such a situation. Threlfall was no ordinary pupil. Harold had met Ann at a B.U.F. meeting and was confident she would support him if things became much more difficult.

"What on earth was that all about?" said Preston, as they walked back to their house together.

"I shall tell you more when we meet later this evening. I can let you know one thing now, though! I am refusing to play against that German team. I shall have nothing to do with it!"

His friends stopped and stared at him.

"But if you refuse to play it will virtually wreck our chances of winning! We couldn't possibly find a centre forward to replace you suitably. You just can't do this!" Hyslow was nearly in tears.

Preston glowered at John. "You've been behaving like a bear with a sore head all day, ever since you had that letter this morning. Let's thrash this all out later."

""Thrash it out we shall!" said John, and strode angrily away, leaving the other two staring after him, completely baffled by his behaviour.

CHAPTER TWENTY ONE

DEBATE

On the Friday evening, as arranged, John, Hyslow and Preston met in John's room. John immediately proceeded to take his father's letter out of his pocket. He held it, unopened, in his hand and then looked searchingly at his two friends.

"Why are you looking at us like that?" said Preston. He was still feeling put out by the way John had ended their last meeting so abruptly.

"I was just wondering whether, when I have told you the news I have received in this letter, you will turn out to be real or just fair weather friends. We've known each other most of our lives, yet I am still able to doubt ."

They looked at him in astonishment.

"What a jolly silly remark!" said Hyslow.

Preston stretched out his legs, clasped his hands together, and glowered at John. "I'm rapidly getting fed up with all this!" he said.

Ignoring these danger signals John persisted, " What do we really know about each other and our families?"

"All we need to know, in my opinion!" said Hyslow, rather curtly.

"Yes, Hyslow, that is exactly what I have always thought, that is until I received this letter. Now I know I was always under an illusion. Let me ask you a hypothetical question, Preston?"

"Go ahead, if it is going to make any sense!"

"Has it ever occurred to you that your father might be a criminal?"

"I knew it wasn't going to be sensible, but that really takes the biscuit! No, of course it jolly well hasn't!"

"No, obviously that is your answer! In fact I doubt whether you would even be prepared to change your mind if you were presented with what seemed incontrovertible proof to the contrary!"

"I certainly would not!"

"And you, Hyslow, you agree with Preston?"

"Oh, for goodness sake, do stop being so ridiculous!"

"But how would you really react if, in spite of everything, it was at last made absolutely certain that what you had been told was true? In other words that you had been deceived, possibly with the best of intentions, even innocently, but, none the less deceived?"

"In such an unlikely case I should need to know a lot more about things!" said Preston, "To me the word "deceived" means having been deliberately misled. I really do not see how one can be innocently deceived."

"Yes, I accept that, but, in the case I have in mind, the eventual outcome is the same."

"Oh, really, Threlfall, this is beyond bearing!" burst out Hyslow. "Do come to the point. What are you trying to say, or tell us?"

"I shall, in my own time! First of all, though, I want to ask you both something else.If you were satisfied that a person you had thought to be a friend had badly misled you would you continue to trust him?

"It is quite impossible to answer such a question without knowing the facts!" said Preston, with growing irritability.

Hyslow, who rather enjoyed this kind of philosophical discussion, said, somewhat enigmatically, "What about "My country right or wrong" or "Blood is thicker than water". Don't maxims like those represent attempts to deal with these kind of situations?"

"Yes, we all have a duty to defend our country, even if we sometimes discover we don't agree with the policies we are being asked to support. We sink our personal opinions in the interests of those of the majority," agreed Preston.

"Would you still think that if you lived in a country which didn't have the freedom we have here?"

"That is a difficult question! I don't know how I should feel if I was an Italian, under that government they have under that man, Mussolini, and told to go and kill Abyssinian peasants with poison gas. There must be a limit where personal responsibility takes over!"

"Is treason only applicable to democracies? Surely not!" said Hyslow.

"Perhaps it all depends on the legitimacy of the government concerned." said Preston, "That's what has caused all this fighting in Spain between the socialists and the Falangists!" said Hyslow. "I am afraid I am not at all sure what I think, now I am faced with the problem! I don't have enough experience of such problems."

"Nevertheless," said Preston, who had been reflecting on the matter, "among one's own family surely it is always right to show a united front? That's where "blood is thicker than water" comes in!"

"What about the position of long and trusted friends?" said John.

"Your family is yours whether you like it or not. Your friends you select for yourself. If so-called friends turn out to be false to you then they are not still the people you thought them to be when you chose them. In the absence of the blood tie such relationships are based on trust alone. If trust goes then, I think, the basis of one's friendship must go with it. But, whatever you may feel about such behaviour amongst your family you cannot dispose of the blood tie like that, it is there whether you like it or not," said Hyslow.

"So, you are saying deceit, or its equivalent, can destroy friendship?" said John.

"Probably but not necessarily," said Preston. " obviously you would look at the former friend in a different way and re-examine your relationship. There might be a reasonable explanation, after all."

"Well, it does seem to me," said John, "you are making a very big distinction between the ties of family and the ties of friendship."

"Yes, I am. After all, as we have already agreed, or I think we have, one chooses one's friends but one's country and one's family are chosen for one. Usually we have no say in such matters, do we?"

"You know, as I see it, everything must depend on whether whatever it is that is supposed to constitute the alleged crime, or whatever it is, is really so unforgivable!"

"I don't follow that line of argument!"

"Well, it's a little hard to come up with a good example, just like this, but I mean something of this nature. Some action may, officially, be considered a crime. Nevertheless the circumstances attending the commission of that action may be such that, whilst not able to exonerate the perpetrator in, for example, a court of law, they might quite possibly be acceptable to me, as a private person, as excellent justification."

"You mean like the early Christians refusing to obey Roman law by offering sacrifice to a heathen god?" suggested Preston.

"Yes, that sort of thing! I often read accounts of trials in the papers and think "There but for the grace of God go I!" said Hyslow.

"Do you agree with Preston about the difference between family and friends?"

"I think one should always try to be loyal to one's family, just like one should be loyal to one's country. But I do think there must be some kind of escape. I'm not so certain now as Preston seems to be."

"But surely, Hyslow, the loyalties involved are quite different?"

"No, as I view the matter, we take all three, family, country and friends on trust. Now I think about it I really cannot see any more reason why we should blindly follow our national leaders or our parents, for that matter, than we would our chosen friends. We have been given individual reason and conscience. We should refer to them."

"Well, that may be as it may be!" said Preston. "What we need from you, Threlfall, are facts! All this talk is little more than hot air! People deceive each other for all sorts of reasons, if "deceive" is always the right word to use. Isn't excusable deceit called "telling a white lie"? It may, I suppose, sometimes be misguided to tell a white lie but it isn't morally wrong, at least in my book!"

"Circumstances alter cases", said Hyslow, rather sententiously.

"Let's call an end to all this!" said Preston. "Threlfall, for the last time, and I mean that, either tell us what it is that you want to tell us, if you want to tell us anything, or let's all go to bed. I, for one, am jolly tired!"

John looked at his friends. "You are both good friends! Thanks for bearing with me. I am aware that I've tried your patiences sorely. I so wanted to clear up these points in my own mind and you have really helped me! Now I shall tell you why I have definitely decided not to play in that German match Arbitant and the headmaster are organising!"

"You don't mean that, do you?" said Hyslow. "You know that if you don't play our chances of winning probably go. Think of the school!"

Preston's patience had worn wafer thin. "Really, Threlfall!" he burst out, "this is ridiculous! First you pick two quite stupid and unnecessary arguments with Arbitant. Then you begin making what seem to me to be silly allusions to skeletons in family cupboards. Then you ask us to engage in a ridiculous debate about friendship and so forth. Just what is it all about?"

"Yes, then you say you are going to virtually betray the school!"

"You owe us an explanation! You know perfectly well that neither Hyslow nor I would ever even think anybody associated with you or your family would behave in the kind of manner you have been suggesting."

"Why did you bait Arbitant, like that, about Shylock?" demanded Hyslow, suddenly. "You know he hates Jews. You were quite deliberately waving a kind of red flag in front of him, weren't you? I, personally, don't happen to like his silly ideas on the subject but that doesn't mean I agree he should be baited like that about them in front of the class. Why did you do it? And what was the purpose of those ridiculous asides about Polonius and Shylock reminding you of your grandmother?"

"There you go to the heart of the matter!" said John.

He opened up the letter he was holding in his hand.

"Now, if you will bear with me, I shall read this letter from my father to you. Then, perhaps, you will understand. Both of you know my grandmother. You know she is the person I love best in all the world, don't you? Anybody who hurts her, hurts me".

"But, surely, nobody has tried to harm her?" said Preston.

"Oh, yes, they have!"

They stared at him in amazement.

CHAPTER TWENTY TWO

LETTER

My dear boy,

I am writing to tell you some news that has come as a great shock to me. It is your grandmother's express wish that you should not, until she agrees, if she ever does, impart what now follows to your Mother. You will understand I must abide by her wishes, even if I do not really agree with her reasoning.

John, the world is often a cruel and unsympathetic place. Sometimes there are things that are better left concealed or unspoken about. Perhaps you have heard the old maxims "Let sleeping dogs lie" and "When first we practise to deceive, oh, what a tangled web we weave"?"

Just recently your grandmother, who has been greatly disturbed by the reports in the newspapers and on the wireless of the possibility of another war, decided to set in train certain enquiries into some private affairs of hers, concerning her side of the family. Until a few days ago I had no inkling whatsoever about such matters. I have, in fact, never known anything about her side of the family..........."

The letter then proceeded to outline, to the best of George's ability, the story of Frederick and Sarah. George then gave a description of Sarah's meeting with Tomkins. The letter continued:

"....the shock of receiving this dreadful information has had the most alarming effect on her health. She is suffering from continuous pains in her chest and is at present confined to her bed. She has asked me to write to Dr. Wisley and obtain permission for you to come back home and see her, as she particularly wishes to speak to you. As I think you know your Mother returns from Germany this Sunday. As I assume that Dr. Wisley will give the necessary permission I shall have Donald drive me up to Bushfield on Monday and bring you back with me. You can then see your grandmother and come back to Bushfield with us the following day. I realise you have to be in good shape to play in this important match Dr. Wisley has asked your Mother and myself up to see on Thursday. Dr. and Mrs. Wisley had already invited us to stay with them over the Wednesday night so I don't suppose they will mind having us for Tuesday night as well, in the circumstances.

As you are well aware your Mother holds very strong political views and is a great admirer of what has been happening in Germany. It is no secret that I absolutely disagree with her but I have never sought to dissuade her from behaving as she seems to feel proper. She has, of course, been greatly influenced by her German cousins, a matter of great regret to me, since my feelings about Germany are common knowledge.

These views of hers are certain to precipitate considerable family problems when she is eventually told, as I suppose will, sooner or later, have to be the case, that your grandmother is of Jewish descent. For the moment, as I have already said earlier, your grandmother has asked me to refrain from informing her. She is, I suppose, hoping that something may happen which will make the revelation unnecessary. That of course was always, it would seem, my father's view. However, quite obviously, he had never foreseen the kind of developments now occurring in Germany."

John stopped reading the letter. "I've read enough to you! Now, what do you both have to say about that?"

"It is a very dreadful position, certainly" said Preston. "However, whilst it is terribly upsetting about your grandmother's illness, I really do not understand how all this impinges upon the points you were raising in the discussion we have just had! What has all this to do with questioning our friendship?"

"And what has it to do with deciding not to play in the match?" asked Hyslow. "Your own parents are coming up to watch it. They obviously don't disapprove, why should you?"

"Because it seems quite obvious to me that any German boy, to be allowed to come over here and play in such a match, representing his country, would have to have proved himself to be a dedicated Nazi! I refuse to play against a team of boys who must be the sons of the very people who are persecuting and probably murdering my grandmother's family and would do the same to her, if they could!"

"Just now," said Hyslow, " you were talking to us about "deceit" and "crimes". Who, in all this, has deceived you? What "crimes" have been committed? Your father has been absolutely candid with you. Your grandfather, and of course your grandmother, were and are perfectly entitled to keep their affairs private. Your grandfather was quite right. What did it have to do with anybody else, or us for that matter?"

"I agree! You have everything out of perspective!" said Preston.

"What was all this about fair weather friends? How does anything in your father's letter affect our friendship or trust?" said Hyslow.

"Don't you appreciate the point? If my grandmother's family were Jewish then my father is half Jewish and I am quarter Jewish. Hadn't you perhaps realised that?"

"Oh, really!" said Preston, " so that's what is concerning you! No, of course it doesn't! Why on earth should it?"

"Jesus and all the Apostles were Jewish until they became Christian. Even then they were still of Jewish origin. That's just the same as your grandmother."

"My father has been saying that horrible things have been happening in Germany ever since this man Hitler came to power there. However, I have an idea that there is more to your decision not to play in the match than you have told us so far. Is that right?"

"Yes, I have come to the conclusion that if Arbitant knew the truth about my grandmother he would say the same things about her as he did about Shylock. That's why I referred to her like that in class. I don't want to have anything to do with something he is organising."

For a moment both his friends could think of no answer to that. Both were realising, very forcibly, the difference between theory and practice when it came to such matters. Then Preston said, "I feel you should do it for Dr. Wisley's sake! He is a good man, whatever you may think about Arbitant. His idea was to expose these German boys to our way of life. He is probably perfectly well aware that he is being over optimistic but thinks it worth the effort, nevertheless. I think you should support him!"

"And by not playing you won't stop the match taking place. You will simply make it more likely that we shall lose. That's a Pyrrhic victory for your ideals, isn't it? Germany triumphs over us!"

"Do you consider this Munich agreement as some kind of capitulation to Nazi ideas?" asked Preston.

"Yes! I simply cannot accept that our own government cannot know what is really happening over there! If this man Tomkins can find out then our highly trained Secret Service must know a lot more! How can people we are supposed to trust, like Chamberlain, make pacts and shake hands like that, with such a regime?

"I suppose that is how politics work!" replied Preston. "I expect Chamberlain received good advice. My father told me that he thought we were totally unprepared for war. He thinks Chamberlain did a good job by buying us time to prepare. Look at the enormous wave of relief that swept right across the country when the news of peace broke. But people have had more time to reflect now."

"You are both really good friends! I just don't know what I would do without you both! But I cannot but help wondering what my Mother and her beastly German cousins would make of all this!"

"So?" asked Hyslow.

"You have convinced me. I shall play. We'll thrash them and send them home with their horrible flag wrapped round them, covered in good old Bushfield mud!"

CHAPTER TWENTY THREE

PREPARATION

On Saturday morning Strong asked John to come and see him. Arbitant was present. "I have had a note from the Headmaster asking me to send you over to see him at The Lodgings as soon as possible. It seems your father telephoned him last night. I hope nothing serious has occurred!"

"My grandmother is very ill, sir."

"Oh, I am sorry!" said Arbitant. " I had no idea. Is that why you were so difficult in class yesterday morning?"

"What is all this?" asked Strong suspiciously.

"Oh, we just had a little disagreement about Shylock's character!" replied Harold, airily.

"H'm!" said Strong.

Then he turned to John and said, "By the way, just before you go over to see the headmaster I think I should warn you that he is going to tell you that the first lesson, that you are due to read in chapel this Sunday, is to be from Ecclesiastes 3, the first eight verses. You had better take care to rehearse them before then. He is attaching a lot of importance to the way they are read. His idea is that you should underline the message they contain of peace and reconciliation."

"Yes, remember, this is to be a very special service! Just you make sure you read the passage with emphasis and feeling!" put in Harold, quite gratuitously.

"Yes, I certainly shall, sir!"

John walked over to The Lodgings.

Left on their own Strong spoke furiously to Harold. "Please leave me to deal with affairs relating to the chapel, Harry! The boy is in no need of advice from you on how he should read the lesson. Also I should be obliged, as I have told you often enough before, if you would keep your anti-semitic opinions to yourself during school hours. Just recollect that, Munich Accord or not, war with Germany is still more of a probability than a possibility. Your proclaimed admiration for Hitler and all his ways could be construed by a lot of people as support for a future enemy of this country. Also remember there are a number of boys in this school who come from Jewish backgrounds. It is quite unacceptable to me that you should cause them distress with such remarks!"

Harold flushed with annoyance. "I think, sir, that if Dr. Wisley has sufficient confidence in me to ask me to carry out the present negotiations with the German Embassy you should, at least, give me the same degree of trust yourself. My exchange in class with the boy was of a purely literary and light hearted nature."

"You stick to teaching German and running your O.T.C. and leave me to see to matters connected with the chapel. Don't mix education and politics!"

"Education without political conviction is quite meaningless!" said Harold, enigmatically but angrily.

"Oh, I just don't have the patience to argue with you, Harry!"

John arrived at The Lodgings. Mrs. Wisley herself answered the doorbell. John was one of her favourites. "The headmaster is expecting you. You are to go straight in to see him. He is in his study."

"Sit down, Threlfall!"

Everybody always felt slightly uncomfortable in Wisley's presence. John chose a straight-backed chair and sat on it, uneasily perching on its edge.

"I have had a letter and a telephone call from your father. He tells me Lady Sarah is not at all well and wishes to see you at Loughbourne."

"Yes, sir, I have had a letter, too."

"I have told your father he can come up here and collect you on Monday morning.

You can stay the night, see your grandmother, and then your parents will bring you back with them on Tuesday. I have asked them to stay here with me and be here to watch you score the winning goal on Thursday! Does that suit you, eh?"

"Yes, sir, thank you very much."

"Has Mr. Strong told you about the lesson I wish you to read on Sunday morning during the thanksgiving service? It is a wonderful prose poem, full of what are called antitheses. If you don't know what those are look the word up in your dictionary! I want you to practice reading it so that you bring out, very clearly, the message I consider it to contain of peace and reconciliation. All the governors will be present to listen to you. Unfortunately your mother will still be abroad on Sunday, otherwise I should have invited her and your father to be with us as well."

"I shall do my best to make it a very special occasion, sir!"

"Who will be looking after Lady Sarah whilst you are all up here?"

"The servants all love her, sir, and she has her personal maid, Violet. She is well looked after!"

"Yes, she is much loved! We all admire her!"

"It is good to hear that said, sir!"

Something in the way John made this comment suddenly struck Wisley as odd. His imagination, he thought. Strange though.

John went back to the house. Hyslow and Preston were waiting for him.

"We all have to go and see Arbitant immediately," said Hyslow.

"Tell us about your talk with the Head later, though." said Preston.

Gathered in Harold's room they found Trevor Polesden, Captain of School, Brian Jason, who was the R.S.M. of the O.T.C., Simon Repton, the school band's band major, Robert Cumberworth, a very senior master, renowned for his musical abilities and Tom Riding.

"I have asked you all to come to this meeting so that we can settle all the arrangements for the reception and entertainment of our guests from Germany."

He proceeded to do just that. He set out, in meticulous and irritating detail, the composition and positioning of the Guard of Honour. He told them exactly what was to be done when the team arrived. He explained how and when the flags were to be flown, raised and lowered, these latter tasks delegated to Tom. He told Repton just what music was to be played. He told David Rumbelow, Captain of Soccer, who had meanwhile joined them, how the match was to be played. He told Polesden how the visiting team was to be entertained. He even told Cumberworth to organise some appropriate musical entertainment for the Wednesday evening. He was very precise, very informative, very dogmatic. He contrived in the process to greatly irritate everybody present, whilst remaining happily in ignorance of the fact.

"Where do I find this flag, sir?" asked Tom.

"I am keeping it, for safety, here in my cupboard." He rose from his chair, took it down from a shelf, and showed it to them. They looked at it curiously and with some distaste. Then he continued, "This flag has been specially loaned to us by the German Embassy, by permission of the Ambassador himself. It must be treated with the greatest respect. As soon as the match has finished make sure it comes back here, to my room, in good condition, Tom. The visitors will be taking it back with them."

When the meeting had finished John returned, by himself, to his room.

He then took out his Bible, opened it at Ecclesiastes, chapter three, and carefully studied the first eight verses.

As he did so he mouthed the words half aloud to himself. A plan began to form in his mind.

Then he pushed back his chair, stretched out in his chair and stared at the ceiling. He had decided exactly what he was going to do.

CHAPTER TWENTY FOUR

CHAPEL

The school began to assemble for chapel at about eleven in the morning that Sunday. In normal circumstances the compulsory attendance there was tolerated rather than welcomed. Little groups of boys began to make their desultory progress towards the chapel. There they waited, shivering in their best suits in the rather chilly October weather, for Tom, who was busily engaged tolling the bell, to throw open the great oaken doors and let them in to the comparative warmth. The chapel always filled slowly, the whole process usually somewhat exceeding half an hour. Officially the service started at eleven thirty and lasted an hour.

On this particular occasion an unusual air of something almost akin to excitement was apparent. The pupils led an almost monastic existence. They were all boarders. Even to go and visit a shop in Bushfield village it was necessary to obtain a special exeat. Parental visiting was strictly limited. Places of public entertainment, such as the local cinema, were absolutely out of bounds. In the circumstances it was scarcely surprising that most of the younger boys were more than a little bewildered by the fuss that was being made by Dr. Wisley about the Agreement just reached by the Prime Minister at his Munich meeting with Hitler and Mussolini. Rumour had it that something much more interesting was going to be announced during the service, possibly involving an extra holiday. Why such an announcement, generally made during morning assembly, should be reserved for chapel was beyond comprehension and served to add to a vague feeling of excitement.

The senior boys, who were encouraged to read approved quality newspapers took a much greater interest in world affairs. The older they were the more immediate was their concern for the future. They realised that if war were to be declared they might be expected to go almost immediately into one of the services and, perhaps, temporarily forego plans to go to university. The prospect of a general call-up, beginning with eighteen year olds, loomed large on their horizons. Some were concerned about fathers, brothers or other relations. Some were wondering whether any war that came would last long enough to involve them. Some hoped it would and some hoped it would not. Not one of them, however, if asked, would, in all probability, have expressed the least doubt that Britain would emerge victorious. The ill-preparedness of their country for war was simply unknown to the vast majority of people, and the Bushfield pupils were no exception.

Those members of the staff who had served in the Great War recollected only too vividly the horrors of active service. It was also evident that the inevitable departure of younger colleagues would throw much greater burdens on those who, because of age or disability, would remain. In many cases long cherished retirement plans would have to be foregone. For these reasons and many others the hope afforded by the conclusion of the Munich agreement came like a break in thunderclouds.

The more junior staff, many of whom had still been children during the Great War, were deeply divided by political opinions varying from the extreme right, as in Harold's case, to as far left as was acceptable in a social environment such as that of Bushfield Abbey. Quite bitter political altercations in the staff room were frequent.

In such a context the thanksgiving service had to be viewed. Wisley intended it to focus everybody's attention on the benefits of preserving peace. In this he did seem to have general support. The opinion most often expressed by younger staff was that whilst they would not lend their support to a government which was prepared to settle for peace at any price they would do so provided they believed any compromise could be regarded as honourable.

Sergeant Tom Riding, at that time forty-six, had been Major Sir Frederick Threlfall's batman and had been at his side when he had been killed at the front. It was he, resplendent in his full dress uniform, medals gleaming, who at last opened the chapel doors. People began to enter.

The teaching staff always occupied the front three rows of pews in full academic dress. The generality of the school, seated by houses, sat in the middle pews and the prefects occupied the rear pews. This invariably resulted in the senior pupils having to wait for about a quarter of an hour before entering. Discussion always flourished whilst they waited. On the present occasion a most unusual altercation suddenly arose between Brian Jason and, of all unexpected people, John Threlfall.

Brian was the son of the school matron, a very popular boy who was currently the R.S.M. in the O.T.C. and well known for his patriotic views. He had just remarked, "My Mother has been describing to me the horrors my father suffered in the trenches. I think we should all be jolly grateful that we seem to have been spared the same experiences because of the agreement. If the Prime Minister truly has succeeded in securing "peace in our time" then this service is really meaningful!"

Suddenly, and to everybody's great surprise, John Threlfall seemed to take great exception to this apparently innocuous remark. "I am sick and tired of hearing everybody bleating on and on about "our wonderful Prime Minister" and his so called "peace"!"

A sudden silence fell on the little knot of senior boys. Such an outburst from Threlfall was entirely unexpected. He and Brian were the best of friends. Both boys equally respected by all those listening.

"So far as I am concerned the wretched man has done our country no service at all.

All he has done is sacrifice our national pride to buy off what are really no more than a bunch of thugs!"

This remark was greeted with a shocked silence. It was John's greatest friend, Hyslow, who was the first to speak. "Really, Threlfall, I, for one, simply cannot accept that! My father has told me that Chamberlain's action had diverted an awful calamity!"

Jason said, good-naturedly, "Of course, Threlfall, you are perfectly entitled to express such views. I do think you are quite wrong, though. I read in The Times that even the Leader of the Opposition said yesterday that we should all be grateful that the threat of war has been averted. Do you know any better?"

At this point Polesden, the revered Captain of School, decided to intervene. "Simmer down, Threlfall! Leave these matters to more experienced people than us!"

John was about to dispute this, even with Polesden himself, when somebody sighted Dr. Wisley and his guests rounding the bend in the gravelled path that connected The Lodgings with the chapel vestry, by the door of which he always entered the chapel.

All discussion abruptly ended and the prefects hastily filed into their pews.

Tom closed the doors, the organ started up, and the service began.

CHAPTER TWENTY FIVE

LESSON

The Bishop, a pompous but very sincere man, knew how to read a lesson and give it meaning. He came to the concluding words of the passage he had selected as appropriate for this service:

"....and he shall judge between the nations and shall reprove many peoples and they shall beat their swords into ploughshares and their spears into pruning hooks: nation shall not lift up sword against nation neither shall they learn war any more."

For a moment an almost palpable silence seemed to hang in the air. There was a visible tension in the front three rows. The passage was familiar to all of those present but never had it made such an immediate impact.

Dr. Wisley, seated in his accustomed place in the choir stalls noted this with satisfaction. It was exactly the effect for which he had hoped.

The Bishop carefully found the pages from which John was to read, when it was his turn, and inserted the marker.

Now it was time for Wisley to preach his sermon. He mounted the pulpit.

"You are probably wondering why it is I and not our own chaplain or the Lord Bishop himself who is delivering the sermon today. They have been good enough to allow me to do so for a special reason. I have news to give you which I felt should be conveyed to you in the context of this special service, the theme of which is peace and reconciliation.

You have just had the text I have chosen read to you but I shall repeat it.

"Nation shall not lift up sword against nation neither shall they learn war any more."

We have, in these last, momentous, days lived through times which, God willing, may come to be remembered as marking the beginning of an unprecedented era of peace rather than, as we so recently feared, of armed conflict.

As you have heard the agreement which was recently concluded in Munich by our Prime Minister, alongside the leaders of France, Italy and Germany has given us, and I quote our Prime Minister's own words, "Peace in our time, peace with honour."

"Those of you who are studying history may already have realised that "peace with honour" were words used by one of our greatest former Prime Ministers, Benjamin Disraeli, when he commented upon the peace between the powers of Russia and Turkey. They are great and inspired words, embodying a high ideal, spoken in each case by great men of whom our nation can be justly proud.

Certain important and painful concessions had to be made to achieve this agreement. That, however, is the way international treaties are made, by give and take. So terrible might have been the consequences if this agreement had not been concluded that I, personally, feel that for once the end justified the means. It is for this reason that we are holding this service to give thanks for the deliverance of the world from the terrible peril of war that threatened.

Now I come to my special announcement. It is but twenty years since the Great War, in which so many of your fathers fought, and many, so sadly, perished. Every day we pass that monument in Heroes' Yard. Because of the names recorded there and on countless other similar monuments throughout the length and breadth of this land there still remains even now, twenty years on, great anti-German sentiment. The scars of war do not easily heal. Whilst such attitudes remain the conditions for creating a lasting peace are stifled.

Just before Mr. Chamberlain made his visit to Munich, to negotiate this agreement, this school received a proposal from the German embassy in London. This suggested that we should receive here, at Bushfield, a team of German schoolboys and play them at soccer. The purpose of the match was to provide you with such an opportunity in the very appropriate context of the sports field. We seriously considered the merits of acceptance. However, at that time, it was considered that the timing was wrong. The war clouds hung heavily over our two countries. We, therefore, for the moment, declined. Then came this break in the clouds. It was agreed that we should accept. I am now able to tell you that the German team will be with us next Wednesday and will play the match against us on Thursday morning. In consequence Thursday will be a special extra day's holiday.

Please remember that our visitors will be playing away from their homeland. They will have no natural supporters to shout for them. Make sure they can return home with warm and friendly feelings both for us and our country. That is the principal reason for having them here. It is not to win, although win we shall, but to mend fences, establish friendly relationships

.The next lesson, which will be read by Threlfall, will convey such a message of peace and reconciliation. Please, therefore, listen carefully to the words as he reads them.

Now let us rise and sing that beautiful hymn, "Praise my soul the King of Heaven". This contains the wonderful line "Rescues us from all our foes". When you come to that line please remember that all of us, whether British or German, Prime Minister, teacher, parent or schoolboy are all in God's keeping."

Whilst Dr. Wisley had been delivering this address it had become increasingly evident that John was becoming very agitated. Prayers and the psalm now followed and everybody now waited to hear what it was that John was to read. The customary practice was for the prefect whose turn it was to read the second lesson to leave his seat during the singing of the last line or so and make a slow and dignified march up the central aisle to the lectern. The ideal was to arrive at the lectern just as the psalm finished.

On this occasion, however, as the final words of the selected psalm, "Thou shalt prepare a table before me against them that trouble me", were still hanging in the air, John was already very rapidly striding up towards the lectern, which, therefore, he reached far too soon. He stood there, his hands tightly gripping the outstretched wings of the great golden eagle on which the book lay. He looked round at the congregation, as though defying them.

He began to read. His elocution was superb. He read, as instructed, with special emphasis on the antitheses. The message he contrived to convey, however, was certainly not of reconciliation.

"To everything there is a season and a time to every purpose under Heaven

A time to be born *and a time to die*

A time to plant *and a time to pluck up that which is planted*

A time to kill and a time to heal

A time to break down and a time to build up

A time to weep and a time to laugh

A time to mourn and a time to dance

A time to cast away stones and a time to gather stones together

A time to embrace *and a time to refrain from embracing*

A time to seek and a time to lose

A time to rend

A time to keep silence *and a time to speak*

A time to love *and a time to hate*

A time for war and a time for peace."

There was no doubt in anybody's mind that he had deliberately altered the meaning he had been intended by Dr. Wisley to convey from one of reconciliation to one of confrontation.

CHAPTER TWENTY SIX

INQUEST

"It seems to me that young Threlfall must have formed a distinctly dim view of Chamberlain's achievements at Munich!" said Simon Franks, a relatively junior master.

"Yes," agreed Arthur Fellows, one of his contemporaries, "perhaps he has seen it as a betrayal to extreme right wing thinking! It is all rather odd though! I am sure I have heard that his mother is an ardent supporter of Hitler and Moseley. I saw something about it in the gossip columns."

"I must say that if those really are his views I have some sympathy with him!" said Franks.

"It was an absolute outrage! It was highly embarrassing for Dr. Wisley, especially with all the governors present!" interposed one of the more senior staff.

"What puzzles me," said Cumberworth, reflectively, " is why a boy of only seventeen, and from his elevated social background, should be so concerned with such matters. I could understand it all if he were at university. Students there do things like that, but not schoolboys! There must be more to this than meets the eye!"

"Yes, indeed!" said Harold, who had been standing in the doorway, listening. "That boy has been behaving very oddly of late!"

"It certainly was odd," agreed Franks. "However, perhaps he acted with the best intentions. I suppose he thought it was a good way to express his disapproval for the Nazi regime. If that were his intention then, basically, I agree with him."

Harold exploded. "What? You are willing to condone such an incident! He abused the trust that had been reposed in him! Why, he even made a mockery of Holy Writ!"

"Oh, really, Harry, that is going a little too far, isn't it?" said the senior master.

"How can he be defended? His conduct was monstrous!"

"There are plenty of people who share the opinions he seems to hold!" said Fellows.

"You should think carefully, before saying things like that!" fumed

Harold. "It was open insolence. I cannot imagine what the Headmaster will do. Whatever else happens he should not be allowed to play in the match!"

At this hubbub ensued. Harold surveyed the arguing staff with contempt. He went back to his rooms.

In the meanwhile Dr. Wisley and the governors, now accompanied by the Reverend Strong, had returned to The Lodgings.

"I must say, Wisley," said the Bishop, as soon as they were settled in the drawing room, "that boy made the most extraordinary exhibition of himself. What on earth got into him do you think?".

"I simply cannot say, Bishop. I do know that his grandmother, Lady Sarah, has just been taken seriously ill. That just might have something to do with it. Why his grandmother's being ill should have such an effect is quite beyond me, though. The boy is, however, absolutely devoted to her. His father is coming up here tomorrow to take him home to see her."

"That may be as it may be, but the fact that Lady Sarah has been taken ill, just on its own, surely isn't sufficient reason to behave like that, dash it!" said Sir David.

"I agree, he gave a very odd slant to the meaning!" said Sir Gordon. "He obviously intended to do just that. It must be looked into, and thoroughly!"

Sir Hubert was more worldly wise. "I think the boy simply came to the conclusion that all this peace talk issuing from Downing Street was nonsense and had nothing to do with honour!" he said.

"That may well explain his actions, but it does nothing to excuse them," retorted the Bishop. He rarely argued with the General but, on this occasion, he had come to the conclusion that since the episode had taken place during a church service, it lay within his domain of responsibility rather than the General's.

"It sounded to me as though the boy was openly stating his disapproval of our agreeing to this German match taking place," said Sir Gordon. "There's something for you to consider, Wisley!"

Wisley could see that the matter was beginning to escalate out of control. People were beginning to take up positions from which they would find it too hard to retreat without loss of face. He was thinking furiously how he could dampen down the fires of wrath. Sir George was a power to be reckoned with when he was so minded. He had always declined to accept a governorship, but he was the Board's eminence grise, ever hovering in the background. This matter directly affected his son.

Sir David, however, had been quietly reconsidering the situation. He now said, "In all fairness, there are certain aspects of German domestic policy, for example their reported treatment of certain minorities, which, if truly reported, give me cause for disquiet myself. Young people often become very emotionally involved over such issues. I wonder whether this has anything to do with what happened?"

"Possibly," nodded Sir Graham, "I, too, have heard reports that the more extreme prejudices of these Nazi chaps against their Jewish citizens, for example, have resulted in some most unpleasant incidents, and worse".

""You have used the term ' prejudice'," said the Bishop. "'Prejudice' surely means they are acting unreasonably and without due cause. Is there any real evidence that such is the case?"

So far Strong had remained silent, not something he had found easy to do. He was only too well aware of his propensity to express himself over forcibly. He always tried to keep a bridle on his tongue in the presence of the Bishop, something he frequently found almost impossible to do. This last remark by the Bishop was too much for him. He opened his mouth to speak at last. He was pre-empted by Sir David.

"As a matter of fact," said Sir David," I did voice my disquiet on this very subject, to a senior member of the Lord Chancellor's staff with whom I had dinner recently at Middle Temple. He told me that, whilst it was undoubtedly true that there had been some very unpleasant incidents, the German government would certainly modify its attitude He said the whole problem was being exacerbated by certain sections of the sensation seeking press. He pointed out there had always been anti-Semitic feeling throughout what is now Germany. The Kaiser always privately detested Jews. He said most of what was being said in the German press and by some of the more prominent German politicians was mere rhetoric for popular consumption. I suppose he knew what he was talking about."

Strong exploded, they all looked at him, startled by his vehemence. "Rhetoric, indeed! 'Full of sound and fury, signifying nothing!' Are the confiscations, arrests, burning of books, expulsions of which we all read daily in the press, in respectable papers, I might add, not the gutter press, are these 'rhetoric'?"

They all looked at him uncomfortably. At least, thought Sir David, who had meant well, he spared me from completing the quotation with "A tale told by an idiot"!

The embarrassed silence which followed Strong's indignant intervention was broken by Sir Hubert. He had decided to bring the discussion to a halt. He was of the same mind as Dr. Wisley. Sir George had to be considered. Furthermore he was one of those Englishmen who instinctively distrusted all foreigners, and, ever since the war, especially Germans. So far as he was aware he had never met, socially at least, anybody who was Jewish, certainly not a practising Jew. "I keep an open mind on these things, although personally I am inclined to think this Hitler fellow is a fanatic. What we have to think about now is what is to be done, if anything, about young Threlfall. He is a Threlfall, you know. I think some of you have overlooked that little point. You never know which way George may jump. We have already been told he is coming up to collect the boy tomorrow. In my considered opinion this is not a suitable matter for us to be debating, it's a matter for Dr. Wisley, as headmaster, and the boy's father. Anybody disagree with me?"

He looked round the room. Nobody uttered a word.

When Sir Hubert spoke in such terms nobody ever argued with him.

Silently Dr. Wisley heaved a sigh of relief.

By mutual if unspoken consent they began to discuss other matters.

CHAPTER TWENTY SEVEN

VISIT

It was a fine October day when Donald drove George to Bushfield to collect John. The leaves were just about to fall, having just attained their fullest autumn glory, still clinging to the trees in one last magnificent display. George usually thoroughly enjoyed the drive from Loughbourne to Bushfield, along the familiar route. He retained the happiest memories of the time his father would take him back to school in the old Daimler. He and Sarah had never since been able to entertain the thought of parting with that car. To that day it stood, side by side with the old family coach, in what had been the coach house but was now called the garage, with the newer Rolls Royce. All were lovingly maintained by Donald but on the first two Wilfred continued to lavish his own especial care. Only Wilfred and Sarah still used the Daimler for the shorter journeys to Crufton or to the Loughbourne church. The coach in which Sarah had made her first grand entry to Loughbourne was, however, now only a curiosity. Wilfred resolutely refused to touch the Rolls Royce. "The Daimler is mine, you can have the Rolls!" he had said to his son when it arrived.

Normally, when alone with Donald in the car, George would tell him to open the glass partition that divided the passengers from the chauffeur and chat away to him about everything under the sun. This particular morning, however, the partition remained inexplicably but firmly closed. George sat in the back, lost in his private thoughts. He was only vaguely aware of the familiar, if now changing, countryside as it rolled by. The roadside was becoming far more built up, particularly as they neared Bushfield village, for Bushfield lay much closer to London than Crufton or Loughbourne, neither of which the urban sprawl had yet reached.

He was wondering whether his mother was dying. The local doctor, Angus McGregor, had been vague in the extreme. Then his thoughts turned to his relationship with Ann. Why, he asked himself, had things so turned out? What a shame it was. He began to worry whether he was to blame. Would it have changed matters if he had not been so insistent on confining himself to Norsex and the P.O.C.s and agreed to her pleas for them enter into the social whirl for which she so much yearned? "To thine own self be true", he muttered to himself.

They had arrived. The car swung into the gravelled drive, through the wide open great wrought iron gates. Tom Riding, who had been eagerly watching out for their arrival, was standing at the door of the Lodge and greeted them with a smart salute. The car crunched up towards the Great Tower, passed the war memorial, and finally came to a halt in front of The Lodgings. Mrs. Wisley, who had been watching its approach from a window, came running out to greet him.

"Welcome! My husband and John will join us very soon. They should both be on their way over here now. We are going to give you both a spot of lunch before you return. Good morning Donald! I've told Tom to take care of you!"

They entered the house, as Donald drove off towards the Lodge, where Tom was waiting for him.

"I am afraid his grandmother's illness seems to have upset John a good deal. He has been showing signs of strain. Very worrying, really. He has been behaving in a very strange manner. I do hope this visit settles him down."

"Oh, how's that?"

"Well, for example, Richard asked him to read the second lesson yesterday, at this special thanksgiving for peace service he had arranged. All the governors came. John read it in the strangest manner. Really most unsettling. A lot of people were very disturbed by the episode."

"Are there going to be any serious repercussions, do you think?"

"It seems not. There was some trouble with some of the governors, and one of the masters, Harold Arbitant, John's form master and assistant housemaster, was particularly annoyed. Richard managed to convince the governors that John's anxiety about his grandmother must have been the cause, coupled with all the responsibility he is carrying for the success of this forthcoming important match. The school puts such reliance on John when it comes to winning soccer matches, you know!"

Dr. Wisley had just entered the room. He now joined in the conversation. "Yes, I think it is as well he is to have this short break. Seeing his grandmother may settle him down."

"This all sounds very alarming. I am afraid my Mother is, in fact, very poorly."

"Whatever has caused it? Last time we saw her she seemed so fit and well and happy!" asked Mrs. Wisley.

112

"I simply do not have an explanation. She went up to London to do some shopping, came back looking absolutely washed out, and collapsed."

"I don't like going to London," said Mrs. Wisley. "A nasty, dirty place!"

"If John is being troublesome," said George, "I shall have to have it out with him. We cannot have this sort of behaviour!" In point of fact George was feeling most uncomfortable with the present conversation. He was not by nature accustomed to prevarication. He felt he was becoming enmeshed in a web of deceit.

At this point John, quite unexpectedly accompanied by Harold, entered the room. Class was just ending when Harold had received a note from The Lodgings asking him to send John across as his father had arrived. That was all he had been asked to do. He had, however, taken it into his head to walk round with him. He was not aware that Ann was in Germany and had rather been hoping she would be present..

"Is grandmother any better?"

"Not at all good, I am afraid, John! But what is all this I have heard about your behaviour in chapel yesterday? What ever were you thinking about?"

"I read the lesson in the way I felt best!"

"That is quite unacceptable, Threlfall!" snapped Harold. "You quite deliberately distorted the meaning. You know perfectly well what you intended!"

"Mr. Arbitant!" said Wisley, very angrily, "Sir George is present! He and I will deal with the matter!"

John stood his ground and repeated, "I read the lesson the way I thought was right. I have heard that because of that Mr. Arbitant wishes me to be dropped from the team next Thursday. I should be happy not to play!"

There was an uncomfortable silence.

"Your impudence is beyond belief!" said Harold.

At that moment the maid entered the room to announce that lunch was ready.

"Could we perhaps continue this over lunch, Dr. Wisley?" said George.

Harold, of course, had not been expected and was not invited. He had to return, very angrily, to his rooms. Why, he fulminated to himself, should a boy, who had behaved so atrociously, who, in fact, in his view, really merited expulsion, instead be invited to lunch with the headmaster? Simply because of his father's social position! If he were in charge he would know how to deal with the matter!

As they took their places round the table Dr. Wisley said very sternly to John who, truth to tell, now he was faced with the prospect of actually lunching with the Wisleys, was beginning to feel distinctly uncomfortable, "Look, Threlfall, I know you have been under great strain. For that reason, and that reason only, I am prepared to overlook all this. Go home, see your grandmother. But come back in a proper frame of mind. I warn you, do not try my patience too far!"

George looked at Wisley gratefully. "A lesser man would have reacted quite otherwise! I am afraid you have been greatly provoked by my son!"

George and John sat silently in the car at first. The glass panel between them and Donald was shut. At last George spoke," John, you and I must handle this position in partnership, like men. You must surely appreciate that the difficulty which faces us is how to tell your Mother about my mother's revelations. Personally I rather think she herself is now sorry she ever told me!"

"Father, I really do not know what to say until I have spoken to grandmother myself. What is the matter with her. Is it her heart?"

"Yes, I am afraid it is!"

"What does Dr. Mc Gregor say?"

"He says she must see a specialist. He thinks it could be serious."

From that point each sat silently, wrapped in their own thoughts, gloomily watching the countryside.

When they arrived they found Ann was already waiting for them. She was quite obviously angry about something. It was not the kind of welcome they would have chosen. After he had returned to his rooms Harold had, on the spur of the moment, made a decision to make a telephone call to Ann. He proceeded to tell her about what had occurred in chapel and all about John's outburst that morning. He knew quite well his call would be uninterrupted by George, who would be safely out of the way in the car between Bushfield and Loughbourne. He knew that when he learned of the call George would be furious, but relied on Ann to protect him. She was both astounded and grateful.

"Thank you so much, Mr. Arbitant! I certainly would never have been told anything about all this otherwise."

"I have just had a telephone call from Mr. Harold Arbitant!" was, therefore, her unexpected greeting to them. "Could we all discuss this matter?"

Without waiting for a reply, and ignoring all other preliminaries, she opened the door to her private room and entered. They had no alternative, in the circumstances, but to follow her. She closed the door. "Now!" she said grimly, "Would one of you be good enough to tell me what is going on?"

John jumped in before his father could utter a word. "What is "going on", Mother, is that I have declined to take any part in this match against this German team. I absolutely refuse to take any part in anything connected with this beastly Nazi regime of which you seem to be so fond. There is a war coming. It is going to involve my friends and myself. They all share my views."

" How dare you speak to me like that! George do something!"

"Ann, I am sorry he used such words to you but you must know that I share his sentiments. The person who deserves a good hiding is Arbitant! He had no right to ring you like that behind my back! You should have refused to speak to him until you had seen John and myself!"

The already very emotionally disturbed John was now close to tears. "Don't you care about England?" he demanded. "All these beastly people you keep on visiting are plotting war against us, quite apart from other rotten things they do!"

Ann's fingers were digging into the sides of the armchair in which she had seated herself. She opened her mouth to respond but John continued, "I hate them all!" He glowered at her, beside himself with anger.

She rose unsteadily to her feet and left the room.

George continued to sit, in helpless silence, gazing at his son.

John went to the door and, firmly closing it behind him, went upstairs to see Sarah.

CHAPTER TWENTY EIGHT

DECLINE

When John entered her room Sarah was lying propped up with pillows in the bed she had always shared with Frederick. The change in her appearance since he had last seen her, before he returned to school, was a considerable shock to him. She was looking much more tired and drawn than he could ever remember. He sat down on the bedspread which had been neatly folded down by the ever attentive Violet, still her personal maid. She had her eyes closed but she sensed he was with her and smiled.

"John, my darling, you have come!"

"Wild horses wouldn't have kept me away!"

"Has your father told you why I want to see you so particularly?"

"He wrote me a letter but if you feel up to it I'd prefer to hear it all again from you."

She related her story to him from beginning to end. It all seemed unreal to him. It seemed to bear no relationship to the world of Loughbourne and Bushfield Abbey.

"This Tomkins chap. he told you that your brother and the men of his family living with him in Berlin had all been arrested and taken away somewhere, but did he know any more about what happened?"

"As a matter of fact he did. I am afraid I didn't tell your father everything, he was becoming so upset and to repeat it just then would have disturbed me even more than I was already. I feel more able to go into details now, especially with you.

He said that the likelihood was that the three of them would have been sent to a place just outside Munich where there is what they call a concentration camp, a place called Dachau. He told me that this was rumoured to be a very terrible place, in fact he had heard that even some women and their children were there, in unspeakable conditions. He said they were there, in the main, either because they held political opinions opposed to the Nazi government or, more usually, simply because they were either Jewish or from what had originally been Jewish families.

You know, John, it seems these horrible people are not content with depriving people they don't like of their businesses and homes and then putting them in these dreadful camps. He told me that it was quite often the practice to make the families, including the children, parade around in the local streets, wearing insulting notices, so that they can be publicly humiliated. He said the bullying of children supposed to be of Jewish parentage at school was actively encouraged. As for my brother and his son and grandson he told me that he had spoken to a witness who had actually seen them being roughly thrown, in handcuffs, into the back of a dirty truck."

"Is anything else known about this Dachau place?"

"People are quite scared to give much information, it seems. He managed to speak to one person, though, a Nazi official, pretending he was a Nazi sympathiser. This man told him, quite boastfully, that their eventual aim was to exterminate everybody in such camps!"

"Exterminate?"

"That was the word Major Tomkins told me the man used, John!"

"My school is going to play a German team at football next Thursday. The headmaster, Dr. Wisley, says the match has been arranged to help to establish good relations between our two countries. The school has asked me to play because I am quite a good centre forward. Do you think that in these circumstances I should refuse to play? I don't want to play, you know, not after all you have told me. I feel sure all the German boys will be Nazis themselves!"

"Yes, I think you should play. Who knows? Dr. Wisley may well be right. If you cannot make friends on the sports field, where can you? As for all of them being Nazis, I just don't know. It seems impossible that all of them can be so awful!"

She was beginning to feel the strain of the conversation, much as she had looked forward to having it.

"I think you should have another rest now, grandmother!"

Just as he was about to leave the room she called him back. "You and your father are both so dear to me! I know your mother has these views that are so upsetting to the rest of us. But you must appreciate that she has many good qualities as well I am sure all will come right in the end. What has happened with me is something which often occurs when people of such different backgrounds as your grandfather and I fall in love and marry. We never consider the consequences! We just live for the moment!"

She closed her eyes and he quietly left the room.

Downstairs his parents were still arguing.

"I simply will not tolerate your behaviour, George. Your actions are inexplicable!"

"I have already explained matters, Mother," cut in John, who entered the morning room at this moment.

"This is little more than a conspiracy! I am beginning to wonder whether even Sarah's indisposition hasn't something to with what is happening. Why did she have this sudden attack? What was she doing in London? I don't believe this tale about going shopping. She hasn't done such a thing for ages. What aren't you telling me?"

"She did go shopping. She simply overdid things. She must have slightly strained her heart. You know she has been a little breathless recently. That must have been a warning sign, if only we had guessed. We are concealing nothing from you!"

There's a white lie, thought John, thinking of Preston's earlier remark.

When John went in to say goodbye to Sarah the next morning she said to him, "You know, John, I have been lying here thinking that if Frederick hadn't made me promise to keep our secret I should in all probability have revealed everything when George wished to marry Ann. Then either he wouldn't have asked her or, when he did, she would have refused him. Then you would never have been born, would you?"

He bent down and kissed her.

"You go back to school and play as well as you can in that match. Don't forget you must have some cousins living in Germany, about your own age. They will be German, won't they? It's just chance where and what you are born. You must never dislike people simply because they are different from you for such reasons. You should choose people you are going to dislike as carefully as you choose your friends!"

"I hadn't thought of it like that! You are very wise, Grandmother!"

"I'm not really very wise, John, but I have lived a long time!"

He went downstairs. The car had already drawn up in front of the house. He climbed in and sat down between his parents. They were seated, one in each corner, unspeaking. The panel between Donald and his passengers remained closed. It might as well have been open for not one word was spoken during the whole of the journey. After what seemed a lifetime to all of them the car, once again, pulled into the drive of Bushfield Abbey.

Donald drew up by the war memorial and John alighted and made his way back to his house. George and Ann proceeded on to The Lodgings. Then Donald went back to the Lodge, where he was, as usual, to be Tom's guest.

That evening Harold arranged a rehearsal for the Guard of Honour. The flag posts were already in place at either end of the school first eleven pitch. Everything was ready for the reception at Bushfield Abbey of the visiting team. Harold went to bed well satisfied.

I may have German cousins, thought John, just as his eyes were closing, I wonder what they are doing and what is happening to them?

He had a bad night.

CHAPTER TWENTY NINE

ELISABETH

Rosemary, the six year old daughter of Sir Francis and Lady Penelope Preston, of Preston Hall, near Leeds, in Yorkshire, had never been in good health since she had been born in 1932. Penelope succeeded in conceiving again twice but each time she had a miscarriage. She was then warned never to try again. After that Rosemary became the most important person in their lives.

Francis, born in 1900, had taken over the management of the famous textile works in 1926. His father, Sir William, recently created a baronet, had died at the age of only fifty-one that year. The active management should then, by rights, have devolved upon William's younger brother, Horace, thirteen years his junior. Horace, however, had been badly gassed during the Great War and felt unable to assume the burden. He, therefore, had requested Francis to take his place, with the title of managing director, whilst he took on the purely nominal responsibilities of chairman. In effect this meant he took no part in the day to day management of the mills.

Horace had not married until 1920 and then had the one son, Gordon, born in 1921. Thus, although they were first cousins, there was an age gap between Francis and Gordon of twenty-one years. The two seldom came into contact. For a large part of his life Gordon had been a boarder, either at Bushcome Preparatory School, which he had entered when he was eight, or, latterly, at Bushfield Abbey School.

Immediately Francis took over he began to consider how he could expand business. Eventually he established an excellent working relationship with Aronbergs, a well-known Berlin based firm of textile importers and exporters, a family concern like his own. Although this firm had a small London office, he preferred, in view of the volume of international trade involved, to deal with their headquarters directly. These were based in Charlottenburg in a large mansion, thath also served as the family residence.

The trips to Berlin were frequent and he was never happy at leaving his family so often. In the course of one of his visits he mentioned to the Aronbergs, whilst having dinner with the family, that he was considering leasing an apartment in Berlin, as a pied-a-terre, so that he could bring Penelope and Rosemary with him in future.

"But, Sir Francis," said Naomi, the wife of the senior director, Samuel," that is quite unnecessary! You can always stay with us. We have plenty of room here. We shall keep a suite especially for you. "

"I understand, Sir Francis," said Rachel, Samuel's granddaughter, who was married to the youngest director, Benjamin Hands, "that you have a daughter of the same age as my Elisabeth. The two could share a room when you came and certainly become great friends. It would be wonderful!"

From that time onwards, whenever Francis made one of his increasingly frequent trips to Berlin, he took the family with him and stayed at Charlottenburg with the Aronbergs. They always travelled by the SABENA 'plane, which flew daily between Croydon and Tempelhof and the Aronbergs arranged for their chauffeur to meet them at the airport on arrival. The two children formed a very close friendship and the much stronger Elisabeth adopted a protective attitude towards the often sickly little Rosemary.

In May 1938 another visit was arranged. This time, it had been agreed that they would bring Elisabeth back to Leeds with them to spend a few weeks with Rosemary, who was greatly excited by the prospect. The chauffeur met them and they drove out towards Charlottenburg. Looking out of the car window it became only too evident that the anti-Semitic propaganda being so actively encouraged in Germany by the Nazi regime was bearing fruit. Slogans were daubed on shop windows and the doors of some houses, their continued presence bearing witness to the fact that the owners of the premises concerned were either too scared to remove them or were no longer there.

The entire Aronberg family resident in Berlin, including Aaron and Rebecca, Rachel's parents, were waiting for them, as usual, when they arrived. Elisabeth immediately took charge of Rosemary and the two left the room together to play.

"She is so looking forward to staying with you, Sir Francis!" said Rachel. Rachel, at that time just twenty-five, was a slender, very beautiful woman, with the strange family characteristic grey green eyes, and dark brown hair.

"And we are really looking forward to having her, Rachel!" said Penelope, "Rosemary now has almost no friends. We only wish you could allow her stay longer!"

"As a matter of fact, Lady Penelope...." began Rachel, to be immediately interrupted by an embarrassed Benjamin.

"Really Rachel!" said Benjamin, "I do not think we should try to impose such a responsibility on the Prestons. It is too much!"

"Whatever is it, Rachel?" said Penelope, absolutely bewildered, for Rachel was looking very miserable. Naomi took Rachel's hand and tried to comfort her.

"The fact of the matter is, Lady Penelope," interposed Samuel, "that the anti-Semitic activity here is not confined to those who still practice Judaism. As you may have heard it is not a matter of religion now, as it was for the main part under the Kaiser, it is a matter of ancestry. I am afraid this has affected little Elisabeth!"

"Affected Elisabeth!" said Francis. "But however can this concern a small child of six?"

"Well," replied Benjamin, "what happened was that a teacher at her little school, where she has always been so happy and popular, suddenly began not only to be very unkind to her but to encourage the other girls there to be unkind as well. We are, as you surely know, of Jewish origin, although we have, for a long time now, been Lutheran Christians. Our name of Aronberg reveals this and we have never tried to hide the fact. Elisabeth became so unhappy that I felt I absolutely had to go and make a complaint. Unfortunately the teacher in question is the wife of a very prominent local Nazi official. To cut a sad story short we have been told to remove Elisabeth from the school on the grounds that they do not want Aryan children mixing with what I was told was an inferior race."

"This is incredible!" expostulated Francis.

"It may seem incredible to you, Sir Francis, but it is by no means so to us!" said Aaron. "Just the other day my father and I put our names to a protest, signed by a number of prominent citizens of Jewish origin but Christian faith, concerning the desecration of Jewish cemeteries, in which, of course, some of our own ancestors are buried. You must remember that there have been Jewish communities here for a thousand years. I am afraid that action on our part, too, has had unfortunate results. We have been placed on a blacklist, branded as anti-social elements. It seems we, not the desecrators, are the hooligans. One never can tell what may happen as a result. People we know have been arrested for similar reasons and disappeared, goodness knows where, probably to Dachau, although one never knows for certain!"

"What is Dachau?" asked Penelope.

"A concentration camp, near Munich. They put people of whom they disapprove there, either on trumped up charges of disaffection or for no reason at all, at least no legally valid reason. People of Jewish origin, communists, socialists, gypsies, a few real criminals possibly. Nobody really knows for sure who is there or what goes on there. Some people are allowed out but they are too scared to talk about their experiences."

"I am so frightened for Elisabeth's safety!" exclaimed Rachel. "Such terrible things are happening. There are all sorts of rumours. What I was wondering, Lady Penelope, was whether you and Sir Francis would consider allowing Elisabeth to stay on with you, in the safety of England, for a while? There has been a report that quite soon people like us will have great difficulty in leaving the country. I have been trying to persuade Benjamin to accept Samuel's offer to put him in charge of the London office. Then we could all come over."

"I think that would be a very good idea indeed," said Samuel, "why don't you agree, Benjamin? It would be an ideal solution and good for the firm."

"Because it looks like running away, Grandfather, Why should we be forced to leave our country? People will come to their senses sooner or later."

"Just like your great grandfather!" smiled Samuel. "He could never reconcile himself to living in England, no more could I! I understand. But it would be good for the firm, as well as please Rachel. She is quite right you know! Things could become much worse here for all of us, very suddenly."

"Well, I am very happy for Elisabeth to stay on with the Prestons for a while longer, if they are willing. I think we should wait ourselves, though, before taking such a drastic step. I feel certain things will improve."

"Rachel, dear," said Penelope, "Elisabeth can stay with us as long as she likes. I don't know what the rules are about people from abroad, even children, remaining over a certain length of time, though."

"Well, I am sure it won't be that long!" said Francis, "But if the need arose I know somebody in the Home Office whom I am quite certain would see that everything was put in order for us."

"I am so relieved!" said Rachel. "I was very hesitant about asking you. I am sure that I shall be able to persuade my obstinate husband to take the London office appointment. However I really don't want Elisabeth to come back until I feel things have really improved. The school affair was very frightening."

"You know," said Francis, " Penelope and I have been visiting you for a long time now, very regularly. Yet even we had failed to appreciate how very difficult things were becoming for you. This makes one realise that if even people like us have failed to understand the gravity of the position then how little can people who take democracy for granted grasp the depths to which things have sunk over here!"

"Grandfather, do you think we are all in real danger?" asked Rebecca.

"I am afraid, dear Rebecca, that I should be foolhardy if I did not reply "Yes" to that," said Samuel. "I think it is more than possible that one of these days one of us, at least, very likely myself, will be arrested on some charge or other. If I could see some feasible way of our all leaving the country I should take it. For the moment, I can only counsel caution. Things may improve, I suppose, although I don't really share Benjamin's optimism."

Rachel took Penelope on one side. Benjamin looked at them enquiringly. "I am only telling Lady Penelope about a few matters concerning Elisabeth, Benjamin," she said. Then she whispered to Penelope, "I have something very special for you. Would you come up to my private room with me please?"

Rachel went to her desk and took out of one of the drawers an envelope. "Lady Penelope," she said, very earnestly, tears welling in her eyes as she spoke, "Benjamin knows nothing about this. I don't even know whether it will be of any legal validity as it is signed only by myself, but it just may be of some assistance. Elisabeth is so precious to me I feel I must take every possible precaution I can. Things over here, for people of Jewish origin, like us, are so uncertain that one never knows what may happen next. For all I know, if I cannot persuade Benjamin to come over to London soon, he and I may soon be arrested, and goodness knows what might happen to us all then! I have, therefore, had this document, for what it is worth, drawn up by a local lawyer. It gives my consent to your adoption of Elisabeth if our family, for whatever reasons, can no longer look after her. Of course I cannot expect you to agree to anything so drastic, and I am really pray it would never be needed anyway, but it would make me happier to know you had it. Will you take it?"

The strain of making this little speech had told on her. Until now she had more or less retained her self-composure but now she sank down on to a chair and began to cry bitterly. Penelope bent over her and kissed her. "Whilst she is with us she will always be as much our daughter as if she were our own."

Through her tears Rachel managed a smile.

For the next three days business discussions continued and then it was time to go back to England.

"The chauffeur will take you to the airport and see you through customs.. You are so well known as important English visitors to Berlin there should be no problems when you board with the two children. We shall be in touch as soon as possible about when she is to return", said Samuel. "Rachel will come with you in the car to the airport to say a final good bye. Let us know that you have all arrived safely. I think you should be guarded in your message and send it both here and to Eli in Munich, just in case of any mishap in Berlin. Just say 'Package arrived safely'/ "

The two children were so excited that the process of farewell at the airport was not as heart- rending as had been anticipated. The great fear they all had had, although none of them had voiced it, not wishing to upset the others, was that Elisabeth might run into trouble at the passport check. Incredibly, however, they were waved through. The man did not even look at Elisabeth's documents. He had merely taken one glance at Sir Francis', whom he knew very well by sight, as a frequent visitor of known importance. He even smiled at the two children as they trotted through, hand in hand. Rachel waited until the craft was airborne. Then she very sadly and very apprehensively returned to the Charlottenburg house to await what ever might be the pending misfortunes that she felt increasingly convinced that fate had in store for them all.

Safely home at last in Leeds Francis wired both the Berlin and Munich Aronberg offices with the same message, "Package arrived safely, Preston." However just three days later, in the middle of the night, Samuel, Aaron, and Benjamin were arrested. For the moment the women were for some inexplicable reason left alone. They decided their better course of action was to join Eli in Munich, if he were still there. That they were being watched was evident. Immediately they were seen to have left the house and were on their way to Munich the Charlottenburg premises were confiscated, the business closed down and a notice appeared outside proclaiming, "This house is now the Property of the German People."

Eli was meanwhile endeavouring to carry on as best he might in Munich. Matters were rapidly becoming impossible for him. His business there was already at a standstill and his communications with Berlin had been cut. All his employees had quit, fearing for their own safety. He had no way of discovering what was happening, or had already happened, to the rest of the family. All he could do was to remain in the house and await what ever fate was in store for him. Then a wire arrived from the Prestons. It read "Package arrived safely". He had absolutely no idea what it meant.

In Leeds, that July, Rosemary's always fragile health suddenly deteriorated rapidly. Tuberculosis had taken a final grim hold on her. She was rushed to hospital but, in spite of every possible treatment, nothing could be done to save her life.

Penelope would probably have lost her reason if it had not been for the pressing need for care for Elisabeth. In truth it was only the presence of Elisabeth which saved the situation. The child's grief almost eclipsed her own.

"She simply cannot return to Germany. We cannot make any contact now with either Berlin or Munich. Their London office seems to have vanished, darling!" said the almost distraught Francis.

"She must remain here!" said Penelope. "

"But I am not even sure about the legality of her residence here! She is a foreign national, even if she is a child!"

"Ask your friend Charles Walton! Surely he can tell you what to do! There is no question of my allowing her to go back or leave here. She is in trust to us from Rachel. If anything has happened to Rachel we must adopt her. In fact if adoption is the only way to keep her here, we must adopt her now."

"But what about her family? We must at least make some formal attempt to contact them before trying to take such a drastic step."

Penelope showed him the document Rachel had given her.

"I shall ring Charles at once!" he said, after he had read it with considerable astonishment.

Charles was a hard bitten and very senior civil servant of immense influence at the Home Office. He had been one of Francis' best friends at school. "My goodness Francis!" he said, when he had listened to the story, "this is like something from the Scarlet Pimpernel' Of course I shall see to everything for you and Penelope. Just leave it with me! Don't worry. It will all be arranged. I shall send somebody up to see you in Leeds. He will have clear instructions what to do."

War against Germany was declared that September. No trace of the Aronbergs could be discovered. They seemed to have vanished from the face of the earth.. Soon thereafter Elisabeth Hands was officially declared to be Elisabeth Preston. Charles had been as good as his word. The adoption documents were there to prove it.

Penelope clung to her like a lifeline.

Although she had been badly traumatised both by the sudden death of her friend and the continuous absence of her mother, the little girl seemed to be adapting to the situation with that remarkable resilience small children so often display in adverse circumstances.

CHAPTER THIRTY

DEBACLE

Von Rohrbach had instructed Schumacher to assemble the just arrived team of German youth in one of the smaller conference rooms in the embassy. "They must be given an appropriate address before they depart. I shall do this myself. They must appreciate the importance of what they are doing, as representatives of the Reich."

The team had, accordingly, been drawn up in quasi-military formation, facing Von Rohrhbach, with Schumacher by his side. Behind the desk where the two of them were seated was an enormous swastika flag and a portrait of Hitler.

"All of you here have been chosen as pure Aryans, members of the glorious Hitler Youth. You represent the Reich! Heil Hitler!"

"Heil Hitler!" responded his enthusiastic young audience, raising their arms in salute.

"Here, at this embassy in London, you stand in the very shadow of the Fuhrer! Our great leader, the man who has taken Germany from the ignominy of treacherous defeat, inflicted on our country by the evil machinations of international Jewry and communism, to world leadership almost single handed! Such defeat for Germany is never again to be contemplated! Each action we take, however small, must be seen as paving the way for further victories. Today you set out to win a game of football, tomorrow you may well be on the battlefield! Remember! You are members of the master race! You play this game for the greater glory of the Reich! Heil Hitler!"

"Heil Hitler!" thundered back his rapt audience.

With this rhetoric of Von Rohrbach still ringing in their ears the team then marched out to their coach. Proudly the embassy staff watched these sons of the Reich board their swastika bedaubed transport. Each member of the team was sporting his swastika armband. Fresh faced, golden haired, blue eyed, they represented the Nazi idyll of Aryan youth.

Von Rohrbach had been given the use of an embassy Mercedes, a landau, for the occasion. It was a warm October day and he had decided to travel with the hood open. From the car's radiator fluttered the swastika pennant. Von Rohrbach, with Schumacher seated beside him, gave the signal to set off. The embassy staff cheered. The ensuing journey was unremarkable until they were approaching the environs of Bushfield village

The village had suffered considerable damage and loss of life during the Great War when the Zeppelin that Wisley had mentioned to Harold had dropped that bomb on it. A very high proportion of its men had also been killed at Ypres, almost all of them being in the same regiment, which had been all but wiped out there. Memories in Bushfield were long and bitter. The news that a German team was to play the Abbey, as the school was known locally, had provoked much adverse comment in the village, which was never on easy terms with the school at the best of times. Bushfield Abbey employed virtually nobody from the locality and, since the pupils were forbidden to shop there without special permission, made little contribution to the prosperity of the residents.

There was only one really feasible route into the village and along this the village had posted its look-outs. As soon as these reported the approach of the flamboyantly decorated car and coach the villagers began to line the roadside to watch. The immediate approach road to the school was still a country lane, passing through open country, leading to thick copses. These fields were separated from the lane by stout wooden fences and on these were perched every child in the village from the age of fifteen downwards, and some older than that for good measure.

These preparations were eyed unhappily by the village policeman who had been instructed by higher authority to take up his position at the school gates and not to leave it under any circumstances. His experienced eye warned him that some sort of trouble was brewing but he could think of no way of dealing with it, whatever it might turn out to be. He was entirely on his own.

At the foot of the Great Tower the Guard of Honour, twenty-five picked cadets, under the command of Polesden and Jason, had formed up. Their uniforms were well pressed, their belts blancoed, their brasses polished. They held their rifles, butts beautifully oiled, at ease, awaiting Polesden's command to bring them to the Present. Their boots shone, surmounted by meticulously wound puttees.

Repton had the band at the ready. The school in general, enjoying the unexpected holiday, swarmed on to the usually sacrosanct grass lawns edging the driveway, eager to greet their visitors and impress them with the warmth of their welcome in accordance with Dr. Wisley's wishes.

On the steps of the Great Tower waited the welcoming party. Dr. Wisley was in full academic dress, with his wife, Sir George and Lady Ann beside him. Harold Arbitant, in his uniform, sword at his side, watched over the Guard of Honour with fatherly pride.

Behind the Guard of Honour was drawn up the band and next to them, kitted out in blazers and well pressed flannels, was the team. From the top of the Great Tower fluttered the Union Jack. The plaque on the war memorial gleamed as only Tom, resplendent in full uniform and all his medals, could make it gleam.

Ann looked at the scene with great approval. "Well done, Harold! We are all very proud of you!"

He glowed with pleasure. This was certainly his day of triumph!

Suddenly sounds of an as yet distant but apparently approaching disturbance penetrated this splendid scene. The village children, with the tacit, or, in most cases, far from tacit, approval of their elders had planned a rude welcome for the visitors. This had been well thought out and brilliantly co-ordinated. There was, undoubtedly, a village Cromwell somewhere in Bushfield village school. In addition to the prevalent xenophobia there was also a long-standing enmity between the village 'erks', as the Bushfielders called the village boys, and the 'toffs' as the village boys called the Bushfielders. The opportunity now presented to the 'erks' was too good to miss. They hit hard, the villagers cheered them on, and the constable watched helplessly.

A volley of rotten eggs, flour and home made stink bombs descended on coach and car. The landau hood was open and Von Rohrbach was struck squarely by first a rotten egg and then a stink bomb, followed by a bag of flour. Then Schumacher was hit by an egg. Faster and thicker the missiles flew. There was no escape for them. The lane was much too narrow for the car or coach to progress any faster. The weather being warm the coach windows were wide open. Several stink bombs landed inside the coach. Closure of the windows merely served to intensify the discomfort of the occupants. The proceedings was accompanied by shouts of "Hun, Hun, dirty rotten Hun!"

Suddenly a whistle blew. The children who had at one moment been perched on the fences were suddenly hurtling towards the shelter and safety of the copses. It was all over. Grimly the constable thought to himself that there was no chance of bringing anybody to book. He knew the village too well. There would be no witnesses and no informants.

The bespattered and furious convoy turned into the drive at last. Their grand entrance had been reduced to a farce. Still unaware of what had occurred Repton launched the band into the regimental march and Polesden brought the Guard to the Present. The boys in the coach, however, were unimpressed. They were occupied chanting, "Swine, swine, British swine!" as loudly as they were able. The Mercedes drew up at the foot of the Great Tower. Out of it stepped a furious Von Rohrbach, covered in flour and smeared with rotten egg. A terrible smell of stink bomb hovered over everything.

"Stay just where you are, Schumacher! No, go over and tell the coach driver to keep the team where they are. Then come back and get in the car again. I shall deal with this!" Only then did he deign to take any notice of the thunderstruck welcoming party. He addressed himself solely to Harold, ignoring all the others. He had never met Ann or he might have been more careful.

"Who are these silly children, playing at soldiers?" he said, looking contemptuously at the Guard. "For goodness sake do tell them to stop that dreadful music! Is this all part of some stupid plan?"

Before the astonished Wisley could say a word Harold responded, "This appalling act has obviously been instigated by Jewish and communist agents. You must realise this. It has nothing to do with us!"

"Ah, so! Well, if you cannot manage your affairs better than this we want nothing to do with the matter!" Without waiting for a reply he turned to Schumacher and said "Tell the coach driver to take them back to their hotel at once. We shall follow!"

So saying he re-boarded the Mercedes.

Within a matter of seconds coach and car were heading back to London. The villagers, having already decided that discretion was the better part of valour, had dispersed. The little convoy left without further molestation.

The erstwhile reception party stood and watched in agonised disbelief.

Wisley was the first to recover his composure. "You must contact the embassy as soon as possible and make an appointment to go up there and see them and explain things!"

Harold looked at him aghast at the thought. Then Ann intervened.

"Look, it so happens that one of my cousins is a personal aide to the Ambassador. If you so wish I shall ring him now and explain what has happened. Then Harold is certain to be seen and they will listen to what he has to say!"

"We should be very grateful, Lady Ann!" said Wisley.

Ann went over to The Lodgings to make the call.

"Everybody is to return to their houses at once!" said Wisley. "Dismiss the Guard and the band and tell the team to stand down!"

Eventually things began to settle. Wisley went into consultation with the constable. Harold returned to his rooms. He had to pass Strong's rooms on the way.

"I gather there was some kind of hitch in the proceedings!" called out Strong as he went by. He was not a vindictive man, but he simply could not resist the opportunity.

"The whole thing was a Jewish-communist plot to wreck everything!" snorted Harold.

"O, pshaw! Here, at Bushfield? Of course it wasn't! It was a village prank that went too far. You're manic about these matters!"

"Prank, indeed!" said Harold and went into his room, petulantly slamming the door.

By this time it was four in the afternoon.

It was at that moment that the telephone in The Lodgings rang. The maid answered and said, "It is a Dr. McGregor for Sir George. He says it is very important, sir."

George took the telephone from her with a feeling of dread.

"McGregor here, Sir George!" came the gruff Scots voice. "I am at the Manor. I won't beat about the bush. Your mother passed away half an hour ago, a sudden heart attack. There was nothing that could have been done. I advise you not to rush back. Mrs. Mitchell is seeing to everything. I suggest you do not bring John back with you just yet. Leave him with his friends, he would be better away for the moment in my view. He can come down for the funeral. I'll expect you tomorrow!"

"Oh, my God," stammered George. "So suddenly, like this, whilst we are up here. I feel we should...."

"Look, Sir George!" responded the doctor decisively, "You must understand that I deal with these situations all the time! Please act as I advise. I am right. I am not going to argue with you. I must get away now. "The line went dead.

For a few seconds George stood as though frozen to the spot, staring at the telephone. Then he carefully replaced the receiver on its hook and went back to join the others. They all looked at him questioningly.

"My mother died at half past three this afternoon," he said in as composed a voice as he could manage. "He has strongly advised Ann and myself to stay here tonight and return tomorrow. He advises us to have John remain here until the funeral arrangements are completed as he thinks he would be better to remain with his friends than to come home just yet."

"Yes, I agree, he would be better here, with his friends," said Mrs. Wisley.

131

"We must go and tell John," said Ann.

George was secretly suspicious that his wife was not at all upset by the news of her mother-in-law's death. In any event he was sure that John would not wish to be told by Ann, or even in Ann's presence. Also he wished to speak to John privately as soon as possible. Even in the midst of his grief it had at once crossed his mind that, now his mother was no more, her story might as well continue to be her secret. In that event Ann would never need to know about it.

"I think that must be my unhappy task, Ann," he said.

He looked at the clock. It was five o'clock. He proceeded to make his way over to Chaplain's House to find John.

First of all he knocked on Strong's door and told him the news. Without any further delay Strong took him up to John's room. John had just returned and was changing from his blazer and flannels. He looked at Sir George in surprise." What are you doing over here, Father?"

"Your father has something very important to tell you, Threlfall!" said Strong. "I shall leave you with him."

George sat down in the rickety old cane chair with which John had furnished his room. George recognised it as one from the Loughbourne nursery, it had originally been Sarah's nursing chair. John perched on the side of the table and looked at him.

"Well, father?"

"John, I have very sad news. I shall come straight out with it. My mother passed away at half past three this afternoon from a heart attack...."

He was prevented from saying anything further. John had suddenly gone white. He had been in a state bordering on hysteria ever since he had first had George's letter. This final blow seemed to push him over the edge of the precipice.

"They have killed her! Those Nazi beasts! They have killed her!"

"John, you must get these things in perspective! It was her heart!"

John seemed not to hear him.

"John," continued George, still desperate to raise the matter, even now, of Sarah's story before Ann somehow learned about it. "Should we harm her memory? Only you and I know her secret, should we not keep it to ourselves?"

But John still seemed not to take any notice, He simply repeated, "They killed her!"

Realising that his son was, for the moment at least, beyond being reasoned with and being quite unable to cope with such an unfamiliar situation George decided the better course of action was to leave him alone for a while. He thought of the advice he had been given to leave John with his friends.

"Go and have a chat with Hyslow and Preston, John. Nothing like friends! I'll talk to you again when you feel better. Come over to The Lodgings if you wish." Quietly he left the room.

John buried his head in his hands and wept uncontrollably.

It was now six o'clock.

CHAPTER THIRTY ONE

CULMINATION

Ann had had a very satisfactory discussion with her cousin at the embassy He had been delighted to speak to her and, much to her surprise, far from being annoyed at what she reported to have occurred, was highly amused.

"I think it was rather amusing. I should have loved to have seen Von Rohrbach! He has absolutely no sense of humour whatsoever! He has not made any report on the episode to us here as yet. I suppose he is sitting in that car we allowed him to use worrying away about what the ambassador will say when he finally tells us. Some important people in Berlin had dreamed up this idea! You can tell your protégé, this fellow Harold Arbitant, to come up and see Schumacher tomorrow and have lunch with him. I shall have things sorted out by then. Just make sure he brings that flag he was lent back, though!"

Harold, having been informed that the way had been cleared for him, although not, of course, of the full content of this conversation, determined to arrive at the embassy in good time. He had no wish to exacerbate matters still further by being late for such an important appointment. He decided to order the Bushfield station taxi and accordingly cycled over there and made sure it would be at the school the following morning to collect him, with his precious parcel, in time to catch the first morning train to London.

He then returned to his rooms and made certain that the flag was still safe. There was absolutely no reason why it should not be safe but, by now, he was in a state of increasing anxiety. So many things had gone wrong already. It had been superbly packaged when he had been given it at the embassy. He looked around for a suitable container into which he could put it. He had no desire to turn up with it in an untidy looking parcel. He then thought of his leather suitcase and decided that would be ideal. It was very heavy, even empty, but quite new, and he was, after all, going by taxi. He pulled it down from the top of his wardrobe and began , very carefully, to pack the flag. He was so engaged when Strong knocked on his door."Harry, I am afraid Threlfall has just been given very bad news by his father. I feel you should know at once. His grandmother died earlier this afternoon. He has taken it very badly his father tells me. I am leaving him alone for the moment. I think it is better that way."

Harold's mind was concentrated on his mission to London. He could think of no suitable response to this information. He heard himself saying, "I am so sorry! I have only had the privilege of meeting Lady Sarah twice. She seemed to be a most charming lady!"

"I am of the opinion," continued Strong, with quite unexpected solicitude," that Lady Ann would probably welcome your company at The Lodgings. She seems to like you and she is on her own, as her husband is obviously taken up with other matters for the moment. She did you a very good turn with the German embassy, I hear. You may not have another opportunity to thank her personally. By the time you return from your London visit she will have returned to Loughbourne."

Nothing loath Harold left the suitcase, with the flag half-packed in it and the lid open, and went across to The Lodgings. Strong was quite right, she was very pleased to see him. The news of Sarah's death had eclipsed all else. Nobody was now in the least interested in hearing about her own recent German experiences, which she had been greatly looking forward to describing to the Wisleys. She and Harold quickly became engrossed in their conversation, for their political views coincided. Time sped by and it was with surprise Harold suddenly noticed it was already half past seven. Staff dinner began at eight. He hurried back to his rooms, arriving there at twenty minutes to eight.

After his father had left the room, an event he had hardly noticed, John eventually pulled himself together and began to attempt to come to terms with the news he had been given. He could feel a great anger building up within him directed against all those people he had by now convinced himself were responsible for his grandmother's death. He was quite sure, in his own mind, that if she had never learned of the fate of her brother's family in Berlin, she would not have had the heart attack. He looked at his watch. It was one minute to seven. He was far too upset to consider joining Hyslow and Preston for dinner. He wandered downstairs. They were all in the dining hall and he was quite alone. He glanced through the door that led to the masters' rooms. Harold's door was standing ajar and, within, he could see the open suitcase, with the half - packed flag lying in it.

On a sudden impulse he entered the room and stood for a split second looking at the hated flag. Then he took his scout knife from his pocket and thoughtfully opened it. With careful deliberation he then proceeded to slash the flag to ribbons. With equal care he then heaped the pieces back into the suitcase, stood back, and surveyed his handiwork with the greatest satisfaction. He had found the whole proceedings cathartic in the extreme.

It was nineteen minutes past seven.

His intention had been to go over to The Lodgings to resume his conversation with his father at eight o'clock. He now calculated that Harold would probably be returning to his rooms from wherever he might be very soon, to change for staff dinner. He would, thought John, then find the mutilated flag and rush over to The Lodgings with it immediately to show to Wisley. It would, he said to himself, be very appropriate if he and Harold could arrive at The Lodgings simultaneously. He would enjoy being a witness to what then happened.

He returned to his room and waited.

Preston and Hyslow returned from school dinner at twenty-five minutes to eight.

"Haven't you had any dinner?" asked Hyslow, opening the door of John's room. "We didn't call for you on the way over as Mr. Strong told us your father was with you. We didn't want to interrupt. Was it anything important?"

"He left some time ago. I shall be going over to The Lodgings to see him again quite soon. I have been sitting here thinking about what he has just told me. Then I did something I felt needed doing. I feel a lot better about things now!"

"You look very tensed up to me. Is there anything you would like to tell us about?" said Preston.

"Oh, nothing much! Just that my grandmother died earlier this afternoon."

They looked at him, amazed by his apparent calm.

"I must go over to The Lodgings now," he said and left the room without another word.

John had just left the house when Harold returned. The vandalised flag was the first thing he saw as he entered his room. His reaction was exactly as John had foreseen. He gathered it up in his arms, holding it as though it were a baby, and ran to The Lodgings.

Although John had had a head start he had been walking slowly and, in consequence, they arrived at the door together. Harold was so stunned by what had happened that he had not had time to give any thought as to who might have done the deed. John rang the bell and Dr. Wisley himself answered the door.

"Headmaster! Look what has happened to the flag!"

Dr. Wisley gazed in horror at the tattered rags being flourished in front of him by the distraught Harold who, closely followed by John, now pushed into the hallway. The others, hearing such a commotion, emerged from the drawing room, where they had been sitting over coffee.

"Look! Look!" repeated Harold. He waved the ribbons that had been the flag in their general direction wildly.

"Whoever did that?" said Ann, the first to recover her composure.

"I did!" said John in a flat, even voice, virtually devoid of expression.

They all looked at him in silence, scarcely believing he had actually spoken the words.

Then Harold went white with fury.

"You? You did this? ". His voice came out, choked with emotion, in an almost inaudible whisper.

"Yes! It gave me a great deal of pleasure!" responded John, staring straight at him, with icy self-control.

"The boy has gone mad!" breathed Harold, looking at the others.

Wisley decided he must take control of this extraordinary scene.

"I suggest you return immediately to your rooms, Harry", he said, deliberately using the first name, something he never did with junior staff, in an effort to calm down the excited young man. "I shall deal with this matter. Leave it all to me and his father."

"What shall I do? What shall I tell the embassy?" said Harold.

"There's a good fellow! Do as I say! I shall be in touch with you later. Off you go!"

He almost pushed Harold out of the door.

Harold returned to his rooms, clutching the wretched remnants to his chest.

The rest of them were still standing, almost petrified, staring at the studiedly nonchalant John.

"Please go into my study and wait there, Threlfall," said Dr. Wisley.

Then he turned his attention to George and Ann to whom he was just about to say something when Ann seemed to come to life again. She suddenly grasped her son's jacket by the lapels, put her face close to his, and said, "You wicked, wicked boy. What have you done! You have disgraced us all!"

John, very deliberately, and using his considerably superior strength, detached her from his jacket.

"The only disgrace attaches to those who bear responsibility for grandmother's death!" he said.

"Oh, George, is the boy really mad?"

"Please go into my study, Threlfall!" repeated Dr. Wisley.

John went into the study and closed the door behind him. Wisley turned to George.

"You must understand, George, that, notwithstanding the obvious embarrassment I feel about all this, I have no alternative but to take the most serious action. He cannot be allowed to return to his house and I cannot permit him, until this is sorted out, to go home with you. He will have to spend the night in the Great Tower room. Could you ask Mrs. Jason to have it prepared at once, please, Patricia?"

Mrs. Wisley sped out the room to carry out her instructions.

"Yes, of course, I understand!" said George. He was beginning to wonder whether he would suddenly wake up and find this was all only a nightmare. He was fervently wishing that Sarah had never begun her investigations and then told him her story. Above all he regretted acceding to her request for him to tell it to John. He realised that it was this that had triggered the whole crisis, but he was unable to confide in anybody present.

Mrs. Jason and Tom had, in the meanwhile, both arrived. They were given their instructions. Mrs. Jason was asked to make sure the Great Tower room was ready for the reception of an occupant. She asked no questions and hurried off to see to everything.

"Tom! I am sorry to have to tell you that young Threlfall is in serious trouble! He is going to spend the night in the Great Tower room. As soon as Mrs. Jason has everything prepared please escort him over there. In the meantime please go and sit with him in my study."

Tom was considerably taken aback by this news but his military training took over. He, too, asked no questions. He saluted Dr. Wisley and entered the study, where John had seated himself in a chair and was staring out of the window. Tom took another chair and sat down in an embarrassed silence, hoping Mrs. Jason would not be too long.

In a very short while Mrs. Jason returned to say that all was ready.

At a quarter to nine Tom took John over to the Great Tower. John was still silent and Tom could think of nothing appropriate to say.

In the meanwhile Wisley had requested Strong to come over to The Lodgings.

As soon as John was reported installed in the Great Tower Tom was instructed to take George and Ann over to see him. They arrived there at quarter past nine.

Left on their own Dr. Wisley said to Strong, "I shall now do my best to explain the apparently inexplicable to you, Alistair!"

Strong listened in astonishment and dismay as the story was unfolded to him.

CHAPTER THIRTY TWO

APOCALYPSE

George and Ann silently followed Tom over to the Great Tower. Tom walked nervously ahead, twisting the big key round in his hand. He could, he was thinking, have spoken to Sir George, if only he had been on his own with him. Lady Ann, however, was quite different. Any words would have dried in his throat. George was preoccupied with his own thoughts. He was sure that everything would now be revealed. Ann was still seething with anger. It was only a very short walk but, to all three of them, it seemed to last for ever.

John, left on his own, had already made a close inspection of the room. It had been provided with a small selection of supposedly improving books, chosen by a previous headmaster of austere tastes. He looked at the collection so provided somewhat despondently. He took out a book at random and began idly to leaf through its not very interesting contents. He was so engaged when his parents were ushered into the room by Tom.

"I shall be in the other room, Sir George. Just call me when I am wanted." He promptly left the room. George and Ann sat down on the two remaining chairs. For a moment nobody said a word. John sat and looked intently at his father. Ann looked from her husband to her son and back again.

"It was those beasts of whom you are so fond, Mother, who killed her!" said John, suddenly.

George sat silent. He had no idea how to react. He just prayed for a miracle.

"What on earth are you talking about? What is all this nonsense?" demanded Ann.

"So Mother still doesn't know?" said John to his father.

George knew that the Rubicon had been crossed. Now he would have to reveal all to Ann. He plunged in bravely.

"Whilst you were away in Germany, Ann, Sarah told me the most extraordinary story after she had returned from her London visit. At the time she was already in the most distressed state. It turned out that the principal reason for her expedition had been to see a firm of solicitors." He paused at this point and glanced at John, almost as though seeking his approval to continue. John simply sat there listening, apparently impassive. George continued, "She instructed them to carry out certain investigations, concerning her family."

"Investigations?" said Ann, very surprised, "Whatever needed investigation about the family?"

"They were investigations relating to her own family, not the Threlfalls."

"Now you mention it," said Ann, " I never did know anything about her family. What were these investigations?"

The entire story had to be related to her. She listened in total silence.

"I did not say anything to you because I felt that was in the best interests of everybody. I was thinking of you, in particular, Ann. I am only too well aware of your professed convictions and prejudices. I knew that her story would greatly upset you."

"Professed? Prejudices?" she echoed him. The full significance of what she had just heard was only just beginning to register with her. "Have I been told everything now?"

"So far as I know, yes."

Ann began to examine her fingernails as though the answer to all their problems was written upon them. This process went on for about two minutes, whilst George and John waited, watching her. Then she spoke.

"Sarah and your father, between them, brought dishonour on the names of Threlfall and Winslow and, by so doing, on Von Runing."

"Dishonour!" gasped John. "In what way did they dishonour us or you?"

"By the blood which flows in your veins and by my union with it!"

"That is quite monstrous!" exploded George.

"It is true!" responded Ann.

She stood up.

"I wish to be taken back to Loughbourne at once!"

She abruptly opened the door and called out "Riding, we are leaving!"

Tom at once emerged from the other room. In his presence it was quite impossible for George to continue the conversation. He could think of no alternative but to follow her. Tom then carefully locked the door of John's room and let them out of the Great Tower, locking the door to that after him. John, left on his own once more, shrugged his shoulders. The enormity of the events of the day seemed to have temporarily paralysed his brain. He gazed blankly at the pages of the book he had been reading. Then he went to the window, that overlooked Heroes' Yard, and stood there gazing out of it, vainly trying to obtain a grasp on the situation.

The Wisleys had accepted Sir George's explanation for returning home so precipitately with their usual diplomacy. They had anticipated that the meeting with John would be very difficult, even stormy. It had, evidently, been even worse than they had supposed. As a matter of fact they were relieved that their guests had decided to go home. Shortly thereafter the Rolls Royce rumbled down the drive. John's barred window overlooked the war memorial. He stood there watching them depart. Then, rousing himself from his quasi-trancelike state with an immense effort, he began to examine the room carefully. He discovered that the washroom, partitioned by some former school carpenter from the main room, had been lined with hardboard attached to laths pinned to the walls with masonry nails. In one place this lining had begun to come loose. He pulled at it and it gave way completely. Behind it was a door, bolted on his side .He pulled back the bolt and pushed, there was a slight resistance. He pushed harder and then there was a sound of tearing. The door opened slightly. Although bolted it had not been locked with the mortise. Another determined push and the door stood wide open. He found himself standing in the corridor that divided the two rooms. The tearing sound had been the encrusted wallpaper which had concealed the presence of the door from the outside. He realised that, whilst he could now leave his room, he still could not escape from the Great Tower itself.

Not much use, he thought to himself, if only I could have escaped I could perhaps have run away to sea or something! Then he smiled at the apparent absurdity of that idea. Despondently he sat down again and reflected on all that had happened since he had received that letter from his father. What, he meditated, lay ahead for him? Was the whole world going to co-operate with this Nazi regime in Germany? It seemed to be that way. Everybody seemed to be so anxious to avoid war at any price. In such a world what place would there be for people like his father, or, for that matter, himself? They would be second class citizens at best, perhaps not even that. Here he was, with a mother who pointedly despised him, perhaps even hated him. All that lay ahead for him was first punishment for what he had done and then disgrace. His depression deepened rapidly. I should be seething with anger but I feel absolutely calm, he thought. Calm before the storm? He closed the book and went over to the bookcase. There was the inevitable copy of Shakespeare. He turned to Hamlet and found the ""to be, or not to be" soliloquy he had so much enjoyed reading recently. He read it again, this time finding a much deeper meaning within the words. He read them out aloud:

> To be, or not to be: that is the question:
> Whether 'tis nobler in the mind to suffer
> The slings and arrows of outrageous fortune,
> Or take up arms against a sea of troubles,
> And by opposing end them? To die: to sleep;
> No more; and, by a sleep to say we end
> The heart-ache and the thousand natural shocks
> That flesh is heir to, 'tis a consummation
> Devoutly to be wish'd. To die to sleep;
> To sleep: perchance to dream:

The words so exactly expressed his feelings. He left the book lying open on the table. He was not absolutely sure that he really knew what he was planning to do, although a frightening but exciting idea was by now hovering at the back of his mind. He was conscious, however, whatever this action might eventually prove to be, that by leaving the play open at that particular passage he had explained everything. Then he walked out through the discovered door into the now dark interior of the Great Tower. At first he tried to fight the awesome idea that Hamlet's lines had placed in his mind. Surely, he reasoned, there was another way out of all this turmoil, some other avenue of escape. All the while, however, he was still steadily ascending higher and higher. Up and up he went, up the stairway that led to the upper gallery. Then higher still, up the narrow ladders, past the ropes, then past the great bell, hanging mute in its loft. Then up yet again, through a trap door. He pushed this open to find himself on the little platform which surrounded the flagpole, with merely a small, ornate railing running round it as protection.

There was a full moon above, hanging in a cloudless starlit sky. He looked up and felt sure he could see his grandmother and hear her calling him. He climbed over the railing. And then he was suddenly sliding down the steep conical roof and then, faster and faster, past the phoenix hovering over its motto. He had made no effort to arrest his descent.

He came to rest, with a dull thud, on the railings around the memorial. A splash of blood spread over the plaque, covering Frederick's name.

It was three in the morning.

At one minute to seven the following morning the young duty bugler, Bob Johnson, aged thirteen, arrived at the memorial to sound Reveille. The sight of John's body drove every other thought out of the boy's head. Sobbing hysterically he ran to the Lodge and banged furiously on Tom's door. Bill, Tom's son, was staying with his father and answered . Bob could do little more than gesture towards the memorial, but Bill had seen enough. He pulled the boy inside and sat him down on a chair. Tom, alerted by the commotion, had looked out of the window from upstairs. He was already running up the drive, in a state of dishabille, in the direction of The Lodgings. He ran straight past the war memorial and thundered on the headmaster's door.

The Wisleys had just finished breakfast. Wisley sprang up and rushed out of the house, to be confronted by a distraught Tom.

"The boy's had a terrible accident, sir" he gasped. Then, without any further enlightenment, he returned to the scene of the accident, followed by Wisley and his wife.

At that moment Bob came out of the Lodge, obviously in a state of shock. Mrs.Wisley ran to him, took his hand and quickly led him back to the Lodgings. Then she rang Mrs. Jason, on the house telephone, to come over as quickly as possible.

Bill was standing at the memorial. "He's dead, Dad!" he said.

Tom gathered the body up in his arms and took it into the Great Tower where he put it down on the bed. Then, before anybody knew what he intended to do, he ran up to the ropes and began to peal the great bell as though, by so doing, he would rid his beloved Bushfield Abbey of the demons which seemed to him to have suddenly invaded it.

The peals aroused the school, indeed much of the surrounding district. It took at least two minutes to persuade Tom to stop. By that time people were beginning to gather. Wild rumours were circulating. Tom had been seen covered in blood. Somebody said he had tried to murder the headmaster. Then somebody else mentioned that Reveille had not been sounded. Perhaps it was young Johnson who had been murdered?

In the meanwhile Dr. Wisley was frantically telephoning the police, the ambulance service,and the doctor. Then, finally, he rang Sir George, who reacted with unexpected calm.He and Ann would come up to the school immediately. They were expected within the next two hours.

Only then was he able to go outside and take complete charge. The Reverend Strong was there, doing his best to control everybody.

"Everybody is to return, immediately, to their quarters!" said Wisley.

Then he beckoned to Mrs. Jason and Strong to accompany him inside the Great Tower .Tom, still sobbing, met them on the steps, "He's dead, sir! He's dead! Fell from the Tower!" he said to Strong. Bill put his arm round his father's shoulders.

"Leave him to me, sir," he said to Wisley. "I'll take him home and settle him!"

The three of them then entered the tower room and stood together, looking at the broken body. Only Strong noticed the open book. Quietly he closed it and put it back in the bookcase. He never referred to the matter again.

In a short while first a taxi and then the village policeman on his bicycle came up the drive. "The police have just arrived, Headmaster," said Strong, looking out of the window.

Wisley hastened out of the Great Tower and made his way across Heroes' Yard towards the constable. At that moment he caught sight of Harold, carrying his heavy suitcase, making for the taxi which had come, as ordered, to take him to the station. Wisley rushed over to intercept him.

The school clock stood at twenty minutes to eight.

PART THREE - THUNDER

CHAPTER THIRTY THREE

RESURRECTION

Ann and George, seated in opposite corners of the car, travelled, unspeaking, through the dark lanes of Norsex.

George was, at that moment, however, regretting he had ever married Ann. She had, he was telling himself, vilified his mother and his son. He felt he would never be able to forgive her conduct. She had so acted whilst his mother was lying on her deathbed and their son was in dire trouble. Her conduct, he repeated to himself, had been monstrous. Paradoxically he knew he still loved her. Loving somebody and liking them was not the same thing, he reflected.

Ann's own thoughts were even more confused than her husband's. In the Great Tower she had spoken in the white heat of anger and, as she had honestly then believed, from absolute conviction. To her alarm, however, she found she was beginning to have doubts. George's use of the epithet ' professed ' was worrying her. She had, at the time, angrily repudiated the innuendo but it had been perceptive. She stole a glance at her husband, hunched miserably in his corner, What have I done? Ann asked herself. Why did I say such things? It had all arisen so suddenly, so unexpectedly. The image of Mrs. Hodge, her childhood governess, came into her mind. She had had a particularly bad childish tantrum and said some very unpleasant things about everybody.

"Just you remember, this little rhyme, young lady, when you feel angry:

'Boys flying kites draw in their white winged birds

But you can't do the same when you're flying words."

"Oh, don't be so silly, Mrs. Hodge!" she had said, "Twaddle! as my father says!"

Mrs. Hodge, faced by her angry and spoiled charge, had resignedly shrugged her shoulders. But, thought Ann, had she been right?

Perhaps, she reflected, for the sake of upholding ideas that I never really understood properly I have succeeded in wrecking my whole family life? Very belatedly it had dawned on her that her family were much more important to her than those arrogant German cousins. However, so bitter had been the altercation in the Great Tower that it had bred an obstinacy in her, she could not bring herself to utter a word. The two of them sat in the car in sullen silence. George could know nothing of Ann's inner turmoil. He saw only a woman he loved yet whose conduct and opinions he abominated.

Their return at such a time was completely unexpected at Loughbourne. The car drew up, nearly at midnight, outside the manor house and Donald sounded the horn. Lights came on and Lily Mitchell, who was now the housekeeper, Mrs. Faming having long since retired, followed by the new butler, Jameson, Goodenough's successor, hurried downstairs to meet them. Both had just been on the point of going to bed.

Then Janet emerged from her room to see her mistress just beginning to ascend the stairs. Ann, whose inner turmoil was now, she could feel, pushing her to the brink of insanity affected to ignored them all. The perceptive Janet, however, at once realised that her mistress was in a highly emotional condition. An immense wave of sympathy swept over her. She watched quietly as Ann went quickly to her room and heard the key click as the door was locked. Once safely secluded Ann lay down still fully clothed. She lay there staring at the ceiling. Janet was just about to knock at the door and enquire if she were needed when her feminine instinct warned her to do no such thing. She stopped her hand in the very act of knocking and then quietly crept away.

"Her ladyship is feeling out of sorts. I am sure she will be better by the morning. All of you please go back to bed."

George now entered his mother's room. Violet Mitchell, Sarah's maid ever since she had first come to Loughbourne, was sitting by her side, watching over her dead mistress. She had dozed off for a moment, even though she had deliberately chosen a hard chair expressly to avoid this happening. She awoke with a start as George entered the room..

"Thank you, Violet! I shall take over the watch now! You go and get some sleep!" said George, noting her confusion

Violet had covered Sarah's face with a sheet. George bent down, pulled this back, and kissed the cold forehead. Then he spoke to his mother as though she were still alive.

"Mother, what shall we do?" He took the dead hand in his own and sat down, still holding the hand. He closed his eyes and then, abruptly, the anxieties of the last two days completely overwhelmed him. He went into a deep sleep.

He woke up, with a start, from a troubled dream, still sitting in the armchair, and still holding his mother's icy hand, to see Ann standing next to him, sobbing pitifully and looking down at Sarah. The faint movement he made as he awoke caused her to turn and look at him. He looked back at her, still only half comprehending that she had entered the room.

She was very pale and completely devoid of any make-up. Her hair was hanging, in a golden cloud, round her bare shoulders. She looked lovelier than he ever remembered. A great wave of love and protectiveness for her engulfed him, only to be at once replaced by the memory of the previous day.

Ann, in a torment of grief and guilt, had passed a dreadful night. The words she had spoken in the Great Tower had combined, in her fitful dreams, with Mrs. Hodge's nursery wisdom. They had echoed through her dreams like a terrible refrain, "Can't do the same..... dishonour...kites." She had risen from the bed, paced the room, and gazed out of the window across Peter's Garden towards the home park where, as a child, she had spent so many happy hours riding with George. What have I done? What have I done? she kept demanding of herself. The question, although only asked silently of herself, seemed be being shrieked at her by a demon within her head. A great blackness, a feeling of complete helpliness decended on her.

She was the product of her social class and her era. The 1920's, in which she matured, had been a time of great reaction by girls of her class against the strictness of their parents' generation. She would have been ashamed to be seen by her smart friends in an act of voluntary prayer. It was simply not 'done' to engage in such activities in the set in which she moved. But her childhood roots were stronger than she knew. In such a crisis she knew that she had to pray. She knelt down by the bed, her hands clasped together as that same Mrs. Hodge had taught her.

"Dear merciful Jesus, help me."

Frantically she besought forgiveness, for guidance.

So that dreadful night slowly dragged by. She knew that which she must now do. As the first faint birdsong penetrated the room she unlocked her door and, still dressed in the same now bedraggled clothes, and with her usually carefully coiffured hair all awry, she crept quietly, almost timidly, along the corridor of the still silent house to George's room. His bed was unslept in and she knew at once that he had spent the night watching by Sarah. She let down her hair over her shoulders and opened the door to Sarah's room. He was in there, asleep, still holding his mother's hand.

He looked so tired but, she thought, so good, so handsome. She had never felt such overwhelming love for him. Very quietly she went over to the bedside and stood there, looking down at Sarah's uncovered face, beautiful even in death. All night the solace of tears had been denied her but now they came. She gave a little sob and George immediately awoke.

She could see the initial look of love on his face replaced by one of suspicion and alarm. She knelt down and took his hands in hers. "George we must return to Bushfield and collect John this morning. He must come back here."

Together they silently weighed up the import of her words. Then Jameson knocked on the door.

"It is the Headmaster of Bushfield Abbey, Sir George. He says it is very urgent."

The bedroom clock was standing at quarter past seven. They looked at each other with an unspoken but mutual dread in their eyes.

"I shall be down at once, Jameson!"

He turned to Ann and said, "Stay here, darling, I shall return as soon as I can!"

The long unused but spontaneously uttered endearment hung in the air like a promise yet to be fulfilled.

Ann left the room and knocked on Janet's door.

"Janet," she said, " Could you possibly do my hair and find me a clean dress, very quickly?"

Janet, astonished at being addressed in such considerate terms, emerged at once from her room. They went in to Ann's dressing room and Janet quickly put her mistress' hair into a coil and found her a fresh dress.

"Thank you, Janet! That will have to do! There is no time for anything else."

The entire matter had taken the deft Janet about five minutes. She had just finished when George returned. He was looking very serious. The conversation on the telephone with Wisley had been extremely distressing.

"I have very bad news, George! Is Ann with you?"

"No, she is upstairs in her room."

"During the night John managed to leave his room. He found a door of which we knew nothing."

"He has run away from the school?"

"No, it is far worse, I am afraid. He seems to have begun to explore the interior of the Great Tower. He managed to find a way out on to the roof. Then he slipped."

"Is he badly hurt?"

"I am afraid it is much worse than that."

"Are you telling me..."

"Yes, I am."

"You said he slipped. Do you mean he jumped?"

"He missed his footing."

"We shall come up to Bushfield immediately."

"The doctor and police are here. I am afraid there will have to be an inquest."

"We shall be with you in about three hours."

He put down the telephone.

"Jameson, please ask Donald to bring the car round immediately. Her ladyship and I are returning to Bushfield. I am unsure when we shall be back. I shall be in touch with Mr. Morton by telephone. Please ask him to expect a call from me some time this afternoon."

Donald brought the car round within a few minutes. George returned upstairs to collect Ann. She emerged from her room, closely followed by Janet. Ann looked at her husband almost pleadingly, as though she were willing away the bad news she knew he was about to impart.

"George, what is it? Is it some thing dreadful?"

"I fear it is very bad, Ann! I think you had better come with us, Janet! The car is waiting outside. We must leave at once, there is no time to pack anything. We must go as we are. I shall speak to you on the way."

They followed him down the stairs and seated themselves in the car, Janet sitting in the front, next to Donald, with the dividing panel closed.

George took Ann's hand in his and held it tightly.

"Tell me, now, George."

"It appears he found another concealed door which he forced open and was thus able to escape from the room in which he had been confined. Apparently he wandered around inside the Great Tower for a time and finally found his way out on to the platform on the top. It was still dark and he seems to have missed his footing and slipped ..."

"He's dead!" moaned Ann, "He killed himself! It was my fault, speaking like that ...." she was almost beside herself. Her grip on George's hand was so tight she drew blood. Gently but firmly he extricated himself from her grasp.

"Nonsense! He slipped as I have just told you! Don't be so foolish!"

She relapsed into quiet sobbing which continued without cessation until the car was turning into the gates of the school. The terrible blackness of the previous night descended upon her once again. Then, just as the school tower came into sight she regained control of herself. The car drew up at The Lodgings. The Wisleys came running down the steps.

From there on it was undiluted agony. How they managed to do what they had to do both never quite knew. But when such things have to be done they have to be done. George rang Alan Morton and broke the news to him, giving him only the barest details. There were meetings with the doctor, the police, the Reverend Strong.

At last all the formalities were completed. A verdict of accidental death had been returned.

A pall of desolation descended over Loughbourne Manor. It was an unparalleled tragedy. A double funeral, attended by the entire county, a large proportion of the school staff, many of the parents, and the whole population of the village followed. Loughbourne church had not been so full since that Christmas Day when Sarah had made her first appearance there.

At last the house returned to something approaching normality. George and Ann were left on their own. Ann took George's hand in hers.

"We are both so tired, my darling, we must go to bed. We both need to sleep, if we can."

Without resistance he allowed her to lead him up the great staircase. At the top of this they had, for many years now, been in the habit of parting. He taking his way to his rooms and she to hers. On this occasion, however, she entered his room with him. Janet was thus discovered laying out her mistress' nightdress on the bed.

"Thank you, Janet! You take the evening off from now on. You must be as tired as we are! We shall see ourselves into bed."

Janet, very surprised, curtsied and left the room. Going downstairs to the kitchen she encountered Donald, who had been for some time now had been making quite clear that he was becoming very attached to her. "My Mum says, 'Even the darkest cloud has a silver lining'. I think there's a silver lining upstairs!"

"They could do with a silver lining!" said Donald and then, very daringly, gave her a kiss.

George and Ann walked across to the bedroom windows. These gave a clear view across Peter's Garden and the home park to Loughbourne church. There, side by side, were the two graves, as yet without headstones. At that moment both felt that speech would have been an intrusion but they were closer than they had been for many years. John, in death, had brought his parents back together.

As they lay down to sleep she began to sob again. "If only..." she began. For a while George lay in silence, agonising in her agony. She reached out and clutched his hand. He, unspeaking, drew her towards him. Gradually, as they lay there, enfolded in each other's arms, a kind of peace descended on them and then they slept.

It was in January, 1939, that Ann discovered that she had conceived again. The new life moving within her seemed to her to be the answer to the fervent prayer she had offered up that terrible night. It was a kind of purgation of the misery of guilt she had ever since endured. It was, she knew, an offer of salvation. The baby in its innocence began to exorcise the demons that had been possessing and tormenting her without ceasing ever since John's death.

In March that year George, in his capacity as Commanding Officer of the Territorial battalion of the Prince's Own Carbines, discussed the international situation with Dr. Wisley, his second in command.

"War is coming, in spite of everything, Richard! That war my son foresaw and dreaded. It will be a just war and we shall all be in it! I fear that poor Dr. Williams will have to return, for you and I and many others will have to go!"

On October the twelfth, 1939, at three in the morning, Ann gave birth to a son, whom they named Roger. By that time Lieutenant Colonel Sir George Threlfall was serving with Major Wisley in his now fully mobilised battalion, preparing for imminent embarkation for active service in France. Dr. Williams had taken up the reins again at Bushfield Abbey.

Every morning Ann, accompanied by Violet and Janet, walked across the park to Loughbourne churchyard and placed fresh flowers on the newly dug graves. The headstones were now in place. On Sarah's were the words:

"Here lies a gracious lady"

On John's she had had inscribed:

"I was, I am, I shall be"

She would nevertheless have been in continuous torment had it not been for Roger. The baby needed and received her attention constantly, for this time she immersed herself in motherhood and in the knowledge that her child had ancestors on both sides of his family of whom he would grow up to speak with pride.

CHAPTER THIRTY FOUR

DEPARTURE

Harold, in a state bordering on trauma, returned to his rooms carrying the remnants of the flag. He put these back into the suitcase and sat down and considered the position in which he had been placed by John's actions. There was no way that anybody at the embassy could as yet be aware of what had happened and how it had occurred. These revelations would have to be made by him to what would be an undoubtedly highly unsympathetic audience of Schumacher and, eventually, Von Rohrbach. Even in spite of the help he had received by reason of Ann's previous intervention he could not expect to escape censure.

He was determined not to compound problems by missing his appointment. He set his alarm clock for six in the morning and then took himself miserably off to bed. In order to be sure to be ready for the taxi he had ordered he would need to be in the staff refectory by seven o'clock, when it opened. He slept fitfully, much disturbed by dreaming, and was relieved to be awoken by the ringing of the alarm.

By a few minutes to seven he was already on his way to the refectory. By force of habit he listened for the sounding of Reveille as this was one of his responsibilities as O.C. the O.T.C. To his surprise it did not appear to be sounded. Notwithstanding his other preoccupations he made a note to check the apparent omission with Repton when he returned from London.

The maids were still finishing their own breakfast and he was served personally by Mrs. Jason. He was just beginning his meal when Mrs. Jason was called away to answer the house phone. He heard her say, in a somewhat concerned manner, "Certainly Mrs. Wisley, I shall be straight over! I only have Mr. Arbitant here at the moment. I shall just ask Doris to take over from me and then I shall hurry across to you."

She opened the door to the kitchen, where the maids were just finishing, and called out, "Doris! Would you come and take over, please! I have to go over to The Lodgings at once."

Then she said to Harold, " One of the boys has been badly hurt. I shall have to leave. Doris will see to you!" So saying she divested herself of her apron and hurried away.

As she left the great bell began to peal out as though being rung by a madman. She looked round and exclaimed, "Whatever can that be?" but hurried off without waiting for his reply, not that he had any more idea than she had.

Left on his own he hastily finished his meal, he had no desire to get trapped into any delaying conversation with any other early breakfasting member of staff. Then he returned to his rooms to finish his preparations for the London trip. The clamour of the bell, which had now ceased, had caused a number of people to come out to see what was happening. His own curiosity was aroused but he sternly resisted the temptation to join them, there was no time. He had to catch that train. He hastily finished his packing, locked the suitcase, put on his overcoat and hat, and made his way towards Heroes' Yard, where the taxi was to pick him up. The heavy leather case somewhat impeded him and he made rather slow progress, arriving just as the taxi was coming up the drive. Rather to his surprise he noticed that it was closely followed by the village policeman on his bicycle. Glancing by sheer habit at the school clock he saw it was exactly twenty minutes to eight.

People, chattering excitedly, were making their way back to their houses. He was still too preoccupied with the mission which lay ahead of him to take much notice. It must, he thought, be something to do with the boy who has been injured. Then he suddenly caught sight of Tom, apparently covered in blood, standing on the steps of the Great Tower, supported by Bill. He looked at him in bewilderment, Mrs. Jason had said that one of the boys had been injured, not Tom. It was then that Dr. Wisley saw him and hurried across to intercept him. Harold was the last person he wanted around at that moment. "Off you go, Arbitant!" he said, "A boy has been very badly hurt!" He deliberately refrained from saying who it was that had been hurt. "No, no discussion now, please! I want you on that train. Please take the taxi and go! Just see that matters at the embassy are settled satisfactorily!" Harold still hesitated. "Look, your train leaves in twenty minutes. Go, man, go!"

For another second Harold continued to stare at him, dumbfounded, then he obediently boarded the taxi.

"What's up, sir?" said the taxi driver.

"It seems there has been an accident, that's all I know!".

As Harold's taxi left the school gates the doctor's little car turned in, the doctor looking tense and white behind the wheel. The policeman was in earnest consultation with Dr. Wisley, Bill and Tom.

153

Harold only just caught the train. He settled back into his seat and a sudden thought struck him, the injured boy must have been Threlfall.

"I wonder whether he has killed himself?" he said aloud.

Fortunately there was nobody else in the compartment.

CHAPTER THIRTY FIVE

RETURN

As the convoy of coach and Mercedes made its dismal return to London Von Rohrbach's anger began to recede and give way to intense anxiety. He was well aware that the match against Bushfield Abbey had been the brainchild of a person of great importance in Berlin. Notwithstanding the provocation he had had to endure he was by no means sure the precipitate decision he had made to cancel the fixture and return to London with the team would meet with approval, rather the reverse he began to fear. The school was a prolific source of potentially important connections. He would probably be called in by the ambassador personally to make an explanation. Naturally he had no idea that Ann had already been in touch with his own superior. He sat in the car wondering whether, by some means, he could manage to put the blame for what had happened on Schumacher, who was sitting, equally glumly, beside him. Sadly he could think of no way of achieving this, to him, desirable end.

He decided that he must give priority to returning the team to their hotel and, for the time being at least, keeping them away from the embassy. He wanted to be able to tell his own version of events before any other found credence there. Accordingly he directed the convoy to go directly to Bayswater. The team was duly deposited back at the hotel they had left earlier the same morning, greatly to the surprise of the management, who had not anticipated their return until Thursday. By way of explanation the management were informed that, for unexpected reasons, the match had had to be postponed. Then he summoned the team captain to come and see him.

"Under no circumstances are you, or any of the team, to tell anybody anything about what occurred, either here in London or when you return to Germany, without my express permission. Any explaining will be done by either Herr Schumacher or myself. That is a direct order! If it is breached the person responsible will meet with very serious consequences! Make sure everybody is quite clear on this matter! This afternoon and for most of tomorrow you are all free to go sight-seeing but make sure they are all back here in time to board the coach which will bring you to the embassy to meet the ambassador in the evening. Make sure everybody is properly dressed for the occasion. You will be held personally responsible for seeing these instructions are carried out!"

The boy saluted him smartly and left. Von Rohrbach knew he could be absolutely relied upon to obey him to the letter and without question. "Behold the advantages of German education and discipline!" said Von Rohrbach dryly to Schumacher.

This settled, the two of them set off for the embassy. "You know," ruminated Von Rohrbach, as the car edged its way down Park Lane, "I have been thinking that that attack probably was the result of a Jewish-communist plot! It was so well planned! It seems impossible that ordinary peasants, like the ones who attacked us, could have thought it all up on their own!"

"Now you point it out, sir, it certainly does seem extraordinary. It was certainly very well thought out and executed!"

"Yes, indeed! I wonder whether there might be some co-ordinator within the school itself? They had very good advance information. I wonder whether there is an active Jewish element in the school? That seems more likely than a communist one."

The more he thought about the matter, the more he convinced himself that the explanation must lie there. The whole episode smacked of what he described to himself, with increasing rancour, as Jewish cunning.

"As soon as we get back to the embassy, Schumacher, have your section run a special and detailed check on everybody at that school, pupils and all staff. Let us locate any Jewish element there. There is certain to be one. I know that that is what is behind all this!"

The receptionist was waiting for them anxiously. "The Chief Secretary wishes to see you as soon as you return, Herr Von Rohrbach. He has asked for you several times already. Please go up to him immediately. I shall tell his secretary you are on your way."

"You go ahead with that investigation as fast as you can! It looks as though the news about Bushfield is already known here!" He hurried off up the grand staircase.

Ann's cousin, the Chief Secretary, was standing at the window of his office gazing out over the Mall, looking longingly at Buckingham Palace. He was an impressive man with a suitably impressive office. Even the much-feared Von Rohrbach was in awe of him.

"Heil Hitler!" said Von Rohrbach, standing to attention and saluting smartly as he was ushered in by the secretary.

"Heil Hitler!" said the Chief Secretary, rather curtly. He pointed to a rather uncomfortable chair, which had been strategically placed in front of his desk, "Sit down!"

Von Rohrbach sat. There was an uncomfortable pause.

"Lady Ann Threlfall, a member of the Von Runing family, of whom, I presume, you have heard, and a personal friend of several people who are very close to the Fuhrer, was in the reception party at Bushfield Abbey which you saw fit to insult this morning! She telephoned me immediately you left!"

Von Rohrbach was perspiring. "I had absolutely no idea she was present, sir! I acted, perhaps rather too hastily, in indignation at the insult that had been delivered to the Reich! We had been assaulted by hooligans! I intended no offence to Lady Ann Threlfall......."

The Chief Secretary had been unable to resist playing cat and mouse with this normally pompous and powerful embassy official. He cut him short.

"Alright! All right! We know all about what happened! The matter has already been discussed with the ambassador and he, in his turn, has been in touch with Berlin. In the circumstances you have been exonerated! It is all very regrettable, though. We had placed high hopes on the resulting contacts.

Your Herr Arbitant is coming up here tomorrow and he will return that flag you lent him. Did you know he was a member of the British Union of Fascists? We think it would be a good idea if you recruited him for the Aryan Friendship Society. We think he could be very useful to us. I have already spoken to their chairman. There is a meeting of his committee here tomorrow. See what you can do. If you can secure him for us we shall forget this episode at Bushfield.

Now then, what do you think caused this trouble at Bushfield?"

Von Rohrbach felt a great wave of relief sweep over him. He determined to enrol Harold into the AFS if it was the last thing he ever did.

"The more I consider the matter, sir, the more convinced I become that there must be a cell of Jewish plotters at that school! Right at this moment I have Schumacher checking things out there to see if we can identify any potential suspects."

"Very likely! Very likely indeed! Well done! Keep me informed. And don't overlook what I said about this man Arbitant. We need good, reliable, German speaking recruits. The AFS meets in Room 100 tomorrow afternoon. Try and persuade him to join them. There will be a number of very influential people there. You are authorised to handle the matter from there on as you see fit. The man has already been cleared as suitable for recruitment by our Munich people."

The meeting was over. Von Rohrbach hastened back to his office. There was a knock on the door and Schumacher came in with a look of triumph on his face. He placed some papers in front of his chief. Impatiently Von Rohrbach picked them up and glanced at them. He was anxious to tell his junior what had happened in the Chief Secretary's office. Then the full significance of what he was looking at struck him.

"My God! This is absolutely amazing! Do you know we arrested this woman's brother in Berlin last May, together with two other members of her family? The rest of them have been under surveillance in Munich ever since! Well done, Schumacher!"

Sarah and Frederick's marriage certificate and Sarah's change of name deed poll had been located by the section's investigations. They had secured copies of everything.

CHAPTER THIRTY SIX

REVELATION

"You are expected, Herr Arbitant!" said the receptionist deferentially, as Harold approached the desk. She beckoned to the porter, who hurried forward to take his suitcase. "Herr Schumacher will be down directly, he has been asking if you had arrived. I shall tell him you are here. Would you be good enough to take a seat for a moment?"

Rather taken aback to be so cordially received he took a seat as indicated and waited. In a very few moments Schumacher appeared, making his way down the main staircase, for he had been closeted with Von Rohrbach. He advanced, hand outstretched in welcome, with a broad smile.

"Good to see you again, Harry! Von Rohrbach is waiting for us. By the way do you have the flag with you?"

"Yes, it is over there, in my suitcase, with the porter, Gregory," replied Harold, still more surprised by such a reception, very different from anything he had been expecting after the previous day's contretemps.

Schumacher signalled to the porter to follow them and they made their way up to Von Rohrbach's office on the first floor.

"Good morning, Mr. Arbitant!" said Von Rohrbach, with great affability. "No hard feelings about yesterday's unfortunate misunderstanding I hope!"

"You are being most kind to me! I had not expected you to be so forgiving!"

"Ah, well! I think we were all somewhat shaken by what happened. I am afraid I myself owe you an apology! Things got out of control. We have all had time to reflect."

He paused and looked at the suitcase, which the porter had placed on a low table. "I suppose the flag is in your case? I shall arrange for it to be returned to stores. I suppose, just for routine purposes, we had better check it. I am sorry you were never able to fly it! Then we should like to discuss some other matters with you, if you can spare the time?"

Nemesis, thought Harold, had just entered the room. He gulped nervously. Slightly puzzled Von Rohrbach waited a little impatiently.

Schumacher moved towards the suitcase. In a rush Harold said, "I am afraid the flag has met with an, ah, an, ah, kind of accident, that is to say, something has happened to it."

"An accident?" said Von Rohrbach, his tone distinctly less amicable. "What kind of accident. Let us see it, please?"

By this time Harold felt quite certain that it had been Threlfall who had fallen from the Great Tower and that he had either committed or attempted to commit suicide. That was the obvious deduction to make from his otherwise seemingly inexplicable conduct over the last few days. He had been hoping to be able to mention this before he was asked to produce the flag so that he could relate its destruction to John's obviously disturbed mental condition. However the sequence of events had gone wrong. He was just on the point of grasping the nettle and opening the suitcase when, providentially, Von Rohrbach had to answer the telephone.

Von Rohrbach listened to the person on the other end without expression. Then he hung up, looked at Harold, and said, "Were you aware before you left to come up here this morning that Lady Ann's son killed himself at the school some time during last night?"

"I was not certain that it was he. I knew there had been a terrible accident but I could only guess that it was John Threlfall. He had been confined in the Great Tower, awaiting punishment. He had already confessed to damaging your flag, you see!"

"You had better show it to us, now, before we go any further with this conversation!"

Tremulously Harold opened the case and pulled out the tattered cloth that had been the flag. They looked at it incredulously.

"Herr Von Rohrbach," said Schumacher, " do I have your permission to tell Herr Arbitant what we have discovered? It must, surely, explain what has happened!

"Go ahead, then!"

Schumacher proceeded to explain to the astonished Harold everything the section had unearthed about Sarah and her parentage. "We not only have copies of the marriage certificate and the deed poll and the birth certificate," he said, " but we also know all about the rest of her family, who are still in Germany."

"Let me add to that," intervened Von Rohrbach. " I am in a position to inform you that, last May, this woman's brother, one Samuel Aronberg, a Jew, together with his son and grandson, were arrested in Berlin on charges relating to public order and are, at present, in detention. She has another brother, who is resident in Munich. The wives of the arrested men are presently with him and are under surveillance. A child, the daughter of the grandson, has vanished. We are still investigating the circumstances. The premises the family occupied in Berlin have been sequestrated."

"But this woman, Sarah, John Threlfall's grandmother, died last week! How is it possible that she married into an aristocratic family like the Threlfalls and nobody seems to have known about it? It seems incredible!"

"We cannot, as yet, answer that. However they were married at a civil ceremony and not in their local church. That indicates some intention to cover the matter up, as does the change of name."

"But this must mean that Lady Ann is married, quite unknowingly, to a half Jew!" said Harold.

"Indeed!" said Schumacher. "The lady has been the victim of a cruel deception!"

"Herr Arbitant," said Von Rohrbach, "has it yet occurred to you that some ill-disposed people at Bushfield and Loughbourne may seek to place the blame for this boy's death upon you?"

"But that would be completely unfair!"

"We are not concerned with fairness or unfairness, dear as those concepts are to the British! We are concerned with the reality of the situation. You are likely to be very badly received when and if you return to Bushfield!"

"But of course I am returning to Bushfield. I must go back. I have nowhere else I could possibly go, in any case!"

"Herr Arbitant! You have been under scrutiny here. Many very important people have been taking considerable interest in you. We have come to the conclusion that your considerable talents are being wasted. You have potential qualities of leadership and initiative that we and some important countrymen of yours believe can be better employed in the interests of your country. Would you like to meet some of these eminent people?"

"Well, yes, I am sure I should. But you are not suggesting I should engage in some kind of treasonable activity are you? I should never agree to that!"

"No! Definitely not! We should not wish to be associated with anything like that. But it is scarcely treason to belong to a legitimate organisation seeking to pursue openly declared objectives for patriotic purposes, is it?"

"No, that is true," replied Harold, impressed by the logic of the response.

"Then come along with me," said Von Rohrbach.

They walked along the corridor and stopped at the door of Room 100. Von Rohrbach knocked and an educated English voice bade them enter. In the room, under the chairmanship of a most eminent British politician, whom Harold recognised at once, were seated a number of well known people, from academe, politics, business, even religion. The chairman looked up and said, "Ah, Mr. Arbitant, we had been expecting you. Welcome to the Aryan Friendship Society! Would you care to take a seat, please?"

Obediently, almost as though mesmerised, Harold drew up a chair at the table and found himself seated between two people of such importance that he had never dreamed of meeting them. They both smiled at him encouragingly. The meeting proceeded. Von Rohrbach withdrew and returned to his office.

"There will be no problem with him!" he said to Schumacher.

For the next ten days Harold never went outside the embassy. He slept and ate there. His mentor was Schumacher. He attended endless seminars. He spoke with people he had never thought he would be able to meet on terms approaching equality. He was briefed on the new vision they had for Britain and Europe.

The increasingly frantic enquiries about him, first from the school, and then from his parents, were met by the embassy with bland denials as to any knowledge as to what had happened to him after he had, so they said, left the building. The receptionist said he had certainly left and produced her register to show the time he had checked out. The police, having no right of entry to the embassy, were unable to make any progress. He seemed to have vanished into thin air.

At the end of his indoctrination period Harold was seen by another official. "Would you like to visit Germany, as our guest, Herr Arbitant?"

"Very much, but I have no passport! I have never been out of England!"

"That is no problem. Herr Schumacher will see to everything. He will go with you."

On October 25th, 1938, Harold was on a German merchant ship bound for Hamburg. On November the first he found himself lodged in a comfortable apartment, with Schumacher for company, in Munich.

For a week thereafter the round of seminars, organised visits to places of interest and indoctrination into Nazism continued. All these were being attended by highly educated and interesting people from English speaking countries. There were twenty-five of them in the group altogether. They were closely thrown together and, perhaps for the very first time in his life, he found himself accepted without question. There was no shortage of funds. He was, in short, happy.

He made no attempt to contact either the school or his parents. This was just as well, had he known it. His activities were being closely monitored by the Gestapo which was taking a great interest in the activities of the group and certainly had no intention of allowing any of them to return to their home countries without their express agreement, which, for the time being, they had no intention of giving. As it was the Gestapo reports on him were excellent.

PART THREE - STORM

CHAPTER THIRTY SEVEN

BRECK

It was late in March, 1938, that Von Rohrbach, already very prominent in the Nazi Party, was invited to attend a high level Gestapo conference in Vienna. He had been given special responsibility for rooting out subversive elements in the newly integrated Austrian dominions of the Greater Reich. He was more particularly concerned with the Jewish underground and their international links, especially in Britain. It was this interest which, in due course, caused him to establish a special section devoted to this work in the German embassy in London.

Whilst attending this conference in Vienna he re-encountered someone he had first met during the Great War. This was a man called Fritz Breck, an Austrian peasant farmer, who had served in the ranks of the regiment in which Von Rohrbach had been an officer. Both, in 1917, had been nineteen years old and both had emerged from the defeat smarting with indignation at the humiliations inflicted on their countries by the victorious Allied powers. Subsequently both had eagerly adhered to the new party founded by Adolf Hitler.

After the Anschluss Breck's long loyalty to the party was well rewarded and he achieved high rank in the Gestapo, being based in Klagenfurt in Carinthia. Thereafter there were very few, if any, people in that area who would have dared to incur his displeasure.

By virtue of this appointment Breck was invited to attend the Vienna conference. The two recognised each other immediately, notwithstanding their different social backgrounds and the intervening period of time since they had last met. They greeted each other like long lost friends. Thrown together in this way they became intimate. So much so that Breck relaxed his usual caution and told his newly found friend of a personal problem which he had never before mentioned to another living soul.

"I have," he said one evening, whilst they were drinking together, "a problem on which I should much appreciate your advice. I have a sister called Heidi and she is the only person in the world about whom I really care. She is, however, seriously mentally retarded. She lives with my mother, whom I heartily detest, on her own, for my father died last year. We have, you see, a small family farm, which lies, in a very remote position, some distance from Klagenfurt.

Now, you Herr Von Rohrbach, are as aware as I am, that it is the policy of the party to purify our race and eliminate people such as my sister. I live in absolute terror that, remote and difficult to find as the farmhouse may be, that one of these days somebody will report her to the authorities and demand action. If that happened I should be in a very difficult position, would I not?"

"How do you provide for them without attracting attention to your sister's condition, then?"

"I have made an arrangement with a Klagenfurt provision merchant, who is greatly in my debt for certain reasons, and whom I know I can trust. Every week he takes a regular supply up to the farm, which he leaves in a hut at the end of the track which leads up to the house. Nobody but this man ever goes anywhere near the farmhouse. I, myself, do not visit them all that frequently. In fact, as I was told only this morning, I have been promoted to a position of much greater responsibility in Munich and my visits will become even fewer than they have been until now."

"Whilst I sympathise, I still do not understand exactly what is your problem? You seem to have her well hidden. Unless somebody finds her, which seems unlikely from what you tell me, she seems safe enough."

"My wretched mother, who has never wanted to be burdened with Heidi and would be only too glad to denounce her and thus be rid of her, continuously complains that she is left on her own to do everything. She wants me to provide her with assistance. You will appreciate that, were I to agree to such a course of action, I should at once make myself vulnerable to blackmail by somebody outside the family. In addition Heidi's condition renders her of uncertain temper, she is very strong and subject to occasional bouts of violence."

"I believe I may be able to suggest a possible solution! You may have to wait a while before you can put it into execution though. Perhaps a few months. It so happens that a short time ago I was privileged to attend a very secret meeting that was addressed by Herr Himmler himself. In the course of this meeting he told us that his eventual plan for the remaining Jewish able-bodied population of the Reich was to create a slave force to put to work in industry and agriculture, thus making an economic asset out of what would otherwise merely be a useless liability. Perhaps we could use such an idea for your private advantage!"

"This is very interesting but, with the greatest respect, Herr Von Rohrbach, I do not follow your proposal. How could this be used to solve my problem?"

"I also happen to know that, as soon as the right opportunity presents itself, there is going to be a great purge of Jewish elements still remaining here, throughout the Reich. We still have to be patient as, unfortunately, it is necessary to pay some attention to international opinion, misguided as it may be. One of the cities which would be especially affected in such a situation would, as it happens, be Munich, where you are going to be in a position of great influence from now on. My proposal is that you select some suitable Jewish person, I suggest a woman would be better for your purpose. When the inevitable riots take place then, under cover of the ensuing confusion, and with my assistance, you could engineer her "disappearance" to your farm without exciting any comment. From then on your mother would have her own private slave force, nobody would be any wiser, and the existence of your sister would remain a secret!"

"It would certainly provide a solution! I shall look into the matter as soon as I take over in Munich!"

"Keep in touch with me in London. Together we can make it work for you. The English have a saying, you know, "Needs must where the Devil drives!" and you are being driven by your devil of a mother, it seems!"

"I certainly am!" laughed Breck.

Breck went away and thought about the idea. The more he thought about it the more he determined to see it through.

He scanned the files that appeared every morning on his desk. In May his attention became focused on one marked "Aronberg". This stated that three Jewesses, the wives of three Jews arrested earlier that month in Berlin, and now all in Dachau, had fled to Munich and taken up residence with a relation, a well-known local commercial figure in Munich, a Jew turned Christian, called Eli Aronberg. He was instructed to keep this household under close surveillance. The business which had been operated from the premises had been effectively closed down. For the time being, however, for reasons not vouchsafed to him, the family still resident there themselves had not been so far molested.

He examined the file closely and discovered that the youngest of the three women, called Rachel Hands, was twenty-five. "She will undoubtedly be in good physical shape and is just the right age!" he thought to himself. Subsequent investigations confirmed him in this view. He earmarked her as his victim.

By October that year the position at the farm was becoming desperate. His last visit had been extremely difficult. Heidi was having more frequent violent fits and his mother was adamant that she was going to denounce her.

"I cannot cope with her any longer, Fritz! She has to go!"

He bullied his mother into waiting a month.

"I have a plan, you must wait a month! I can make things very unpleasant for you here if you defy me! Do what I say!"

"Right! One month, then I shall go into Klagenfurt and tell them about her! I'm not frightened of you!".

He rang Von Rohrbach on the private line he had been told to use at the London embassy. "Are these "developments" likely to occur soon? The situation at the farm is desperate. My mother has given me one month to find her some help or she is going to the authorities in Klagenfurt. I cannot think of any way I can prevent her carrying out her threat!"

"Have you found a suitable candidate for the position?"

"Yes! A woman called Rachel Hands."

"You could not have selected anybody more suitable! I know all about her and her family. She is a member of Eli Aronberg's household, is she not?"

"Do you know everything?" said Breck, much impressed

"Yes, I know most things! Remember that! However, as I have just said, you could not have made a better choice. I have a personal score to settle with members of that family. Just be patient and keep your mother at the farm. Things will happen very shortly, trust me! I shall be in Munich the first week in November. Just wait for me."

Early on Wednesday, November the ninth, 1938, the news broke that a deranged Polish Jew, a man called Grynsban, had shot and killed a Third Secretary, an official called Von Rath, at the German embassy in Paris. This was the long awaited excuse and signal for an outbreak of unprecedented violence throughout Germany against the Jewish population.

That night appalling acts were perpetrated, Munich being particularly badly affected. A horrified reporter for the London "Times" wrote:

"seldom had [such acts] had their equal in a civilized country since the Middle Ages"

In the midst of these disturbances Von Rohrbach, who had meanwhile arrived in Munich with Schumacher, and was staying with Breck at his house there, having made carefully thought out plans to carry out their scheme, acted. He took some plain clothed storm troopers, Schumacher and Breck and two unmarked trucks. In these they went to Eli's mansion.

"I want them all taken alive, if you can, but especially I want the youngest woman, named Rachel Hands, brought to me, as unharmed as possible. I have something special in store for her!"

The storm troopers, misinterpreting his intentions, grinned at each other.

CHAPTER THIRTY EIGHT

DISAPPEARANCE

Apprehensively Eli, in Munich, answered a light knock on his door. There on his doorstep were Naomi, Rebecca and Rachel.

"The men have all been arrested, Eli!" sobbed Naomi falling into his arms. "We came here, hoping against hope that you would still be safe, as we could not think of anything else to do."

"But where is Elisabeth?"

"The Prestons took her back to England with them," said Rachel. "It was all arranged, fortunately, for her to go for a holiday with them. I waited at the airport and there didn't seem to be any trouble about her being allowed to embark. Oh, dear, I would like to know she has arrived safely though! I was hoping there would be some news here for me from Leeds."

"So that's the meaning of the message I've received. It was from the Prestons but I couldn't understand it. It said, "Package arrived safely".

"Oh, thank God! Elisabeth is safely with them.""

"I have paid off all the staff. The business has been closed down." said Eli."The Gestapo is certain to know you are here with me. We shall have to wait and see what transpires."

Increasingly venomous articles attacking the Jewish population appeared daily in the newspapers. They heard, via former business contacts, that the three men had been consigned to Dachau and that the Charlottenburg house had been sequestrated but, beyond that, nothing. They lived in a state of perpetual dread.A month went by. Then, on November the ninth, terrible rioting suddenly erupted, stirred up by the assassination in Paris of a junior German embassy official there by a deranged Polish Jewish refugee. The police and fire services stood by and did nothing. Rioters roamed the streets unchecked. The pavements were deep in smashed glass. Jewish owned premises, business and private, were on fire, being looted by apparently otherwise ordinary people, egged on by uniformed Hitler Youth. Dispossessed families were wandering the streets. Hitler Youth, often mere schoolchildren, were chanting," Germany awake! Death to Judah!"

It was rumoured than an edict had been issued expelling all Jews from Munich.

The four of them, alone in the great house, gathered in the morning room and listened in terror to the every nearing tumult of the mob.

"We must put ourselves in the hands of God!" said Naomi.

Eli had quietly slipped out of the room. He went to his study and opened the safe.

From this he took out a loaded revolver and then returned to the women, with it concealed in one of his pockets. . Then he suddenly pulled it out. His intention was obvious.

Rachel screamed out "No, Eli, no! I have Elisabeth to consider!" She had fled from the room before they could have stopped her, even if they had attempted. There was no time left. Tumult was practically at the gates. Eli shot Naomi and Rebecca through the back of their heads and then, putting the barrel in his mouth, himself. Almost as he fell the door of the room flew open and Von Rohrbach and his party entered.

Behind them were the four storm troopers. Another had been posted outside to deflect the crowd. This he moved on to another house to loot. Von Rohrbach inspected the three corpses. Then he said to the waiting storm troopers, "There is another woman, still in the house. If she is alive bring her here to me, as unharmed as you can, quickly!"

Rachel was cowering in the study, and made no attempt to conceal herself. She was dragged into the morning room, and stumbled over her mother's dead body. In so doing she knocked against Breck, who roughly slapped her back, knocking her over by the force of the blow so that she fell on to Eli's blood covered corpse.

"Put a sack over her head and take her out to the first truck! Put her in the back and tie her up!"

She was hustled out.

"This house is now the property of the German people! Put up a notice to that effect and see everything here remains undisturbed. Take these four bodies out to the back. Pour petrol over them and burn them, then distribute the remains all over the area!"

"But, sir," said the senior storm trooper, "there are only three bodies!"

"I said there were four! Surely you can count, man! If you can't you aren't fit for your rank! How many bodies are there?"

"Four, sir!" said the bewildered storm trooper.

"That's right! Four! Make sure you say four when you make your report to me!"

"Heil Hitler!" said the man, saluting him.

The bodies were dragged from the room into the garden.

"The advantages of German military discipline, as I have said before, are manifest!" said Von Rohrbach to Schumacher.

Then he continued, "Breck here and I will deal with the woman from here on, Schumacher. You return to your duties and see what Arbitant and the others are doing. I have given orders that none of them are to be allowed out of their quarters this evening. I hope nobody disobeyed. I order you to say nothing about what you have seen here tonight, to anybody, at any time. And remember that there were four bodies discovered when we entered the house. Those of three women, all murdered by the criminal Eli, and his own, dead by his own hand. Is that clear?"

"Heil Hitler!" said Schumacher, saluting him.

He left the room and returned to his quarters.

Left on their own Von Rohrbach said to Breck, "As I have said just now, behold the advantages of German discipline! He will never reveal anything other than the discovery by us of four corpses, none of them killed by us!"

Then he and Breck went out to the waiting truck. Rachel was slumped in the back, the sack pulled over her head and pinioning her arms and hands. Her feet had been securely fastened. They ignored her once they had satisfied themselves she was still alive and completely helpless.

"I shall drive!" said Von Rohrbach to the stormtroopers. "You report back to your corporal. But remember you have not seen this woman! Is that clear! If you say anything about this to anybody, anybody, mind you, you will have me to answer to and I shall make my business to see that you regret it."

"Heil Hitler!" said the two storm troopers, saluting. Then they returned to the grisly cremation in the garden of the house.

"The advantages of German discipline, again! If you cannot trust them, then terrify them!" said Von Rohrbach.

Breck looked at him admiringly.

"Well, Mother is waiting!" he grinned. "Let 's hope she hasn't lost patience. I should hate to think it had all been a waste of time!"

"Well, it has been exciting, hasn't it!" said Von Rohrbach as he drove off.

CHAPTER THIRTY NINE

DARKNESS

The officer who was in charge of the airstrip for which they now headed was deeply obliged to Von Rohrbach, as were so many other potentially useful people, for past and, so he hoped, future favours. He could be absolutely trusted by him. He had agreed, well in advance, to have a suitable small 'plane waiting.

"The whole of this operation is top secret!" Von Rohrbach had impressed upon him. "Speak about what you see to absolutely nobody!"

"You can rely on me!"

Rachel, still hidden from view inside the sack, was rapidly bundled on board and the pilot took off with his three passengers. It was only a relatively short trip to the secret airstrip just outside Vienna. Here a car was waiting in readiness. Nobody present dared, or for that matter even wished, to enquire what was going on. Breck was well known here. There was a short delay whilst Rachel was allowed to have something to eat and drink and walk around for a while, well out of view of anybody other than Breck and Von Rohrbach, who never left her on her own for a moment's privacy.

""We don't want her dead!" said Von Rohrbach, "What a waste of effort that would be!"

Then the car took off, driven in turns by Von Rohrbach and Breck. It was a very long way and the roads, for the most part, were by no means good. They stopped only infrequently. Rachel, slumped across the back seat was mercilessly bumped up and down but they took no notice of her whatsoever.

After an absolute eternity, during which she passed out from sheer exhaustion, the car finally arrived at their destination and turned into the muddy track which led up to the remote farmhouse. In the distance the frantic barking of dogs could be heard.

At last the car finally came to a halt in front of the house. The dogs were two gigantic black alsatians, tethered by ropes to wooden posts in the farmyard. They snarled ferociously at Von Rohrbach, a stranger to them. Normally these animals roamed loose on the property, a most effective deterrent to any intruder. Frau Breck, however, had heard the sound of the approaching vehicle and taken the precaution of tying them up.

The door of the house opened and Frau Breck, with Heidi peering out from behind her, emerged to meet them. Frau Breck's sixty-four years had not been kind to her, they had been long and arduous. What small amount of human kindness she might have possessed had long since evaporated. She was tall, gaunt and weather-beaten. Her once flaxen hair had turned a dirty grey and hung down over her fierce blue eyes in unwashed straggles. She was wearing a shapeless dress and heavy and very dirty farm boots. Heidi, who appeared to be little more than an almost shapeless mass of flesh, was similarly clad. She hovered behind her mother, obviously pleased to see her brother, yet scared in the presence of the visitor.

"This is my friend, Herr Rudolf Von Rohrbach!"

Heidi pushed past her mother and struck Von Rohrbach with her open hand across his back. He staggered forward, reeling under the force of the blow.

"Oh, take no notice!" said Breck, "She is only saying "Hullo!" to you!"

"My God!" said Von Rohrbach. " Do you mean to say you have put me to all this trouble to preserve that! My sympathies lie with your mother!"

"You see the sort of treatment I have to put up with?" cackled Frau Breck. "That's why I want something done about her!"

"I have brought you some help, mother!"

Frau Breck looked around. "I can't see any help!" Her gaze fell on Von Rohrbach. "He wouldn't be any use!" she said, eyeing him contemptuously. "Are you mocking me again? I'm still capable of giving you a good thrashing, you know!" She advanced on her son threateningly, evidently with every intention of doing just that.

Breck just stood and laughed at the furious woman. "I do assure you, mother, I have brought help for you! We'll show it to you later! Let's eat first. We are both famished!"

They entered the filthy house. There was certainly no lack of food or alcohol. The Klagenfurt merchant had seen to that. Every week the two women took a wheelbarrow down to the hut at the end of the track and collected the provisions he had left for them, first of all making quite sure there was no one around to see them. He had instructions never to approach the house, not that he would willingly have done so in any event, for fear of the dogs.

They sat down to an ample if not particularly appetising meal, at least from Von Rohrbach's viewpoint. He had never before in his life been entertained in such a disgusting place.

"Well? Where's this help you have brought me?" she asked at last.

"It is in the back of the car, mother! Come outside and we'll show it to you!"

Mystified, Frau Breck went out to the yard and stared at the car.

"All I can see in the back of your car is a bundle of rags!" she announced.

"It's a kind of intelligent animal, mother. You'll find it can do everything, once you've trained it! It just needs enough food to keep going. It can sleep with the dogs, once they accept it! We don't want them killing it, do we? That would be a waste! After all the trouble we've had getting it for you! There is one condition, though! You are on no account to let anybody know you have it. If anybody ever comes here you are to hide it away in the cellar and not let it out until they have left. If you don't do that the supplies will stop! I mean it! Then you would both starve!"

"But what and where is this thing? What have you brought me? Some kind of trained monkey?"

"No, mother, not a monkey! We have brought you this!"

So saying he opened the back door of the car and pulled out Rachel, still in the sack.

He proceeded to rip this covering off with his jack-knife and removed the shackles from her legs. She lay prostrate on the ground. She was dying of thirst, starving and absolutely traumatised.

"There!" he said proudly displaying the wretched Rachel, giving her prostrate body a kick, "that's it!"

"Why, it's a young woman!"

"That isn't a woman. That's a Jewess! Your very own slave! She'll do anything you tell her. If she doesn't then beat her! But don't kill her! I expect to find her alive and able to work every time I come. I've been to a lot of trouble to get her for you! Don't ever forget that nobody else is to know you have her! Everybody would want one!"

"What is she called?" said Frau Breck. The idea of having a slave appealed to her. It seemed a fine idea.

"Call her "Scum!" suggested Von Rohrbach.

"Scum", said Frau Breck." That's a good name." She turned to Heidi. "This is "Scum" she said to the girl, "She is going to look after us. We won't have to do any work any more. Say "Hello" to her, Heidi."

Heidi came over and looked at the prostrate Rachel. "Why is she lying on the ground?" she said. "Get up!" She gave Rachel a hard kick. But Rachel could not get up.

"Oh, leave her!" said Breck. "I'll put some food and water over by the door in one of the old dog's dishes. She'll get herself over to it when she sees it, soon enough."

"Then I'll introduce her to the dogs!" said Frau Breck. "Once they know she is meant to be here and know her smell she'll be alright with them. Then she can sleep with them in their kennel."

She was right. The dogs did accept her. They soon proved to be the only friends she had. From that date she slept with them and shared their food with them. She washed herself as best she could at the farmyard pump, winter and summer. Her hair hung matted and uncut. Her nails wore away. Her hands became callused with work. She did everything on the farm. She collected the provisions. She cleaned the house. She washed the clothes. She tilled the field. She tended the dogs. There was nothing she did not do. Frau Breck began to look quite well dressed and even Heidi 's appearance improved. Heidi still had her attacks of violence but it was now Rachel who bore the brunt of them. Rachel looked like a scarecrow, but Frau Breck, mindful of her son's warning, made sure she had enough to eat and was always able to work, although she was also generous with her blows.

Quickly Rachel came to terms with the situation. She had heard of conditions in the concentration camps from somebody she had met, who had once been in one. She reflected that her condition was probably no worse and possibly even better than those of many others. "At least I am still alive", she told herself, "and one day, I promise myself, I shall see Elisabeth again. "And so, clinging to that thought as a lifeline, for endless year upon year, with no knowledge of what was happening in the outside world, she endured her pitiless captivity. Very, very occasionally Frau Breck had reason to think somebody was coming up the track and at once threw her, none too gently, into the cellar in complete blackness. She was taking no chances with the supplies. Usually the alarm turned out to be a surprise visit from Breck, whereupon she was unceremoniously summoned up to be inspected by him before being kicked out of the house to resume her labours.

The house, the farmyard and the field began to assume a cared for look.

Even Heidi began to respond to her. The dogs were inseparable from her. Only Frau Breck remained impervious. Her soul was encased in steel.

For Rachel there was always the vision of once again seeing

Elisabeth. She was sure she had been spared for that reason. Every night, when she sank down exhausted beside the dogs, she tried to concentrate her mind on that thought and that was her rod and staff through those terrible, apparently endless, years of torment.

CHAPTER FORTY

CONFLICT

By April, 1939, it was quite evident to all thinking people that war between Britain and Germany was increasingly likely. The now Lieutenant Colonel Sir George Threlfall was working hard with his second in command, Major Wisley, on mobilisation plans for their Territorial battalion of the Prince's Own Carbines. The previous month Wisley had made it clear to the Governors of Bushfield Abbey that he would no longer be able to continue as headmaster if full mobilisation were to be declared, as he now expected to be the case. It had then been agreed, as he had always anticipated, that in such an event Dr. Williams would be invited to resume as acting headmaster "for the duration".

Wisley summoned another staff meeting at the school at the end of that month.

He told the silent and attentive audience, "In the event of the outbreak of hostilities many of us here, all volunteer members of the Territorials, are more than likely to find ourselves engaged on active service very shortly thereafter. My own assessment of the situation is that it is not unlikely that we may discover that this year's summer camp prolongs itself into permanent service for the duration of a war. As you will all know by now Parliament has already enacted a Conscription Act and, with certain exceptions, everybody between 18 and 41 is now liable for military service. Of course Territorial Army units would be mobilised automatically. We must be prepared.

So far as Bushfield Abbey is concerned the school would immediately lose the services not only of myself but also of Mr. Cumberworth, Mr. Franks, and Mr. Fellows, who already all serve with me in the P.O.C.s. Both Polesden and Jason have made it clear to me they would at once postpone their university careers and join me.

Dr. Williams has volunteered to return and re-assume the acting headship during my absence, if it becomes necessary.

The rest of you will have to pick up the burden, lay aside retirement plans in some cases, and thus play your part in the national effort."

When the meeting ended he was approached by Tom Riding. "Could you find a place for Bill with you, sir? As you know he is in the regular battalion, but he would much rather be with you!"

"I shall speak to his commanding officer this afternoon, Tom. I think you can anticipate that he will agree to the transfer. By the way, Tom, I hope you both realise that, when the time comes, your position can be passed on to Bill, if he would like to have it!"

Preston and Hyslow, both approaching eighteen, left the meeting discussing their own plans.

"Shall we postpone university and volunteer right away, like Polesden and Jason?" said Hyslow.

"I don't think it will last that long! Polesden and Jason were both going to read classics, just as John would have done. We are going to train to be scientists. I think there is going to be a great need for young scientists. They are certain to cut the length of the university courses, in any event. I think we should graduate and then join up, if there is still a war on then!"

"My ordination will have to be shelved for the time being!" He spoke with a certain satisfaction. He had resigned himself to his church career, but he felt that his parents might have consulted him before committing him to it. He was determined to graduate in science first and he had no intention of serving in the forces as a chaplain, not that he anticipated the war lasting long enough for that to ever become even a possibility.

At Loughbourne George and Ann assembled the staff in the drawing room.

"If mobilisation is ordered I shall be leaving to take up command of my battalion of the Prince's Own Carbines. In that event I shall entrust the management of the estate to her ladyship, assisted, of course, by Mr. Morton."

Alan Morton was now fifty-nine.

"Mr.Henry Morton, together with Donald Mitchell, will be coming with me, as will the Reverend Alexander Tapping, who will be joining the battalion as our chaplain."

Jameson, who was unfit for active service, would be staying on at the manor, for the time being.

As the staff dispersed Janet and Donald approached George and Ann.

"May we have a word, please your ladyship?"

"Certainly, Donald, what can I do for you both?"

"Me and Janet would like to get wed before I have to go, if I have to go, that is!"

"That is wonderful! Congratulations! We'll do everything here! We'll pay for everything!" said Ann. Then, to the delight of all the staff, she gave Janet a kiss, causing the embarrassed young woman to turn scarlet.

"You will look after him, Sir George?" she said anxiously.

Her naive question broke the tension. Everybody laughed.

"Wherever I go, Donald will go, Janet! He is coming as my personal driver! Are you not, corporal?"

Activity was also proceeding in Leeds. Sir Francis, just thirty-nine, had conceived the idea that his excellent command of German might be put to good use in some way. Accordingly he telephoned a friend, high up in the War Office, and put the idea to him.

The man at the War Office was enthusiastic. "I think I know just the right thing for you, Francis! Could you come down to London and see me? I shall then introduce you to somebody right up your alley!"

Francis walked down the long corridor at the War Office later that month, accompanied by his friend. They came to a halt at a door marked "Intelligence". In response to his escort's knock a gruff voice called out "Enter!" There, sitting behind a large desk, was a florid faced man in the uniform of a major.

"This is Sir Francis Preston, of whom I spoke to you briefly a few days ago, Major Tomkins. He speaks excellent German and may, perhaps, be of some assistance to you in your special section."

"Leave him with me".

Tomkins rose and came forward with outstretched hand. "Tell me, Sir Francis, do you have any first hand knowledge of Germany?"

"Well, as you may perhaps have been told, I run a large textile business..." began Francis.

"Yes, Sir Francis, I think there can be few people in this country who do not know Prestons Textiles!" smiled Tomkins.

Much encouraged by this acknowledgement of his firm's prestige Francis continued, "We have now, for very many years, operated an arrangement with a German firm of textile merchants called Aronbergs. The business we conducted with them was so important that my wife and I, together with our little daughter, used to visit them, at their home and headquarters, in the Charlottenburg district of Berlin, very frequently. That, in fact, is how I acquired my knowledge of German. Our last visit there was in May, 1938. We then brought home with us a daughter of one of the junior directors. She was the same age as our own daughter. and they were great friends. She was to spend a few weeks with us in Leeds"

He paused for a moment.

"This had very strange consequences", he continued. "Do you wish me to tell you about them?"

"Very much, if you do not object, Sir Francis."

Francis told Tomkins the entire story.

Tomkins heard him out to the end. Then he said, "Now, I shall tell you a story, Sir Francis!"

He proceeded to tell the astonished Francis of Sarah's enquiries and what he had discovered as a result of them.

Francis listened incredulously. "I simply cannot understand why Sarah Threlfall, who is the mother of George, and whom I have known since childhood, should be interested in the Aronberg family! It is an absolute mystery to me! By the way, were you aware that George's boy, John, died in a rather strange accident at Bushfield Abbey School last October, shortly after Sarah's own death? A very strange business! Well! Well! Do you know, now I think of it, Ann, George's wife, has German ancestry, very aristocratic I believe."

He reflected on this last comment for a while and then added, "Do you know, Sarah's maiden name was Avondale! George once asked me to witness a document for some reason and I happened to notice it! There's a kind of similarity, isn't there? Avondale and Aronberg! I wonder whether Avondale is an Anglicisation of the German? Perhaps there is a family connection and there is Jewish blood in her family? That could explain her interest, couldn't it?"

Tomkins, very intrigued by this theory, diplomatically decided it was time to change the subject. He wanted more time to think about all this new information.

"Would you mind if we continued this some other time, Sir Francis? For the moment let us just complete the matter you came to see me about. We need well-connected expert linguists with knowledge of various countries, especially Germany. The work here is vital and could entail some degree of personal danger. It seems obvious we are going to get along famously. Would you consider joining me?"

"I should be delighted!"

"I shall be in touch as soon as matters are sorted out, mere formalities!"

They shook hands and parted.

But Tomkins immediately put in hand certain investigations. Within a few days he had uncovered the entire Sarah story. For the moment he was unsure of its significance and usefulness. The newly adopted daughter of his future assistant was, he now knew, Sarah's great great niece.

In the meanwhile Francis had returned to Leeds where he had at once paid a visit on the chairman, Horace.

"Horace, if war comes, and I think it is more or less a certainty now, you are going, I fear, to have to take a more active part in the management! I shall shortly be joining a special section at the War Office! Don't worry too much. You can have Petworth to carry you." Petworth was the company secretary and knew the business backwards. At the age of sixty he was exempt from call-up. "Jessica and Penelope can be appointed directors! Too many women but that's the price of war!"

"Oh, well!" said Horace, reluctantly, "Needs must where the devil drives! I just wish I could have had Gordon to help me! But maybe there won't be a war!"

"Oh, yes, there will!" said Francis

Five months later he was proved correct. By that time he was already with Tomkins engaged on highly secret work at the War Office. Tomkins, however, decided to remain silent about his researches into the intriguing Aronberg affair. There were other pressing matters requiring their attention. He did not wish to distract his new colleague. He felt sure, however, that the information would ultimately prove to be of considerable importance.

PART FOUR - BRIGHTENING

CHAPTER FORTY ONE

ENLIGHTENMENT

By the close of November, 1938, it had been become painfully apparent to Harold that in politics, as in everything else, there was a world of difference between theory and practice. The foreign members of the AFS had all been kept locked in their quarters during the November the ninth riots, but the after effects were only too apparent. In any event they had been able to see the rioting through their windows, and the noise had been audible, to say the least. They did not discuss what they had seen but he, for his part, was filled with revulsion. This was quickly detected by Schumacher.

"You English never have the stomach to see anything right through to its logical conclusion! I remember that saying of yours, "Put your money where your mouth is!" What is the good of professing adherence to the tenets of a philosophy if, when it comes to action, you find you cannot proceed? You English are all theory and no action! Frankly I despise the English part of myself! Fortunately both my parents were of pure German descent. If that hadn't been the case I could never have become a party member, let alone had my present rank!"

This diatribe sickened Harold. Until he had been confronted with the realities behind Nazism he had been in a state almost bordering on mesmerism. He was amazed to find how shocked he had been by what he had been able to discover. However, he had by now realised the very difficult and dangerous position in which he had been placed by his own folly. He was possessed by an absolute determination to extricate himself and return to Britain, whatever fate might await him there, but realised that to do this he would meanwhile have to play a cunning and cautious game. He grimly concluded that he now had no other course open to him but to prevaricate.

"Well, serious errors were made in 1919 by the Allied Powers but we must forget all that now, get together and create a new kind of Europe. There is no point in raking over old embers, is there? For goodness sake don't let you and I fall out over what is, after all, simply an internal policing matter?" he replied in a placatory manner.

But Schumacher had not yet finished. "In any event it was American power, backed by Jewish money, that won the last war! Even your so-called British Empire was accumulated by skulduggery and thievery, by unprincipled rogues like Clive of India, Rhodes, and, above all, that Jew you all admired so much, Disraeli!"

It was apparent to Harold that Schumacher had for some reason worked himself up into a rage. Perhaps, he surmised, he too had been disturbed by events he had actually witnessed that night and was using this opportunity to convince himself that they had been justified. He replied, therefore, in what he hoped was a diplomatic fashion.

" I made it quite clear when I joined the AFS that I did so in order to help to convince my fellow countrymen that they should adopt and support the system of government advocated by them and you, by all legitimate means at my disposal. Those are still my intentions. I don't understand why you are speaking to me like this."

"You didn't like what you saw and heard to be happening on November the ninth, did you?" responded Schumacher, reverting to his original theme." Why was that?"

"You seem to overlook the fact that I didn't actually see anything. Obviously I knew there was rioting and that it was provoked by the murder of one of your diplomats in Paris by a Jew. Surely you would agree that the rioting did seem to get rather out of hand, though?"

"I don't need to explain or defend anything that happened that night to you!" responded Schumacher hotly. " Ordinary people were justifiably outraged by the support given to the perpetrator of that foul murder by the Jews of this and other cities of the Reich and elsewhere. The Party supports such popular expressions of outrage. It acts always in the best interests of the German people. Any actions which directly flow from that concept must therefore be justified automatically!"

"You are attributing ideas to me which I am very far from holding," lied Harold. "Why do you think I came over here in the first place?"

By this time Schumacher was beginning to have second thoughts. Recruiting Harold into the AFS was, to a great extent, his own responsibility and, for the moment, something for which he had been accorded a good deal of credit. To denounce him for no good reason would serve no useful purpose and would, more than likely, be held against him as a serious error of judgement. He decided to make his peace with him.

"I accept your explanation, Harry," he said stiffly. "I agree you have behaved loyally and done fine work for the AFS. I do feel strongly about these matters, you understand?"

"Indeed, as do I!"

Solemnly they shook hands.

Harold had been given a well-paid position with the AFS Secretariat. This organisation was, in actual fact, notwithstanding its ostensible pretensions, totally funded by the Gestapo. Harold honestly if naively still believed it existed simply to co-ordinate the efforts of Nazi and Fascist sympathisers world-wide, and particularly within the Empire and Commonwealth, to ensure continued peaceful coexistence with the German and Italian regimes and give support to Franco in Spain. The real purpose the Gestapo had in mind was to create a gigantic and very effective international espionage network. The AFS was directed by Herr Heinrich Schimmelpfennig, who had his headquarters in Munich, and to whom Harold was acting as personal assistant.

Harold had been persuaded to join the AFS, as had most of his fellow members, by a mixture of flattery and false promises. Thereafter nobody had felt able to voice openly any subsequent misgivings. Not one of them had, it seemed, been able to accept that their actions might be verging on the treasonable. "It is not as though we are at war!" was the stock argument.

Schimmelpfennig went to great pains to labour this point.

"Herr Arbitant, your countrymen are being deluded and betrayed by international Jewry and communism! Your invaluable work here helps to provide a counterbalance and is a patriotic service to your country. You mark my words, a day will soon come when you will be well rewarded by your country for the services you are rendering!"

Harold had heard similar cases put many times before by fellow AFS members. At the outset he had been totally convinced. Now, however, he was in a very difficult, perhaps even, he acknowledged to himself, an impossible position. He had dug a pit for himself and he had no idea how to climb out of it. He was very comfortable. He had plenty of money. To try to return home would certainly raise problems. For one thing he had no passport. It would mean having to answer all sorts of awkward questions. He would, in any case, have the greatest difficulty in finding suitable employment in England. He could scarcely expect a satisfactory reference from Bushfield Abbey. He was, in short, much better off where he was. There seemed to be no alternative but to remain until some opportunity arose to escape, for escaping was what he now realised it meant. So he played his cards cautiously and remained, doing his allotted tasks well.

This was just as well for him. He was under constant scrutiny by the Gestapo. If he had tried to leave he would not have been allowed out of Germany and his ultimate destination would, undoubtedly, have been Dachau. As it was reports on his work were very favourable and he was classified as highly reliable. So much so that soon after Christmas, 1938, he was sent for by Schimmelpfennig.

Schimmelpfennig was in a most unusual state of excitement. He actually smiled at Harold. "I have some excellent news for both of us, Herr Arbitant! It has been decided by Berlin that you and I are to establish the AFS Secretariat within the German Embassy in Berne, Switzerland. We shall be posted there ostensibly as third secretaries, replacing two people who are being brought back to Germany especially to make room for us. It is felt in Berlin we shall be able to operate from Switzerland much more effectively than from Munich. You have been given a diplomatic passport and will have to assume, for this purpose, a different identity. You, obviously, cannot take such an appointment and be seen to be a British citizen. You will be known as Adolf Adenbauer."

"But why have I been selected for such an important assignment? I should have thought there were plenty of genuine German citizens, all good party members, capable of doing such a job!" Harold, whilst absolutely delighted by the idea, had decided it would be much safer to appear to accept cautiously.

"You have been specially recommended by me! You combine ideal qualities. Your German is excellent. English is your native language. You have first class knowledge of the manners and customs of your countrymen. You have been closely observed since you have been here and we know you are trustworthy and first class at your work. You are, it is agreed, ideal for the position. I trust you accept?" Harold had at once realised that residence in Switzerland, even within the German Embassy, could provide him, at last, with the hoped-for chance to escape. "I most certainly do!" he replied enthusiastically. It was early in March, 1939, that Harold and Schimmelpfennig arrived in Berne. On entering the embassy they were immediately ushered into the presence of a very senior official there. For the moment this official completely ignored Harold and addressed himself solely to Schimmelpfennig, almost as though Harold were not present.

"Does this man understand the conditions under which he is allowed to remain here?"

"No, I have said nothing to him, sir! I felt it was better he should be within the embassy precincts before he was told. I was sure you would wish to speak to him yourself!"

"You were correct on all counts! Well done!" Only then did he deign to acknowledge Harold's presence.

"Your devotion to the excellent and important work of the AFS has been noted in Berlin, Herr Adenbauer," he said, addressing Harold by the name by which he would from now on invariably be called by everybody. "You must be aware that here, in Switzerland, outside the embassy, you would not enjoy the kind of security we are able to provide you with in Munich. It is not by any means impossible that there are people in Berne who might recognise you and even attempt to abduct you. This could give rise to problems we wish to avoid at all costs. You will appreciate that British Intelligence would like very much to know what has happened to you. Were you to be discovered here, working under an assumed name, with a German passport, you would, to say the very least, excite a great deal of interest on the part of your own Secret Service! They would have a great number of questions to ask you! For your own safety, therefore, as well as reasons of embassy security, you will, from now on, be strictly confined to the embassy precincts, On no occasion are you to leave the embassy other than in the company of Herr Schimmelpfennig. Such occasions will be limited to AFS essential business, authorised by myself, and, during them, you will never leave Herr Schimmelpfennig's sight. Do I make myself clear?"

With that Harold had to be content. He was made very comfortable. He did not make, and, in any event would not have been allowed to make, any attempt to contact anybody outside the embassy other than in his official capacity as Adenbauer. His temporary assumption of fictional German nationality was an additional cause of concern but he managed to convince himself that, since Britain and Germany were not at war, he had committed no criminal offence of which he could think. So far as he was aware he was doing nothing which could be regarded as treasonable. The AFS, even if he no longer agreed with its views, was, so far as he knew, a perfectly legitimate organisation.

At the end of April, that year, he and Schimmelpfennig listened together to the wireless as Hitler denounced the Anglo-German Naval Treaty. That was the moment he began to realise that there might really be a war. Until then he had convinced himself that the Munich agreement had effectually prevented such an occurrence. He had been insulated from anything other than German propaganda for a long time. Even then Schimmelpfennig assured him he was worrying quite unnecessarily.

"Germany and England will stand together, rock solid, against Bolshevism, Herr Adenbauer!" said Schimmelpfennig, with absolute assurance. "But Germany must have a strong navy!"

At the end of August came the news that Von Ribbentrop had signed the German-Soviet Pact concerning Poland. Harold was genuinely opposed to communism. He felt betrayed. He said so, in no uncertain terms, to Schimmelpfennig.

"Such matters are determined by the Fuhrer himself, Adenbauer! As a loyal subject you must not question such decisions!"

"I am not a German subject!" said Harold rather crossly and unwisely.

"Adenbauer, you are most certainly subject to the Reich! To whom else are you subject?" He did not bother to keep the scorn out of his voice.

On September the third Britain declared war on Germany. Schimmelpfennig listened to the announcement with him.

"Now, my dear Adenbauer!" he said, "The British would really hang you if they caught you here! You are now certainly a traitor in their eyes. You had better double your precautions!"

Harold said nothing but he was now more determined than ever to escape and face the music, whatever might be the legal position. For the moment he could only wait for an opportunity, he was sure one would present itself. He just hoped it would be sooner rather than later. The longer he remained the worse things would look.

Two weeks later the two of them were authorised to make one of their rare excursions outside the embassy to attend a meeting of AFS supporters being held on the other side of the river. For this purpose they were provided with an embassy limousine driven by a chauffeur. The car made its way towards the Kirchenfeldbrucke to cross the Aare. As it entered Helvetiaplatz from Thunstrasse two cars ahead collided and their own car ran into them, coming to an abrupt halt. Simultaneously the car behind them, unable to stop in time, rammed into them. The chauffeur alighted and began to argue with the people in front. The damage to the rear of the limousine had also been considerable and Schimmelpfennig decided to inspect it. He opened the door, saying to Harold as he did so, "You stay where you are! I shall send the chauffeur to find a taxi!"

As he went round to the back of the vehicle Harold, who had not failed to note the British Legation as they had passed 48, Thunstrasse, found himself left on his own and, of course, outside the embassy.

By this time two policemen were on the scene. One was speaking to the furious chauffeur, and the other was deeply engaged with Schimmelpfennig, who had been remonstrating with the driver of the car behind. Very quietly and quickly Harold got out of the car and slipped away up Marienstrasse. He was now only about 600 yards, he calculated, from the British Legation. At that moment, by good fortune, a taxi came by. Frantically, he hailed it. He had a few Swiss francs on him, a precaution always taken when they left the embassy. "The British Legation, 48, Thunstrasse!" he gasped, looking anxiously towards Helvetiaplatz, where the arguing was still in progress. The taxi moved off.

He had thought long and hard what he would do if an opportunity presented itself to escape. He had determined that, in such an eventuality, he would immediately report to the British Legation. He realised that the longer he remained in his present position the worse things would look for him. He had even coined a little catch phrase to 'encourage' himself. "Better a British rope than a German bed." He said this now to himself, half smiling, even in his present predicament, at the sheer crudity of the thought. He was unlikely ever to have a better chance. The embassy would redouble its precautions after this mishap. He might never be allowed outside again.

Once again he had crossed the Rubicon.

CHAPTER FORTY TWO

RECOIL

Francis had finally joined Tomkins at the War Office in July, 1939. He found that the section within which they operated was especially concerned with combating espionage. Within this the now Colonel Tomkins had a special and highly secret department of his own devoted to keeping a close watch on known Nazi and Fascist sympathisers resident in the country. These investigations had immediately caused them to take a very close interest in the activities of the AFS.

"Events are moving rapidly to a climax!" he said to Francis as they listened on the wireless to the announcement that Chamberlain had reaffirmed the British pledge to Poland to honour the treaty signed in May. "The very fact that Hitler had now denounced the Polish Non-Aggression treaty will, at least in my opinion, inevitably lead us into war. All these people who have been openly or clandestinely expressing sympathy with the Axis Powers are going to find themselves in a very difficult position. I think we should be particularly concerned with this AFS. It seems to have attracted some very powerful backers. An intelligence report has just come in that it is now being run from inside the German Embassy in Berne but we do not have enough firm evidence to be certain. The people who are supposed to be running it, ostensibly there as third secretaries, never break cover. It seems to have activities covering the whole of the Empire and Commonwealth and even further afield, including the U.S.A. I think it would be advisable for you and I to pay a visit to our own Legation there and see what we can discover for ourselves."

The following month the news broke of the signature of the German-Soviet Pact. The mobilisation of the British fleet followed quickly. By this time Tomkins and Francis were in Berne. British citizens who had been caught touring Germany, or on business there, or even resident there, were already flooding into Switzerland, on their way home or waiting to see what was going to happen from a safe vantage point. Most of these people were beyond suspicion but, among them, inevitably, were some whose motives for their previous presence in Germany, at such a time, were, at the very least, questionable.

Tomkins had been provided with details of certain persons it was considered should be carefully watched. There was still no actual state of war, Switzerland was firmly neutral, and the whole matter had to be carried out with the greatest diplomacy.

On September the first Germany invaded Poland. Two days later Britain was formally at war with Germany.

On September the fifteenth Tomkins received a message from the legation security chief. "I have a man here, Colonel, you should see at once. He is from the German embassy, here in Berne, but he swears he is really English. He says he has escaped from them and had been held there under duress. I have him under close guard for the moment."

"Have him sent up here immediately!"

Ten minutes later a legation guard brought Harold into Tomkins' office.

"The identity documents you were carrying," Tomkins said to Harold, " clearly state that you are Herr Adolf Adenbauer, a third secretary at your embassy. Yet you have told our chief security officer that you are really a British citizen. You had best explain this extraordinary tale to us."

"My real name," said Harold, " is Harold Arbitant."

"Stop!" said Francis. "Before you say another word. Tell us, what were you doing immediately before you went to Germany?"

"I was teaching at an English public school called Bushfield Abbey, sir."

Francis turned to Tomkins. "I should like us to have a private talk about this matter."

Harold went out with the guard.

"I must tell you, Robert, that I myself was educated at Bushfield Abbey School as were all my family. Although I have never met this Harold Arbitant, whom this man is either impersonating or actually may be, I do have a young cousin, my uncle's boy, who was actually in the house at the school of which he was assistant housemaster. A very strange episode is connected with him. He went up to London, one day, to see somebody in the German embassy on a matter connected with school business. Thereafter he vanished without trace. He was known to be a Nazi sympathiser but nothing was ever discovered."

"Now you mention it I do remember reading some reports about the case. Didn't his disappearance coincide with that mysterious death of George Threlfall's boy, who fell from the school tower? This seems to connect up with that matter which we both discovered we were mixed up in when we first met!"

190

"You mean the Sarah Threlfall and the Aronbergs affair!"

"Yes. After Sarah died the son decided to discontinue the investigations she had asked me to conduct. Then I was brought back into the army and my energies were directed elsewhere. It was not until I had that discussion with you that I began to put two and two together. I have to tell you that I did have some further enquiries made. They yielded some very interesting information, which I felt it better, at the time, not to divulge to you. However, in view of this remarkable development, I shall now tell you what I have learned. You remember you were beginning to speculate as to why Sarah should be interested in the Aronberg family. You mentioned her family name was Avondale and theorised that that might be an Anglicisation of Aronberg, thus explaining her interest and even a Jewish background. It all seemed highly improbable to me but I did decide to follow the matter up. I was concerned because, in the course of my first interview with you, you had told me that you and your wife had brought back with you from Berlin one of the Aronberg children, actually Elisabeth Hands, whom, as I now know, you have since adopted. You know as well as I do that anything like that needs careful checking out."

"Yes, that is why I was completely open about it all from the outset!"

"I discovered you were, to a degree, correct. The fact is that she had changed her name by deed poll. Her maiden name was Aronberg. She was the sister of the Samuel Aronberg you knew in Berlin. Your adopted daughter is her great great niece."

"But why ever did you not tell me all this much earlier?" said the astonished Francis.

"I was in a cleft stick! I realised we both had a great deal of interest in the matter. But yours was personal and mine professional. We have such a close relationship that I felt it was better to keep what I had discovered to myself. I acted with the best intentions, Francis!"

"But why do you select this moment, just when we are about to interrogate this man, whoever he turns out really to be, to reveal all this to me? Do you really feel there is some connection?"

"I admit it may seem a little far-fetched but, in this business, I have learned the more unlikely something is the more often it turns out to be something like the truth, Francis! Yes, I do think there could be a link. It all arises from the order in which these events of which we know took place. At the end of 1938 Von Rohrbach is insulted by the attack which took place at Bushfield. He probably convinced himself it had been masterminded from within the school. Then, I am, of course, only theorising, he in some way discovered about Sarah's parentage. This could have made him connect John Threlfall with the supposed masterminding of the attack, as John would have been half Jewish."

"You say you are only theorising but I know you must feel you have strong grounds on which to base your theory!"

"Their attention would already be focused on John, wouldn't it? They would have learned from Arbitant, when he returned their flag, about the extraordinary attack John had made on it. Then the boy dies by falling from the tower. I know a verdict of accidental death was brought in but it did look rather like suicide, didn't it? They were looking for a mastermind at the school. They could easily have made a search at the Births, Marriages and Deaths registries. They were known to be making systematic searches there. These would have quickly revealed Sarah's background; after all it took my people no time at all to come up with the same information. Anyway, for the sake of this discussion, let us assume that is what happened. This man, Von Rohrbach, a very influential person, whom we now know to have been high in the Gestapo, for this reason decides to initiate a personal vendetta against all Aronbergs. He does some investigations and is informed that the Berlin end of the family has already run into serious trouble. Then he discovers there is a Munich branch and he begins to take a malign interest there."

"Well, this all makes sense but I still don't see where this man Harold Arbitant fits in to the picture!"

"Perhaps he doesn't, but it was he who had been specifically jeopardised by John's destruction of the flag! It was he who had to face the music at the German embassy. If, by that time, Von Rohrbach and this man Schumacher, who was known to work with him, had discovered Lady Sarah's background it seems reasonable to suppose they then revealed it to Arbitant. If they did they might have used that to scare him off from returning to the school. Possibly they recruited him, perhaps into the AFS, and smuggled him out of the country and back to Germany. That would account for this man's extraordinary presence here. Also he may well know more about what happened in Munich to the Aronbergs. Since your adopted daughter's mother was one of those who, we assume, went to Munich after her husband's arrest, that would be of immense concern to you, Francis!"

Francis sat back and digested all this reasoning.

"Right, let's have him back in and see what he has to tell us!"

"Please take a seat, Herr Adenbauer, if that is your correct name, and, starting from the very beginning, give us your version of events," began Tomkins.

As the interrogation proceeded it became increasingly clear that he was indeed Harold Arbitant. His story checked out against all the facts known to them. Tomkins' hypothetical reconstruction of what had happened was accurate it seemed.

"But why on earth did you elect to remain within the London embassy instead of returning to Bushfield?"

"They really convinced me that I was going to be held to blame for John Threlfall's death!"

"But that was plainly nonsensical!"

"They convinced me! I didn't know what else to do! Then they offered me this opportunity to work with the AFS. I genuinely believed this to be a bona fide organisation devoted to promoting accord between the Axis powers and the United Kingdom. At that time I had no idea, and certainly no intention, of leaving the country and going over to live in Germany. I naturally thought I should be working in London. My intention was to resign my position at Bushfield Abbey. Then, when the Munich trip was proposed, I was under the impression it was merely a training session. It never even occurred to me that I would not be able to return. I gave no thought to the passport matter. After all it wasn't as though we were at war nor, since the Munich Agreement, did I think war was likely. It didn't seem to me that merely working for the AFS was in any way treasonable, quite the reverse, in fact."

"If all this is true, and now I really do not know how to address you, you are or were quite remarkably naive! However, let us leave this for the moment. We should like some more details about what happened after you arrived in Munich. Why, if you had such honest intentions, did you not make any contact with anybody in England after you arrived there? Surely you could have telephoned, wired or written? You must have realised the worry your disappearance was causing to many people, including your parents and colleagues."

"The fact of the matter is that, whilst it may seem rather a lame excuse sitting here, with all the knowledge of hindsight, I was not at all happy at Bushfield and I never had much love for my parents. My relationship with my senior housemaster was bad. I was unpopular with many of the staff. They knew of my political views and many disliked them a great deal. The boy's death, whether it was suicide or not, clinched the matter for me. The job I was given in Munich seemed quite innocuous to me. I was well paid; I had good accommodation and the people with whom I was working were all, so far as I knew, very agreeable. So I decided to stay. As for why I didn't contact anybody back at home I suppose this was partly cowardice. On the other hand I now believe that even if I had tried I should have been prevented and in all probability arrested, but, of course, I cannot prove that."

His interrogators sat and digested this response. Then Tomkins said," I am going to arrange to have you sent to London. You will there be subject to much more investigation. Major Preston and I shall be returning to England ourselves within about four weeks. We shall see you again then and, by that time, there will be more known about your story and its ramifications. We do have another matter, however, concerning which you may have some knowledge as, if your story is true, you appear to have been in Munich at the beginning of November. It could help you to help us.

We have reason to believe that certain of the Aronberg family, of which you now know Lady Sarah Threlfall was a member, fled to Munich after the Berlin arrests. Do you have any idea what happened to them? You have told us that both Von Rohrbach and Schumacher and this man Breck went off by themselves, leaving you confined in your quarters, on November the ninth, when the riots took place. Obviously two of these men had their personal reasons for seeking to harm these people under cover of the anti-Semitic activity perpetrated that night."

"When I was with them in London they made it quite clear that they held John Threlfall to blame for the organised attack at Bushfield. They attributed this to his Jewish ancestry. Since both he and his grandmother were by that time dead and they could see no effective means of harming Sir George they focused their attention on the Munich household. That I know. I was only too well aware of the violence that erupted on November the ninth, which absolutely appalled me. Fortunately for me I was not in any way involved since I was locked in my apartment for the entire day and night .If that had not been the case I should have felt unable to participate. If I had been asked to do so and refused then, with the benefit of hindsight, I now honestly believe I should have ended up in Dachau. As it was Schumacher detected my antipathy and challenged me afterwards. I had to pretend in order to remain free to escape as and when I could. I had already by then determined to face up to whatever was coming to me, just as I am now. I had put myself into an impossible position by my own folly. You surely realise what a dangerous position I was in. I really have no idea what part Von Rohrbach and Schumacher, and probably that friend of Von Rohrbach's called Breck, actually did that night. I can, however, only speculate that certainly they would have been presented with an ideal chance to wreak some kind of private revenge under cover of the riots. I can add no more than that, I am afraid."

Harold was returned to England. Once again his identity was changed for reasons of security. He was discreetly accompanied throughout the return trip by a legation guard. As soon as he was safely back in England he was despatched to a special location, where he was kept under close guard, whilst further interrogations and investigations proceeded. These were carried out, in conditions of great secrecy, by members of Tomkins' section. Nobody was informed of his presence in England. His information about and knowledge of the structure, membership and the work of the AFS proved to be extensive.

As soon as Tomkins and Francis had completed their Swiss mission they returned to London and reinterrogated Harold. The report which had, meanwhile, been prepared from the information he had given proved to be invaluable. Tomkins went to see his chief.

"I have come to the conclusion, sir, that this man could be very useful to us. He speaks German excellently and has a first class knowledge of the inner workings of the AFS. So far as I know his ex-employers have no knowledge we have him. I understand they are still looking for him in Switzerland. They had convinced him he would be charged with treason, if he gave himself up to us, and hanged. They probably succeeded in convincing themselves as well. In brief, sir, I am convinced the man was simply naive. I think his value to us here outweighs any possible benefit of a prosecution. In fact, sir, I should like to recruit him into my section, and retain his present cover. That means his presence in England would remain a secret and he would not be allowed to communicate with anybody outside his work.

Do I have clearance?"

"Yes! If anything goes wrong, however, I shall hold you responsible, Colonel!"

In this manner Harold, now with yet another identity, found himself operating for the remainder of the war from a secret location, way out in the remote English countryside, on intelligence work, under the command of Francis. He was permitted no contact with the outside world. Thrown so closely together the two apparently very diverse men came to know each other very well and, gradually, a close friendship began to develop between them. Harold had learned a great deal of sense from his traumatic experiences.

In due course there came the end of the war in Europe.

In May, 1945, Tomkins and Francis were despatched to Klagenfurt in Austria on special duties. The entire surrounding district was in a state of chaos. There were displaced persons, escaping from the Russians, Russian army deserters, units of the German army composed of émigrés, elements of the Yugoslavian Chetnik forces, escaping war criminals, ordinary criminals, released concentration camp inmates, all intermingling. Tomkins and Francis had the unenviable task, as Tomkins had put it, "To attempt to sort out some of the wheat from the chaff."

The town major found them billets in the old Gestapo Headquarters. This, they soon discovered, they were sharing with the officers' mess of a battalion of the Prince's Own Carbines, which had just arrived there, fresh from the Italian campaign. The battalion adjutant, Captain Cumberworth, came in to see them.

"The Colonel presents his compliments. He requests the pleasure of your company at our mess, sir, during your stay in Klagenfurt!"

"That is exceedingly kind of him, Captain, we should both be very pleased and honoured to accept!"

That evening the first person to greet them as they entered the mess was Lt. Col. Sir George Threlfall.

"Good gracious, Francis, what ever are you doing here?" said George, shaking his old school friend's hand warmly.

"It's all rather hush, hush, George! May I introduce you to my senior officer, Colonel Tomkins, of Intelligence?"

"We should be very much obliged, sir," said Tomkins to Sir George, " if after dinner you could possibly spare some time for the two of us to have a discussion with you and Major Wisley. We are here on a very important mission. I am sure you could be of very great assistance to us if you are willing."

"Nothing would give us greater pleasure!"

He beckoned to Wisley to accompany them. The four of them went into George's office.

"We have an astonishing tale to tell you, gentlemen, " said Tomkins. "You will all be interested. It concerns one of your ex-colleagues at Bushfield Abbey School, Major Wisley!"

"An ex-colleague?" said Wisley, looking blank. "What on earth do you mean?"

"Colonel Tomkins is referring to Harold Arbitant!" said Francis.

"I had rather hoped I would never hear that man's name again!" said Wisley. "He always seems to spell trouble."

"It is quite a story!" said Francis.

They all looked at Tomkins in anticipation.

CHAPTER FORTY THREE

LIBERATION

The end of the war in Europe had found the Prince's Own Carbines stationed in Klagenfurt in Austria. Sergeant Donald Mitchell was still Lt. Col. Sir George Threlfall's personal driver whilst Bill Riding, to his father's immense pride, had achieved the rank of Regimental Sergeant Major. The Reverend Alexander Tapping was the battalion chaplain.

The very last person Wisley had ever expected to hear about, amongst all his present problems, was Harold. The pressures and anxieties of the Italian campaign, throughout which he had been Sir George's second in command, had considerably dimmed the appalling memories associated with Harold. Now they came flooding back.

He and Sir George sat there waiting to hear whatever it was that was about to be revealed.

As succinctly as he was able Tomkins proceeded to outline what appeared to have happened when Harold had paid that ill-fated visit to the London embassy. Then he told his astonished listeners of Harold's secret removal to Germany, his involvement with the AFS and, finally, of his appointment to and subsequent escape from the German embassy in Berne and its aftermath.

"And you mean to tell us that, notwithstanding this extraordinary record, he is now actually working, under an assumed name, within British Intelligence, under your command!" exclaimed Wisley.

"He was most carefully investigated, Major Wisley," said Francis. "He operates under my personal supervision, mainly for his own security. His assistance to the war effort in uncovering what was already a very effective international espionage system has been immense. I assure you that he is now a very different person from the one whom you knew"

"Well, I suppose the powers that be know best!" said George, "I must say, though, if I hadn't been told the tale with such authority I should have had difficulty in believing it."

Francis said to George, "Look, old man, I have some other news, connected with this affair which directly concerns you personally. It would also, I know, be of interest to Major Wisley here, as it relates to that affair at the school, in October, 1938, when your boy died in such tragic circumstances! Can I tell you about it?"

"If it relates to that affair at Bushfield, something that concerns both George and myself very much indeed, please tell us everything, Major Preston, " said Wisley.

Francis now said to Tomkins ,"May I go ahead? I don't think there are any security problems, are there?"

"I take it you are going to tell them about the Aronberg affair?"

"That is my intention!"

"Right, go ahead! It affects everybody in this room. I am pleased we have this unexpected opportunity."

"George, because at the time you were so utterly devastated by the concurrent deaths in your family, you may not have realised that my own little six year old daughter, Rosemary, died earlier that same year!"

"As a matter of fact, Francis, I did not. I suppose John must have known. It is unlikely that Gordon, his best friend, would not have mentioned it to him. He never told either Ann or myself though. You know he was passing through a very critical phase just then, with tragic results. I am so sorry!"

"Just before my daughter died my wife and I made a business trip to Berlin. We had established a very close working arrangement there with a firm called Aronbergs, engaged in the merchandising of textiles. The Aronbergs, who were of Jewish origin although practising Lutheran Christians, used to put us all up at their house during our quite frequent visits. We had, in consequence, become close friends. The senior director was a man called Samuel. His son, Aaron, and his granddaughter's husband, Benjamin Hands, were both junior directors. His granddaughter was called Rachel and she had a six-year-old girl, Elisabeth, the same age as our own Rosemary. The two children were very attached to each other. Our last visit to Berlin was made in May, 1938. At that time the Nazi persecution of people of Jewish origin was beginning to become much more evident to us. Rachel had previously arranged with us for Elisabeth to come on holiday to Leeds to spend some time with Rosemary. Indeed there was even a possibility that Benjamin might come over to London to take charge of the office there. Just before we left Rachel told my wife that she had been extremely frightened by some recent developments which had brought the family into trouble with the Nazi authorities, a very dangerous situation at that time. She asked Penelope if she would, in the circumstances, be prepared to keep Elizabeth, in the safety of Leeds, until things settled down. In fact, as I subsequently found out, she even gave my late wife a letter agreeing to our adoption of the child should anything happen to her.

After we had returned to England we learned, through the Aronberg's small London office, with which we normally had little contact, that the three Berlin based directors had all been arrested and taken away to some place unknown, but in all probability Dachau. Their wives were all thought to have found some kind of temporary refuge with Samuel's brother, Eli, who had a large house in Munich, from which he ran another branch of the business.

Shortly thereafter it we found it to be impossible to communicate with the Munich office. Their London office had apparently vanished. We never discovered what had happened to the wives, but presumed the worst.

In July I regret to have to tell you Rosemary finally succumbed to the T.B. with which she had always been afflicted and died. By that time I had already taken steps to arrange for Elisabeth to be allowed to remain with us in Leeds and had, in fact, begun adoption proceedings, assisted by a highly placed contact I had in the Home Office.

By the time war broke out the official adoption papers were finalised."

"This means, then, " said George, " that your adopted daughter is, I presume, related to me, through my mother. "

"As a matter of fact, Colonel Threlfall," intervened Tomkins, "we have established conclusively that Francis' adopted daughter was your mother's great great niece. We have now, however, since the end of the war, had access to certain official files which were captured intact in Munich and, in consequence, know a great deal more about what happened to the Aronberg family, both in Berlin and Munich."

"Just one moment, though, Francis!" interjected George. "You said "my late wife" just now. Do you mean to tell us that you have not only lost your daughter but also your wife?"

"I am sorry to have to tell you all that Penelope was killed by one of those terrible V2 rockets. Elisabeth, our adopted girl, was with her at the time. It all happened just before the war ended in Europe."

"Do you mean to say they were both killed? said Wisley.

"No, sir! My wife died in the blast. Elisabeth, however, survived, but very badly injured. She has, in fact, lost the ability not only to walk but also to speak. One day, they tell me, it is possible that something may be done for her, but medical knowledge has not yet reached that point. For the time being she is confined to a wheel chair. Otherwise she is as well as can be supposed, but she will not utter a word. The doctors say it is a shock symptom and may right itself in due course."

"Good God!" said George, "I just do not know what to say to you, Francis!"

"I think, Francis," said Tomkins at this point, " we had better complete the story, so far as we are able to piece it together, of what happened to the Aronbergs. The files were discovered in the offices of one of the Munich Gestapo chiefs, a man called Fritz Breck, currently on our wanted list for alleged war crimes. These reveal that Samuel died shortly after entering Dachau. Aaron and Benjamin were sent to Auschwitz and are shown as "executed" there. The three wives, who had all taken refuge in Munich, with Eli, died during the notorious riots which took place on November the ninth, 1938. The story is recorded in meticulous detail in the files. For some reason Breck seems to have taken a special interest in the family. All their bodies were, it says in the files, discovered in the house by looters, who had broken in, but what exactly happened to them is not stated. The official story is, however, that Eli had, apparently, shot the three women, presumably with the intention of saving them from probable rape, and then taken his own life. The record is quite specific that four bodies were found and identified."

Francis was shaking with emotion. "I have seen some terrible things since this war began," he said, "but have never before heard a tale like that! Oh, my God! So poor Rachel is really dead! I had been hoping against hope that she might have survived, perhaps in Ravensbruck or one of those other awful places, but survived! Thank God I at least still have her daughter safe in my keeping!"

"What is it that you and Major Preston are doing here, in Klagenfurt, if you are able to answer that question?" asked Wisley, feeling it was time to find a new direction for the discussion.

"Yes, we shall tell you and, at the same time, ask you if you can help!" responded Tomkins. "We have been given a list of certain people we believe may be in the area and who are urgently wanted for alleged war crimes. In order to assist us in the search we have been provided with very detailed aerial photographs of the surrounding district. It is our intention to set out, hopefully tomorrow, on what we have termed a "trawl" to see what we can unearth. I have already been allocated the services of a reliable ex policeman from the Klagenfurt civil force, who knows the topography and inhabitants of the outlying and remoter farms, in which we are especially interested. For the moment we only have this policeman, our driver, one truck and the two of us. If you could furnish us with any reinforcements it would be very greatly appreciated!"

"I am afraid that much as I should like to help I, personally, cannot spare the time," replied Sir George, "but I should be more than happy to have Major Wisley go with you. In fact you can also have another truck and my personal driver, Sergeant Mitchell, and our R.S.M, Bill Riding."

"I can assure you, Colonel Tomkins," said Wisley grimly, "that having heard your tale catching war criminals is going to be a very attractive occupation for me!"

Early the following morning the little party assembled and set off into the surrounding very rough terrain in their two fifteen hundredweight trucks. Overnight Tomkins and Francis had made a detailed examination of the photographs. They had pinpointed one very remote smallholding that they now pointed out to the policeman.

"Do you know anything about this place?"

"It belongs to a man called Fritz Breck," he told them, to their astonishment.

"If that's the man we think it is then we've hit a bullseye!" exclaimed Tomkins. "Tell us more about this man, please."

"He used to be very high up in the Gestapo, here in Klagenfurt. Then he was promoted to Munich. He is, or rather was, greatly feared around here, indeed his influence extended as far as Vienna! The holding has been in the family's possession for a very long time. His mother still lives there with his sister, a woman called Heidi. Nobody ever sees either of them but she is reputed to be mentally retarded. Nobody ever interfered with them though. They were sent regular supplies by a local merchant. He once told me his orders were to leave the provisions, which were paid for by Breck, in a little hut at the end of this track," he pointed to the track on the photograph," and never to approach the house, which, he said, was guarded by huge dogs. I suppose the deliveries must have stopped now. Perhaps they are running short!"

"That's our man! I wonder whether he has gone to earth there? It is such an obvious place it seems unlikely, but perhaps he has gone there for the moment, hoping to slip across to Switzerland one night!"

The roads steadily became worse and worse. Eventually the hut and the track were located and the trucks turned in. Some distance ahead they could hear a dog barking frantically as it sensed their approach. Then the house itself came into view. An enormous black alsatian dog was tethered to a wooden post, just outside the front door, straining wildly at its rope in its endeavours to reach them.

"I don't fancy having a set-to with that!" said Donald, as they pulled up.

"This place looks remarkably well cared for!" said Tomkins, surveying the yard with an experienced eye for detail. "It looks to me as though there is a very hard worker around, probably a man. Mark my words, sergeant, there are more people here than just an old woman and her dim-witted daughter! Take care!"

They alighted, weapons ready. The dog barked louder than ever. The door opened and an elderly woman emerged, followed by another, evidently the daughter. Although their appearances were by no means prepossessing they were both reasonably clean and dressed. They were wearing good shoes and looked far from hungry.

The woman addressed herself to the policeman, ignoring the others. "This is private property! It belongs to Fritz Breck! If he finds you here there will be hell to pay! Clear off!"

She obviously had no idea the war was over. Indeed so isolated had they been that she had scarcely been aware there had ever been a war. The name of Fritz Breck was so feared that it always acted as a most effective deterrent. She assumed these people were some special troops from Klagenfurt and would be familiar with her son's name.

"She doesn't seem much concerned by our presence, does she sir?" said Bill.

"Tell her who we are!" said Tomkins to the policeman.

"These are British officers! The war is over! Germany has been defeated! You must obey their orders!"

The woman showed no emotion at this intelligence. She just stood and stared at them, without moving a muscle.

"Stand aside!" said the policeman.

She moved reluctantly back into the house. They followed her. It was spotlessly clean. There was a heavy wooden table in the middle of the room, standing on a large rug, and at this the younger woman now seated herself and gazed at them. Bill Riding, who had been outside looking at the outhouses, came in and crossed over to peer into the rear room. As he did so Heidi suddenly sprang up and gave him an enormous buffet, just as she had once done to Von Rohrbach. Gasping he staggered backwards, taken by surprise. Donald sprang forward to restrain her and, in the ensuing melee, the table and chair moved, pulling back the rug. Then Heidi suddenly quietened down, put back the chair, sat down and began to moan quietly to herself.

"Who else lives or works here?" said Francis, speaking in German.

"Only my daughter and myself. There is nobody else here!"

"But who does all the work? You couldn't manage it all, I'm certain!"

"I do! Who else do you think does it? She doesn't do anything!"

"She's lying!" said Tomkins, in English. "She couldn't possibly do all the work and look after that girl as well, even if she is as tough as she seems to be! There must be somebody else here! Search the place from top to bottom, and be careful! If there is anybody here they are sure to be armed."

By this time the dog outside was beside itself with frustration. It was pulling harder and harder at the rope, which was giving signs of breaking under the strain.

"Colonel!" exclaimed the policeman, "I know these dogs! They are very dangerous! If that rope breaks somebody is going to be killed!"

"Shoot it!" said Tomkins to Bill.

Bill went outside. There was a shot and, for the moment, silence.

Then, to their amazement, the barking began again.

"It's coming from under the floor, sir!" said Donald. "It must be down in the cellar!

The dragging back of the rug had revealed the trap door over which it had been spread. Bill and Donald pulled this up and peered down into the black hole below. The barking doubled in its intensity. Donald ran back to his truck and returned with a powerful torch. He shone this down and its beams revealed two yellow eyes. Tomkins took the torch from him and methodically moved the light around to see if he could discover what else was down there. At first he could see nothing. Then he saw what he thought was a bundle of rags.

"There seems to be a large bundle of something down there! Behind the dog! Is there a ladder around?"

The policeman hurried out and returned with one. This they proceeded to push down into the cellar.

"But we can't send anyone down there!" said Wisley. "The dog would kill them! We'll have to shoot it!"

"Just a moment, sir" said Bill, "I wonder whether that bundle of rags you saw, was somebody hiding down there? You said it was a large bundle, sir! If it is a man he may be armed!"

"Good thinking, R.S.M.!" replied Wisley.

Tomkins peered down into the cellar again. "You're right, you know! I saw it move! There is somebody concealed down there! Francis, speak to whoever is down there, in German, and tell them to surrender!"

Francis knelt down, put his head inside the opening and, shouting as loudly as he could, to be heard over the noise the dog was now making, called out, "We are British officers! Come to the foot of the ladder and climb up. I warn you that you are covered by my pistol!"

Then a voice came up, as the bundle of rags slowly moved past the dog, which it seemed able to restrain from barking by saying something to it, and made its way to the foot of the ladder, preparatory to slowly ascending. The effect was astonishing, for the voice quite obviously belonged to a well-educated woman. The English was perfect, if slightly accented.

"Please don't shoot the dog! I can control it! I am coming up! I am unarmed!"

The unexpected and rapid approach of the two trucks had taken Frau Breck by surprise. She had only just had time to push Rachel down into the cellar and conceal the trapdoor with the rug and table. Rachel, during her long enslavement, had become fast friends with the dogs, who never left her side. Although Frau Breck had managed to tether one of them she had been unable to prevent the other from jumping down into the cellar after Rachel. There was, thereafter, no means of making it come out. It had had to be left there with her. For a while it had remained quiet, secure in Rachel's presence. Rachel had heard the commotion above, during the first fracas, but, fearing that it was being caused by boisterous local soldiery who had somehow found their way into the farmhouse, and who would probably end up raping her if she were discovered, had remained as quiet as she could, subduing the dog's growls. It was most unpleasant working with Frau Breck but at least she was still alive, she was taking no chances. When the shot was fired, however, the dog became uncontrollable, probably sensing that its mate had been killed.

She emerged into the light. She was filthy. Her matted hair hung across her emaciated face. She had a black eye from a recent skirmish with Heidi. Her back was covered in marks from beatings, clearly visible through the tattered rags in which she tried to conceal herself. Her feet were bound up in paper and rags. Her hands were scarred and her nails worn down.

She stood, blinking in the light. Then her eyes fell on Francis. She couldn't comprehend what had happened but she knew who he was. She simply said one word,"Elisabeth!"

Then, as Francis, realised who it was that they had found, and rushed towards her, she stumbled and fell into his arms.

They stood there, almost petrified, looking at them, in utter bewilderment.

"This is Rachel!"

CHAPTER FORTY FOUR

REUNION

Francis could, when he chose, call upon the assistance of many friends in high places.

Rachel had already been taken, at his expense, to a private clinic in Vienna, where every effort was being made to nurse her back to something approaching normality. He had, however, been told quite bluntly by the doctor in charge of her case that resources available locally were so limited that it would be advisable, if at all possible, to have her taken to England or America and as quickly as possible.

"She has endured six years of this dreadful treatment." said the doctor, who had been appalled by her condition when she arrived. "She appears to have been sustained almost entirely by her determination to see her daughter again. Her release, however, has achieved what her captivity did not. She is at present in a state of virtual collapse, both mentally and physically. She can recover, but she will need both care and understanding."

Francis took himself off to Army Headquarters. Here he sought out a very senior officer, a man he had known at school, somewhat older than himself. He explained what had happened.

"I simply must get her back to a clinic I know about in Leeds. Is there any advice you can give me as to how I can do this?"

"I don't suppose there is any way you can claim she is a British subject?"

"No, although she has been so grossly mistreated, I suppose, ironic as it seems, that she is actually classified as an ex-enemy alien!"

"Well, we might overcome that particular objection, but it could take time! It would have helped if she had been able to claim British nationality. You say you have actually adopted her daughter by legal process?"

"Yes, I have been wondering what weight that would carry."

"I think we could manage something, but the problem is that these things take time."

Francis had been thinking.

"If I married her, which I can now I am a widower, provided there is no other legal barrier to doing so, she would automatically become a

British citizen as the law stands at present, wouldn't she? Then she would have the right to come back with me to Leeds!"

"If that is indeed the present law and so far as I know it is would you really be willing to go to those lengths, Francis?"

"Yes, of course I would. She is the mother of my adopted daughter! My late wife always maintained that we were simply holding Elisabeth in trust for Rachel, if she ever returned."

"Provided you are correct, Francis, once she is your wife I shall personally see to it that both of you are on the first available 'plane back home. Invite me to the wedding!"

Francis hastened back to Klagenfurt and sought out the Reverend Alexander Tapping to tell him of the proposal.

"So far as I know you are correct, Major Preston. Provided I am satisfied that this lady knows what she is doing, concerning which I shall first have to satisfy myself, I should be only too pleased to marry you to her."

"In all honesty," said the doctor at the clinic, "I am not all that certain that she is as yet capable of completely understanding what is being proposed, you can but try! I think you had better do so in the presence of witnesses, who could later, if necessary, testify to the fact that she was of sound mind when she made her decision. I suggest the chaplain and myself should act in that capacity."

He had to wait several weeks whilst his Leeds lawyers checked out the legal position. Then, reassured that various possible problems had been overcome, he asked the doctor if he could propose to Rachel.

Privately the doctor had his doubts that Rachel would really understand, but he deemed it better to conceal them. "Go ahead!" he said encouragingly. It seemed to him the very best thing that could happen for his patient.

On being asked she smiled at him and said, "Of course I will, Sir Francis!" and then promptly closed her eyes and went to sleep.

"Are you satisfied?" he said anxiously to his witnesses.

The chaplain grinned and winked at the doctor. "Well I am satisfied!"

"I concur!" said the doctor, who had already made his decision in the interests of his patient.

It was agreed the wedding should take place as soon as Tapping had had time to complete certain formalities. In the meanwhile Tomkins had arranged for him to go on indefinite compassionate leave with his new wife. In the intervening time Francis explained to Rachel as best he might that, although Elisabeth was alive, Penelope had died. He did not go into details and Rachel seemed to be satisfied with what she was told. She asked no questions. Her mind seemed to be completely concentrated on seeing Elisabeth again. She never asked when she was going to see her. She appeared to be completely content now she knew she was alive and that they were going to be reunited. Whether or not she really understood what was happening was unclear. Nobody probed too deeply. They had all succeeded in satisfying themselves that the marriage was in order and were not at all anxious to upset that situation.

"I advise you not to try to explain too much, Sir Francis," said the doctor. "Little at a time! On no account tell her about her daughter's condition, until she is much stronger! It is the euphoria which is keeping her going at the moment. Just take it slowly!"

The marriage ceremony, when it took place, was a very low-key affair. Prompted by Tapping Rachel made all the correct responses and signed the register. Whether or not she had the least idea what she was doing nobody was too sure, but she was thereupon declared by Tapping to be well and truly wed to Francis. The necessary documents were issued and, Francis' friend being as good as his word, Sir Francis and the new Lady Rachel returned to Leeds. Rachel travelled on a stretcher as, for the time being, she appeared to have lost control of her lower limbs.

"It is only a temporary effect!" said the doctor. "It is all due to delayed shock. There is nothing else physical seriously the matter, apart from the malnutrition, from which she is now slowly recovering."

Once safely installed in the Leeds clinic Rachel made a very slow recovery, punctuated by alarming relapses. Francis sat by her bedside almost all the time. Elisabeth had not been told her mother was back in England. It was felt that it would be better to wait, just in case some unexpected development occurred. Occasionally Rachel would look at him and say "Elisabeth!" and smile. She never went beyond this. He would smile back and nod. Then she would go to sleep again.

One morning he was sitting there as usual when she opened her eyes and said, in English and very distinctly, " Sir Francis I have just had a very strange dream!" She always addressed him, at this time, as 'Sir Francis'. "I dreamed that you told me that Lady Penelope was dead and that you were going to marry me and reunite me with Elisabeth!" She began to cry.

He quickly took her thin hand in his own and said, very gently, "Dearest Rachel, it was not a dream! It is fact! You will soon be seeing Elisabeth!"

She looked at him, uncomprehending, and then said, very weakly, "Lady Penelope..." before going again to sleep.

This time, however, her sleep appeared to Francis to be of a different quality, much sounder and more natural than had hitherto been the case. He went out of the ward and asked the nurse to call the doctor. They came in and listened to her heart and felt her pulse.

"She has turned the corner, Sir Francis! Just have patience!"

Now she began, each day, to ask where Elisabeth was and when she was going to come and see her. Each day Francis produced fresh excuses. She was in London, she had been delayed, she was on her way. Finally, to his relief, the doctor said Rachel was well enough to be told of Elisabeth's condition.

"You should tell her about the wheel chair but not the speech loss, Sir Francis. The speech loss is a psychological phenomenon and most unpredictable. She may recover quite suddenly. One thing at a time!"

Francis returned to the bedside and took Rachel's now visibly stronger hand in his own.

"Rachel, do you remember that I told you that Penelope had died?"

She nodded. "Yes, Sir Francis! I do! Then you told me that you had married me! I thought it was all a dream but you said it was true! Then you said I was to see Elisabeth again soon! Where is she, Sir Francis? I do so want to see her!"

"Rachel, Penelope was killed by a bomb, just before I discovered you!"

"Oh, poor dear Lady Penelope! I remember now! It was she who saved Elisabeth that day! Oh, Sir Francis, I am so sorry!"

"Elisabeth was with her the day she was killed, Rachel. The same bomb very gravely injured Elisabeth. She is alive and well but she has lost the use of her legs. She is in a wheelchair. She is here, outside this room. She has no idea you are here. We have told her she is visiting a sick friend of mine. We did not want her over excited!"

Rachel sat there, propped up by her pillows, and looked at him as though she were transformed. "She is here!" she breathed. "Oh, Sir Francis, please, please let me see her!"

Francis rose and opened the door. There, in her wheelchair, sat Elisabeth. She was just thirteen years old and had not seen her mother for seven eventful years. She had not uttered one single word since the day Penelope had been killed. The nurse wheeled her in. Mother and daughter saw each other at last.

"Mother!" said Elisabeth, in German, loudly and clearly, "Mother, you have come back! Oh, dearest Mother!"

It was July, 1945.

CHAPTER FORTY FIVE

WIMBLEDON

At the end of 1946 the veil of secrecy which had surrounded Harold's wartime career was lifted and he was told he was to be allowed to return home. He was given this information by Tomkins, who had taken over his direct supervision from Francis, who then said, "I think that it is only fair that you should have my support in what may prove to be rather a difficult encounter with your parents, whom, I presume, you will now be contacting. They have had no news about you since you disappeared back in 1938, since absolute secrecy concerning your activities has been observed. Would you like me to write to them and ask them to come up and see me? Then I could, as it were, break the ice for you?"

"The fact is, sir, that I have never had a good relationship with my father. He is absolutely certain to put the worst possible interpretation on everything that happened. However, for the time being, I can see no other choice for me than to go and live with them, provided they will have me, until I can find my feet again. I do not suppose for one moment that Bushfield Abbey are going to have me back again, and I doubt if they will give any kind of reference, in the circumstances."

"As a matter of fact we have already discussed your case with Dr. Wisley, who has now been allowed to leave the army and return to his duties at Bushfield. Whilst it is certainly correct that you would not be offered your post back there, nevertheless, in view of his knowledge of subsequent events, he is quite prepared to give you a reference, and even try to assist you in finding another position. Initially he suggests you should apply to a small private preparatory school."

"That is very generous of him. In the meanwhile, sir, I should be most grateful to take advantage of your offer to speak to my parents. The explanation would come with so much more authority from you!"

And so it was that, one morning, a letter carrying the O.H.M.S., War Office, insignia dropped on to the doormat at the West Wimbledon home of Albert and Doreen Arbitant. Doreen picked it up and looked at it curiously. "Whatever can this be, Albert? " She passed it across the breakfast table in the kitchen.

Albert had been a leading figure in the local civil defence during the war. He could think of no other reason why anybody at the War Office should write to him. Perhaps, he thought to himself, I have been recommended for some special decoration? Rather expectantly he opened the envelope. He proceeded to read the contents with little grunts of astonishment, much exciting thereby his wife's curiosity.

"It's about Harold!" he said, at last. "It's from a Colonel Tomkins at the War Office. He wants us both to go up and see him. I'm to 'phone for an appointment!"

"What, to see Harold?" said Doreen, looking amazed.

"No, Doreen!" said her husband irritably. "Not to see Harold, to see this Colonel Tomkins! I'll wager that boy's been up to no good! I was always suspicious when he disappeared after visiting that Nazi embassy place in London. I always said all those politics of his would bring him to a sticky end!"

"Oh, Albert, how can you talk like that about our son! But I had become used to the idea of his being gone! Now it's all going to start all over again. I wonder what this is all about? It must be important by the sound of it! A Colonel, you say!"

"Well," said her husband, philosophically sucking on his pipe, "we'll soon know. I'll telephone this colonel now."

Three days later they were seated in Tomkins' office in Whitehall.

Very carefully and thoroughly Tomkins detailed as much of Harold's story to them as he felt needful. He made a point of stressing Harold's subsequent valuable contribution to the war effort after his return to England. This, however, made very little impression on the indignant Albert.

"Are you telling us, Colonel," he snorted, "that when you first met him he'd been working for the Nazis? That my son was a traitor?"

"Treason, Mr. Arbitant, is a very serious matter. It still carries the death penalty, as I am sure you know! Your son was very, very carefully investigated. His subsequent services to the country were invaluable to the war effort."

"That's as may be!" retorted Albert, still far from happy at what he had been told. "The whole business has a nasty smell to me! I don't want him to come back to Wimbledon and be with us. I never liked either his politics or his friends, not that he had many, except that creepy German bloke he once brought home from university, Shoemaker or some such outlandish name he had, nasty bit of work, I thought!"

"Really, Albert!" intervened his normally placid wife, moved to speech by this vitriolic attack on the return of her prodigal son. "That's enough! Where is the boy, colonel?"

Albert, thus uncustomarily humiliated, lapsed into a sullen silence.

Tomkins went to his anteroom door and opened it. "Come along in, Harold!" he said.

The three Arbitants looked at each other, for the moment struck dumb. Then Harold said a prosaic "Hullo Mother, Hullo Father!" The fact of the matter was that, notwithstanding all that had happened to him since he had last seen them, he could think of nothing else to say to them. He felt no affection for either of them.

His mother went up to him and, rather awkwardly, embraced him. His father stood there looking at him in a hostile fashion. At last Albert found words, "So you've come back!" and he extended a rather limp hand to be shaken.

It could not be described as a joyous occasion. Tomkins afterwards described the reunion to Francis as one of the most dismal and embarrassing occasions of his life. Eventually the trio left and caught the train from Waterloo to Raynes Park. It was a miserable journey, not one of them even attempted to open their mouths in case somebody overheard them, there were too many local people in the carriage. They sat in awkward silence.

By now Harold was thirty six and his parents were both in their sixties. They were both old well beyond their years and very set in their ways. They were not at all happy about his living with them. He was a disturbance to their routine. Although the house was Harold's childhood home he had never been happy there. The very act of embracing his extreme political views had been occasioned by his father's opposite dogmatism. He had always had a poor opinion of his mother, despising her for her subservience to his father.

A period of extreme misery followed for him. He kept out of reach of the inquisitive neighbours and local shopkeepers. His mother, after her initial show of independence, rapidly returned to her normal compliance with her autocratic husband. Harold was left to sit alone in his badly furnished little bedroom. He listened to the wireless, tried to read books, and studied the newspapers from end to end. He took to rising very early, walking to the windmill on the common, buying his breakfast there, and then spending much of the rest of the day looking at one of the ponds, watching the children sailing their boats. He felt no desire to look for a job. Such money as he still had left over from the pay he had received whilst with Francis was beginning to run out. He had no savings.

He even began to wonder whether he should commit suicide.

****

Francis, in Leeds, had by now been demobilised and, in the intervals available to him from managing the business, which he had now taken back from the exhausted Horace, was devoting himself to domesticity.

"As soon as Gordon becomes available I suggest we ask him to join me, Horace. He'll be twenty-five soon. It would be good to have him on board!"

Some time after this conversation with Horace, Francis was sitting at home with Rachel and Elisabeth.

"Francis," said the now apparently recovered Rachel, "I have been thinking about that man, Harold Arbitant, the ex-Nazi sympathiser, who renounced them and then worked with you uncovering all those fifth columnists. You became very friendly with him, you told me, in spite of his earlier activities."

"Yes, that is true, Rachel. He told us he was so utterly horrified by what he saw and heard that terrible night in Munich, when you were abducted and your family murdered that it was as though scales had literally dropped from his eyes. He swears that from that moment on his only desire was to return to Britain and face whatever might be the consequences for him. It took us a long time to be convinced but, once we were, and gave him the opportunity to prove his worth, he proved himself an excellent man. His assistance to the war effort in helping us to uncover what could have been a very dangerous spy ring was tremendous. I had many long conversations with him and came to understand and like him. I believe him to be a good man who was led astray by beliefs he held sincerely, if mistakenly. If everybody who has ever held mistaken views is to be branded as a pariah ever afterwards, whatever their subsequent actions may be, then it is a poor outlook for reconciliation. I, personally, have never believed in any policy that wins battles and loses wars. That is sheer folly."

"What happened to him, Daddy?" said Elisabeth.

"I have been told by Tomkins that, for the moment, he is living with his parents in Wimbledon. Tomkins met them and explained things to them. He told me that the father was most unsympathetic. If he hasn't found a position yet, and I doubt if he has, I should think he is most unhappy there. As a matter of fact, Rachel, it is curious you should mention him. I have been wondering whether I could find something for him in the firm. I have been hesitating, however, because I didn't know how you would react. He didn't have any direct connection with your own tragic experiences, but he was involved with the perpetrators, as we now know. Why was it, darling, that you brought his name up like this, so suddenly?"

"Because, Francis, I, too, believe that the only way in which we are ever going to avoid a repetition of such terrible events is if people such as myself and Elisabeth, who have been so terribly wronged, can bring ourselves, in the right circumstances, to make genuine gestures of meaningful reconciliation. I believe such an opportunity now presents itself to me."

"So, Rachel, you would like me to try and find him a position with my firm?"

"No, Francis, I have been talking about this with Elisabeth. We have another proposal to put to you. We think that it should be possible, with your help, to recreate the former Aronberg business network. Almost all the pre-war contacts must still exist. It just needs a lot of hard work to rebuild the business. If that could be done what a wonderful memorial that would be to all those of my family who died."

"But the amount of work involved would be enormous! In any event what has this to do with Arbitant?"

"He speaks perfect German and he is apparently without a job. You, personally, like and vouch for him. He, like me, has been through the fires of hell. If I preach reconciliation I should practise it! I should like your agreement to my meeting with him. If I feel he is suitable I should like him to come here and join with me in such a project. I am sure, if it were successful, as I am sure it would be, it would prove to be of immense benefit to Preston's."

"Go on, Daddy! Give him a chance! You helped me, you helped Mummy, now help him!"

"It's the most extraordinary proposition I have ever had put to me! But if you two are so insistent, why not? He can come up here and be interviewed by you, Rachel, if you so wish. It can't do the man any harm. I'll speak to Colonel Tomkins on the telephone tonight about the matter!"

"I think it is a marvellous idea, Francis!" said Tomkins. "The man must be in a kind of hell in Wimbledon. I'm sure he'd jump at the chance. Do you know how to contact him?"

Two weeks later there was another letter on the Wimbledon doormat. This time it bore the Leeds postmark and was addressed to

Harold. His mother handed it to him across the kitchen table at breakfast. He read it with immense astonishment.

"I've been invited to go up to Leeds and see Sir Francis Preston about a possible job!" he exclaimed. "Look, he's even sent me twenty pounds for expenses!"

"Oh, yes!" said his father, apparently addressing his open newspaper, his mouth full of toast. "When are you off then? Sooner the better. You've battened on me long enough!"

"The boy's always paid his way, Albert!" said Doreen, in a last show of independence.

"I'll go and make sure you have some things ready to take with you, Harold!"

She hurried out of the room to begin packing his case, although he hadn't yet said when he was going. The fact was she couldn't wait for him to go. The strain of living with the two of them was too much for her.

It was then early 1946.

Two years later Albert died followed, in 1950, by Doreen.

Apart from returning to Wimbledon for a few days to oversee the winding up of their small estates Harold never visited the house again.

CHAPTER FORTY SIX

LEEDS

Harold was met at Leeds railway station by the Preston chauffeur, who deferentially took his small travelling bag. His mother had packed a few things, not seriously expecting him to stay in Leeds very long or, for that matter, to secure the appointment, notwithstanding her husband's expressed optimism that they had seen the back of him.

"He'll be back, Albert! "

"Humph!"

"Where are we going?" asked Harold as they walked towards the car park.

"Why, sir, you're going to Preston Hall!" said the chauffeur in a surprised voice. "Lady Rachel is waiting for you in the car."

The chauffeur put Harold's case in the boot, opened the door and said, "Mr Harold Arbitant, my lady!"

"Hullo, Mr. Arbitant! Do get in. I do hope you had a pleasant trip!"

He climbed in, a little awkwardly, and sat down beside her.

"You are going to stay with us, Mr. Arbitant, if that's convenient to you. My daughter is so looking forward to meeting you. She's really excited! We don't have many people to stay, and we've so many rooms in the house."

"I had no idea you were going to put me up, Lady Rachel. I had come expecting to stay in an hotel. I don't want to be any trouble to you!"

"Trouble! I am sure you will be the reverse of trouble! I am hoping you are going to prove to be the person I have been seeking to help me, but let's talk about that much later, shall we? Have you ever been to Yorkshire before?"

She sat there and chatted to him about the beauties of Yorkshire. Whilst she did so he studied her. It was unbelievable that this was the woman who, as he knew, Sir Francis and Colonel Tomkins had discovered in such appalling conditions on that Austrian farm as the war was ending.

Everything that human resource could do to eradicate all traces of that experience had been brought into play. Her face, her hands, her clothes, her poise were all perfect. Only her strange grey green eyes, that Aronberg trademark, betrayed the ordeal through which she had been. Within them he could, he was sure, perceive the anguish she still felt.

How, he marvelled, could anybody, let alone this beautiful creature beside him, have had such an ordeal and yet be able to look and behave like this? In his imagination he conjured up a vision of an oyster, protecting itself from an irritating grain of dirt, by covering it in layer upon layer of iridescent beauty. The appalling memories will always be there, he thought, how could they ever go? Why had she invited him, who had been so closely associated with the scoundrels who had murdered her family and enslaved her?

"My young daughter, Elisabeth, will be waiting for you," she said. "I suppose you know she is confined to a wheel chair. She was injured during the war by the same bomb that killed my husband's first wife, Penelope. It was Penelope, you know, who rescued Elisabeth from the Nazis in 1938.""

"Yes, your husband told me the story when I was working with him during the war. I am so sorry about the terrible injuries she suffered when that V2 fell."

"Oh, well, I know that both you and I have learned to take life as it comes, haven't we?"

"Yes, Lady Rachel, that is certainly true! But I think your experiences far outweigh my own. In any event I was responsible for my own misfortunes. You were the victim of the criminal act of people with whom I am utterly ashamed to say I was once associated." As he spoke he was thinking of her dreadful confinement on that farm, and, perhaps, in some ways, even worse, the appalling scene she must have witnessed in Eli's house that November evening in 1938, before she was abducted.

Without saying a word she put out her hand and put it on his tightly clenched fist.

He looked at her in amazement.

"Mr. Arbitant you have been asked here because I wanted us to be friends. Let us both do our best to forget the past! Perhaps you did build a bonfire for yourself but you have been purged in its flames, haven't you? Please don't refer to those events again. I certainly shall not!"

Harold sat there silently, choking back tears. Into his mind flashed the image of the Bushfield phoenix. What I was, I was, he thought, now I am something else and that it what, God willing, I shall be from now on.

She smiled at him and continued to point out the sights as the car wound its way through the peaceful countryside in the general direction of Harrogate. At last it turned in through great wrought iron gates, strongly reminiscent of Bushfield Abbey, and began its progress up the long gravelled drive. Its approach had been observed. Elisabeth, sitting excitedly in her wheel chair, was awaiting them.

The chauffeur opened the car door and Rachel, closely followed by Harold, alighted.

"Elisabeth, this is Mr. Harold Arbitant."

Elisabeth's eyes, those strange grey green Aronberg eyes, were sparkling with excitement.

"I've been so looking forward to meeting you, Mr. Arbitant! Isn't it exciting! Do you know I'm just fourteen! This is a lovely birthday present for me, isn't it? I'm so sorry I can't get up. It's these silly legs of mine. Aren't they a nuisance?"

She held out her hand to be shaken. Without thinking what he was really doing he bent down and pressed it to his lips. She glowed with pleasure at thus being treated like a heroine in a work of romantic fiction. Nobody else had ever before kissed her hand like that.

"We are going to be best friends," she announced. "I know that for certain. Come along, I'm going to take you inside!"

He had never before had in his life such a welcome. All of a sudden the accumulated pressures and anxieties of the past years utterly overwhelmed him. The warmth of his reception at Leeds by these two so deeply wronged people had been so unexpected. To be greeted like this by this almost elfin-like, crippled child, whose father had been murdered by a regime he had once applauded, and whose own enjoyment of the normal attributes of life had so cruelly been taken away by them, was beyond belief. To his intense embarrassment he found he was crying. He pulled out his handkerchief and wiped his eyes.

""I'm so, so sorry...." he gasped.

A soft hand touched his arm. "We understand only too well about these things, don't we Mummy? We are all going to be your friends here."

Once again, almost instinctively, he bent down and kissed her hand.

Elisabeth was not absolutely bound to the chair. The very best surgeons had not as yet been unable to provide any effective remedy for the injuries she had suffered. She had been provided with a newly invented but rather cumbersome device, which enabled her to walk, very slowly, provided she had some assistance from an attendant.

When she attempted this it was pitiful to see this otherwise vibrant young girl struggling so gamely with it. Her face when in normal repose possessed a tranquillity, which at once enchanted all those, she met. When she used the device a look of absolute determination to succeed dominated her expression.

At that time neither she nor her parents had ever seen the famous portrait of Lady Sarah Threlfall which showed that same tranquillity, behind which, in paradox, lay a hint of tragedy.

She began to attempt to get up from the chair. The attendant nurse produced the walking device, ready to assist her.

"No, no!" she said, "I wish to take Mr. Arbitant in myself! May I call you Harold, Mr. Arbitant? It is so much friendlier!" She held out her arm and he gently helped her.

In this manner Harold made his first entry into Preston Hall. From that time onwards, though he did not then know it, Preston Hall was to be his home.

Later on that day Francis returned from the mills. Rachel and he were soon satisfied that Rachel's project had found a very suitable and enthusiastic administrator.

"You are to remain here at the Hall with us, Mr. Arbitant," said Francis, "until you are settled and feel able to find somewhere convenient to live."

"I am so pleased you are so enthusiastic about my idea, Mr. Arbitant!" said Rachel.

"Now it is all settled can I, like Elisabeth, call you Harold?"

"Yes, indeed, " said Francis," this is Yorkshire, you know! Inside the family we don't stand much on ceremony. Rachel and Francis is good enough for us, so far as you're concerned my lad! Regard yourself as one of the family. Elisabeth seems to have adopted you already!"

"I simply cannot find words to express how grateful I am to you all!"

"Words don't mean anything, my lad! By your works we shall know you!"

Nothing could have been more different from the small house in Wimbledon than was Preston Hall. Quite obviously it was incomparably more spacious, but it was the atmosphere of the place which made all the difference for Harold. The dour philistinism, which accompanied Albert wherever he went, like a black cloud, was replaced by the sweetness and light which seemed to emanate from both Rachel and Elisabeth. For the first time in a very long while he felt happy to be alive.

The house had been built by the firm's founder, Josiah Preston, in the 1880's. Ten years later, in his fortieth year, he had had completed the family chapel, the last building to be erected within the grounds. The principal buildings were constructed from a pleasant red brick. The architect Josiah had engaged had contrived to avoid most of the excesses which had plagued the work of many of his contemporaries. He had been unable to resist adding some turrets and a few pseudo-battlements to the three storied, many windowed, house but, on the whole, the effect was pleasing. In the sixty years of its existence it had had time to acquire a certain patina which greatly enhanced its appearance. The windows had been particularly well proportioned as had the grand portico, which formed the main entrance to the Hall.

Inside was a gigantic drawing room, very sensibly furnished, with a great log fire at one end, the windows looking out over the extensive park, mainly laid out to grass, rhododendron woods, and silver birch, ending up at a small lake. A large and pleasant kitchen, at the rear of the building, gave way on to a brick paved yard; around which were grouped numerous outhouses. Standing on its own, some small distance away, overlooking one end of the lake, was the chapel. This was a building of considerable size.

Rachel, with Harold pushing Elisabeth in her chair, was showing him round the grounds. Together they walked down from the house, along the long straight gravelled drive, up which they had been driven when he arrived. Then, at the gates, they turned back and began to cross immaculate lawns, edged by flower filled beds, making their way towards the chapel. On their way they paused to show him the little rose garden that Francis had had created especially for the use of Rachel and Elisabeth. In the centre of this little private enclosure was a small fishpond fed by an ever-running waterfall.

"I come and sit here whenever I can, with Elisabeth by my side, Harold. I sometimes feel that it is as near to Paradise as I shall ever be in this life! But come and see the chapel!"

"It is beautiful!" he exclaimed, "But why is it so large? It does seem enormous for a family chapel!""Do you know I asked my husband the same question! He told me that Josiah, the Preston who built this house and the chapel, was such a devout man that he wished it to hold all the Church of England employees at the mill! It became virtually compulsory for them to attend with their entire families, twice each Sunday! He told me the practice didn't lapse until the thirties! It is hardly ever used now, but it is still a consecrated church. Every now and then the local vicar holds a kind of token service here. It would be pleasant, would it not, if one day, it could be used again, just as it was, but I suppose that is unthinkable these days!"

He became completely immersed in his work. Between them, with Francis' encouragement and financial backing, he and Rachel began to re-establish the old Aronberg network, greatly to the advantage of Preston Textiles business. Rachel saw to the administration and Harold travelled the world. The years seemed to fly past.

Whenever he returned from a long and arduous trip Elisabeth would be eagerly waiting for him, aching to be told of his "adventures", as she called them.

"I don't suppose I shall ever be able to see these places for myself!" she said, rather despondently. "You are my eyes, Harold!"

In this way three years went past. Elisabeth had grown to young womanhood. Newer and more sophisticated devices had by now been devised and she was able to walk a little with their assistance. She had by now acquired the latest in electric wheeled chairs, but she still preferred Harold to push her whenever he was at home. They always engaged each other in long and engrossing conversation whilst he pushed her round the grounds or sat together in the rose garden.

"I think it is a waste of time dwelling on the past, Harold!" she said one day. "The words "if only" are silly! One always imagines that something much better would have happened, but it could just as well have been something much worse, couldn't it! You could say I was unlucky to be injured like this, but you could equally well say I was lucky not to be hurt much more badly, let alone not killed! I read in a book the other day "The best is yet to come!" I think that's a wonderful thought, don't you?"

"When I was a teacher at Bushfield Abbey School, Elisabeth, if I can mention that bit of my past for once, the school crest and motto was a phoenix arising from the ashes over the words "I was, I am, I shall be", below."

"That's just what I mean, Harold! You, Mummy and me, we're all phoenixes, aren't we? We've all risen from the ashes of our past, haven't we?"

They went back into the house. Rachel and Francis were waiting for them in the morning room. Rachel had a look of serene happiness on her face and Francis could scarcely restrain his excitement.

"We have some wonderful news, you two!" said Francis.

"What is it Mummy? What is it? Oh, do tell me, quickly!"

"Darling, a marvellous thing has happened. I am going to have a baby!"

"Oh, Mummy! A little brother for me! Oh, Mummy! How wonderful!"

"She was still in her chair but gestured frantically to Rachel to come and be kissed.

"But why do you say "brother", darling? Why it could be a little sister?"

"No, Mummy, I know he will be a brother!". Then she added, "But if it were a sister I should love her just as much!"

They all laughed with happiness.

In due course she was proved correct. The baby was a boy and he was christened Martin. Elisabeth, now seventeen, sat in her chair holding the baby, gazing at him with wonder. Her maternal urges surged strongly through her crippled body.

"Oh, isn't he a miracle! Oh, I do wish he was my very own!"

Rachel, watching, observed Harold's eyes filling with tears. At that moment she guessed his carefully guarded secret.

"Francis!" she said, as they were getting into bed that night." Harold is in love with Elisabeth. I know for certain!"

"You're not the only one, darling! I've realised that ages ago!"

"You never said a word to me!"

"I thought it better to give it time. Things have a way of sorting themselves out, don't they!"

"Yes!" agreed Rachel. "Life certainly does take unexpected turns!"

By unspoken agreement neither of them ever referred to the past these days but he knew what she meant. Penelope, Rosemary, Benjamin and all the others were always there with them.

In 1950 Harold received the news that his mother had died. He told them over breakfast.

"You are all the family I now have. In some ways I feel you are all the family I ever had!"

"We are glad to have you in the family, Harold!" said Rachel.

"I know I am, Mummy!" said Elisabeth.

In 1948 Gordon Preston had finally come out of the army. He was at once invited to join the Preston Textiles Board. Very soon thereafter poor Horace, worn out by his wartime exertions, died.

"Gordon," said Francis, after an appropriate period of mourning had gone by, " I am only fifty but I would very much like to pass the burden of management here on to you, if you are willing! I do so want to devote myself much more to Rachel, Elisabeth and Martin. My suggestion is that we appoint you as managing director at the next board meeting and I take over as chairman. I shall take a more active part than your father, of course, but the main responsibilities would be yours. What do you say to that?"

"Francis! I feel as though I have entered the Promised Land. This has been my ambition since boyhood!"

One sunny May morning in 1952 Harold accompanied Rachel to her favourite bench in her rose garden. Here she said to him, very firmly, "Please sit down, Harold, I have something very serious to say to you!"

Very puzzled and more than a little apprehensive, he sat down next to her on the bench and looked at her questioningly.

"Harold! You are now forty-two! You have done so much for us, but what have you ever done just for you?"

He began to say something, but she held up a restraining hand.

"No, Harold, hear me out! Francis and I are concerned that you have never been loved as a man needs to be loved. You know what I mean, Harold!"

He moved restively, embarrassed by the remark, so unexpected from her.

She continued, relentlessly, "Francis and I both know that you are in love with Elisabeth!"

His heart was thumping so hard it felt as though it would burst from his body. He felt physically sick at so abruptly having his secret exposed.

He was scarlet with embarrassment. "Rachel! I have made a fool of myself! I never realised it was so obvious. I have tried so hard not to give any signs. I feel I have betrayed the trust you placed in me. What can I do? I assure you my love is absolutely honourable. I don't deny anything. I do love her! I love her so much I am willing to go away if that is what is required of me, but I shall never stop loving her! As long as you believe that I could, I think, bear the pain! Rachel, believe me, I know it is ridiculous of me. I'm forty-two and she is twenty! Even if you were to allow me to ask her and she were to agree I know people would say I had only married her for my own benefit, and taken advantage of her, too!"

"Dear Harold! What is all this worry about your respective ages? We have never paid any attention to such trivia in this family. As for advantage and benefit who is taking advantage of whom and who benefits? Francis is thirteen years older than I am and look what I was when he married me!"

"But Rachel that was all quite different! And just think! When I am eighty she will be in her fifties! There's a world of difference between a thirteen year gap and a twenty two year one!"

"What matters is what you both want now! Who knows whether either of you will ever reach either eighty or, for that matter, fifty? It's the here and now that matters. That's what Francis and I think!"

"Do you really think she would accept me?"

"That, my lad, is for you to find out!" said a voice behind them. Francis had come up unobserved and been listening to the conversation. "You're an honorary Yorkshire lad now, Harold! None of your London ways here! No time for sitting around thinking of reasons for not doing what ought to be done. That's not the Yorkshire way! If you want something and its worth having, then go and get it!"

Without further ado Harold rose from the bench and went into the house. Elisabeth was sitting in her chair in the drawing room, pretending to read a book. When he entered she looked up and smiled at him.

"I wondered where you were?" she said.

Half an hour later Harold emerged from the house pushing her in her chair. She was absolutely radiating happiness.

"Congratulations!" said Francis.

Then Rachel kissed them both.

CHAPTER FORTY SEVEN

UNION

"To whom do you feel we should offer the school chaplaincy now that Alistair has decided to retire?" enquired Sir George, now chairman of the Governors of Bushfield Abbey School, blandly looking round the table, in the boardroom at Bushfield Abbey..

It was June, 1959 and he was chairing his first meeting of a totally new board. The other newly appointed governors present were Sir Francis, the Right Reverend Kenneth Hyslow, bishop of the diocese, and the Reverend Alistair Strong .

"You know perfectly well, chairman," said Dr. Wisley, present in his capacity as headmaster, "that it has to be offered to William Hyslow. That has always been understood! In any event Baldock made it quite clear that that was what he expected to happen when he ordained him. You were there when he told me!"

Sir George smiled at him. "I have to go through the motions, Richard! I am not allowed to act as a rubber stamp! Do you agree, Francis?"

"Of course, I do!" said Francis.

"What about you, Alistair?"

"Oh, me, I bow to the will of the majority!"

"And how are you going to vote, Bishop?"

"Who am I to defy you all, chairman!"

William Hyslow had married his childhood sweetheart, Valerie Bentham, in 1947, when they were both twenty-six. He had graduated from Cambridge with a good science degree, as he had always stated he would, and then proceeded to his theological studies as his parents had promised on his behalf. Mercifully he had found that he really did have a vocation for the ministry. He was quite sure that, whatever the cost, he could not have proceeded if he had not been satisfied on that score. He was ordained in 1952, at the last such ceremony ever conducted by the Right Reverend Baldock before his death at the age of seventy-three later that year. He and Valerie had had one daughter, whom they named Marion, born in 1950. For a while they had faced a considerable financial struggle, somewhat eased by the unexpected receipt of a legacy from those very same godparents who had assisted his education so generously. The going since had, however, been hard. The curacies he had held had not been at all well paid. Although, secretly, both William and Marion felt sure that one day he would be offered the Bushfield Abbey chaplaincy they discounted this as an immediate source of relief. The Reverend Strong was only just coming up to seventy. They had every expectation that he would remain at his post for another five years, seventy-five being the normal age for retirement for senior staff at Bushfield at that time.

Strong, however, suddenly and unexpectedly, announced that he had had "enough of schoolmastering" and was going to retire. With some evident reluctance he agreed to being recruited to the Board of Governors.

This appointment descended upon the William Hyslow household like manna from heaven. The chaplaincy not only carried a very satisfactory salary but it also provided them with a home, as the chaplain automatically became housemaster of Chaplain's House and had accommodation there for himself and his family. Life became distinctly rosier.

The matter of the chaplaincy, which had been the last item on the agenda, satisfactorily settled, George proceeded to declare the meeting closed. The governors began to gather their papers together, looking forward to the usual pre -luncheon cocktails always provided on such occasions, prior to the very satisfactory meal, which followed. It was, therefore, with something approaching irritation they heard Francis suddenly exclaim, "Just a moment, just a moment, I have something I want to say!"

"Really, Francis!" said Sir George, "The meeting is over! Whatever it is will have to wait over. You should have spoken before I closed it!"

"Oh, fiddlesticks to the meeting!" said Francis jovially.

This was such an uncharacteristic utterance on the part of the normally rather serious minded Francis that they all looked at him in surprise.

"I have something to tell you all! Mrs. Jason, bring 'em in would you, and join us yourself!"

Mrs. Jason, at fifty-four still the school matron, had been waiting outside for the signal. She now entered bearing a silver tray on which were arrayed brimming glasses of champagne, which she proceeded to hand round to the surprised governors.

"I have the greatest pleasure, gentlemen, in announcing the engagement of my daughter, Elisabeth, to Mr. Harold Arbitant! The marriage will take place in the chapel at Preston Hall this coming September! I hope you can all attend!"

****

That September witnessed an unprecedented gathering of Bushfielders and people from Loughbourne at Preston Hall. For many of them it was the first time they had re-encountered each other since the war years. Everybody seemed to be there and everybody seemed to know or know of everybody else. Roger Threlfall, by now a rather shy thirteen year old, in his second year at Bushfield Abbey, was there with his parents. He had been asked to be the page of honour, a position that conferred upon him the duty of wheeling in the bride's chair as she entered the chapel for the ceremony. He was feeling distinctly conspicuous in his page's outfit. To his consternation he found himself being addressed by the bridegroom.

"So you're Roger Threlfall!"

As he made the remark Harold looked at Ann, standing fondly by her son. It was the first time the two had set eyes on each other since that day in 1938. Both had been dreading the inevitable meeting for neither knew how either they themselves or the other would react. Both had changed so radically in their outlooks. Roger, however, seemed to act as a kind of catalyst. Quite suddenly they both felt at ease in his presence.

"He's in his second year at the school, Harold. Actually he's in Chaplain's House. You know, I suppose, that the chaplain is now William Hyslow? Alistair Strong has retired. He is around somewhere. Has he spoken to you yet?" Then she added, almost shyly, "It's so good to see you again, Harold, in such happy circumstances. I am so pleased for you!"

There was a pause whilst they both looked at each other rather lost for further words. Both knew that the other was thinking of John, but neither felt able to mention his name.

Then Harold said, "What a fine boy you have, Lady Ann!"

There followed another pause. Roger, sensing their unease, shifted unhappily from foot to foot, wondering what was happening.

Then Ann said, "If it can be managed, somehow, Elisabeth must come down with you and stay with us at Loughbourne. We should love to have you!"

"We'll take you up on that Lady Ann!"

Then somebody else came up to speak to her and they became separated. He drifted off to speak to other guests. Across the room he watched her chatting to them. It was like a dream that had never happened. Elisabeth's words came back into his head. What were they now? "Live for the future, forget the past" or something like that! Ah, yes! " 'If only is a silly thought". No good the phoenix rising from its ashes, he thought to himself, if it promptly dives straight back into them!

Gordon, who was to be best man, came up to him.

"Have you seen that young Roger, Harry? Are there you are, young feller! You're wanted!"

Roger was whisked away. Observing this, Ann, across the other side of the room, caught Harold's eye and shot him a quick smile. George, unusually observant, said,

"So you two have met up again already, then? What a turn up for the book, eh, Ann?"

"George, did you know that Gordon was John's best friend?"

"Yes, he and that vicar chap over there. That's William Hyslow. The three were always inseparable!"

"Yes, I've just been talking to William! He's conducting the service today."

She was misty eyed. Sir George took her arm and walked her over to the window, where they stood gazing, almost unseeingly, out at the gardens. After a moment she said, "It's alright, George, I've got over it now! We must make sure this is a happy occasion for them!

Oh, George isn't it wonderful! The Arbitants, the Prestons and the Aronbergs all being united like this in this marriage. I just wish that somehow we could complete the circle! George I'm so proud of your mother. I'm so proud her blood runs in Roger's veins and in yours. You do believe that, don't you?"

He squeezed her hand comfortingly. He was perfectly well aware that another crisis had just been overcome. Ann had been subject to these regularly ever since John's death. The recollections of that terrible time, periodically and quite suddenly, combined to overwhelm her. Over the years they had both had to learn how to deal with these recurrent attacks of regret and guilt.

Over the other side of the room Francis was standing with Rachel at his side. Ann caught her eye and smiled. Rachel came over to her and said, "Ann, dear, it is wonderful to have you with us. What a lovely boy you have. Do you know I can see a resemblance to my father!"

"Oh, Rachel, how painful that must be for you..." began Ann.

"No, Ann, dear, he is the future, why should that be painful? He, like Martin and Elisabeth, is of my blood."

"You are a very wonderful person, Rachel!"

"We have both known sorrow, Ann. Perhaps it has done something good for both of us. Let's just look to the future. I try to bury the past."

Impulsively Ann kissed her, frantically endeavouring to restrain her tears.

"None of that today, Ann dear," whispered Rachel. "Just be happy for them!"

The ushers were now moving around asking the guests to make their way into the chapel. Harold was already in place at the end of the aisle, Gordon beside him. The chapel, long without such a congregation, began to fill.

George and Ann filed into a pew.

"Look, George, that's little Martin Preston over there playing with Marion Hyslow, don't they make a perfect couple! His nurse was telling me he is just three and a half!"

Several guests were wondering who the tall, distinguished man, in full dress Brigadier's uniform might be. "That", said Cumberworth to his wife," is Brigadier Tomkins. He was Sir Francis' chief at the War Office during the war! I met him at the end of the war when we were in Austria. He came into our mess together with Sir Francis. It was he and Sir Francis who rescued Lady Preston from the Nazis."

The organ had struck up. The bride was entering. They all stood.

Roger, who had found his courage in Elisabeth's own radiant happiness, entered, pushing her in her wheelchair. She sat in it with such a look of absolute joy, a bouquet of roses on her lap, that it seemed as though an extra light had suddenly been switched on as she entered. By her side walked Sir Francis, looking every inch like one of his Viking ancestors.

Harold, resolutely resisting the temptation to look round at his approaching bride, waited.

William began the service.

****

One year later, with no problems, Elisabeth gave birth to Esther.

CHAPTER FORTY EIGHT

ENCOUNTER

"Have you heard the news, Ann?" said George, one January day in 1971. "Martin Preston has announced his engagement to Marion, William Hyslow's girl! There's going to be another wedding at Preston Hall, next September. I was told the news last time I was at Bushfield. There's an invitation on its way for us!"

"Oh, dear, George! I do wish Roger could find somebody for himself! He does nothing but sit in that stuffy office of his with Henry, looking over estate accounts."

Henry Morton had taken his father's place as land agent in 1946, as soon as he had left the army.

"If he doesn't find somebody soon," agreed her husband, "the manor looks like being inherited by some blighter nobody's ever heard about! What can we do? He's thirty three already, dash it!"

"They say engagement parties generate other engagements! Why don't we throw a party here for Marion and Martin? I'm sure everybody would come! That could start Roger thinking, couldn't it? And it would be fun!"

"Right, let's do it!" said George, only too pleased for her to have produced such an idea of her own volition. She really is beginning to be her old self again, at last, he thought.

"Oh, for goodness sake, Father!" protested Roger, when he was given the news, "That's a terrible idea! We don't want a lot of people trampling about all over the house and grounds. They'll ruin the place. Let old Cumberworth give them a party at Bushfield, he'd love to do it!"

Cumberworth had been appointed Headmaster of Bushfield Abbey, in succession to Dr. Wisley, who had retired in 1965.

"You seem to have a poor idea of the behaviour of our friends and relations, Roger!" laughed Ann. "We are going to give it and you are going to be the life and soul of it!"

"Oh, no I am not! Anyway where are they all going to sleep?"

"We have all those empty rooms. It will be wonderful to wake the house up again!"

"Oh, fiddlesticks!" said Roger, and returned to his little office.

The party took place that April. There were people everywhere. The servants absolutely loved the commotion.

"Isn't it all wonderful?" said Lily Mitchell to Jameson. "The house hasn't seen anything like this since Lady Sarah's days!"

"It makes a fine swan song for me, Lily!" agreed Jameson, who was due to retire at the end of the year.

Roger, however, was appalled. He retreated into the estate office and firmly shut the door. He had, he felt, been betrayed by Henry, who was cheerfully throwing himself into the jollities. He sat there on his own.

"All this and it hasn't worked!" grumbled George to Ann. "Oh, well, let's enjoy ourselves, anyway!"

Some time later Roger was sitting in his office, which was in an outhouse situated between the main house and the servants' quarters, when he was roused by a soft knock on the door. Then the latch lifted and he found himself face to face with a young woman of about nineteen. He recognised her at once. He had seen her photograph. It was Esther Arbitant, the granddaughter of Sir Francis Preston, the textile magnate, one of his father's oldest friends .It was quite obvious, however, that she had no idea at all who he might be.

She came in and looked around the dusty office of which he was so proud with something approaching horror on her face.

"Goodness! Why don't the mean old things give you a proper office? You should see the one our land agent has at Preston Hall. I suppose you are the land agent? But then you should be at the party! Do you mean they didn't ask you! I didn't think anybody would be expected to work today!

I came out here, on my own, sort of exploring. Then I got a bit lost. Luckily I saw your light on and noticed you sitting here. I looked through the window but you didn't see me.

By the way, I'm Esther Arbitant, I'm Sir Francis Preston's granddaughter. We're all here for the party they are giving for Martin and Marion!"

All this was delivered almost without pause for breath. He sat there, gazing at her, transfixed. He had met comparatively few young women of his own class. This one had made a very big impact on him. He felt an overwhelming desire to please her.

"I recognised you as soon as you came in. I've seen your photograph. I'm Roger Threlfall, George and Ann's son. I had to do some work on some overdue accounts, but I'm finished now!"

"Oh, isn't that good! I was wondering where you were. Everybody has been asking for you. I've been longing to meet you. If you've finished whatever it was you were doing could you take me back to the party, please?"

As they made their way across the cobbled yard she slipped her arm through his.

"These high heeled shoes I'm wearing weren't made for walking on cobbles!" she said by way of explanation.

"Good old cobbles", he thought to himself. He was enjoying the experience.

In this manner they made their entrance into the drawing room, where the party was now in full swing. At the far end of the room Martin and Marion were dancing together, to the strains of a gramophone record, oblivious to everybody. These two had first met when they were very small children at the wedding of Elisabeth and Harold. Since then they had seen each other as frequently as possible.

Esther looked at them enviously. "Lucky things!" she said.

Esther's parents and grandparents were seated talking to George and Ann. They all looked up with considerable surprise and interest as the two young people made their unexpected entrance together. Roger was looking embarrassed but far from sulky. He shot a smile at his mother. George noticed at once.

"Well, well!" he said to nobody in particular.

"Too young, I fear!" sighed Ann.

"It doesn't look to me as though either of them are worried about their ages!" said Elisabeth.

Roger and Esther came up to the group.

"Look who I found, Mummy," said Esther. "He's going to show me round the house!"

She slipped her arm back into his and they left the room, Roger looking slightly sheepish.

They entered the library. "Isn't it gloomy!" said Esther. She began to wander rather vaguely round the book-laden shelves, looking at them with slight distaste. "I hate libraries and bookshops, in fact I don't read much at all, certainly not these kind of books!" she said. Then she caught sight of Sarah's portrait and gave a gasp. "That person looks like my grandmother! Who is she!"

"That's my grandmother, Lady Sarah. She died here, the same year as my older brother John, just before I was born. I never knew her, I'm afraid, but I do know that all her family except one, I think, were killed by the Nazis."

"Do you know it's a strange thing but my grandmother's family were all killed by the Nazis, too. My grandmother was made a prisoner by one of them and rescued just after the war ended by Sir Francis, who I call my grandfather. He had already rescued my mother, when she was in danger as a child in Berlin, before the war. He adopted her as his daughter after my real grandfather was murdered and my grandmother was kidnapped and disappeared, nobody knew where. Then at the end of the war his first wife, Lady Penelope, was killed by the same V2 rocket that so dreadfully injured my mother. That's why he was able to marry my grandmother, after he had rescued her. My grandmother's maiden name was Aronberg. It's all terribly sad and complicated and a bit exciting isn't it? Martin and I are both terribly proud of our Aronberg ancestry! Was your grandmother's story anything like that?"

"Yes, in fact, Esther, it does seem that our grandmothers must have been very closely related. Both my father and I are proud of the Aronberg blood in us, too!"

"We must ask our parents to tell us the whole story. You and I seem to have an awful lot in common!"

They stood, hand in hand in front of Sarah's portrait, fascinated by this discovery.

In her agitation Esther reached up to one of the shelves near the portrait and started to examine, for no very good reason, an old book her hand happened to alight upon.

"What a strange book! It has a French title but is written in funny old English, like the Bible. "She turned to the flyleaf. "Look, somebody has written something here!" She slowly deciphered the faded brown ink writing. "True love, Bk 18, xxv, For SA from R 1884".

She began to turn over the pages excitedly. "This is just like detectives, isn't it?"

"Let me find the passage for you! Ah, here it is! Why, this is Sir Thomas Malory's "Morte D'Arthur". It's a mediaeval account of the legend of King Arthur. I didn't even know it was here. Look here's the quotation you were looking for. Do you want to read it out aloud to me?"

She took the book and began to read, at first rather self-consciously theatrical. Then, for some reason, she began to feel the portrait was listening to her critically. She suddenly became serious. ""How true love is likened to summer", that's how the chapter is headed." she paused and said, "I think that's rather lovely, don't you Roger?" He nodded. She proceeded, trying her best to give expression to the words, as she had been taught in her elocution lessons at school. The library lighting was not good, the print was old fashioned, and they had difficulty reading the text. They bent forward, straining to make out the words. As they did so their heads touched, very lightly, and he felt as though a small electric shock had just been delivered to him, a very pleasant sensation. "For then all herbs and trees renew a man and a woman and in likewise lovers call again to their mind old gentleness and old service and many kind deeds that were forgotten by negligence."

She ceased reading and said, "Wasn't that really beautiful?"

"Not as beautiful as you!" he thought to himself, at least he intended only to think the words, but, subconsciously, his lips moved with the thought and she knew what they were. She gave no sign that she had guessed but she felt a glow of pleasure within.

She put her arm through his again and they began to leave the room. Hastily he put the book back on a different shelf. Normally he was almost manic about replacing books in their correct places but she seemed anxious to leave. I can come back later, he thought, and put it back properly.

She paused again in front of the portrait. "We must go and get them. I must find out more about all this. She does look so like my grandmother!"

The group was still sitting, just where they had left them. "Mummy, Grandmother! There's a portrait in the library of Roger's grandmother. She looks just like you, grandmother! Everybody, do come and see it!"

"That is my own mother, Sarah, " said George. "As a matter of fact she was your grandmother's great aunt. I am so sorry Rachel and Elisabeth, I should have shown it to you earlier. I kept forgetting to do so in the general excitement. Come and see it now, all of you!"

Harold pushed Elisabeth's chair into the library whilst Rachel and the others followed. Rachel went up to the picture and they could see her begin to tremble violently. Although Esther had seen her mother in the portrait, what Rachel could see were the faces of Aaron, Samuel and Eli. With a tremendous effort she regained her self -control and said, "Thank you, Esther darling. I agree the resemblance is very striking, isn't it Elisabeth?"

It was quite evident to them all, however, that she was deeply moved, although only George and Francis divined the true reason for the disturbing effect the portrait had had upon her. Somewhat subdued they returned to the gaiety of the party. Esther and Roger realised that now was not an opportune moment to ask for further enlightenment. For one moment a dark shadow from the past, so long concealed, had fallen across them.

Roger remained behind for a moment. He was still anxious to put the book back on its correct shelf. He looked at the place where it was supposed to be and, to his amazement, saw that it had apparently returned there of its own accord. Then he realised there were two copies, virtually identical. He took down the second copy and opened it at the flyleaf. The inscription written there said," Bk 18,xxv, true love, from FT to S,1896". He put the two books back together, side by side. As he did so he had the strangest feeling of satisfaction. He had the sensation he had stumbled upon something very private and wonderful.

Thoughtfully he returned to the party. Esther was talking excitedly with the others.

"My grandparents have had a wonderful idea, Roger! Your father has just said he can easily spare you to come up to Leeds and stay with us for a few weeks. You can help my father do some cataloguing he's working on in our own library!"

"But what about the Loughbourne work, Father!"

"Fiddlesticks! What do you think Henry does? You can start worrying again about Loughbourne when he retires and goes to live in that place he's bought for himself. Then, if you're capable of looking after it, you can move into the Dower House. You'll need someone to look after you there, though. It's a big place!"

He needed no further encouragement.

Exactly what the mysterious cataloguing might be with which he was supposed to be helping Harold he never discovered. He did, however, enjoy himself immensely. The longer he stayed at Preston Hall the more he fell in love with Esther.

Esther, for her part, certainly made no efforts to discourage his attentions.

One evening he took his courage in his hands. Esther was up in her room, having her hair done by her maid. He grasped the opportunity of being alone with her parents.

"I know I am a lot older than Esther, but would you mind if I asked her if she'd think of marrying me?"

"Why don't you ask her and see what she says!" said Elisabeth encouragingly.

He did, as soon as he could.

"What took you so long?" she demanded "I want to be married side by side with Martin and Marion. A lovely double wedding, right here in our chapel. Won't it be fun!"

"But that means we shall only be engaged for a few weeks!" he laughed.

"Waste of a few good weeks! Who cares about silly old engagements? It's marriage or nothing for us!"

Then they went in to tell the others.

For some reason they showed no surprise.

The news was received at Loughbourne with rapture.

"My wish has been granted, George," said Ann, "the circle is completed. "

"What do you mean by that Ann?"

"Don't you remember what I said at Harold and Elisabeth's wedding? That their marriage united the Aronbergs with the Prestons and the Arbitants. Now we complete the circle with Roger and Esther. How pleased John would have been, I know he would."

He took her in his arms and kissed her.

CHAPTER FORTY NINE

CIRCLE

"Half an hour to go!" said Francis to the Right Reverend Kenneth Hyslow, who, although retired, was, nevertheless, splendidly attired, being about to escort his granddaughter, Marion, up the aisle.

Francis, Harold, and the Bishop had sought temporary refuge in Francis' study at Preston Hall and were enjoying a pre-nuptials glass of champagne. Outside the sun shone down from an almost cloudless sky. They stood at the window and watched the guests trooping across the lawns in the direction of the chapel. Major General Tomkins, now also retired, passed by, Mrs. Jason holding his arm.

"Perhaps we'll all be receiving another wedding invitation soon!" remarked Francis as he watched them. "Better late than never, eh? Dash it, they're only seventy three and made for each other!"

The Wisleys went by, accompanied by Alistair Strong, then the Mortons, the Tappings, the Ridings, the Mitchells, more and more familiar faces, some old, some young.

"I believe everybody I have ever known is here today!" said the Bishop.

"Well," said Harold, after a pause, "I suppose we had better go and seek out our charges!"

William Hyslow was performing the ceremony for Marion and Martin, whilst Alexander Tapping was to officiate for Esther and Roger. Gordon Preston, who was married only to his beloved mills, was to be best man for Martin, and Henry Morton for Roger.

At ten minutes to eleven the two bridal parties began to make their separate ways across to the chapel, once again packed with a full congregation, as it had been for Harold's and Elisabeth's wedding twenty years before.

The organist gave the signal, everybody stood up, and the two bridal parties entered, first Marion and then Esther, each preceded by their officiating clergyman. Marion was proudly escorted by the Bishop, in loco parentis for his son, and Esther by Harold.

At the end of the aisle the two bridegrooms waited. The last time either had been in that chapel had been at Harold's wedding, when

Roger was fourteen and Martin three and a half. At that time Martin and Marion had spent their time playing a mysterious game Marion had invented, comprehending virtually nothing of what was happening around them.

The double wedding proceeded much as such ceremonies always do. Ann read the first lesson and Rachel the second, William gave a splendid address. Then the wedding parties, having signed the register, made their emotionally charged exits from the chapel.

Tom Riding, a hale and hearty seventy-nine, was not to be deprived of this moment of glory. He was in full dress uniform, his medals shining on his chest. He threw open the great doors and the congregation streamed out, chattering excitedly. The photographer began to marshal the newly weds into those wedding group permutations so beloved of wedding photographers, gesticulating as such photographers always do. Obediently they arranged and re-arranged themselves, almost dazed with the happiness and excitement of the occasion. There was much laughter.

Ann and Rachel stood there, watching, side by side, with their husbands holding their hands. Harold, as ever, stood by Elisabeth's chair, one hand resting on her shoulder.

Ann's free hand slipped into Rachel's and held it tightly.

"They are all here with us, Rachel, I know they are!" she whispered.

"Yes, Ann dear, they were and they are and they always will be!"

THE END

ARONBERG FAMILY TREE AS AT 1971

JOSEF	MARRIED	RUTH STEIN	(SISTER OF REUBEN)
1817-1895	1838	1819	1825-1905

ISAAC	M	MIRIAM	
1839-1925	1863	1842-1925	

SAMUEL	M	NAOMI	ELI	SARAH	M	FREDERICK THRELFALL
1865-1938	1887	1866-1938	1866-1938	1874-1938	1896	1871-1916

AARON	M	REBECCA		GEORGE	M	ANN WINSLOW
1888-1940	1911	1889-1938		1901-	1920	1902-

RACHEL	M(1)	BENJAMIN HANDS	JOHN	ROGER	M	ESTHER ARBITANT
1913-	1931	1911-1940	1921-1938	1939-	1971	1953-

ELISABETH	M	HAROLD ARBITANT
1932-	1952	1910-

(ELISABETH WAS ADOPTED BY FRANCIS AND
PENELOPE PRESTON IN 1939)

ESTHER	M	ROGER THRELFALL
1953-	1971	1938-

(RACHEL HANDS (Née ARONBERG) SECOND
MARRIAGE TO FRANCIS PRESTON)

RACHEL	M(2)	FRANCIS PRESTON
1913-	1945	1900-

MARTIN	M	MARION HYSLOW
1949-	1971	1950-

GENEALOGIES (ii)

THE PRESTON FAMILY TREE AS AT 1971

JOSIAH	MARRIES	VICTORIA
1850-1920	1874	1853-1922

WILLIAM	M	MARGARET		HORACE	M	JESSICA
1875-1926	1898	1876-1950		1888-1950	1920	1891-1970

FRANCIS	M(1)	PENELOPE		GORDON
1900-	1927	1902-1944		1921-

ROSEMARY
1932-1938

BY ADOPTION BY FRANCIS AND PENELOPE
FROM RACHEL HANDS (Née ARONBERG) IN 1939

ELISABETH	M	HAROLD ARBITANT
1932-	1952	1910-

ESTHER	M	ROGER THRELFALL
1953-	1971	1939-

(FRANCIS SECOND MARRIAGE)

FRANCIS	M(2)	RACHEL HANDS (Née ARONBERG AND NATURAL MOTHER OF ELISABETH)
1900-	1945	1932-

MARTIN	M	MARION HYSLOW
1949-	1971	1950-

239

GENEALOGIES (iii)

THRELFALLS AT 1971

ROBERT	MARRIED	MARY
1845-1896	1870	1842-1896

FREDERICK	M	SARAH AVONDALE (Née ARONBERG)
1871-1916	1896	1872-1938

GEORGE	M	ANN WINSLOW
1901	1920	1902

JOHN

1921-1938

ROGER   M   **ESTHER ARBITANT**

1939-   1971   1953-

WINSLOWS AS AT 1971

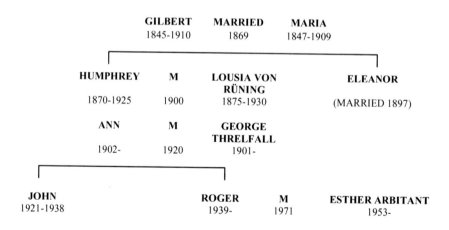

GILBERT	MARRIED	MARIA
1845-1910	1869	1847-1909

HUMPHREY	M	LOUSIA VON RÜNING	ELEANOR
1870-1925	1900	1875-1930	(MARRIED 1897)

ANN	M	GEORGE THRELFALL
1902-	1920	1901-

JOHN
1921-1938

ROGER   M   **ESTHER ARBITANT**
1939-   1971   1953-

Printed in the United Kingdom
by Lightning Source UK Ltd.
121718UK00001B/235-264/A